Liam McIlvanney was born in ... Professor of Scottish Studies at the University of Otago, New Zealand. He won the Saltire First Book Award for *Burns the Radical* in 2002, and his work has appeared in the *Times Literary Supplement* and the *London Review of Books*. He lives in Dunedin with his wife and four sons. *All the Colours of the Town* is his first novel.

Praise for *All the Colours of the Town*:

Longlisted for the 2010 Authors' Club Best First Novel Award

'An exceptional debut novel . . . McIlvanney manipulates his hero into a series of tight spots with a deftness that bodes well for the future.' *Daily Mail*

'Pulse-racing . . . excellent.' *Metro*

'A remarkable debut . . . More than a cut above the average thriller.' *Independent*

'The sense of belonging, willingly or not, to a city, to its territories and its allegiances, is what lingers underneath this tale of political exposure and is what gives it its real weight . . . McIlvanney has a great deal to offer and I look forward to seeing more from him.' *Scotsman*

'Distinctive and striking . . . One quality that makes the novel stand out is McIlvanney's portrait of the deep-rooted tribal tensions in Glasgow and Belfast.' *TLS*

'*All the Colours of the Town* is dark fiction, plumbing the abysmal depths of human behaviour in a scorching crime-mystery tale.' *Dominion Post*, New Zealand

'Dialogue is McIlvanney's forte in a highly proficient first novel recalling the work of Denise Mina.' *Sunday Times*

'McIlvanney successfully delivers a powerful thriller, rich in colour and skilfully imagined.' *The List*

'A thoughtful and evocative debut thriller.' *Big Issue*

---

by the same author

BURNS THE RADICAL

All the Colours of the Town

Liam McIlvanney

faber and faber

First published in 2009
by Faber and Faber Ltd
Bloomsbury House
74–77 Great Russell Street
London WC1B 3DA
This paperback edition first published in 2010

Typeset by Faber and Faber Ltd
Printed in England by CPI Bookmarque. Croydon

A CIP record for this book
is available from the British Library

ISBN 978-0-571-23984-9

2 4 6 8 10 9 7 5 3 1

For Valerie

Prologue

Already she is smiling, one foot on the stairs. She stops to listen. She isn't scared. This is a game they play most nights. It's important to have a story, a pretext. This is part of the game. She stands on the top step and listens for a sound, for something she can use when she gets downstairs, when her mother will turn towards her with that expression. 'I heard a noise,' the girl will say. 'I was scared.'

Her mother is the problem. Her dad will let her stay. If she makes it to his chair before her mother chases her out of the room. Then she'll curl up in his lap, in the flicker of the telly, and later he'll carry her up to bed.

It's dark on the landing.

The light on the landing is off. She isn't scared. She thinks of herself as a ghost. She can spook her parents – she knows this – when they come on her at such moments, barefoot and pale, out of context, moored in some halfway space, the staircase, the hall.

She creeps down, step by step, feeling the carpet on her bare feet, twisting her soles a little with every step, flexing the fibres. She feels invisible, almost, so little noise is she making.

Some nights there are parties. She hears the laughter in little sips when the lounge door opens, when somebody goes to the bathroom. On those nights she avoids the lounge. Instead she makes for the guest bedroom, where the coats cover the bed in a layered pyramid. The women's are soft, woolly, with collars of fur which give, when you root in their lifelike depths, a womanish sting of perfume. Their silk linings, slippery cool, feel wet against the backs of your fingers. The men's are sterner, textured tweeds and twills, with the sharp assertive stench of stale tobacco; or crinkly raincoats with belts and buttons. She lies on the bed, among the coats, her hand traversing them like a fish, dipping in and out of flaps and pockets. Her fingers trace train tickets, paper hankies, loose coins, stiff folded banknotes, glasses-cases, bubble-moulded sheets of aspirin. They pat car keys and ballpoint pens and cigarette lighters. Their probing tips brush crumbs and lint and grit in the seams of pockets.

Only once did she take something. A book of matches. The slim glossy packet swelling to its jerky spine, its cover tucked snugly into the jutting lip with its cold smudgy strip where the matches sparked. The embossed logo troubling the ball of her thumb. An object both worthless and exquisite. Who would miss it? She folded her fingers over it, made for the door.

The banister is smooth beneath her palm. She thinks, as ever, about sliding down it, as they do in the movies, as they do in cartoons, as she has never yet done. The paint is thick, smooth; her thumb catches a bubble, a little runnel that has dried and hardened, that she feels with her thumb now every night.

She knows every step. The loose stair-rod and then the landing, and then the bend in the stairs, and then the man. A man in a green jacket, standing in the hall. And he must have heard her – maybe she is not so silent after all – because his head turns. At first the flash of his glasses is all that she sees but he steps to the side and shades his eyes and she sees him, a man like her father, with brown hair and glasses, but younger. His face is kind, he has a kind face, and she smiles at him, a smile that expects his complicity, a smile that says, *Don't tell*.

He smiles back, and says something in a voice that is, not foreign, exactly, but guttural, thick – and though she doesn't catch the words she nods.

Behind him, the front door is ajar. He will let the cold in, she thinks. The man looks at her. She isn't scared. They often have visitors at this time, Daddy's clients, men who stand sparely in the hallway till Daddy can see them. When she comes downstairs on these nights, the men grin, almost shy, patting their pockets for coins. When their business is finished and the men leave, she stands by her father's legs as they say goodnight. But tonight, stalled on the landing, poised to take the last few stairs she hears a noise, there's a noise from the living room, like furniture being shifted, and a man comes briskly out and the two men are gone.

She wants to call out, to bring the men back, the green man with the nice smile. But though the door is ajar and the night air – cold and sharp, Novemberish – tingles on her ankles, what she smells is the harsh burnt stink from the living room.

She glances into the dark street. For a moment she thinks about leaving, escaping into the night. Already, the bright room at her back is a foreign land. It's not the living room but a room in a fairy tale, a dragon's cave. And now, for the first time she can remember, she regrets having left her bed. She can feel the duvet's warmth, the girl-shaped hollow that she's left, but there is no way now to get back, to climb backwards up the stairs and into the past. She closes the front door and leans against it, counting to ten.

Her mother is kneeling by the sofa, at the far end of the living room. Is it the rosary? is what the girl thinks: are they saying the rosary? But her mother is beside the sofa, not in front. There is something on the floor; her mother is bending over something. She flitters across but pulls up short. She's standing in something. Her feet are wet – sodden, as though her bladder has emptied – and she flexes her toes, arching them free of the sopping rug. But when she looks down, when her strained toes sink back to the carpet, what rises between them is black, brown, a cola-coloured puddle. Without moving her feet she leans right over, canting her body to see beyond the couch, beyond her kneeling mother, to whatever has caused the mess.

And now her bladder does empty, the water loosed in a startling spatter, like radio hiss, the warm turning speedily cool on her inner shins.

He looks drunk, he looks like she's seen him one time at New Year's, slumped on the couch, pouting and heavy, impervious to her nudges and shunts. Now, though, he lies on the carpet, his head against the wall-unit, his chin forced into his neck. And around him, sustaining him it seems, is a black little lake, a darkling pool. She looks to her mother but her mother is busy, frantic, pushing her dad in the chest, two-handed, once and then again, serious thumps that bounce his head against the wood.

'Get someone!' her mother is shouting. 'Get someone!'

The girl turns, too quickly, skidding in the mess, down on one knee and one hand, before righting herself and skittering out. There is sky, stars, branches against the street lights. There is shouting now, clamour, a girl in a bloody nightdress whirling in the roadway, the sound of her shouting and animal cries. And now the doors are opening, lights coming on, stripes of yellow light along the paths.

Book One

Chapter One

'We're like football players,' Rix liked to say. 'Doesn't matter what we do all week. Just get it right on Saturday.' He'd trot this out, early shift on Saturdays, out on the floor in his shirtsleeves, and we watched stolidly from our workstations, watched him gesture and pace, before swivelling back to our screens. It was Rix's shtick, motivational crapola, but how wonderful, it struck me now, tracking my screensaver's tropical fish, how wonderful if this were true. All week to idle in boyish play, and then one bright flurry of achievement. Handshakes and drinks and the stereo loud on the drive home.

The telephone rang. It was Tuesday morning, quarter to twelve. I'd been sat there since eight, cursing in turn every portion of our fledgling legislature, from the ruling coalition to the inoffensive Greens. Conference was at twelve. For an hour I'd been trawling the news sites for stories. Holyrood had been in recess for a week and already the leads had dried up. The MSPs had scattered, gone to ground in Portugal and Cyprus, shielding their eyes from the poolside glare. First Minister William 'Banker Bill' MacLaren was taking his annual, ostentatiously frugal week on the Isle of Mull. I was sitting it out till my own break began, five days from now, when the boys and I would be heading west; five days' furlough on Carradale beach. Currently, on a document headed

'Schedule', I had four curt lines of text: 'Post office closures'; 'Knife crime statistics'; 'Smoking ban challenge'; and 'Gallup poll: support for Independence spikes'. If each of these stories panned out, I might make a couple of nibs, a wing column. Forget page leads. Forget splash.

I'd spent two fruitless hours trying to raise my contacts. Everyone's email had an out-of-office autoreply promising prompt attention to your message at a specified future date, two weeks down the line, and giving a mobile number for urgent enquiries. But the mobiles all rang out and went to voicemail. I pictured them throbbing forlornly on hotel dressers while their owners piloted lilos with swipes of a trailing hand, or coaxed the next coarse-grained page with a lotion-free pinkie. By now I was on to the blogs, sifting for dirt.

On the fifth ring I picked up. The click of the newsdesk secretary, putting someone through.

'Gerry Conway?'

'Speaking.'

'Must be a helluva story.'

'What's that?'

'It must be a big story you're working on, you're too busy to return your calls.'

'Who is this?'

'No time to follow a lead, even when it's served right up to your desk.'

'Who is this?'

'It's Hamish Neil, Mr Conway.'

He left a pause. I left it too. Finally he sighed, heavily.

'I phoned you last night? I phoned again this morning. I emailed you.' He blew out some air. 'About Peter Lyons?'

His tone had flattened to a petulant bleat.

'Hamish, is it? OK. Thing is, Hamish, it's a busy week. I mean, if Lyons is poking his research assistant or taking his R&R in Blythswood Square, it's not really our thing. Why don't you try somewhere else? Give the *Record* a call; the number's on the website.'

The silence had a wounded quality. I could hear his lips working, the tongue detaching itself from his teeth.

'It's not your thing?' He laughed. 'Is that right? Not your thing. It's not sex, Mr Conway. It's better than that. It's –' he let the word come to him – 'it's a bit *graver* than that.'

'Graver than sex?' I snorted. Something in his tone put my back up. 'Let's have it then. Amaze me.'

His laboured breathing filled the silence.

'The thing is,' he said finally. 'I'd rather not do this over the phone.'

'No? I'd have thought you did a lot of this over the phone.'

'What?'

'Wanking off. Try the *Record*, Mr Neil. Thanks for your call.'

Every day they plagued you. Cranks and timewasters, slanderers and fantasists. Breathless grievance merchants. Whispering grasses. People with the inside dope, the horse's mouth, on various ministers and mandarins. Rumours and smears and did-you-hear-the-one-about so-and-so. They floated this stuff on the blogs, but it wasn't enough. They needed the validation of a forty-point headline, the tangible tarnish of newsprint. Every day I took a dozen of these calls. Statistically, yeah, a portion would fly. Some of them would hold water. But how could you tell? In the absence of evidence you were down to rules of thumb, intuition, the timbre of someone's voice.

I turned back to the screen but I couldn't focus. I kept hearing Neil's flummoxed laugh, the bewilderment in his throat as I pulled the plug on him. At the start of the call his voice was hearty, voluptuous with assurance. He was practically purring. And this is the flip side of smugness: he would hardly have sounded so smug if he didn't have something good. He had mentioned an email. I opened Eudora and clicked on my inbox.

I scrolled down my messages. Aside from layered swathes of spam, highlighted in tangerine font, my inbox was clogged with comments on last week's copy. Points of information. Bulletins from interest groups. Obscene rants and sectarian slurs; flamboyant denunciations in wide-eyed capitals. I was harried by madmen. Indignant missives from halfway round the globe. The letters page was no longer enough; now people weren't happy till they'd made it personal, till they'd helped you to a perception, point by pernickety point, of the manifold levels on which your work sucked.

Finally, amid the promises of penis enlargement, offers of Viagra and cheap non-prescription drugs, I spotted it.

To: gerryconway@tribuneonsunday.com
From: neilh66@scotmail.com
Subject: Peter Lyons.
Mister Conway,
I have some information on your friend in Justice. Don't tell me you're not interested. You can reach me on 07909 738326.
Hamish Neil.

I hit 'delete' and exited Eudora. Piss or get off the pot, Mr Neil. I clicked on my bookmarked page from Visit Carradale. A hilltop view over Carradale Bay: the great white curve of sand, like the head on a pint of Guinness; the petrol-blue Kilbrannan Sound, and the five jagged peaks of Arran.

The House Under the Sea. There's a cousin of mine who isn't quite right. There were complications when Aunt Jude was giving birth. Dunc needed oxygen; someone fucked up and he got it too late. Now his features are a little squashed, and the motion of his limbs is out of true, as if he were moving underwater. He's a little slow, but mainly what he is is a guy who can't be mean. As a kid he wouldn't eat chocolate animals. His action men fraternised in an endless Christmas truce. All he really liked to do was look at fish. He watched nature documentaries. The turquoise screen; the yellow-and-black fish volte-facing smartly; the magical flourish of bubbles; the camera panning over ruined groves of coral. These images enthralled him. But when the voiceover started, when the narrative kicked in, he gave up. The words killed his interest. He'd be gawping at a sea-porcupine squirting away from a Moray eel, and then – 'The house under the sea . . .' – and that was it. He'd get up and leave the room. It became a family catchphrase; when something was boring the pants off you, when your attention had started to wander, someone would ham the Cousteau accent and mumble it into your ear.

It came to me now, as Rix soldiered on through his weekly address. He'd been at it for twenty minutes, moving his big hands around on the table like he was shuffling and setting a stack of toy bricks. The words, in his patient estuary whine, seemed to vaporise before they reached our ears, and I watched instead the meaty pale lips, the quaking pink cheeks, the bouncing blond wedge of feather-cut fringe. He was only thirty-nine, but he had the girth, the commanding upholstery, of a senior banking executive. When he spread his arms, a tremendous lemon shirt, tethered at collar and cuffs, blazed like a local sun.

We'd been through the schedule. Fiona Maguire had spoken to the news list, and I'd kept my gaze lowered while she covered politics – my four paltry offerings – in her sceptical monotone. We'd done features, foreign, sport. Neve McDonald had bestowed her grudging preview of the magazine. Rix had rallied the troops. We were nearly done. Before we rose, though, Rix liked to spring a couple of questions on one of his editors, quiz them about recent pieces, plans for the coming weeks. My turn was about due, and I'd prepared some plausible codswallop about upcoming party conferences, a possible rift in the coalition, but it wasn't required.

'Thomas!' Rix's voice was hearty now, his palms flat on the table, ready to lever himself up. 'What happened, Tam? Three pages of footie. No interviews, no Old Firm transfers. Did your guys take a collective sickie? Was there an outbreak of salmonella that I didn't hear about?'

Tam Logan's folded arms slid forward on the desk. He was shaking his head as it slumped to the wood. Logan spent the whole close season with a haunted, guilty look. For the months of June and July he did little else but smoke. When you entered or left the building, there he was, gaunt-cheeked, hunched by the revolving doors, sucking viciously on a B&H. With no Celtic-and-

Rangers, the paper could drop 5,000. Logan felt person-
ally responsible.

He raised his head wearily.

'Can only pish with the cock I've got, Norman.
Nothing's happening. If we'd qualified for bloody
Portugal we'd have something, but this is it.'

'You can't speculate? Throw some names around.
Who's unhappy at Inter, Real Madrid? They're always
unhappy, aren't they? Beckham? Adriano? The Old Firm
couldn't be in for these guys? Take a flyer.'

'They don't have any money, Norman. It's not plausible.'

Rix goggled.

'So make it plausible. Hint at takeovers. New
investors. Give me fucking something, Tam. Not endless
profiles of diddy teams.'

Logan straightened up, tossed his pen on the table. He
had stains on his hands, orange stripes down his fore and
middle fingers.

'Fine. Right.'

Two wet diamonds appeared when he laced his fingers
behind his head.

Neve McDonald was sitting across from me, doodling
on her schedule. I tried to catch her eye. She wasn't especially good-looking but she had a sulky mouth I found
appealing. I wanted to share a look, flick my gaze smartly skywards – twinkle, if I could achieve it – to signal my
wry detachment from the proceedings. She kept her eyes
on her drawing.

Rix rose, his PA scuffling papers into a bundle. There
was a ferocious crackling as everyone crumpled their
sandwich trays.

*

At my desk I checked my emails and shut down my computer. I shared a desk – a cluster of workstations – with the other specialists: energy, health, environment. What else? Education.

Tuesday conference was, for most of the working week, my only commitment. In truth, I didn't even have to turn up to this, so long as I got my schedule in to Fiona. But I made a point of attending – to keep up with what was happening, and to make sure that my stories (when I had any) got a decent show. After conference, I'd take the afternoon off. A trawl round Borders. Daniel Auteuil at the GFT. Rembrandt's *Man in Armour* at Kelvingrove. On Wednesday and Thursday I'd be at Holyrood (when Parliament was in session) or working from home (when it wasn't). It was Friday evening before I'd be back at the office to write my stories. Saturday we put the paper to bed. Sunday and Monday I saw the boys.

I was packing up to go when Martin Moir came along and sat on my desk.

There were four empty chairs – the other specialists had already left, for the back nine at Eaglesham, or a stool in the Cope, or wherever they went on a Tuesday pm. But Moir was always perching on your desk. He shifted his hams as if dropping a fart.

'Neve said there was a little *frisson* this morning?'

'Oh aye?'

Moir never went to conference but he liked to know the dirt.

'It go OK?'

'Wonderful, Martin. Really first rate.'

'He's not the worst, Gerry.'

Moir was touchy about this. A year ago, Rix set up an

'Investigations Unit' – three reporters whose brief was to develop major stories and report them in a run of double-page spreads. The unit reported directly to Rix, not to Fiona Maguire. Martin Moir headed it up. It made him look like Rix's golden boy, which is what he was. It wouldn't have bothered me, but it bothered Moir.

'He's actually pretty fair. Once you know him, I mean.'

'Who is?'

Moir smiled.

'This is something. It really is.' He had lifted one of the photos on my desk. The Sinatra. Black and white. Outside Green's Playhouse in fifty-two. My teenage old man with his arm around Frank's shoulder; Sinatra looking tousled and wry, feigning diffidence but still flashing a killer smile. The old man grinning with manic brightness.

'He really played in, Paisley was it?'

'Ayr. He played the Piv in fifty-two. The place was three-quarters empty. He was more or less a nobody at that stage. This was before the comeback. *From Here to Eternity*. All that.'

'Wow.'

He put the photo down.

'Hey. The horse's head in the bed, right?'

'In the movie, aye.'

Moir put his hands in his pockets, flapped his fingers so that his silver jiggled.

'Whatever else, Gerry, he did a real job on the *Mail*.'

I reached for my bottle of Volvic.

'It's not that bad a paper.'

'A lot of people buy it,' I agreed.

Rix had put 10,000 on the *Mail*. When everyone else was in freefall, he'd boosted the *Mail* by 10,000 a day. It made him untouchable. It made him look like a *Tribune* editor, to certain people.

'You're not being fair, Gerry. He's got ideas. If anyone can turn it round, you know? He's got a feel for the paper. He knows the culture's different, that we're not a red-top. He's actually pretty sensitive. In my experience.'

'That right? It's not your arse he'll be canning, though, is it? Your experience probably won't include picking up your books.'

It got Moir off the desk.

'That's not fair, Gerry. It's not your arse either. He actually likes you. He thinks you're sound.'

His vowels got more Ulster when you got him riled. *Soind*.

'Well that's good to know, Martin.'

He might think I'm sound, I thought. But does he think I'm any good?

Moir mooched by the desk. He wouldn't sit back down, now that I'd insulted Rix, but he wasn't ready to leave. He lifted the other photo.

'Hey. How's the Hey You?'

Moir grinned, put the picture down.

'Good. It's going really well, in fact.'

At conference, when he mentioned the Investigations Unit, Rix had started calling it the 'I.U.'

'They still think we're cops, though.'

The Hey You's current project was organised crime. Gangland Glasgow. They spent most afternoons in the East End, trying to find someone who would talk to them. At first they'd taken a car and worn their office clothes – Austin Reed suits and glossy oxfords. Even when they wised up, when they swung down from buses in their Sambas and jeans, their distressed leathers, they weren't fooling anyone. Wee boys on stairwells would hum cop-show theme tunes. They were polis, or they were social workers, or maybe journalists. They sure as fuck weren't local.

'Oh here, look at this.'

He had his wallet out and was fishing for something.

'I meant to show you earlier.'

A slippy square of paper. I couldn't make it out at first, this smudgy black expanse traversed by spidery lines of white. Then I saw it. The dark mass of the skull, edged in brilliant light, like a planetary eclipse. A narrow nub of heel. A tiny fist, upraised as if in victory or protest.

'We had the twenty-week scan on Friday. Unbelievable, eh?'

'That's great, Martin. Really. Look at the wee hand. Do you know what it is?'

He slid the photo back into his wallet.

'Nah, we just decided to wait and see. Clare thinks it's a boy, though. What about you: how's your own two?'

'Great, Martin. First class. We're going to Carradale on Sunday.'

Depending on mood, my stop was Hillhead or Kelvinbridge. The flat on Clouston Street was equidistant between the two. Tonight was a Kelvinbridge sort of night. Coming out of the station I turned left onto Great Western Road and bought a fish supper at the Philadelphia Café.

On the way up I passed the Mormons from the second floor, a blond, well-spoken twosome. As ever, they were winningly polite, wishing me well in frank Midwestern accents. With their neat haircuts, preppy short-sleeved shirts and matching satchels they looked pretty gay, which may explain the trend – surely a recent one – for laminate, corporate-looking name tags clipped to the Mormon shirt pocket. I like Mormons. There was a duo living near us where I grew up. I used to stop them in the street, quiz them about their lives. I asked about the clothes, the smart, navy duds: were these standard-issue from Mormon HQ, or did you get to choose your own? There were guidelines, it turned out, but, yes, the guys were free to assemble their wardrobe, and though the clothes were spruce they weren't expensive. 'Good enough,' said one, nodding. 'Good enough for getting doors slammed in your face,' said the other, with a wry-ness that surprised me. It was like Israeli national service: they did a two-year stint, a tour of duty, pressing door-bells in a far-off land, and then they got to go home and get on with their lives.

They were good guys, with one damning flaw. At that time I had a milk round in the mornings before school. I'd trot up people's paths with bottles wedged between my fingers (you could carry three in each hand, their short necks lodged between your knuckles) and I'd walk back down with the empties. To carry the empties you stuck a finger in the neck of each bottle: they clacked together as you walked, like the trilling of happy glass birds. Everyone else on my round knew to rinse the bot-tles in hot water before putting them out on the step, but the Mormons – whether from ignorance or indifference – never bothered. Every morning, these twin unwashed bottles, a crusted swirl round the shoulders, a curd of yel-low gunge inside the neck, and I'd be forced to plunge my fingers into these foul, sour-smelling receptacles. Every morning I cursed the Church of Jesus Christ of the Latter-Day Saints, though it never occurred to me, or else I was too diffident, to raise it with the Mormons when I saw them in the street.

For me, in any case, the gunky bottles said it all. The futility of the Mormons' mission. How could you hope to convert a people to your religion when you couldn't do something as simple as rinse a milk bottle? What kind of theology ignores the basic principles of domestic hygiene?

They don't sell milk in bottles any more, so I couldn't tell whether my current neighbours shared this foible of their predecessors. But I suspected them of grave and heinous lapses, sensational breaches in elementary sanitation, and when I saw them at their door, I tried to glimpse, beyond the neat, well-barbered heads, the chaos and squalor lurking within.

Back in the flat, I took down the new DeLillo and flicked through the pages. It was Elaine who put me onto him; she bought me *White Noise* for my twenty-fifth birthday. This is the problem with divorce: your whole life is suddenly steeped in irony. The books on your shelves. The shirts in your wardrobe. The photographs lining the hallway. Even my job was ironic. I was Scottish Political Editor for the *Tribune on Sunday*. It was my job to know the dirt on the nation's leader, to sniff out the factions and fault lines, the party cabals, the imminent splits. All this I dissected for our readers. But I couldn't do the same for my own house. The face that scowled out with such sceptical robustness from my byline photo, the cleft chin and hooded eyes that promised *I've got the down*, were those of a clueless sap: he didn't know the politics of his own front door.

It turned out my marriage was in trouble – had been for a couple of years. This was news to me and maybe right there is the problem. But at the time I didn't think there was much amiss, and even now, if I'm honest, I still don't. We talked it through, or at least we faced each other over the kitchen table one night when the boys were in bed, and Elaine spoke to the polished wood, looking up from time to time as if to check I was still listening. There was a bottle on the table between us, and two glasses, but I did most of the pouring and drinking. She covered a lot of ground in that oration, and the problems, which were partly about me, were about other things too. Things I couldn't have helped. Though there was no want of things that I could have helped, either.

I put down the DeLillo and fetched a beer. It was hard to relax, lacking distractions. I tried not to notice the quiet of the flat, its menacing stillness. Silence can impinge on you like a persistent noise. It can seem to fill the room, rising like a fluid, forcing you to act, to assert yourself against it.

When I was a kid, my dad used to take me to Mureton Baths. He had this ability to float on his back, to lie there in the pool with his hands behind his head, as if he was lying in bed. I could never do it, and for a long time this unmanageable feat was my private definition of manhood: when I was a man I'd be able to float on my back. But it never happened. My heels still drop, my neck stiffens, and I have to start kicking to stay afloat.

The silence in my flat was like this. It overwhelmed me, and soon I was out of the chair, clattering dishes in the sink, banging cupboard doors, and cranking up Elmore

James on the Bose. I thought about Elaine, the house on Monument Way. In Conwick the noise was constant. Even when the boys were in bed, we would interrupt each other. 'Wait a minute,' she'd say, her hand upraised for silence. 'Sorry. I thought I heard him crying. On you go.' We'd do this all the time. Pulling up short, halting mid-sentence, straining to hear. As the kettle clicks off or you close a cupboard door, something flares briefly behind the noise; you freeze, head cocked like a spaniel. Nothing. But when they do cry, when that heaving rhythm fills the house, there is no mistake: at its first gathering note something dips behind your chest.

I still hear it, sometimes, late at night. There's a baby in the building, in the flat above or next to mine – it's hard to tell. Late at night, a baby's wail, and the parents moving through to calm it. And sometimes it wakes me, in the early hours, and my feet are on the carpet before I realise my mistake. It sounds like Roddy, it sounds like James. A crying child always sounds like your own.

I remember my surprise, through the first few months of Roddy's life – just the power of this noise, its ardour and intensity. A baby crying. What did it signify? A full nappy. An empty stomach. And yet it carried the world's own weight of woe. It made every utterance – all the novels and epic poems, all the death-bed confessions and battle orations; it turned all this to a meaningless gloss. When he cried, the sound that came from Roddy was universal. When he stopped, when we'd lifted and patted and soothed him to sleep, the crying would continue somewhere else. I came to think that this was what we were hearing, those times when we'd thought he was crying; we'd caught a gust of that universal lamentation, had tuned in to the frequency where the crying never stops.

I gave out at the time, but secretly I relished those nightly disturbances, padding through to retrieve our crying child. When I eased him from the cot and cradled him close he'd crane round, rooting against my T-shirt, the little head bumping my chest, the mouth worrying my nipple.

'Cannae help you there, wee man. Sorry.'

In the bedroom Elaine would have fixed the pillows and sat up, tugging open her jammy top. A pillow across her lap. She pats it. I lay him down and he clamps on straight away, the crying mouth instantly plugged. There is no silence like it. No silence like that of a child no longer crying. I get back into bed and the last thing I see, between sagging lids, inches from my nose, are the baby's twitching feet, these little spasmodic kicks of satisfaction.

Thursday lunchtime. The office was quiet, the monitors blind, their dark screens latent, waiting to be touched to whiteness by the nudge of a mouse, a three-fingered tap on the space bar. Someone's television gave out the financial report. Money is important, the voice implied, but not serious; the newscaster's tone lacked the gravitas of the regular news; the timbre was peppy, bright, the light modulations of the showbiz slot or the sports round-up. There was something secret and promising in the stilled room, some echo of afterschool classrooms, and I had a vision, fleeting and sepia-toned, of brown-and-orange carpet tiles and chairs upturned on desks. A white Speedo clock on a wall.

Almost everyone had gone to lunch. A few heads bent to take bites from wrapped sandwiches or tipped to swill coffee from styrofoam cups. Burnt, bitter, mocha laced the air. The moist warm smell of focaccia.

I'd put in two good hours' work. I'd eaten lunch and was ready to nip out for a smoke, a sly toke on the Liberator, when I spotted the mail, overlooked on my desk. The biggest item was a brown, card-backed envelope, locally posted.

Inside it was a single sheet of A4. It was a Xerox of a photograph. It's a photo I have studied in some detail, and even then, as I laid it on my desk, it seemed familiar, something I'd known for years.

It's an interior shot. Seven men are grouped against a bare white wall. The two men in the foreground wear black balaclavas, army pullovers and webbing belts. They stand with their legs apart and their hands clasped in front of them. The clasped hands grip pistols, the barrels pointing to the floor. The other men, unmasked and in civilian clothes, stand behind the gunmen. Two of them hold up a UVF flag. The head of one of the men has been ringed with a marker pen, and the words 'Minister for Justice' have been written beside it. At the foot of the page, in the white margin beneath the photograph, are the digits of a mobile telephone number.

I lifted the handset and punched the number.

'Uh-huh?'

'Gerry Conway.'

A whistle. A scratchy laugh.

'Hallelujah. You're a hard man to impress. Did I finally get your attention?'

The lift door opened and Martin Moir stepped out, shrugging out of his jacket. I lifted my hand to return his wave.

'It could be anyone,' I said. 'It could be me, in those specs.'

'You think so? It's Peter Lyons all right.'

Moir draped his jacket over his seat. He pointed to the lift door and then tapped his watch; held up five fingers. I nodded, gave him the thumbs-up. We'd arranged to meet for lunch.

'So what do you want?'

'You mean, what do *you* want. You don't want to know more? Your curiosity isn't piqued?'

I met Hamish Neil that afternoon, at the Costa Coffee in Queen Street Station. Moir and I had lunch in the Merchant City and then I strolled on down to the station. There were solitary men at three of the tables in the forecourt, but I knew which was mine. I knew the smile. It went with the voice. I bought an Americano and sat down.

'Just so you've seen it,' he said, and opened his satchel. He slid a seven-by-nine across the table.

It looked a lot different. Lighter and paler, like someone had upped the brightness too far. The black smudges, the violent chiaroscuro of the photocopy had gone. The five civilians had features now, eyes and mouths in place of savage black holes. Everything was sharper, more professional, but something vital had gone, some quality of impromptu brutality, a sense of the makeshift and illicit. The figures looked almost innocuous, posing there in the adequate light.

The man in the glasses was certainly Lyons.

'Assuming it's even him,' I said. 'That's twenty years old, maybe more. What's it meant to prove? That he used to know people who liked fancy dress?' I tossed it onto the table. 'That's not a story.'

'Isn't it?' He took back the photo. 'Anyway, the photo's not the story.'

'What is it then?'

He was putting it back in the satchel.

'The story is the New Covenanters. Ever hear of them?'

I nodded, circled my wrist in a wind-it-on gesture.

He sat back, frowning.

'Yeah, of course you did. You know everything, Gerry. You know all about them. You know that our friend was involved.'

All at once, in front of the screens, a large group of passengers lifted their bags and moved off smartly for the far end of the concourse.

'Do you know that?'

'You think I'm making it up?'

'What's "involved"?'

'What?'

'You said he was involved. Involved how? Doing what?'

'Doing what they did. Fundraising. Safe houses. Going over on the Stranraer boat with a jangle of rods where his spare wheel should be. Use your imagination, Gerry. You're supposed to be a journalist.'

When he grimaced, the furrows were deep round his mouth. A scurf of white in the stubble. He'd be early forties, I figured. Ages with Lyons. Maybe a year or two younger.

'What's your angle, incidentally? Hamish. If I can ask.'

He held my gaze. He swept the back of his hand down the front of his jacket. I took in the bald leather, the frayed neck of the T-shirt, the grubby jeans.

I snorted.

'Have you not heard? There's no money in papers any more. You cannae get decent eccies now, even. I'll be lucky to get claiming for this.' I waggled my empty cup.

He swung the satchel over his head, settled the strap on his shoulder.

'You're not the only hack in Scotland, Gerry.' He jerked a thumb towards the platforms. 'There's a service to Waverley every fifteen minutes now. Four times an hour.'

'I'll see what I can do.' I stood up. 'I'll talk to my editor. If something comes of it, I can maybe get you something. A tip-off fee. Five hundred, tops. And I'd need the photo.'

He zipped his jacket, turned up the collar.

'Let me ask you something, Hamish. You said it yourself: I'm not the only show in town.'

He was bending to fasten his satchel and he looked up, flushed, incredulous.

'Christ. You really don't want this story, do you? What, are you related to this guy? Is he *paying* you? I mean: fuck.' He shook his head.

'I never said I didn't want it. I'm just intrigued. Why I'm so special. Why I get singled out for special treatment. Why is that?'

His head rode the question like a punch. Then he smiled, an ecstatic disclosure of tainted whites.

'Can't you guess, Gerry?' He stood up to leave. 'I like your work.'

In the office I googled 'New Covenanters'. Nothing came up. A few nostalgic namechecks on loyalist websites, and a deluge of evangelical pages devoted to biblical covenants. I tried Lexis-nexis, the UK newspaper archive, but it only goes back to the mid-nineties. I sent an email to Daniel Galt in Research, asking for any references to the New Covenanters in *Tribune* articles between 1981 and 1994.

What else? I thought. Then: *Lewicki.*

Jan Lewicki was a cop. I'd known him since my time on the newsdesk. Even now, it was me he brought his tips to, when he had them, and I passed them on to Maguire. I also arranged his tip-off fees which, being a cop, he wanted in cash. These days it was harder to get away with cash payments to 'anonymous' sources, but for the time being Lewicki did all right by us. I put in the call and he promised to get back to me.

'Who was that?'

Fiona Maguire was at my elbow. I wondered why my eyes weren't nipping; her perfume usually announced itself about halfway across the room.

There wasn't time to come up with a lie.

'Lewicki.'

'Yeah? Something happening?'

'Who knows? Might be nothing. Might be something.'

'Something big?'

'I think so. Maybe. I'll let you know.'

'Good.'

She walked away. She didn't even turn her head, just raised her voice to a measured shout.

'You're due it.'

Chapter Two

Skip James was the only blues singer. All the others sang about pain, they sang about trouble and woe, how their woman left them, how they couldn't pay their rent, how another mule was kicking in their stall. But the music itself was happy. It buoyed you up, got you going. It eased your pain. None of this happened with Skip. Skip James brought you down and kept you there, pinned you to the floor with clean runs of notes in a minor key. A high, complaining voice that scared you when it didn't depress you: *I'd rather be the devil than to be that woman's man.*

The *Complete Early Recordings* was playing while I fixed breakfast. I was cracking eggs into a bowl when the telephone rang.

'Is that Conway Enterprises?'

I looked at the wall-clock: quarter past seven. Lewicki was on nightshift.

'Hold on, Jan.'

I wiped my hands on a dishcloth and killed the volume on Skip's lamentations. I fished my notebook from my jacket pocket.

'On you go.'

The toaster sprung with a violent crash.

'On you go.'

'You got a pen?'

Jan had called in a favour from Special Branch. He had contacts there. Yes, there was a file on the New Covenanters, but it didn't amount to much. No one was even sure what the New Covenanters might be. It wasn't a paramilitary group. It wasn't even a street gang of the Billy Boys type. It was difficult to know what to call it. A pressure group, maybe. They sent menacing letters to Catholic MPs and known Republican sympathisers. They disrupted Republican marches, wrestled banners to the ground. The group seems to have disbanded, so far as anyone could tell, around 1983. Probably it was a tiny operation, a few guys in someone's back bedroom. The New Covenanters was mainly a name, Lewicki offered, something to spray on garage walls.

'Thanks anyway, Jan.'

'There's something else,' he said. 'They put out a newsletter. There was a guy lifted for a breach at a Troops Out march in eighty-two. He had a shoulder bag filled with copies of this magazine.'

I opened the notebook again.

'What was it called?' I said.

'*Rathlin.*'

'As in the island?'

'What?'

'Rathlin Island?'

'I suppose.'

'Good. What about the guy, the vendor; what was his name?'

'Thomas Deans.'

'He still about?'

'He's dead, Gerry.'

'Bollocks.'

I had filled the filter cone with hot water and now it would be close to overflowing. I tried to reach it but the phone cord wouldn't stretch.

'Yeah.' Lewicki sighed. 'But here's the thing. This guy had a brother: Jacob.'

'Uh-huh?'

'Jacob Deans.'

Coffee had spilled over the lip of the mug, pooling on the breakfast bar. Lewicki was waiting.

'I'm sorry, Jan, You've lost me.'

'*Dixie* Deans?'

'Right. Jesus.'

I wrote 'Dixie Deans' on the pad. Then the word 'Maitland'. Deans was a gangster, a local face. One of the Maitland crew. Since Rix had corralled us along the red-top road, we'd seen a lot of Walter Maitland in our pages. According to Martin Moir's increasingly florid copy, Maitland was the overlord of Glasgow crime, the Clydeside Moriarty. He lived in Cranhill and most of the 'business' in the East End – girls, smack, racketeering – went through Maitland. In my own days on the newsdesk I'd covered some of the trials, Maitland's soldiers, his scuzzy lieutenants. I'd seen them taken down, cuffed hands held aloft in gestures of effete defiance. But mostly they walked, emerging onto the steps amid a sidling scrum of reporters, arms spread in benediction to deliver the victory speech, cheeky-boy grins on their chib-marked maps. This was the photo the papers would carry next morning. People can't get enough of these stories. It took me a while to appreciate this, but the city likes its gangsters. A certain civic affection has always encom-passed them, the Fullertons, the Norvals, the Boyles.

Gangsters are a local speciality, like charismatic socialists and dour-faced football managers. People connect them to an older Glasgow, a darker, truer city before the stone-cleaning and the logos, Princes Square and the City of Culture. We take solace in their formalised acts of violence, these murders in which everything – location, timing, the disposition of the corpse – has an emblematic aptness, a rhetorical neatness. Bodies dumped in cars, the bullet up the anus, the dead tout clutching a bag of dogshit: the codes are being respected, you feel, protocols observed.

'So what was Deans's involvement? Was he part of it, the New Covenanters?'

'Nah, not that we know of. It seems a bit, *cerebral* for Dixie.'

I could see his point. I'd last encountered Deans at the Sheriff Court, when he'd answered a charge of common assault. The victim had lost four teeth and a part of his ear. Deans had walked – forensics were inconclusive – but no one was fooled. When he passed the victim's family in the public gallery – they were on their feet and shouting abuse – Deans had cupped a hand to his ear.

'So, what, is Dixie still to the fore?'

Jan laughed. 'Christ, you are out of it, Gerry. He's breathing, but he's not earning. He's doing a seven in Saughton. Attempted murder. He tried to pull a guy's tongue out wi a meat hook. Guy nearly drowned in the blood.'

'Nice.'

I rang off and mopped up the coffee.

After breakfast I phoned Doug Haddow at the Mitchell. I'd known Doug from my postgrad days, when

I'd studied in Special Collections during vacations. There was no mention of *Rathlin* in the online catalogue – I'd checked it on the laptop as I drank my coffee – but I knew that parts of the Glasgow Collection were still uncatalogued. Doug came on the line, and, in his smoker's pneumatic rasp, confirmed this. He told me there were substantial holdings of political ephemera – pamphlets, election leaflets, party newsletters and so on – that they'd only begun to process. He'd have a look when he found a spare half-hour.

Two hours later, I was sitting at my desk when the phone rang again. He'd found it. Issued fortnightly for the best part of a year. *Rathlin: The Magazine of the New Covenanters*. I rang off and grabbed my jacket.

The Mitchell Library on North Street. Ten yards from its entrance the traffic churns past in a vast concrete trench. The lorries and cars make the building look transient; at any moment it might take flight in search of its proper context. I paused on the flyover. Even in the fifties, before the motorway ripped through the city, marooning the West End, the Mitchell must have looked incongruous, rising in its pompous bulk above the tenements of Charing Cross. An enormous dome; two vast assertive wings; the balconies and balustrades and columns: it looks less like a library than a presidential palace, the Capitol of a toppled dynasty. Inside, attendants in lugubrious green uniforms would be stationed in the chequerboard corridors, pacing the lacquered leagues of panelled mahogany, glancing through sheets of gilt-lettered glass. They should have sited it here, I reflected, the new Parliament. It looks more like a parliament than the Parliament does.

I climbed the steps and pushed the heavy doors, took the stairs to Floor 2. Archives and Special Collections was empty, and I chose my old desk, beside the windows on the back wall. Within a minute Doug Haddow was padding across from the counter, gripping a brown cardboard box-file.

'It's not a complete run,' he said. 'There are three or four issues missing. Still, it's as good as you're going to get.' He hovered for a few seconds, ran his hand through his sparse hair, primping the sandy tuft at the front. He looked as if he was about to ask me something, maybe reminisce about old times, but another reader had materialised at the counter. 'Let me know if you need anything.'

'Good man, Doug.'

I opened the box and riffled through the magazines, laid them out on the desk like a game of patience. There were nineteen issues, running from September 1981 through to July 1982. Three rows of six and one left over. I slipped my jacket over the back of my chair and started to read.

The early numbers were winningly crap. Issue 1 was eight typewritten sheets, folded and stapled. Photocopying had thickened some of the font and obliterated all gradations of shade in the photographs, lending them the starkness of Reformation woodcuts. The cover price – fifty pence – had been added in marker. The title was shakily stencilled over a hamfisted logo depicting a handshake.

Still, things picked up quickly. By the fourth number there was a glossy cover, and the title appeared in bright royal blue. But issue seven was where it really changed.

Now the format was A4. The four-colour cover was nicely composed, a long-shot of Edward Carson's statue at Stormont flanked by cover lines flagging that issue's themes. A set of interlocking hexagons provided the logo beneath a title in forty-point Arial. Inside, the copy was laid out in neat double columns, with photographs in high resolution. The cover price had doubled, but either sales had been notably brisk, or someone had thrown money at the magazine.

For the rest of that afternoon, I never stirred from my seat. I read *Rathlin* all the way through – nineteen issues, a nearly complete run. It was a weird, heterogeneous mix. The editorials assessed the state of play in Ulster, both military and political, with a plausible – if partisan – logic. But then there were scare stories of clerical abuse, tales of priestly concupiscence – nuns ravished by cardinals, their bastard babies smothered at birth – that might have been fashioned by Melville or Knox. In between there were interviews with paramilitary spokesmen, and messages of support for Loyalist prisoners. There was a poetry corner, full of doggerel ballads in praise of fallen comrades. A lot of the articles were unattributed, and a colourful range of pseudonyms – 'Cuchulain', 'Ulster Defender', 'John Knox', 'Peden the Prophet' – was pressed into service. But I spotted one article, and then another, seven in all, that carried a by-line: 'Gordon Orchardton'. I tried to think what the name might signify, what resonance it possessed. Was it the name of a famous Reformer, a Protestant martyr? I didn't think so. It looked to me like an actual name. I put it in my notebook.

It was six o'clock when I turned the last page of Issue

19. Doug's shift had finished – a middle-aged woman was at the issue-desk computer – and the reading room was empty. I put the magazines back in the box-file and carried it across.

'Thanks a lot,' I said. 'Tell Doug I owe him one.'

Something in her smile made me pause, and I wondered if she and Doug might not be an item.

'A pint, would that be? Whyn't you buy him it. He'll be over the road.' She hefted the box-file. 'As ever.'

'Thanks. I might do that.'

I left the Mitchell by the side entrance. The Avalon Bar is across the way, on the corner of Kent Road and Cleveland Street. Above the curtain on its bright brass rail I could see the heads of the drinkers. There he was, sure enough, on a stool at the bar, his bald crown shining under the gantry spots, nodding at something the barman was saying. I turned away and walked towards the M8. I fancied a drink but I knew, if I got ensconced with Doug Haddow, the next time I'd see pavement would be when the bar staff were shouting 'Time'.

I crossed the expressway and headed into town. Bath Street was deserted, the office workers finished for the night, the basement antique shops shuttered and dark. It was the lull before the onslaught, the furious merriment of Friday night. The few pedestrians moved quickly, as if observing some secret curfew. I lit a number 3, with its oddly effete, short-sighted-looking portrait of Simón Bolívar – 'The Liberator' – on the band, and rolled its creamy smoke around my tongue. I liked this time of the week. The whole city knocking off work and me with it all still to do. Three stories and an editorial. It gave me a virtuous glow, but no harm, I figured, in topping it up. I looked in at the Horseshoe for a pint of Deuchars and a pie-and-beans at the bar. Outside Central I took a cab and leaned back as we crossed the river.

My wallet was pressing into my back. I tugged it from my hip pocket and felt the folded sheet of paper. I spread it on the seat beside me. There was a tension in the group, an air of suppressed hilarity, as if they'd been joking ten seconds before, and had to compose themselves for the camera. There was something too emphatic in the sombreness of the faces, the shadowed tightness of the mouths, the brows' deep compression. Only Lyons was different, his features caught in a midway blur, a sinuosity of the lips suggesting laughter. His face was somehow clearer than the others, as if the flash had fallen full on him or else a mirror had thrown its refulgence his way. His eyes behind the lenses were bright. It was the face of a tourist, an autograph hunter.

The cab had stopped. The 'B' of TRIBUNE had gone out, the neon shorted. I fished in my wallet for a note.

On Sunday evening I stood in the kitchen, making the boys' tea. Muddy Waters on the sound system: 'You Can't Lose What You Ain't Never Had'. James was playing with his action figures on the kitchen table. Roddy was through in the living room; incidental music from *Harry Potter and the Philosopher's Stone* rose in intermittent crescendos above Muddy's slide work.

Pasta and smoked haddock. It's my speciality – at least, it's something I can do, something quick and unfuckupable that the boys appear to like. I took the smokies out of the fridge. These were the real thing: blackened, stiff, the tails still bound with twine. I loved to prepare them. You microwave the fish for sixty seconds. Then you prop it on a plate and press down firmly on the spine. You feel a crack and the whole fish subsides, collapsing into itself. When you flip it over the haddock opens like a missal. You peel the spine like a silk ribbon and the flesh comes away in moist flakes, thick bite-size discs.

The day had gone well. In the morning we'd been to the Botanics and played hide-and-seek in the Kibble Palace, dodging around the primeval ferns. We lunched in McDonald's and played a game where we pretended that James was invisible. Then we took the Underground into town, James woo-hooing in the echoey tunnels ('Dad, another James is copying me'), and Roddy straphanging in the half-empty carriage. On Buchanan Street Roddy put a pound in a busker's guitar case and walked back with that stiff-legged, sheepish look that always makes me want to laugh. In the toyshop I vetoed Rod's initial choice – a Ninja sword that made electronic slashing sounds – and steered him to a Playmobil motorbike. James chose a pair of jousting knights. In the bookshop we bought *Tintin in Tibet*.

The fish was prepared and the pasta was coming to the boil. I was unstacking the dishwasher and setting the table while James improvised savage unhorsings and pro-tracted gory spearings amid the cutlery.

'That's like Adam,' he said, pointing at me.

'What is?'

'That.' He leaned across and touched my chin, pursed my lips between his fingers.

'Jaggy!'

'Oh the beard? Right.'

I hadn't shaved for a couple of days.

'Adam's got a 'stache.'

He made a neighing noise and cantered a horse across his side-plate. I added salt to the pasta.

'Do you like Adam? Is Adam nice?'

'Yes he is.'

A hissing burst of gunfire – the lances had turned into rifles – knocked one of the knights off his mount.

'He's Mummy's friend.'

'That's right.'

The windows were blanched. Condensation showed up the patterns of dirt – a mess of streaks and spots and runnels.

'Dad?'

I was stacking bowls in the cupboard when James spoke, so what he said next came through a bright ceramic clatter. But I still heard him.

'Adam pushed me.'

I turned round – too abruptly, for he looked up, wary.

'Say it again, son?'

His shoulder came up and he buried his face in his neck.

'Adam pushed me.'

I remember looking at the pasta – spiralli, it was – swirling in the boiling pot, and finding it hard to draw breath. I wanted to sink to my knees, a feeling prompted by two consecutive thoughts: *this might be true*; and *I have no way of knowing*. I crossed to the table and hunched down beside him.

'What happened, kid? When did Adam push you?'

My voice was soothing, low: if I spooked him now, it was over; I'd never get to the truth of it.

'Don't know.' He looked at the ceiling where the steam was massing. 'Smoke! Daddy, I want pineapple juice!'

'OK.'

I fixed his drink and then held it away from his outstretched hand.

'James. Listen to Daddy. What happened, James? Why did Adam push you?'

He reached for the plastic cup, his little fist flashing open and closed.

'Want it!'

'James!'

I touched his shoulder.

'Kid. This is important. This is really really important. Did Adam push you?'

'What?'

'Did Adam *push* you?'

'What, Daddy!'

'Was he kidding on? Was it just pretend?'

He looked up and seemed to decide. He nodded. His lips stretched in a coy grin.

'Just p'etend!'

He took the cup in both hands and buried his nose in it.

I opened the window and steam billowed out.

That night, when the boys had their bath, I studied their bodies for signs of abuse. They stood on the mat in their blithe nakedness: damp, fuzzy-duck heads; big goose-bump-stippled bellies; tiny pricks; and plump, slightly knock-kneed legs. Once I'd patted and rubbed them dry I scooped my fingers into the big tub of Epaderm, rubbed my hands together and then smeared their bodies till they shone like seals. Then I unscrewed the tube of Fucibet and dabbed a spot of cream on wrists, elbows, ankles, the joints of the fingers, the backs of the knees. Then I worked these in with my thumb.

There was nothing – other than the eczema patches – to cause concern. Roddy had a fading, pistachio-coloured bruise at the top of his leg, but Roddy always had bruises and when I asked him about it he couldn't remember. Probably he had fallen off his scooter.

I phoned Elaine when the boys were in bed.

'Don't be daft, Gerry. It's just something he says.'

'You think?'

'He says it all the time. He said it about Stacey, remember?'

This was true. Stacey was the 'tweenie-room' supervisor at the Rocking Horse. When Elaine took the nursery manager aside, and then Stacey was summoned, there was a difficult scene, with tears and testimony and earnest declarations. Stacey's shock was so patently genuine, her hurt so real, that Elaine felt embarrassed, and sorry for having mentioned it at all.

'It's something kids say. It doesn't mean anything.'

'I don't know. The way he plays with his knights, the little action figures? Was he always this . . . *bloodthirsty*?'

'What are you saying, Gerry?'

'I'm just saying.'

'Gerry. If my boyfriend was hitting my children, believe me, I would know. I'm not some junked-out lassie on a sink estate. He's not a hitter, Gerry. He doesn't even raise his voice. He doesnae swear.'

Unlike you, said the silence.

'Right.'

She rung off shortly after, sounding a little sore. I sat in the living room with the *Weekly Guardian* and a bottle of Rolling Rock. But I couldn't read. I kept picturing Adam standing over my sons, his black eyes narrowed, white teeth bared below a black moustache. From the boys' perspective, the figure foreshortened, he'd be as tall as a building.

I finished my beer and fetched another. I thought of Big D. I was already in my teens when Big D came into the picture – Derek Maxwell, Mum's post-divorce boyfriend – and the question of discipline never arose. Though on one occasion it nearly did. We were in London for a weekend break, one of Big D's minutely planned excursions. This one involved a Saturday-night dinner and West-End-show combination. The restaurant was a fancy one and I was supposed to wear a shirt and tie. I actually liked wearing a shirt and tie – getting dickered up, as Mum called it – but I was kicking up stink. I wanted to wind Derek up, force him to intervene so I could tell him he wasn't my dad and where he could stuff his poxy show. Mum kept on at me in this ineffectual wheedling voice, until finally she turned to Big D with a help-me-out-here shrug. Big D wheeled round from the mirror, where he was briskly folding a four-in-hand, and surveyed the scene. Then he turned back to the mirror, still knotting his tie, and, addressing no one in particular, announced: 'He'll do what his mother tells him.'

This was cute, I thought. It sounded decisive and authoritative, but it still left the onus on Mum. If I'd really wanted, I could have picked a fight at that point, but I went to my room and got ready.

I was fifteen when this happened, a surly six-footer in a

cut-off T. Roddy and James were still babies. What chance did they have if Adam turned heavy?

My acoustic was propped against the fireplace. I ran through some blues riffs but they sounded stale – I'd played them too often and I was a shade out of tune. I footered with the tuning pegs for a while but it was no good; something was always a semitone out.

What worried me was Roddy. I knew what Roddy was like, how maddening he could be in that wild half-hour before teatime. He would leap around on the furniture and howl like a coyote. And I knew how quickly you could lose the rag. It was scary how abruptly I could turn. One minute I'd be asking him, in a tone of studied evenness and balance, to please not climb on the sofa, and the next I'd be springing from my armchair in a crash of crumpling newspaper and yanking him by the arm right up the stairs.

It startled me as much as it did him, this instant murderous rage. Where did it come from? And this was my own son, a boy I would cheerfully die for, a boy whose life's load of pain I would gladly endure in his place. If your own kid could rile you like this, what about someone else's? Every day, the inside pages carried the same scenario: a toddler shaken to death, a baby taken to hospital with multiple injuries. And always, without fail, it was the boyfriend, some boorish lummox with a Friday-night skinful, the big cat who killed off the other cat's cubs.

I thought about this, taking big pulls on my Rolling Rock and forcing myself to imagine it. I opened another bottle and something struck me. What if Elaine was right? What if Adam *was* this big benign guy? Captain

Benevolence. Mister Pacific. Wouldn't they choose him over me? Wouldn't they be right to? Maybe I'd got it all wrong. Maybe my departure wasn't a burden to the boys. Maybe it was a deliverance. I had lightened everyone's load.

I sat for a while, not knowing which worried me more – the mean Adam or the good one. I opened the last beer. The couple from the flat below came home. There was a splash of dropped keys and some laughter and the guy's voice, low and smooth and sexual. Then music came on, low, an alt/country thing with pedal guitar. I listened till the beer was done. I checked the boys and went to bed.

I woke in the small hours, panting, hunched on my side, sweating like a racehorse. My knees were stuck together and as I raised one leg and flapped the covers the night air rushed wetly in. I was in a house. It was our house in Conwick but also it wasn't: it was a large, wood-framed mansion of a kind familiar from black-and-white films. *To Kill a Mocking Bird. It's a Wonderful Life.* Elaine was there with the boys. Some people were coming to kill us and we were looking for a place to hide. From an upstairs window I watched two men come down the path. One of them stopped to close the gate, and as he turned back to the path he glanced straight up to my watching-place and nodded.

They wore full-face balaclavas, and heavy revolvers swung at their sides. They had bowler hats on top of the balaclavas, and instead of army-surplus jumpers and jeans they wore dazzling white suits of a beautiful cut.

When the men passed out of sight on their way to the front door I found myself in a kind of closet at the end of the first-floor landing. Elaine and the boys huddled behind me. I could hear the gunmen moving around downstairs. I was watching the top of the stairs from a keyhole in the closet door. Then there was a heavy, creaking tread and then one of the gunmen appeared. Just the one. 'He's killed the other guy,' I remember thinking. Smoke was lifting in plumes from his handgun. Suddenly I was alone: Elaine and the boys had escaped. There had been some sort of tunnel or trapdoor, but it was no longer available; I would have to face the gunman on my own. With his free hand he took off his bowler and skimmed it, Oddjob style, across the landing. Then he gripped the hem of his balaclava and tugged, peeling it free, tossing his hair and baring his teeth in a dazzling smile. It was Adam. He was looking straight at me, as if he could see right through the keyhole, and he moved towards me in great clipping strides. I saw his hand reach for the door-knob as I scrambled back against the closet wall, and then a flash of white as the door was tugged free and I woke.

It was almost light. The bedroom, still unfamiliar after five months, took a moment to remember itself, to settle into its established contours. *It's OK*, I thought. *I'm all right*. Then I heard a hiss, a slurping suck. Shallow breathing, close, right behind me in the room. Panic swelled and died, like boiling milk coming off the heat. I reached behind me and found a foot, a warm parcel of flesh which I gripped and squeezed. I laid the back of my forefinger against the sole, feeling the pudgy creased coolness. Glissade of the instep, the crust of eczema over his ankle. The foot moved and James inhaled noisily, settling down with little slurps of mastication.

Chapter Three

I clattered downstairs to Floor 3. There was an under-standing, our own floor being busier, that we could use the subs' facilities. They hated it. They viewed us, not even as the enemy (we weren't clever enough for that), but as salaried schoolkids whose mess they cleaned up. Their communal areas were full of snidey notices, tacked up like cards at an exhibit:

THE MICROWAVE IS NOW CLEAN. PLEASE LEAVE
IT THAT WAY.
CLEAN ALL 6 SURFACES.

IN THE INTERESTS OF HYGIENE, PLEASE FLUSH
THE TOILET AFTER USE.

This wasn't internal Floor-3 housekeeping: you could tell these were directed at us, the interlopers. They probably wanted notices that read 'FUCK OFF AND LEAVE US ALONE', but this was the next best thing.

The coffee had done its job but I sat on, wallowing in my stink, feeling the blood prick and fizz along the backs of my legs. There was a frosted dormer at my back but I left it closed. Twice, the handle rattled and footsteps dwindled up the hall. When I was finished I took out my pen and subbed the notice over the cistern. I put a line through everything except 'PLEASE FLUSH'. Then I left without flushing.

When I got back to my desk the phone was ringing.

'Gerry, it's Darren.' The voice was languid, suave. 'Darren Bryce.'

'You think I know two Darrens?'

Bryce was a senior aide at Justice. Lyons's bagman. *That was quick*, I thought. Does he know already? Is he *in* on it?

'Peter's in town,' Bryce said. 'He wonders if you're free for lunch.'

'He has to, what, negotiate for lunch now? He can't pick up the phone?'

'He's tied up, Gerry. Busy busy. But he's very keen to see you.'

I opened my desk drawer. The photograph was still there, under a couple of magazines.

'Sure he is. So, what: the Townhouse?'

'Yeah? Peter was thinking maybe the other place.'

The other place was Ferrante's, an old Sicilian basement in the Merchant City. It was some sort of Party haunt, the place they chose for their victory dinners.

'I don't know. It's a little cramped.'

'Peter was hoping Ferrante's.'

I sighed.

'Was he hoping a particular time?'

'One-thirty, we thought.'

I slipped the photo out from under the magazines, put it in my briefcase.

'Bryce?'

'What?'

'Can he eat the stuff himself? Can he do that much?'

'He'll see you at half-one, Gerry.'

On sunny summer afternoons, Glasgow is Manhattan. The buildings instantly lofty, colossal. Black diagonals of shade bisect the traffic, cut across the cabs on St Vincent Street. The city looks like a photograph, black-and-white, something out of Berenice Abbott, Bleecker Street or Union Square.

Fratelli Ferrante was packed. Usually, on visits here, I'd be shown to the toilet corner, where the two-seaters clustered like bubbles so that you ate with your elbows pressed to your sides. Today, though, I followed the waiter's twisting hips to the sunflower centre of the floor, to a table right below the bladed fan.

Lyons was finishing a phone call. He half rose from his seat, his hand raised in greeting and deferral. As I reached the table he snapped the phone shut, glanced at his watch.

'Gerry Conway,' he said. 'The late edition.' The smile showed he was joking. His fingers wiped mine in a brisk shake. There was skittishness, a little flourish to his movements. The eyes were bright, brief scintillas of light fizzing in the blackness. He's on something, I might have thought; the guy's buzzed. If I hadn't known better.

It was cool: even on a day like this, when shoppers wore the plaintive gaze of martyred saints in Renaissance paintings. Fan-freshened air on my nose and cheeks. You wanted to press the back of your hand to all the restaurant's surfaces: the dark wood of the chair-backs, the tabletop's pink marble, the starched napkins that gave off the cool of hotel bedsheets, the blades of the big-handled butter-knives.

There was no menu on the table.

'The special's sole. And it *is* special, in here. I took the liberty.' He had fished a bottle from an ice-bucket beside the table and was filling my glass. 'I hope that's OK?'

I hung my jacket on the chair. 'That's great, Peter. Spot on.'

He laughed. 'It is Friday after all.'

The wine was cold, sharp, appley. It tasted pleasantly neutral, as if the chill had dulled its flavours.

The place was busy. Business suits and well-heeled shoppers. A toothy woman three tables away had noticed Lyons; she was leaning over to her companion, fixing Lyons with that furtive, hungry squint that is so much more blatant than a stare.

'What's the occasion?'

Lyons chuckled, shook his head. 'I'm meeting an old friend,' he said. 'Do I need an excuse?' He lifted the bottle again. Lyons didn't drink, but he made sure your glass was full. I'd noticed this about him, how he was always buying rounds, pouring wine, as if his continence wasn't enough on its own; it needed the relief of the other guy's indulgence.

'All right. Keys, OK? I've a couple of things I thought you could use.'

I pushed my cutlery aside to make room for my note-book. Lyons sighed, then leaned towards me. I wrote while he talked, getting it down, stopping now and then for a gulp of wine. He spoke in a low tone, unhurried, matching his words to the speed of my pen. He gazed off while he spoke, glancing down now and then – I could sense the big chin tipping towards me – to check on my progress with an air of slightly pained distraction, like he was waiting for someone to finish pissing. As summer stories go, these ones were worth a punt. Lyons was announcing a review into 'slopping out' in Scottish jails. He also leaked me a report into private prison finance. These were fine, but the third was a page lead. A sex offender on early release had assaulted a woman in Queen's Park. The news would break tomorrow and the tabloids would go for Lyons, calling on him to intervene. He wanted me to draw the sting on Sunday with a piece blaming the Lord Advocate. When I tucked the notebook away, Lyons clapped his big hands and rubbed them together.

A waiter bore down on us, promisingly, and passed on, his two plates bound for other stomachs, and I rode the little stab of disappointment.

'How're things down there, then? How's Rix?'

Lyons's phone jiggled on the tablecloth, like a beetle trying to right itself. He opened it, checked the number, and closed it again.

'How's Norman?'

A smile was already snagging his lips. He loved to hear Rix getting slagged.

'Rix? The Englishman abroad?' A vegetable smell – asparagus? fennel? – rose from the table behind. I hadn't realised I was hungry till the waiter passed us over. The bread basket was empty.

'Stormin' Norman. He's, like, the worst news we've ever carried. This sentimental cynicism. He's a fucking zealot. I'm right and you're all wrong. Doesn't matter the numbers don't back him.' I looked over Lyons's shoulder; a head flashed past the porthole in the kitchen door. 'In a month or two he'll be flying round the Quay, handing folk their cards. He'll still be wrong, but the numbers'll look better.'

'Heavy weather, eh? The new regime.'

'What can you do? They don't last for ever.'

'You said it.' He was smiling.

'What?'

'I'm saying nothing.'

His smile wouldn't be quelled. Even when he frowned at the tablecloth it kept springing back.

'MacLaren?'

He rolled his eyes innocently.

'You mean, you wish?'

'No.' He shook his head briskly. 'No, he told me himself. He doesn't want to fight the next election. He's standing down next month. He wants to announce it at conference.'

'Why? What is it?'

'I don't know. His wife's ill. He's had enough. He wants to spend more time on Mull. He's nearly sixty, Gerry. He's by with it.'

I sighed. 'Tch. And no one waiting to fill the breach.'

He grinned. The waiter was back and this time it was us. He set the plates down and the warm bland reek of the tatties rose with the uriney tang of the fish.

'Who else has it?'

I had my notebook out once more. He put down the salt and swept his hand towards me in a showman's flourish.

'For real?'

'Would I trust such an item to anyone else? Only, don't sit on it; if he's told me, you know?'

I lifted my knife and fork. The waiter was back again, with a peppermill the size of a rifle. He presented it to Lyons, gave its base three sharp twists and then clutched it diagonally to his chest. I waved him away.

'By the by, Gerry, the photo? The one you used last time? Desperate. I'll get Bryce to send one over.'

'Uh-huh.'

Leave the big shots, Eric told me. Eric Aitken, this was. My first week at the *Tribune*. Don't waste your time. The leaders, the lieutenants. They'll only spill what suits them. Look to the new ones, the up-and-comers. It's like the cuddies, he said. Study the field. Pick out a couple. Cultivate them. Take them to lunch, slip their names into your copy, talk them up a little. When they rise, they take you with them.

He was right. The only advice I was ever offered, and I took it. And I chose well. Not the others, maybe, not the two or three rookies I'd coaxed and flattered, but Lyons, whom I'd rated from the start. It was pure luck. I caught him at the City Halls, at the start of the referendum campaign. It was a yes-camp rally: 'Scotland United'. He took the stage like a boxer, his big shoulders rolling, and faced the mike. Nobody knew him. But he frowned out into the crowd and started to talk. The big flat hand – chop, chop – falling in time with the words. He had the trick of rhythm, starting low and calm and then throwing out phrases, beating the air with his hand, till he signed off on a strong indignant quiver. As he built to each crescendo the hand fell faster, till it seemed he was chopping a log, and then the log gave way in a crash of applause. His hair was longer then, a swart pelt, and with every juddering salvo his fringe worked loose, till it dropped across his eyes and he forced it back with a swipe of his paw.

When he finished, when he left the stage to the stamping

of feet, his plum shirt black and a long damp leaf up the seam of his jacket, I was waiting at the stairs, my card between two fingers. We ate lunch the next day. For the rest of the campaign I looked out for him. He wasn't around much. I caught him at a hustings in Ayrshire. He spoke from an open-top bus in George Square. And then I saw him at the count in Edinburgh, before the big screen with a Coke in his hand, raising his glass as the votes thumped home.

And then he just vanished. Not vanished, exactly, but he dropped out of sight. He'd been promised the nomination to one of the Glasgow seats, and when this didn't happen he took it badly. For four years no one saw him. And then he was back, elected on the Glasgow list, rising in Holyrood to give his maiden speech. The speech was special. It had none of the rancour, none of the field-preacher cadences of the referendum tour. He was witty, dry; nervous at first, you could see that, but enjoying himself, in full control. He spoke without notes, in a courtroom style, swinging round suddenly and pointing his finger, spreading his arms in cajoling appeal. His voice carried, an educated baritone, dropping an octave for prickly little asides in Glasgow Scots. Afterwards, in the Garden Lobby, everyone pouted and shrugged, leafed through their press-packs. But the hacks were stirred, skittish as horses, tossing their heads as they kept an eye on the members' door. I listened to the talk and kept my mouth shut. And that Sunday we ran a profile, a full page with quotes from his law-firm partners and wry reminiscences from primary teachers.

He was holding the bottle now, tipping it towards me.

He's missed the boat, I had thought, when he lost the

nomination. But watching him now, I could see it had made him, the four-year delay. It looked like precision timing. By the time he got elected, the country was yearning for someone like Lyons. The new dispensation had waned. The promise had dimmed, the lustre dulled, and here came Peter Lyons, with his rational charm, his chat-show eloquence, his Mafioso neckties. Peter Lyons, who was new, untarnished, and yet a link with the old brave days, the calendar of hope.

I put my hand over the glass.

'It's only going to waste.' Lyons waggled the bottle.

'They can put it in the gamberoni,' I said. The second glass had made me sleepy. Already the thought of the office was turning sour, like the first twinge of a headache.

'Anyway, we're not all demob happy. Some of us have our work to go to.'

'Yeah?' The bottle clanked as Lyons set it down. 'It seems to me I've just about done your work. I've just about sorted you out. Or is that not right?'

He was nettled. I'd only meant to josh him, find a tactful way of declining the wine. But his face was dark now, with sullen bumps below his mouth.

The glass wobbled as I pushed it to the centre of the table.

'Yeah, you're right. It's only three thousand words, Peter. It writes itself.'

'Bryce'll send you the quotes.' He was smiling again. 'Drop him an email. He'll send them over. You string them together; top and tail.' He laughed. He leaned forward, telling me a secret. 'Nobody reads it all the way through, Gerry.' He leaned back, raised his hand for the check.

His smile failed as the money fluttered down. Two twenties and a ten.

'That cover it?' I put my wallet back in my pocket.

'Gerry. *Gerry*.' He caught my sleeve as I negotiated the tight table, chairs squealing on the tiles. 'I'm kidding, all right? I'm kidding. Jesus. Touchy, Gerry.' He clapped his shoulder. 'Sit down for Christ's sake. You're worse than MacLaren. Come on, Gerry. You know what I think of you. You know I rate you. Did I help out a wee bit? Did I help things along a little?'

What could I say? I shrugged. A waiter was waiting to get past; he stood before me with three desserts balanced on his arm; a tiramisu and two elaborate ice-cream structures. I sat down.

'That's all I'm saying then.' He folded the banknotes, lodged them in the pocket of my shirt. 'That's all I'm saying.'

The waiter squeezed between the tables, twisting his hips like a matador.

We ordered coffee and talked about nothing; Party gossip; Celtic-and-Rangers. At one point the lights went out and a fizzing, orange ball wavered into view, and a man's reddened features, savage in the ruddy glow. Then the music started and everyone joined in, craning round to see. Lyons was beaming. The voices thinned when it came to the name – Timmy, it might have been, or Cammy or Terry – and then we all rallied round on the final line. The kid's round mouth raked the conflagration – there were sparklers in there, and four or five candles – and everyone clapped as the lights came back on.

'How's your own two?' he asked. 'Ricky and James?'

'Roddy. They're great. I'm taking them up the coast next week. Carradale.'

'Nice.'

Lyons's phone rang again.

'Do you mind?' The phone perched on his outstretched palm, open, like a black plastic bird. 'I sort of need to take this.'

'On you go.' I needed a piss in any case.

When I got back Lyons was signing a napkin for the toothy woman.

I called for the check.

At the birthday table the kid was sulking, his chin deep down between the wings of his polo shirt. As his dad leaned in close, the boy flinched, hunching his shoulders as if he was cold, as if his clothes were suddenly wet. I could hear the dad's tone, coaxing and low – a tone that the kid himself would come to master, the tone of a man letting somebody down.

The waiter arrived with the check and presented it to Lyons.

The street was cooler now – a breeze had come up off the river – and as we strolled towards George Square the tension between us passed, as if the restaurant were to blame, its enervating cramped formality, and here in the open air we were easy as ever.

Lyons stopped to light a torpedo; the flame flapped whitely, twice, like a butterfly's wings, as he sucked and puffed and got it to draw. A great white cloud plumed skywards.

'Oh yes.' He shook his head. 'Smoking ban. Fucking politicians. Listen, Gerry.'

'What?'

We paused at a junction.

'About the wine. Back there. It was stupid; I should have thought.'

'What?'

'It never occurred to me. I'm sorry.'

We stood at the kerb. A bus rolled through the junction, its fumes blue in the afternoon sun. I'd been in rehab, briefly, a year or so back – there were alcohol issues after the split – but I didn't see how Lyons could know this. I was about to ask him what he meant when the signal changed and the crowd pressed forward. On the far pavement a man in a red wooden booth called '*Evening Times*' in a stylised bark. Lyons strode ahead, his free hand rooting for change. A backdraught of smoke gusted into my face and the two things – the smoke and the bright hot sun – pitched me back a quarter-century. Sunlit water on wooden planks. I'm in the Howard Park, half in and half out of the gloom beneath the footbridge, reclining on the earthen bank. I'm eleven years old, smoking a Regal King Size and the petty, tea-dark river is majestic with light; its reflection sways on the planks of the bridge, crossing and twisting like ropes of shadow-glass. I watch the pattern through half-shut eyes, through smoke and sunlight, sleepy and alert.

'Here.'

I opened my eyes. Lyons was poking me in the belly with a rolled-up *Times*.

'Phone Bryce. And Gerry? See it gets a good show.'

He was off down Argyle Street, heading for Queen Street Station. He walked on, slapping his leg with the *Times*, then turned to wave, his hand cresting a sun-shot fug of blue cigar smoke.

I turned back towards the East End. At the Cross, I turned down the Saltmarket, keeping to the shady side. I could feel the notebook in my pocket as I walked, its discrete weight, as if the MacLaren story was rippling its pages, the kinetic gravity of news. It felt good to have a story again – not a sloppy wodge of comment but a hard bright newsy nugget. A scoop. I could see their faces already – Rix and Moir and Fiona Maguire; the spreading smiles as I broke the news.

I passed the High Court with its sinister columns. Banker Bill MacLaren was jacking it in: that in itself was a splash. But the real news, the big, billowing indistinct story, was just edging into view. Lyons as First Minister: I had backed the right horse there. But then Lyons as Loyalist conspirator. The First Minister-in-Waiting and a nest of paramilitaries. Who were the New Covenanters? A complete run of *Rathlin* had told me precious little. I knew who old ones were, the martyrs and saints of the Covenant: hardline Presbyterians who fought the British state. They wouldn't have bishops. They worshipped in the open air, on rough bits of moorland, with armed sentries guarding the faithful. The redcoats chased them through barren glens, coursed them like deer in the late sixteen-hundreds. They were shot and hanged in the 'Killing Time'. But who were their namesakes, the New Covenanters? I would have to turn redcoat myself – Trooper Conway – and run them to earth.

The sun hammered down on the High Court steps. On Glasgow Green the grass was thick with bodies, couples reclining on jackets, clerks and junior counsels with their Marks and Spencer sandwiches. Two boys with squeezy bottles were chasing in and out of the bushes. Their laughter issued in fluent spurts. As they passed me, the boy in front turned and planted his feet, squaring off to his onrushing foe. But his bottle was empty; it wheezed hoarsely as he pumped it with both thumbs. His laughter scaled up to a choking joyful shriek as the other kid drenched him, waving his bottle from side to side, the water fizzing on the laughing boy's chest. Then the victor turned his bottle skywards, and sent a thick jet skooshing high in the air, a glistering arch that hung a moment in the sun.

Chapter Four

Two days later I was on the train to Irvine. The carriage was almost empty. Then, two minutes before departure, in they pushed, seven flushed roustabouts, heading home from Aberdeen, wedging holdalls into the luggage racks and squeezing round adjacent tables, bursting the cellophane on a slab of lager, seven ring-pulls hissing in gaseous syncopation. I closed my paperback, slipped it in the seat pocket.

You had to wonder how much Lyons knew. Should I have sprung it on him, I wondered, back in Ferrante's? Pulled the photo from my briefcase and slapped it on the table? That had been the plan. But every moment, as we talked, I was sure he was about to spill. He *had* to know; that was why he called me, that was why he was acting how he was; that strange excitement, a kind of girlish tizz. But then he mentioned MacLaren and I knew he wasn't spooked at all, he was high, exultant at the top job suddenly swinging into reach. By then, of course, the moment had passed. And anyway, the MacLaren angle altered things. Lyons as First Minister? This was a whole new scale of story now. I would have to think it through, decide how to play it. So the briefcase stayed shut.

A station flashed past, too fast for me to read the sign. The oilmen were quieter now, their cropped heads swaying above the sports reports. A kid had started babbling at the far end of the carriage, a forthright, oriental-sounding harangue that sang out with startling purity in the mid-journey lull. The sounds were raw and unformed, but the tone was comically definite and swung abruptly from the plaintive to the bitterly indignant and then on to a sunny sing-song equanimity.

One of the oilmen turned a page and then nudged his mate across the aisle.

'That wean's making more sense than you were on Friday night.'

His pal looked up from his paper, cocked his head.

'Hi, the state I was in on Friday night, I'd've understood that wean. Me and him would have hit it right off.'

They bent to their match reports. I thought of a morning, a year or two back, when James was still a toddler. He'd been in his room and had heard me climbing the stairs. It was a sunny morning, the upstairs landing a buttery haze. He stood in his doorway and roared, gently, like a secretive lion when I came into view at the top of the stairs. I roared back. He roared again, louder, an extended version, the original roar with a little curlicue, and he laughed aloud when I did it right back. We stood there for the next few minutes, tossing this roar back and forth, shaping and twisting it, putting in growls and little crescendos. Sometimes Jamie would introduce the new element, and sometimes I would. In the end I could hardly roar for laughing, not at the humour of the thing but out of sheer ecstatic joy, this spell of blissful concord with my son. Enjoy it, I remember thinking; this is as good as it gets. I knew then that no conversation, no mere exchange of words, would top this festival of roaring on the upstairs landing.

At Irvine I took a cab from the rank outside the station. From the driver's narrowed eyes in the rear-view I guessed that Orchardton's wasn't the best of addresses. But the driver said nothing, just lodged his *Sun* behind the sun-visor, found first and pulled out into the sparse, pre-rush-hour traffic.

I'd phoned Orchardton the night before. There were nine Orchardtons in the Glasgow directory. None of them was him but the seventh – a spry-sounding biddy on Maryhill Road – turned out to be his second cousin. She put me through the wringer a bit but finally she gave me the number. I went online and found the address. I thought of turning up blind but I didn't fancy a wasted trip. When I explained who I was, Gordon Orchardton was polite but chary. I told him I was researching a feature article on Ulster–Scottish connections. Our talk would be confidential, and real names wouldn't be used. He gave me directions from Irvine Station, told me he'd expect me at four.

It was five to four now. I braced my arm on the door as the cab leaned into the curve. We were skirting a housing scheme, long grey lines of corporation semis. That morning's rain had left dark shapes on the gable ends, like urine stains on grey school trousers. I looked out for the acronyms, the spray-gunned logos, since this was an arterial route, a boundary line. A posse would be headquartered here, a Young Team with this street in its name.

The cab swung right and then left, nosing deeper into the scheme. The streets were neater here, well-tended crescents with close-cropped hedges, the houses finished in white instead of grey. It looked like the street where my gran used to live, in a 'good' council scheme with a long waiting list. As a kid I spent most Sundays there. One of the neighbours had a boy my age, and we'd play for hours, stroking a football back and forth beneath the 'No Ball Games' sign on the crescent's central disc of turf. It seemed a safe place to me then, happy – the pensioners walking their terriers, the houses with their wedding-cake walls. A world of local newspapers and corner shops, where all the front doors were exactly the same. Then Thatcher got in and everything changed. Suddenly the doors were different – they were bright-blue or scarlet instead of dark-green, or they were fancy panelled affairs from the home-improvement centres. This was what you did when you bought your council house: you changed the front door, because now you could.

And who could blame them? Not me, who lived in a 'bought' house – still, in eighties Mureton, a sign of posh-ness. Why shouldn't my granny's neighbours own their homes? But it depressed me, on my Sunday walk to Gran's, the sad brashness of these lacquered doors, the hanging baskets and carriage lamps. The doors were too big for the houses. They altered the scale. They made all the houses look like Wendy houses.

The cab had slowed to walking pace, the driving cran-ing out at the numbers.

'Thirty-seven? Here we go.'

I paid up and got out.

I was halfway up the path when a head poked out of the door.

'Gerry Conway?'

'That's right.'

The door closed and then opened and a white dog land-ed on the top step, skittered down onto the path, barking.

'He's due his walk.'

The door clapped shut and the man came down the path, zipping his jerkin. I swithered about shaking hands but his hands were already jammed in his pockets so I lifted my chin to his own curt nod. He walked at a ferocious clip, his heels in their glossy derbies striking the pavement, and, short as he was, I'd a job to keep up. A couple of times I tried to bring up the subject of *Rathlin*, the New Covenanters, but he turned aside, or yanked the dog's lead, and cut me short. At one point the dog hunched on a grass verge and squeezed out a long thin caramel-coloured shit, which we simply left, nestling in the uncut grass.

At the top of the brae was a line of shops. A chippy, a Spar, an off-licence, a bookie's. Outside the Spar, Orchardton handed me the leash.

'Two minutes.'

I went for a walk while he shopped. I lit a Bolivar no. 3 – the first of the day – and strolled down the wee parade of shops. At the far end was a patch of gravel and a bus stop. Some kids were hanging around, teens in lurid white sportswear and some smaller boys. Sandy stopped at the bus shelter, cocked his leg. The shelter was fairly new, with scuffed Perspex panels, magic-markered in a cursive female hand: 'Jody B f's Ryan M.' A wee boy of five or six was poking the ground with a coloured stick.

One of the youths broke off from the group.

'Get us a carry-out, mister?'

His tone was perfunctory, bored, like this was a formal exchange with ordered responses.

'I don't think so, son.'

It was ten past four in the afternoon.

He kept coming, leading with his shoulders, arms hanging loose before his torso in a manner familiar from rap videos.

I could smell his breath – fiery, rank – when he stopped in front of me.

'Gie's a light then.'

I tapped my pockets for the plastic lighter, handed it over.

'Cheers.'

He lit his cigarette and then tossed the lighter towards his mates. One of them stooped to pick it up, stowed it in his tracksuit pocket.

'Later, big man.'

He turned and swung back to the group.

The wee boy was crouched down beside me, petting Sandy. I noticed his stick: it was a miniature baton, a half-sized mace, its shaft patterned with tiny Union flags.

Gordon Orchardton came out of the minimarket holding a carrier bag. He raised his arm in an awkward, oddly poignant salute. I tugged on the leash.

Back at the house, he unclipped the dog and it scrambled up on the armchair, standing on the headrest with its front paws on the windowsill.

'Hey!'

He swept the dog to the floor and motioned for me to sit.

'Wait there a minute,' he said. 'I want to show you something.'

He came back grinning, holding it out on his open palms.

'What's this?'

It was a toy gun, a rifle, full-sized, carved from a light-coloured wood. I turned it over in the light from the window. The workmanship was basic, the edges blunt; it was home-made, something a dexterous uncle might knock up for a boy.

'I used to play with that when I was a kid,' Orchardton said. 'I ran about the back green, kidding on I was a commando. All the other weans had proper guns – toys, I mean, die-cast replicas that fired caps, but I loved that thing.' He smiled at the memory. 'My da used to say to me, "You watch what you're doing with that, Gordy. That stick saved Ulster." That's what he always said: "That stick saved Ulster." For years I never knew what he meant. Then one day he told me the story.'

He motioned for the rifle and I handed it back. He gripped it in his fist and shook it.

'It's a dummy rifle,' he said. 'It's not a toy, it's a dummy. My granda used it in Carson's UVF. Before they got the real guns, they trained with these. He took it on manoeuvres. All these men marching about the hillsides with kid-on guns.'

'Your grandad was in the UVF?'

'This is the original UVF I'm talking about. In 1912. Not the current lot. Not the gangsters. It was like a people's army, to resist Home Rule. Then the war happened and they all joined up together. The whole UVF. One minute they were getting ready to take on the government; next thing they're in France, ready to die for King and Country.

'The army let them stay as a unit. They called it the 36th Ulster Division, but basically it was the UVF. My granda went out with the Armagh battalion. He fought at Thiepval Wood. He was with Blacker's Boys – the

Armagh lot. Six hundred of them went over the top and only sixty came back. There's a letter in the drawer there, where he tells my granny. He says he's the only one in his street still alive: all the boys from Scotch Street joined up together, and he was the only one left. They went over the top with their sashes on, shouting "God Save Ulster" and "Fuck the Pope".' He shrugged. 'That's the story, anyway.'

The dog was at his feet now, sniffing his shoes, and he squatted down to pet it, gripping the gun by its stock.

'After that, there was no way the Brits could force us into a republic. So the six counties stayed British.'

He straightened up.

'Anyway, there it is.' He frowned at the hunk of wood in his hands. 'The stick that saved Ulster.'

We took our coffee in the conservatory. Like his fancy front door it was too big for the ex-council house, ending six yards shy of his wooden back fence. In next-door's garden a wee boy was playing on a plastic chute, scrambling up the ladder, dipping down the short slide and tearing round to start again.

Orchardton didn't touch his coffee. The biscuits he'd bought at the Spar lay neglected on a side plate. He just spoke, almost without drawing breath, looking across to the blue Garnock hills. Now that we'd started he seemed to find relief in talking. His voice was unhurried, authoritative, as if he'd expected such an encounter for years, and had marshalled his memories in preparation. He lit a cigarette and told me about his family, about his childhood in the East End, the boyhood trips to Northern Ireland, summer holidays in Bangor and Portstewart. In next-door's garden the wee boy played on his chute, up and down, up and down. At one point I took out the Dictaphone and mimed setting it on the coffee table. Orchardton's eyes tracked from the window to the device and he nodded, once, the flow of his talk never breaking, moving on to the next anecdote.

Later that night, at my desk in Clouston Street, I tried to piece it together, put his spooling memories into order. Orchardton's dad had come over from Belfast in 1946 with a suitcase and a demob suit. He had friends in Glasgow so he settled there, in a model lodging-house in the Calton. A friend got him a start in Templeton's Carpet Factory. He married a local girl and they flitted to the top-floor flat of a Brigton tenement. This is where Gordon was born, the middle kid of three, in a two-room-and-kitchen in Baltic Street.

He spoke fondly of Brigton, of the tight, hard life of the tenements. The smoky stone. The stink of shit from the stairhead lavvies. Aunties and uncles passing in and out all day, the front room always busy. Brigton was the known world, a place unto itself. There were old guys in the pubs who could remember when it was a separate village and still spoke about 'going into Glasgow'. In Baltic Street some of the families were from home; you'd spot Orange lilies in the windows every Twelfth, little twists of colour like votive candles. Gordon's father joined the Orange Order and the Brigton Burns Club. Gordon joined too, when he turned sixteen. He was asked to join a gang – the Baltic Fleet, a posse of housebreakers and petty extortioners from the neighbourhood – but declined. The Order was strict about this – you didn't run in gangs. You didn't swear. You aspired to lead an upright

Christian life. Anyway, the gangs were on the way out, everyone said. It was nothing like the old days. Even the Billy Boys was just a name, a song you sang on the subway to Ibrox. *Up to our knees in Fenian blood, Surrender or you'll die!* 'King' Billy Fullerton was still around, though, working the door at a local snooker club. You saw him on the street sometimes, standing on the corner of Orr Street and London Road, a short man in a brown suit, chatting with the men beside the bandstand, leaning back to spit into the street.

Then the sixties came and they tore the district down. Whole streets reduced to rubble overnight. It was worse than the Blitz, the old ones said. Folk moved out, to the new schemes at Drumchapel and Easterhouse, or away altogether to a New Town maisonette. The Orchardtons moved to the coast, to a pebble-dash semi in Irvine New Town. A postage-stamp lawn and an indoor toilet. Salty air and the peaks of Arran. Gordon was eighteen at the time.

Everything changed when they moved to the coast. Gordon's da got a job in a local hotel, where he worked as porter and receptionist and odd-job man. Every morning he left for work in a shirt and tie instead of his carpet-factory overalls. He was a different man. He seemed precipitately old, a diminished figure, spruce and obliging, with his pullovers and his neatly shed grey hair. He swore less. He joined a bowling club and fell away from the Lodge. Their neighbours, in the council semi on a split new estate, were a Catholic family, a retired couple with grown-up daughters. Jimmy Farren was a former train driver. He'd fought at Monte Cassino. He and Gordon's da went bowling together. They walked their dogs on the moor on Sunday mornings, traded shorts and light ale chasers in the Spinning Wheel in the afternoons. Suddenly, the old animosities had lifted. The heavy weather of bigotry had cleared. It seemed something they had left behind in Glasgow, something mixed up with football crowds and blackened stonework and the rattling of trams, something that had no place amid the hopeful geometry of the new estate. When the new Trinitron brought images of the latest Ulster mayhem, Gordon's da changed channels, reached under his armchair for another tinnie.

Everyone was thriving: his ma and da, his wee sister; everyone adjusting to the new life. Gordon wasn't. He hated Irvine. He felt like an alien in the coastal town, walking its narrow streets. He never got used to it, the racket of the gulls, the fresh dirty whiff of the sea. The naff accents, the slow speech of the locals. They said 'ken' instead of 'know', like something out of *Doctor Finlay*. He stood on the walkway of the bright glass shopping precinct, staring at the river, at the spire of the old sandstone kirk, out of place amid all that newness. As often as he could, he caught the bus back to the city. He still had friends in Brigton, uncles and cousins, in streets waiting demolition. He kipped on their floors, in their old boxbeds. On match days they'd travel out to Ibrox and then hit some of the old pubs – the Grey Mare, the King George – before Gordon caught his bus back to the coast. There was an Uncle Ian, who took Gordon to the pub after every home game. He was a foreman at Arrol's steelworks and sometimes, when they met up, he'd tap a folded fiver into Gordon's top pocket. He knew all about whisky, single malts, the features of the various regions, how a Lowland differed from a Speyside, the protocol of tasting, how a tulip-shaped glass was best, and a little splash of water released the nose. Islays were his favourites: Ardbeg, Laphraoig, Lagavulin. The reek of peat and iodine. 'Hospital bandages,' he'd gasp, a wash of ecstasy on his face, as he lifted his nose from a tumbler of malt.

Then one day Gordon came home to a different house. A queer tightness in the air as he closed the door behind him. No answer to his shouted greeting, though both his parents were home. He found them in the kitchen, a paper on the table between them. Uncle Ian: his strange familiar face on the cover of the *Evening Times*. Headshots of five other guys. According to the story, Ian was OC of the Brigton UVF cell that bombed the Clelland Bar. They hit another bar on the same night – the Old Barns in the Calton. Celtic pubs. No one was killed but they might well have been. The buildings were gutted. The getaway driver shopped them and the whole cell went down. The trial at the Sherriff Court lasted barely two weeks. Nobody walked. Two of the gang got sixteen years: the rest – Uncle Ian among them – landed eighteen.

When Uncle Ian went to jail, that's when it started for Gordon. That's when he gave up on home, more or less, on his ma and da and sister and the house by the sea. At home, Uncle Ian was never mentioned. It was as if he didn't exist. Gordon's da wouldn't hear the man's name in his house. He wouldn't let his wife visit her brother in jail. Only Gordon went, once a month at first and then every week, sitting across a table in Barlinnie. Uncle Ian in his pinstriped prison shirt, footering with a box of matches, asking about streets that no longer existed. They talked about Brigton. Gordon asked about Belfast on the Twelfth. Uncle Ian told him the stories, going over on the ferry, the things you could stash in a Lambeg drum – sticks of gelly, detonators, TA pistols. Over the months Gordon got close to his uncle. He moved back to the city. He found a bedsit on Alexandra Parade, and hung around Bridgeton, the UVF pubs, holding court at the bar, trading on his uncle's name. One Saturday he queued in Terry's Tattoo Parlour, had a red hand done on his shoulder, 'For God and Ulster' in a scroll underneath.

It was in one of these bars that the idea struck him. A kind of secret society. A coven of Scots Loyalists, dedicated to the cause of Ulster. Something needed to be done. Anyone could see it. Since the Hunger Strikes, the city had been changing. The Taigs were organising. Flute bands had sprung up in Coatbridge and Dumbarton, with names like the Crossmaglen Patriots and the James Connolly Memorial. Every few weeks there was a rally in the city centre: Troops Out; Time to Go. His own streets were falling to the enemy.

So he fought back. He invented the New Covenanters. It started small and stayed that way; never more than a score of members. Guys from the Criterion. Guys from the Lodge. Just guys he thought might be interested. They were flattered to be asked. They took it seriously, the military structure, the weekly roll-calls in Orchardton's flat, before adjourning to the pub. One of the guys had been a sergeant in the Royal Scots, and he led monthly classes in weapon handling and fieldcraft. Manoeuvres on the Fenwick Moors. There was 'intelligence'. They collected information on RCs in sensitive jobs. RCs in politics and the media. They compiled lists of names and addresses.

I smiled. 'I'd have been one of your targets.'

He looked round from the window. He didn't smile.

'You'd never have got the job.' He stubbed his fag out in the saucer. 'Not in they days.'

Sometimes they printed the names and addresses in their newsletter. They hawked the paper in the match-day streets, in the pubs round Ibrox. Some nights they took a collection; they jiggled tins with 'Loyalist Prisoners Welfare' on the sides. The money poured in: loose change, folded fivers and ten-spots. Everyone eager to give to the cause. The landlords would weigh in with something, a couple of fifties from the till. It felt good to be doing something.

He leaned forward, flicked his ash into a saucer.

'It was different then, it was all different. There was no peace process or any of that. It was murder, pure and simple: naked bloody murder. Our side as well, but we'd been getting it for years. You saw it on the news, every other night; our people getting slaughtered right and left. Bloody Friday? I was *there* son, the week before, for the Twelfth; I was barely home a week and I turn on the box. The polis scraping the bodies affy walls. Filling bin-bags wi skittery bits of people. Our people. And who's helping them?'

Some ash had spilled onto the table and he swept it into a cupped hand and shook it into the saucer.

'Maggie Thatcher? She's talking to the Provies. Haughey, a fucking gun-runner. A Provie gun-runner, sipping sherry in Downing Street.'

He sat back, peering out to the blue hills. 'The Taigs had it all, son, no offence.' He turned to face me, thumb and fingers flicking up as he counted it off: 'The South. The Yanks. Ted Fucking Kennedy. Guns from Libya, Semtex from the Czechs. Who did our boys have?' He opened his arms, as if he might embrace me. 'Us. And if we didnae step up? Pwhh.'

He turned back to the window. The wee boy next door had gone back in.

'Did Peter Lyons step up?'

He looked round.

'Peter Lyons?'

'Aye. Peter Lyons. Did he step up?'

Orchardton leaned back in his chair. For the first time that day he really looked at me, his chin tipping jauntily back, the tight brown jowls almost creased in a smile. Over his shoulder a jet climbed the sky, its fuselage glinting pinkly in the failing light. Chimes sounded thinly in the distance, the perfunctory tones of an ice-cream van.

'You want to know about Peter Lyons?' he said. He leaned over to the Dictaphone, pressed the off button.

'I'll tell you about Peter Lyons.'

Chapter Five

It started with the flutes. Thin, high, silvery – a sound that seemed too high for human ears, as if you'd acquired the hearing of a dog. The flutes were what carried furthest, not the drums, whose distant footfall kicked in shortly after. Up close, the drums were all you could hear, and the flute-players – eyes flashing irritably between visor and busy lips – might just as well have been miming. But in those first seconds the flutes held their own, and their wispy, weightless whispering was the loudest thing of all.

You heard it fitfully, at first, in gusts and snatches. There was a moment of uncertainty, a spell of anxious head-twisting when the music seemed to ring from all directions. Then some internal radar pointed down a canyon of vacant street and you ran, at a breathless gallop, to the oncoming clatter.

When the Walk turned the corner it pulled you up; you stopped short, winded by this glorious irruption. Youths in scarlet tunics and feathered caps swung onto Crosskirk High Street six abreast. Their buttons flashed. Their trouser-legs had stripes up the sides. Burnished flutes were pressed to their lips. They had the shallow perfection of figurines. Behind them came the walkers, in dark suits and clean shirt-collars, tasselled sashes, the women in churchy hats, some of them clutching Bibles and umbrellas. Above them the banners pitched and swayed:

dark likenesses of martyrs and reformers, the white smudge of King Billy's charger.

The onlookers whooped and clapped as the band approached, the air already pulsing with the drum. Out in front, drawing the roars of the crowd, came Jack the Lad, Cock of the Walk, the boy who swung the stick. He was talisman and witchdoctor. All the fervour of the crowd, all their sense of favour and entitlement was focused on his mobile frame. His specialness was there in all he did: in his rolling monkey-walk; how he crouched and sprang and strutted and twirled. You saw the beauty of it, his wayward figures-of-eight setting off the marchers' ordered tread, how their gait looked all the straighter for his flourishing arabesques. Grimacing, lolling, acting the goat: he might have been the town drunk were it not for the precision of his hands, the quick wrists busy with the stick. He stretched to send it spinning into the air and then stooped to let it roll across his shoulders or twirl in florid cartwheels round his back. I could watch for ever the sluggish tinkle of his fingers as the baton rode the knuckles of one hand.

A girls' accordion band came next, teenagers in pleated kilts and crisp white fitted shirts, and the roaring was different now, lower and more throaty, and the girls lips twitched, as if with incipient laughter, their eyes sliding to take in the crowd.

I had an urge to cross, to step right out between the bands, make a break for opposite pavement. You couldn't cross a Walk. You couldn't pass in front of it. We'd had this hammered into us as kids. The marshals would lift their truncheons in white-gloved hands and the polis would watch them strike you down.

I didn't cross. I watched the rest of the parade, the bands from Ayrshire and Ulster, the Toronto band with its maple-leaf flag, marching down the low-roofed street, and when the last drummer banged past the Hall and the crowds moved off behind him, I followed too, down the hill to the Green.

Two days before this I was in Rix's office. Jenna, his PA, set a coffee down in front of me. On his desk, where the smirking offspring ought to have been, was the snap of Vinnie Jones reaching behind him to squeeze Paul Gascoigne's testicles. It was autographed in the bottom corner. Rix's windows faced west. He left me time to admire the downriver vista – the Armadillo, the Finnieston Crane – before emerging from his inner office.

Rix didn't rate me. I knew without him telling me that he thought my stuff was useless. Ponderous, he no doubt deemed it. Wordy, worthy, deficient in – let us say, bite? Malice? The note of personal enmity? Rix's own editorials had an unruffled viciousness that I enjoyed without wishing to emulate. Someone had told him I'd studied at Oxford and he was eager to let me know that he wasn't impressed. Why should he be? But I liked to wind him up. As the weeks passed, my copy grew pompously Latinate, I quoted from Bentham and Mill. I dug out my college tie when I knew we'd be meeting.

I was wearing it now as I told him the story. The story was Peter Lyons. I had a source who could connect him to loyalist paramilitaries in the early 1980s. I knew Rix would jump at this, so instead of talking it up, I found myself demurring: the details were sketchy; the source an unknown, most likely nursing a grievance. Probably it was horseshit.

Rix let me talk, his smile widening. He'd only been here two years, but he knew his readers. In this part of Scotland, sectarianism sold. It was better than sex. Then I showed him the photograph: Peter Lyons – or a man who looked like a younger version of Lyons – in a row of scowling men; the two figures in the foreground, sporting full-face balaclavas and pointing Webleys at the floor; and behind them on the wall, the claret-and-amber UVF flag.

Rix appraised it like a connoisseur. He got up from his seat, closed the connecting door to Jenna's office, and brought his chair to my side of the desk. There was a deliberation to Rix's movements. He never hurried. He seemed to relish the simplest physical action.

I liked his composure. It reassured me. If the office rumours were right, he had six months to turn the *Trib* around, two of which had already gone. We were bumping along at 55,000, same as when he took over. Every Tuesday, morning conference was a stampede of suggestions; ruses and stratagems for adding the four or five thousand that might save the title. The mood was hysterical. We were more like a self-help group than a conference of editors. Only Rix stayed calm, shirtsleeved elbows on the table, setting out the week's agenda with slow chops of his big hands, smiling all around the anxious circle.

He was smiling now.

'The Boy Wonder,' he said. 'Paramilitary of the Year.'

Two weeks ago, Lyons had won Parliamentarian of the Year at an awards dinner in the Copthorne Hotel. Rix and I had been sitting at his table. He bought us champagne to celebrate. We'd run a profile of him in that Sunday's paper.

'Who's the source?'

'That's what I'm saying, he's an unknown. There's no form.'

'What do you think?'

I turned up my hands.

'I think he's telling the truth.'

'OK. Let's find out. Have you spoken to any of the others, the old associates?'

I mentioned Gordon Orchardton, the New Covenanters. I told him about the Walk that coming Saturday, the big parade in Lyons's hometown.

'Perfect,' he said. 'Talk to the punters – get them oiled, sing the bloody Sash. See what turns up.'

I nodded. I ought to go to Belfast too, he said. Do some digging. He could send Martin Moir (he'd cubbed on the *News-Letter*, after all), but he'd rather I did it.

'I'll think about it.'

'Gerry.' I stopped at the door. He smiled up, back on his own side of the desk now. 'No old pals act this time, yeah?'

At my own desk I booted up and checked my emails. Rix thought the whole of Scotland was an old pals act, press corps and politicos deep in each other's pockets, so that only an Englishman – maybe only Norman Rix – could claim to be independent. He wasn't entirely wrong, but he wasn't right either. Peter Lyons wasn't a friend. I'd played Royal Troon with him a couple of times. His kids were the same age as the boys, and he'd brought them to our Paddy's Day softball game one year. And he was usually good for off-the-records. But he wasn't a friend, and that wasn't why I liked him. We all liked Peter Lyons. He was a good politician. He gave good copy. In a parliament of cloggers, he was Georgie Best. To hear some of his acolytes talk, he had saved the new Parliament from dying of embarrassment.

Lyons was elected to Holyrood in its second term, when the note of disillusion was deafening. Nobody had a good word to say about the Parliament. All the talent had stayed at Westminster. We had gone through three First Ministers in four years, each more mediocre than the last. The building was still just a hole in the ground, a gluttonous sump of public money. The MSPs themselves were a shambles. Spooked by the cameras, awkward in their stiff three-pieces and trouser-suits, they mumbled and stuttered through slapdash debates. Even our scandals were second-rate – stooshies over office rents and fiddled taxi claims.

Then Peter Lyons was elected on the Glasgow list. Nobody knew him. He hadn't been a councillor or Party researcher. He hadn't even been a member of the Party until the year before. Within a week he was Deputy Minister for Transport; half a year later he was Justice Minister. By the following winter, the scandal had broken. Someone unearthed a photograph of Lyons in the regalia of an Orangeman. He'd been a member of the Order in his teens and early twenties. He threw the stick in the Orange parades. A spokesman for the Catholic hierarchy expressed his sadness and alarm. The Record ran a mock-up of Lyons as William of Orange, astride his white charger. 'Can You Ride This Out, Peter?' was the strapline. Remarkably, he did. He went on *Good Morning Scotland* and spoke about his childhood. Since he'd been a kid, he said, he'd dreamed of being an Orange drum major. In other parts of the country, the wee boy's dream was playing for Scotland; in Crosskirk it was throwing the stick on the Twelfth. Eventually he'd come to see that there were bigger ambitions, worthier dreams. He'd gone to university, his horizons had expanded. He'd come to see the Order for what it was, and he'd left. He wasn't a bigot. He had married a Catholic; his two kids were at Catholic school. The story became one of triumph over circumstance, the bright boy rising above the meanness of his origins.

Lyons had grown up in Lanarkshire, in an ex-mining village gone to seed, a sleet-stung bunker of cold grey stone. As Catholics, we mythologised these places, spoke of them with a shiver of dread. Harthill. Larkhall. Crosskirk. Even the names had a spondaic bluntness, a fearsome Prod foursquareness. You shook your head when you spoke them, made that noise you make when you've swallowed something burny. Now I was heading down the M74 on the morning of the Twelfth, peering through the smirr for the Crosskirk turn-off.

I'd never been to Lyons's home town. 'Bitter' was the term you'd hear. A bitter town. We had a kind of league table of bitterness, with all the shitty towns of Ayrshire and Lanarkshire graded by how much they hated Catholics.

The turn-off appeared, and I swung onto a B-road. The rain was clearing now, claustral shafts of sunlight falling on hedges and fields. Lanarkshire was shining in the rinsed air, nothing at all like the slagheap I'd envisioned.

The road skirted a field, and through a break in the hedge I saw a hare skittering off down the furrows. I opened the sunroof to birdsong and branches.

I thought about Mureton. On our bitterness league table, my hometown wasn't high. No one ever called me a Fenian bastard. I never felt menaced coming home from school. That doesn't mean we weren't keeping score. You knew how many Catholic bank managers there were in town, how many Catholic GPs, how many lawyers. The pub I drank in – the Star Inn (prop. J. Molloy) – was known as the Vatican. There were occasions when someone, hearing your surname, would narrow his eyes – 'Conway?' – and roll your name around his mouth, tasting something sour, and his silence would have the shape and weight of four unspoken words: *That's a Fenian name.*

St Michael's, Mureton's Catholic Church, stood on a hill beside the train station, in what had been a slum quarter. For decades it had been hidden from view by the great black facade of the town's Infirmary, but when the hospital was demolished and the chapel stood alone against the skyline, visible from almost everywhere in town, the town didn't like it. People complained about the old Infirmary, what a shame it was to see it go. What really riled them was the view it left behind, the papish chapel, *brazen* there, at the crown of the brae. Let them go to the devil in their own way, if that's what they wanted. Did they have to shove it down your throat?

But did I ever feel threatened or even put upon? You knew you were different, and when St Michael's played away, and we took the field in our Milanese red-and-black stripes, there was an edge to some of the touchline shouts. All those urgings to get stuck in, get intae this shower; you wondered if this vehemence was matched at every fixture. But our sense of grievance was sedulously nurtured, stoked more by tribal memories of shipyard gangers and hiring fairs than by anything in our daily lives. Our ire was reserved for SPL referees and perceived acts of bias against Glasgow Celtic Football Club.

The sky had cleared. Up ahead some walkers turned to watch me approach. Three lassies – they had mounted the grass verge at the sound of the car, and now their skinny arms stuck into the road. A thin cheer rose as I slowed just beyond them. There was a bit of confabbing and then two climbed into the back as the other – the pretty one, evidently – slid in beside me.

'You going to the Walk, mister?'

'Yep.'

'Can you take us right into Crosskirk?'

'If you'll help me find it.'

'You've never been?'

They were relaxed now, proprietorial, leaning forward in their seats, pointing out the turnings. The smell of them – lemony, chemical – filled the car.

'You've never been to the Walk?'

'Not this one.'

'It's major, man. There's bands from Ireland, all over. Canada. The Walk goes on for ever.'

'Scooby,' said the one right behind me. 'Nice ride. Is it turbo, mister?'

'Afraid not.'

'Hey, he looks like a pimp now,' said the one beside me. 'We're his bitches. D'you feel like a pimp, man?'

'Not especially.'

'You're mental, Diane.'

'What's your name?'

'Gerry.'

'Gerry!' They mugged disbelief. '*Gerry?* You a pape?'

'I'm a journalist.'

I slowed for an oncoming lorry.

'Are you writing it up for the paper; the Walk?'

'That's the idea.'

'Will you put us in?'

'What paper is it?'

'Where's your photographer?' Diane struck a pole-dance pose, hands above her head.

'It's the *Tribune on Sunday*. I don't have one.'

'Too bad.' She pulled the visor down, checked herself in the mirror, rubbed a finger along her teeth.

'Hey, you got anything to drink?'

'There's some water.' I nodded towards the glove compartment. 'In there.'

'He's looking at your legs, Diane.'

'Dirty bugger.'

She paused with the bottle in her hand.

'Are you looking at my legs?'

'No, I–'

'How no?'

The three of them sputtered, the two in the back leaning together till their heads touched. I looked around at Diane again. The set of her lips, or the line of her nose: something was familiar. I seemed to know her. Before I could place it we had reached Crosskirk, its long main street of brown sandstone.

'Can you drop us at the puggies?'

At the amusements arcade they climbed out and were swallowed up in the dark and noise and coloured lights.

Two boys in Rangers tops by the door turned to check out their arses then glared back at me. Diane spun round, once, a cute 360 turn: a flash of teeth, a quick twist of the wrist, a ripple of white pleated skirt.

I drove up the High Street, past Boots the Chemist, the Masonic Lodge, Blockbuster Video, the British Legion. A stylised eye on a billboard advertised the current series of *Big Brother*. I passed a mural, stiff-limbed figures in bala-clavas and black combat jackets, hardware held aloft: 'UFF 2nd BATT C COMPANY'. A knot of boys at the war memorial turned to watch me pass. Old fears began to surface. How Catholic did you look? Could people tell? Was the Forester's dark bottle-green green enough to arouse suspicion?

Near the top of the hill, tied to a lamp-post was a card-board sign with an arrow, a capital P and the logo of an Orangeman (bowler hat and chevron-shaped sash). I fol-lowed the arrow to a big stretch of wasteground in what looked to have been an industrial estate. It was busy already: buses and cars parked in makeshift lines. I left the Forester beside a Parks of Hamilton coach and head-ed out to see the fun.

I like the Walk. I know you're not supposed to. I know it's a throwback, a discharge of hate, a line of orange pus clogging the streets of central Scotland. But I like it any-way. I like the cheap music, its belligerent jauntiness. I like the crisp gunfire of the snares. I like the band uni-forms and the hats and the apocalyptic names stencilled on the Lambeg drums: Cragside Truth Defenders; Denfield Martyrs Memorial Band; Pride of Glengarnock Fifes and Drums.

For most folk, a parade's an excuse to throw off

restraint. In most parades, the participants take their cue from the bands; you think of Rio, its swirl of sequins and ostrich feathers, the bobbing phalanxes of militant Sowetans, Pamplona's neckerchiefed *riau-riau* dancers. And then there's Scotland's Orangemen. Here they come, in their Sunday suits, dark, with just that grudging flash of colour at the shoulders, step by dispassionate step, Bibles closed, umbrellas rolled. Lenten faces and tight, teetotal lips. It's a carnival of restraint, a flaunting of continence. The music rolls past, sends out its invitation to swagger and reel. But the marchers step carefully on, unmoved, without the least roll of the hips.

All except for the drum major, who dances enough for everyone. He takes up the shortfall, whirling and spinning, knocking himself out. All their sinful urges, all the demons of the tribe: he takes them into himself and dances them out. He's the leader, but there's something sacrificial too, like he's some kind of outcast or scapegoat. He's a mock monarch, the King of the Wood, raising a bandaged fist to pluck his sceptre from the skies.

On the sidelines, parts of the crowd catch the infection. They surrender to the music, cavorting on the pavement, drunkenly Stripping the Willow. But after all, these are only spectators, and the Order, in its official pronouncements, likes to stress its disapproval of hangers-on. Is this what bothers the high-ups, I wonder? Not the drunkenness and the battle songs, the tally of cautions for breach of the peace. Just the sheer enjoyment, the looks on the faces? The music plays and people dance.

When the march was over we went to the Green – a stretch of parkland down by the river. The speeches had already started: a small man in a tight suit was talking sternly into a microphone on a platform draped with Union flags. Those nearest him nodded and clapped. You knew when to clap because he left a space. The Green looked like an encampment. The bandsmen had laid down their drums and flutes and were cracking open cans and bottles. The smell of fried onions carried from the food vans. Bannerettes were laid out on the grass, side by side, like the frames of a comic strip. Two toddlers in kilts were swordfighting with flutes. A man strolled between the groups, handing out little booklets. 'Have You Met Your Redeemer?' I stuck it in my back pocket. Three guys sitting on a Union flag were playing pontoons for matchsticks.

At the far end of the meadow a kick-about was underway on the flat ground by the river: a fat man rushed to keep the ball out of the water and landed on his arse once he'd hooked it clear. His raised arm acknowledged his comrades' cheers.

People had brought flasks and tartan rugs, jumbo bottles of cider and fizzy juice, towers of plastic cups.

I passed a family of five enjoying a full-scale picnic. The father had the coolbox open and was twisting a can of lager from its plastic loop when my shadow fell across him. He looked up, nodded hello, and held out the can; gave a no-worries shrug when I shook my head.

I kept an eye out for Diane, but the field was thronged. Teenagers were necking behind the burger vans. A boy with stringy hair was puking into the river. I picked my way back through the fallen bodies. It was hot and sticky. I thought of the can of cold beer and wished I'd taken it.

*

At the Cross Keys Inn, a solitary barman skidded back and forth behind the counter, stretching to press the optics, squatting to snatch beer bottles from crates. He kept at least three taps in motion, flicking each one just before it overflowed. In between he plucked banknotes from fists and dropped change into palms. Compared to the barman the drinkers looked static. Jammed in tight, they could barely move. They turned their heads fractionally to slurp from pints or tear bites out of filled rolls. Up close, there was something camp about the bandsmen. It was the uniforms, the military cut twinned with toyshop colours – superhero reds and blues. They looked like pantomime soldiers, their jackets loud with piping, gold braid criss-crossing the chests, running in garrulous spirals round the cuffs.

Filled rolls wrapped in cellophane were piled on the counter. Spilled beer formed muddy slicks on the brick-coloured lino. The smell was high: top notes of sweat and flatulence over the radical pub stink of slops and stale baccy, pish, disinfectant. I fought my way to the bar and held out a tenner. Ten minutes later, Mary Slessor still in hand, I needed to piss. I pushed back to the exit and joined the row of marchers lining the back wall. By the time I made it back, the place was starting to empty. Pints and whiskies were swilled and sunk and the bandsmen moved out, fastening collars and cuffs, pulling Glengarrys from their epaulettes.

'Where's the fire?' I asked my neighbour.

'It's the return leg: they march back up to the kirk.'

'You not marching yourself?'

'No me.' He added water to his whisky. 'My job's done.'

'How's that?'

'I'm a marshal, son. We bow out at this point, and

they're glad to see the back of us. Let the boys cut loose a bit. Do the blood-and-thunder stuff.'

He seemed to think of something.

'What's yours, anyway?'

He added my order to his own and the barman shouted, 'Got it.' He was rushing around as if the bar was still busy, though only the regulars were left – a few pensioners nursing tumblers of Bell's, ponies of seventy shilling.

'There you go, son.'

'Good man.'

'Frazer Macklin.'

I shook his hand.

'John.'

'OK, John. You coming over?'

I helped him carry the drinks.

We joined the others, three men in dark suits at a corner table. They seemed unsurprised at my arrival, jerked their chins in tepid greeting as if I drank here every day. They had the bored, competent air of petty officials – ticket inspectors or shop stewards. Their sashes and white gloves were folded in two neat piles on the windowsill behind them. Without their regalia they seemed closer to the elderly regulars than to the departed bandsmen. They didn't have much to say. One of them told an anecdote about his grandson and a pet shop. There was a half-hearted colloquy about Rangers' latest transfer target.

The man sitting across from me wore white training shoes. He saw me notice.

'I've got bad feet,' he said. 'The Walk's a killer.'

I got a round in. They all drank heavy, except for one who was on Black-and-Tan. He looked at me queerly when I set it in front of him.

'Is that not right?'

'What? No, it's fine, son. Spot on.'

The barman aimed the remote and the racing came on, a close-up of galloping fetlocks swathed in white tape, then a long shot of the field.

The Black-and-Tan man was staring: I could feel his gaze on the side of my face. Finally he leaned forward.

'Do I know you, son? Are you a Brother?'

I'd already clocked the signet ring, the compasses and square.

'Naw.'

'Do you work in IBM?'

'I don't, no.'

'I've seen your face.' He shook his head. 'It'll come to me.'

Frazer went out for a smoke and when he came back we were still discussing the smoking ban. For the first time since I'd joined them, the Orangemen were animated. They came alive in the clamour to bad-mouth their new politicians, to bemoan the peerless nullity of the Parliament. The smoking ban was the least of it. An infringement of civil liberties, said one of them. The thin end of the wedge. They spoke about creeping totalitarianism, the need for constant vigilance.

'That's right. One day you cannae spark up a Regal; the next it's popery and wooden shoes.'

'That's no funny, son.'

Everyone slags the Parliament: it's a staple of bus-stop small talk, like the weather or the state of Scottish football. But the Orangemen had their own slant, their own angle of grievance.

'Have you seen the names?' said the man with the

training shoes. 'Fucking Kellys and Connollys and Maguires and fuck knows what. Scottish Labour Party? Scottish Sinn Fein.'

'Behave yourself, Turner.'

'Home Rule is Rome Rule. We said it all along, and guess what? It's true.'

'Yeah, but they're no all like that,' I said.

Turner shrugged.

'This was Lyons's lodge, wasn't it?'

'What's that, son?'

'Peter Lyons.'

Nobody spoke. Finally Frazer peered into his half-pint glass, swirling an inch of seventy.

'It's a long time since Peter Lyons threw a stick.'

'But did you know him then? What was he like? Was he a good Orangeman?'

'Of course I knew him. He was a bloody good drum major, that's what he was.'

The others nodded.

'The best,' said Turner.

'So what happened?' I looked round the faces. 'Why did he leave?'

'He sold the jerseys,' said Black-and-Tan. 'He wanted his name on election posters. He wanted a red rosette and his picture in the papers. He knew the comrades would-nae wear it, the selection committees, what have you.'

'Yeah, but you never really lose it, do you?' Frazer tapped on the tabletop. 'He'll always be an Orangeman.'

'Don't kid yourself, Brother.'

'I'm not kidding. I'll tell you one thing. I remember his face when he led the band, the look in his eyes when he brought the boys down that High Street. I don't care what he does, I don't care if he becomes prime minister, the bloody Pope, he'll never get a feeling the like of that.'

'Do you never see him any more?' I said. 'Does he never come down, for the Twelfth?'

Frazer set the empty glass on the table.

'Why'nt you ask him.' He nodded at an old boy sitting at the bar. 'That's his faither.'

We all looked across. The old man rose to his feet and edged out from behind his table. I thought at first he had heard us and was leaving, but he walked past the exit, heading for the lavatory. Then the barman had his arm out, pointing across the pub:

'That'll do you, girls. Not another step.'

Three lassies in short skirts and heavy eye make-up stood just inside the door. Diane was the leader. She held up a card, brandished it like a referee.

'What's this look like? You cannae bar us, mister. We're eighteen. We've got ID.'

'It's your bus pass, hen. You're no coming in.'

He was out from behind the bar now, approaching with outstretched arms, shooing them out.

Diane looked around.

'Hey, Gerry! There's Gerry. Tell him, Gerry. We're eighteen. Tell him.'

'Out.'

The door swung shut on their protests. The barman stayed where he was, making no move to go back to the bar.

Black-and-Tan was nodding. He reached for his drink and then stopped.

'You're Gerry Conway. I fucking knew I knew you.'

'Who's Gerry Conway?'

'He writes for the *Trib*. You write for the *Tribune*.'

'You're a journalist?'

I nodded.

The man who was Peter Lyons's dad had come back from the toilet now and he too stopped, waited for what would happen.

There was a long, slack moment of silence, during which I studied the scuffs on the lino and Turner's incongruous training shoes, and then the breeze was cool on my face, lifting my fringe.

The barman was holding the door and the others had got to their feet.

'Time you werenae here, son.'

I couldn't find the car. I walked from one end of the wasteground to the other. More than ever, it looked like a football match; all the buses in a row, Rangers placards in their windows: Garscube Loyal; Tradeston True Blues. Then I turned a corner and there it was.

The parade had finished: the pavements were filling up once more, as bandsmen and marchers went back to their coaches. I inched through the streets, stop-starting, gently beeping the pedestrians. I wanted out before the streets clogged altogether, and I turned, without proper attention, onto the High Street. Straight off I clocked it: the blue disc, the white arrow, pointing the wrong way. Shit. I looked for a side street, but they were thick with bodies, the crowds spilling into the thoroughfare. Fuck. I threw the car into reverse and swung round.

At first I thought I'd hit someone: shouts of protest sounded from the rear. Something banged on the roof. A hand appeared beside me making the 'wanker' gesture – no; he wanted me to roll down the window. No chance: I shook my head. He jabbed his finger at me, then at the 'One Way Street' sign. *I know*; I nodded. The crowd was thick on either side now, the car stuck sideways across the white line.

Two middle-aged guys stepped round the bonnet, and one of them paused: the Cross Keys guy, the Black-and-Tan drinker. He grabbed the other's sleeve and pointed. The second man turned, gestured to someone behind him.

I leaned on the horn; the sound was thin and somehow effete. It brought more onlookers round the car. I revved the engine but nobody moved. Black-and-Tan stayed out in front with his palms on the bonnet, as if waiting to be frisked. His eyes were dull with drink.

Pointlessly, as if a winking yellow light would bring everyone to their senses, I applied the left indicator.

A gob splattered the windscreen. Someone was trying the door. There was an icy tinkle, barely audible, that I knew was a headlight breaking.

My bag was on the passenger seat: I scrabbled in the side pocket, fingers paddling for my phone. More spit slid down the glass. The banging on the roof started up once again. I saw a man lean backwards to give himself room, and a shoe sole the size of a suitcase came pistoning towards me.

I found the phone.

As I thumbed the buttons a different noise cut through the hubbub, a thin slicing sound, hissing at the window. I craned round. For a moment the whole scene – the jostling bodies, the opening mouths – had a barley-sugar tinge, an orangey film, and I was back in my childhood sickbed, viewing the world through the cellophane wrapper of a

Lucozade bottle. Then the window cleared and a brown cock jiggled comically for a second before flipping into a waistband.

The cabin darkened: someone was up there, blocking the sunroof. Then he was down again and my ear was hurt, stinging, as if something had struck it. My bag thudded down from the passenger seat and the mobile jumped out of my hand. The glove compartment slumped open and my CDs skittered out. Through the front windscreen the sun was swinging into my eyes and out again, like a torch clicking on and off.

They were rocking the car.

Three or four bodies on either side, working together, hitting a rhythm. Each time the car rocked to the right, the window thumped into my ear. I braced my right arm on the door frame and gripped the handbrake with my left. The windscreen kept pitching like a boat on heavy seas, a little steeper with each new heave. Then the sun flared in my side window, not the front, and I was rising, floating, suspended in air as the car tipped onto its fulcrum.

Even then, as a rhombus of blue sky paused in the window, and a vast protracted second gave me all the time in the world to review my situation, I didn't feel afraid. That I might be seriously hurt, in a small town in Lanarkshire, on a sunny weekend afternoon, by a crowd of militant Calvinists in blue suits and sashes, seemed – even then – unrealistic. How serious were these people? How angry? I don't think they themselves were sure. Had something happened, had the car tipped over and the windows shattered, with shards and splinters and blood on the roadway, they might have claimed it as a joke, a prank, a piece of wayward fun. And they might have been right. At that point things could have gone either way.

Then the chassis was bouncing with the shock of impact and ironic cheers greeted my landing.

I waited for the rocking to start again but the bodies had moved away, the cabin suddenly bright, and a policeman's face – incredulous, angry – loomed at my elbow. He rapped on the window.

Out front another cop – arms spread wide in a green fluorescent jacket – was moving back the crowd. A blue light whirled mutely from a squad car.

I pressed the button.

'Are you all right?'

'Yes.'

'Jesus Christ.' He glanced round the cabin as if hoping to spot whatever had riled the crowd. 'Right. Let's get you out of this. Stick close to us. All right? We'll take you the Uddingston road.'

The window scrolled up.

I put the car in gear and eased round. The squad car pulled off. The crowd closed behind me, raising its noise.

On the motorway, once the cops had taken the exit and I merged back into the city-bound flow, I still felt shaken. The backs of my arms prickled with shame. The rocking of the car hadn't bothered me. It was the slow drive down Crosskirk High Street, the hard laughter of the crowd. The street had seemed to go on for ever. At one point, when the cop car braked without warning, I stalled. The crowd hooted and cheered. I saw the camera phones, the hands cupped around shouting mouths. For a second I was lost, I no longer knew how to drive a car. Then I closed my eyes and opened them, talked myself through it: turn the key; find first gear. I followed the Land Rover's bumper down that hostile mile, beneath loops of coloured bunting. It felt like an expulsion, the town purging my unclean presence. I wasn't the victim but the culprit, the scapegoat, the treacherous Lundy.

The faces stayed with me, on the drive back to Glasgow, and the smirking grins on Crosskirk High Street meshed with those in the photo of Lyons. These were Lyons's people, this was his hinterland. This is where he preened and swaggered, tossing his stupid stick. Suddenly I was rooting in my pocket, yanking out my phone. I stopped in a lay-by and punched the number.

'Norman Rix.'

'I'll need a week,' I told him. 'I'm going to Belfast.'

Book Two

Chapter Six

What Gordon Orchardton had told me in his gleaming conservatory, when he leaned to switch the Dictaphone off and turned his back on the blue Garnock hills, was this. There was a time in the early eighties, Orchardton said, when Lyons was in Belfast every month. Things were happening then, and Lyons was close to the action. He had contacts. Names were never mentioned, but you got the idea that these were the high-ups. The top boys. Lyons never let on. This was the whole UVF thing, said Orchardton. You never spilled. The UDA were different, they sat in pubs and flapped their lips, talking large about things they'd never done. But the Blacknecks were tight, Blacknecks never talked. You never knew for certain who was in it and who wasn't.

But then something happened. There was a rift, a falling out, between Lyons and the guys on the other side. Lyons came back in a hurry. It was Guy Fawkes Night, 1983. Bangers and firecrackers snapping in the street, rockets whistling up in the dark and crackling in green-and-purple bursts. That's how he remembers the date: Lyons was upset, agitated – he jumped at every bang and muffled crump, perched there on Orchardton's sofa, his big hands clamped round a mug of toddy.

'I'd never seen him like that,' Orchardton told me. 'Peter Lyons is a big strong man. But that night he was beat; he was a whipped dug. The guy was scared. He came straight to mine's off the ferry. Still had his holdall. He was shaking like stink, really chittering. Like he couldnae get warm. "That's me," he kept saying. "I'm finished. I'm bye with it." Shaking his head and staring into his mug: "Bye with it." Blackneck to the last but.'

Orchardton smiled. 'Wouldnae tell me what was wrong. But something had happened. Somebody'd put the frighteners on him. Somebody *daunted* him. There were no marks on him that I could see but I think they fucked him over.' He looked at me and nodded. 'Yeah. I think they gave him a seeing-to. And maybe something worse. Or else the threat of it. And that was him. He never crossed the water again.'

I told all this to Rix, in his big corner office, the day after the Walk. 'And that's his theory?' Rix said.

'Yeah, he thinks Lyons had a falling out with the Belfast guys. He'd let them down in some way, maybe crossed them, and they ran him out of town.'

Rix nodded. 'But it's not your theory.'

'No.'

'What do you think happened?'

I crossed to the window and leant against it.

'I don't buy it. Lyons falling out with the Shankill UVF? He's got a temper, yeah, but the guy's a politician. To the soles of his feet. That's what he is, even back then. He'd never have rowed with these guys. And he wasn't dumb enough to cross them. I think he was scared all right. But I think it was something else. I think maybe they took him on a job. I think he saw something or he did something that frightened the shit out of him and he wanted out.'

Rix thought about this. The meaty lip edged out and the breath rasped in his nostrils. Then he slapped the desk with both hands and got to his feet. 'Fuck him,' he said brightly. He loped across the office, planting his palms on the windowsill and then straightening smartly up. 'Let's take him,' he said. 'Let's jump the fucker. Put a ferret up him.' I never knew what to say when Rix talked like this. I nodded gravely, tried to look earnest and predatory. 'OK,' I said. 'Great.'

A week in Belfast. Seven days of cooked breakfasts and starched bedsheets and expense-account bar-bills on the strength of a worn snapshot and an old-fashioned hunch. Even I could see how thin it looked. It was the kind of grand, barely warrantable gesture – a big, swinging-dick thing to do, as he would phrase it – that Norman Rix relished. Rix had been hired to straighten us out, slim us down. Enforce the new austerity. The newsdesk had a staff of ten when I started; now three of them droned morosely into phones while Rix scowled down from his glassed-in eyrie. The Brussels correspondent, our stringers in Washington and Paris and all but one of the London bureau had lifted their cards. 'Lunch hour' now had a literal ring, and foreign trips were blue-moon and coach. That was Rix's regime, but from time to time he liked to break out in an old-style splurge, take a flat-out punt on a story.

Which is why, on that Sunday evening, I was clutching the guardrail of the Larne Seacat, watching the Antrim hills get bigger. I was a little aggrieved at how Scottish they looked, as if their green – or ours – might have been more exclusive. The wind smacked my forehead, pasted salt on my lips, blued my knuckles where they gripped

103

the rail. A spray that might have been rain or spume blew over my cheeks. I thought: I could stay here for ever. Then the tannoy ordered us back to our cars and I took the steep steps to the bluish gloom.

The car deck was crowded. It felt adventurous and safe to be back behind the wheel in that echoey dark, encased in two hulls of metal – the car's and then the ship's. That thrill we felt as kids when the Clyde Tunnel closed over-head and the car sped on through the strip-lit gloom. It felt like that. The thought of all that water overhead.

It was almost eight. I'd be too late for dinner but should make it down to Belfast by nine; sign in, snort a few halfs in the bar. I might even manage to phone the boys. The tannoy gave out a migrainey whoop of feed-back and a voice said something I didn't catch. A family of four climbed into the CR-V in front, hauling shut their doors in clunking syncopation. Two mountain bikes were fixed to the back and their misaligned wheels squinted at me like vast, out-of-focus eyes.

The crossing had been fine. I spent it in the observa-tion lounge, watching people read the papers. Of those who had the *Toss*, most were engrossed in the sports or flicked irritably through the magazine, but I did see one – a black-haired girl with a rucksack and a cocker spaniel – frowning over the politics page. I had written up the MacLaren story in eight hundred words: 'FM to Quit Within Weeks: Justice Minister Poised to Succeed'. They had flagged it on the front page. On page 7 I had the story, plus a revamped profile of Lyons and a brand-new photo supplied by Bryce. It was an action shot: Lyons in full oratorical flow, teeth bared like a mastiff, dark locks dropping moodily over one eye, the fingertips of a chopping hand just creeping into the frame.

I checked the other Sundays. Lyons was as good as his word: none of them carried the story. The dailies would pick it up tomorrow and Lyons – you could bet – would be unavailable for comment. It set things up nicely for next week's copy.

We'd been late leaving Scotland. A family in the boarding queue had let their engine idle – to keep the air-con blowing, or the CD playing – and their battery failed. As the testily revving traffic negotiated their stricken Espace, the parents faced front and smiled tightly, incarnating cluelessness.

Still, we had made up the time – the crossing took barely an hour – and now we were ready to dock. The boat juddered and stilled and men in hard hats and fluorescent yellow jackets went from car to car loosening floorstraps. They wore walkie-talkies clipped to their belts and joked with each other across the aisles, raucous and unshaven.

It was years since I'd been in Ulster, Northern Ireland, the Black North, the Wee Six. When I worked on news I was there all the time. Over on the late-night ferry in the wake of some outrage. All the firemen in the forward lounge, throwing it back, cracking atrocity jokes. The last time was 1993, the dark days before the ceasefires, everything nervy and raw. The Shankill Bomb had dropped the UDA war-room into a lunchtime fish shop, killing nine. The UFF returned the serve at Greysteel: two trick-or-treating gunmen in the Rising Sun Bar, raking the drinkers with automatic weapons. Seven dead: six Taigs and a Prod. A lot was made of the lone, ironic Prod, and how his killing showed up the gunmen's folly. As if the other six deaths made perfect sense. The mood was grim, right across the province. After dark, Belfast was a movie-city, a post-apocalypse ghost town. I felt like Leonard Meed when I ventured onto Great Victoria Street, flinching at the sound of tyres, the swishing black taxis and gurgling tanks, the single-deckers shuddering off down arterial routes. *Day of the Triffids. Mad Max.* The Europa was the most bombed hotel in Europe, but it felt safer to hole up in the Whip and Saddle Bar than to cross the ten yards to the Crown. You were waiting with half-shut eyes for the next spectacular, the next outrageous raising of the stakes.

But that was all gone now, a bad dream.

The ferry door dropped open and daylight rolled over us like the future. All the cars started up at once, engines revving, and we waited in a sunshot fug for our line to be called forward.

I bumped up the ramp onto solid ground. I felt that lightening, that release that always comes on disembarking, as if you'd been detained against your will and have somehow made good your escape. The car was nimble and slick on the tarmac and I swung up the road tight behind the CR-V. It turned right at the junction, north to the Glens of Antrim, the coast road to Donegal. I hung a left, down through the Sunday streets.

Larne is a watery, whey-coloured town, the dirty grey of drying whitewash. Bunting hung in the streets, strung in sad diagonals from gable to gable. Pennants flipped and snapped in the brackish air. I was glad to get onto the motorway. Seventeen miles to the city. Even the names were losing their fluorescence – Belfast and Portadown simply words on a road sign, barely less bald than the numbers beside them. The road was quiet. I overtook a camper van with a yin and yang symbol stencilled on its side and opened it up on the long empty stretch.

I thought back to the stories I'd written in the nineties, the tales of sectarian carnage. They hadn't all been Irish. In the mid-nineties a boy had his throat cut in the East End of Glasgow, on London Road, outside the Windsor Bar. He died on the pavement from loss of blood, just a boy coming home from the football. His Celtic scarf wasn't even on show. His killer was a teenage Loyalist with family connections to the UVF. The story came back a year later when the UVF's political wing put in a transfer request. They wanted the killer to serve out his sentence in Ulster. He'd have political status and be eligible for early release. There was an instant, ardent outcry – we splashed on the story two weeks running – and the plan was dropped.

The story had haunted me, and not just because of its grimness. All through the eighties I did what this boy had done. I walked back from Celtic games down London Road, through Brigton Cross and on to the Trongate. You were warned not to do this. It was an accident of geography that placed Celtic's stadium next to the city's bitterest Loyalist enclave. But it was the quickest route home and I didn't see why a huddle of witless bigots should put an extra mile on my journey. At the full-time whistle, 60,000 people would spill out of Parkhead, squeezing through the narrow streets, jostling and shoving. There were bodies all around you, jammed in tight, but by the time you'd walked six hundred yards to Brigton Cross you were on your own. The crowds had evaporated. It was an eerie feeling and though I kept my colours hidden under my jacket I couldn't disguise which direction I'd come from. Most Saturdays I would hurry through Brigton Cross without a hitch but sometimes there were comments and looks and once an old lady in a rain-mate stepped smartly from a doorway to spit in my face.

I lit a Café-Crème and slotted *Highway 61 Revisited* into the CD player. It was good driving. Late sunlight lay in stripes across the waves, like shipping lanes on a map. I reached for my sunspecs in the overhead bin and thought of the bicycle-eyes on the silver CR-V. It ought to have been me, tooling to the shore with a backseat-full of kids. I'd phoned Elaine the night before and got it over with. She did her spoken laugh – a soft, low-frequency *ho ho ho* that spelled something like, *Boy, you've done it this time*. 'You're on your own,' she said. 'If you think I'm going to break this to them you're up a gum tree. The sad thing is, why am I even surprised? Go ahead and break their hearts. Be my guest.' It took an hour, a tropical storm of sobs and huffs before the weather started to clear. I would make it right, I told them. I would take them away later in the summer, before the schools went back.

The night was fine. I reached up for the button and the sunroof neatly withdrew, flooding the cabin with pink evening air and the foul-fresh smell of the sea. I snuffed it up and pushed the pedal down and generally felt less bad about being me. It was good to be back in harness, chasing a story. I'd spent too long shifting my hams on swivel chairs, glossing gimcrack debates. Sitting in the Garden Lobby with my Dictaphone whirring as some bored frontbencher recited his answers. Writing columns, op-ed pieces. The whole dreary business of framing opinions. Was there anything less necessary than venting an opinion? Across the blogosphere, everyone with functioning forefingers was tapping out their prejudices. Why add to the racket? Maybe I should quit, shut the fuck up, or else just report things, get it down in black and white, tell the truth as I saw it. Bang out a story with Strunk and White's *The Elements of Style* open at my elbow. *Use the active voice. Omit needless words. Do not inject opinions.*

Low hills loomed at my shoulder, turning blue in the failing light. Pylons in their gunslinger's pose. Sheep with their legs tucked up beneath them.

I had the Forester at eighty, coming down the dual carriageway with Dylan's 'Tombstone Blues' squealing and whooping through the speakers. The sun was sinking wrong – into the hills and not the sea. Everything looked like home, only all switched round like a mirror. You could see Scotland, out beyond Islandmagee, tissue-paper mauve, and then the road swung round to meet Belfast Lough. Seagulls wheeled in the smoky air, their undersides pink in the last of the sun.

Rix had warned me not to blab. To tell no one I was going to Belfast. It would get back to Lyons soon enough; but the later he learned, the better my chances of getting the story. Rix was really buzzed. We were on to something big, he could feel it. The photo had piqued him but what really got him was the story that Orchardton told me.

Carrickfergus. I'd heard the song so often, at parties and lock-ins, that the town itself, with its round, grey, English-looking castle, seemed implausible. I stopped for a wayside slash in a lay-by near Newtownabbey then joined the motorway into the city. In a little while Belfast loomed out of the night, a stipple of silver. The street lights were on, and the neon signs, but the dusk had yet to deepen into dark. A livid stripe of sky, frog's-belly yellow, lowered on the western hills. The squat skyline stood out blackly. I swung through the darkening streets, scouting for landmarks. The place had changed. Across the Lagan a burnished rotunda would be Waterfront Hall. Glassy new apartment blocks had mushroomed in my absence. But it was still the same old city: open, low, curled like a dog in its basket of hills.

Something else hadn't changed. The police station at the top of Donegall Pass still looked like a badly wrapped parcel, swathed in wire and grille-work. I turned up Botanic, past the newsagents and minimarts, the smart bars and tatty flats and the late-weekend revellers, the strutting, short-sleeved lads, the microskirts and clacking heels.

Grania Lodge was near the top end of Botanic. I parked beside a silver Audi. A mumbling bald guy with a Vandyke beard signed me in and gave me a plastic key card. I took my bag straight to the bar and ordered a Baileys. Large. A girl brought it over on a tray with a complimentary bag of nuts.

The bar was quiet. A middle-aged couple had low bedroom voices for each other in the far corner. A solitary business type in a polo shirt let his lager go flat as he tapped on the keyboard of his book-sized Sony Vaio. I'd almost finished my Baileys. The girl broke her stride as she passed my table but I waved her off. I drained the glass and shoogled the ice cubes, let them rest against my upper lip, numbing the flesh. I left a folded fiver under the glass and headed for the lift.

Even now, my nights were defined by twin itches, paired anxieties that traded places around nine o'clock, like shift workers. Before nine I was anxious to call the boys, to hear their voices, get a fix of their innocent nonsense before they went to bed. Bedtime was half-past eight. If I phoned before nine I could usually count on the thumping of bare feet and the vehement whispers as they fought for the phone. After nine it was too late to call. But after nine, especially when nine o'clock found me in the snug of the Cope or studying the damp patch over my sofa with a bracer at my elbow, it could seem like a good idea to call anyway and speak to Elaine.

'The boys are in bed,' she would say on these occasions, though we both knew I knew this. Sometimes I'd pretend to have lost track of time. Elaine had developed, I came to realise, a strategy for dealing with these phone calls, a code of conduct. The code didn't permit her, for instance, to cut these calls short, to put me off with an excuse, even when she might have company. These calls were a duty: I was still raw, still hurting, and she felt obliged to see them through, to fill a respectable space with small talk. At the same time, she resisted all attempts to nudge the conversation into murky waters, and met my innuendos, my coaxing remember-whens with a caustic briskness. The deeper, the more night-time fuzzy my tones, the crisper grew her diction. There was something operatic in these exchanges, my lumbering *basso supplicato* dogging her bright evasive trills. Even when I knew that Adam wasn't present, it sounded as though he was listening in.

The next morning, these calls to Elaine pained me more than my hangover. I'd come to treat them as lapses, to count the days between them like someone in rehab.

In the hotel room I dumped my holdall on one of the twin beds and crossed to the window. Good. A decent view: a long curved street and cars parked up both sides. The beds had that tight, starched, angular look. The bathroom was clean, the minibar full. I took a miniature Red Label and a bottle of Beck's. The beds were firm. I chose the one nearest the door. My Nokia was open on the other one. I took a pull on my Beck's and then snatched up the phone and with my free hand scrolled down to Lainie's number, still filed in my address book under 'Home'. The number was engaged.

I called John Rose instead. Rose was the *Trib*'s Belfast stringer. He'd be showing me round for the next few days. He didn't answer. I left a message. I opened the whisky. I stood at the sink and added some water. There was salt in my hairline, a frosting of white on my spectacle lenses. I took the glasses off and rubbed my tired face. When did I get so old? I looked like my dad in the striplit glare. Something broad and brutal in the features. I looked like one of the men in the photo.

Chapter Seven

The Crown Liquor Saloon. The one Belfast boozer that everyone knows. Corinthian pillars, snib-locking snugs, aproned barmen. It's like the set of a costume drama, some Edwardian extravaganza with high velvet collars and brown bowler hats. I had aimed for a note of irony when proposing it to John Rose, over the phone, on my first night in the city. It was late when I reached him; he was tired-sounding, curt; and though I'd been to Belfast before, and had drunk my way up and down the Golden Mile, there was only one name I could muster.

It was a little after one when I got there. I stood across the street, heels on the kerb, while a gearshifting cab ground past. As I crossed the road I slowed and paused and stopped right there on the broken white line to take it all in once more – the foursquare glinting jewel-box, its enamelled facade a Pompeii of lacquered tiles, aqua, cornelian, emerald, pearl, glinting like a bag of midget gems – before an elongated blare stung me onto the pavement and in through the pinned-back doors.

The place was heaving. I plunged in to the gloom, doggy-paddling through the lunchtime crush towards the gantry and flung a hand on the bar. An apron loomed and I ordered a Guinness.

I didn't know John Rose. No one at the *Trib* had met him. He'd been stringing with us for barely a year. His copy was good. A little flashy, a little heavy on the power-chord intros, but he knew his way round a sentence. We didn't use him that much, since nothing much was happening, but Ireland still sells papers in Glasgow and every few weeks I'd see his by-line under a six-hundred-worder.

My pint appeared on the bartop, a brown commotion settling upwards to the creamy head. I lifted the glass but a young guy was squeezing through to the counter, his Action Man crew cut bobbing under my nose, his bleached denim shoulders almost bumping my pint. I eased back to let him through but he turned and brought his face right up to mine.

'Sorry?' I missed what he said. He had an earring in his eyelid, a silver hoop below a tonsured eyebrow.

'Gerry Conway?'

'Aye. Yes!'

'I'm John Rose.'

I put my pint down to shake his hand.

'Good to meet you, John. Jesus, for a minute there I thought I was claimed.'

He ran his hand across his scalp.

'Yeah? Well, the night's young. Never know your luck. Come on, we're over here.'

He led me to one of the snugs, the wooden booths that lined one wall. We sat down and he reached over to turn the snib that locked the door. Peace. The hubbub muffled.

'This is my first.' He lifted his half-drunk pint from its beermat. 'I don't like drinking on duty.'

'Well, I wouldn't worry,' I said, lifting my own. 'Anyway, you couldn't come into the Crown and drink tomato juice. What's your background, John?'

'Background?'

'How'd you get into this game?'

He shrugged. 'Same as anyone else. It was kind of a growth industry around here at one time. We made a lot of news. There was plenty to go around. Sorry, is this like an audition? I thought I'd got the gig.'

'You have, John, you have. I was just curious.'

A head appeared briefly at the partition. I reached for my drink. Rose was frowning at his pint, twisting the glass on its beermat. I asked him for his verdict: on the peace process, the current situation. He brightened a little and gave me his spiel, the potted briefing he'd prepared for these occasions.

I didn't interrupt. I nodded weakly and buried my nose in my pint as he spoke about the ceasefires and Good Friday and the various agreements. He had a lot to say about the paramilitaries. There were so many acronyms he sounded like an adult spelling out words so a child won't hear. He took a pull at his beer every few sentences and wiped his palm down his mustard Fred Perry. I'd known he was new, of course; but why had no one warned me? He looked barely out of his twenties. Our previous Belfast stringer was a proper hack, an old-school ex-Street staffer called Maurice Brand. Maurice Brand news-edited the *Mirror* for twenty years and then came back to Belfast in semi-retirement. He had a string with us and with one or two English papers. He boosted his Streeter's pension by driving Yanks and Brits around the city. I only met him once – bigfooted him, in fact, in the early nineties. When a story grows arms and legs a paper wants its own guy on the case. They parachute you in and the stringer gets bumped. It happened to Maurice with the Shankill Bomb. Maurice broke the story and I stepped in. He wasn't bothered. He met me at Aldergrove airport and drove me into town. He took me to the shattered shop, the street still smoking in rubble and dust, the great jagged hole in the heart of the terrace, a torn line of bricks like a crow-stepped gable.

I spoke to a couple of truculent locals. Maurice fixed a meeting with the RUC investigating officer, who gave me ten minutes in his mobile incident-centre and answered my questions with polite contempt. Then we had a pint in Benny Conlon's A1 Bar, and Maurice spoke out of the side of his mouth, making eye contact from time to time in the big whiskey mirror. He sucked peppermints – he may have been giving up smoking – and the whiffs of mint and whiskey mixed with his droll reminiscences of torture and death. He gave me the low-down on various celebrated killings of the early Troubles – the betting shop murders, the Black-and-Decker case, the Markets crucifixion; eerie details that never made it to the papers.

John Rose would have been skiting Matchbox cars across his kitchen lino when all this happened. Watching *Animal Magic* with a bowl of Smash in his lap. We talked it through anyway. He'd been briefed about Peter Lyons, the New Covenanters, Lyons's retreat from Belfast, the three killings in the week before Guy Fawkes Night, 1983. Until last week he'd never heard of the New Covenanters. Why should he have? He knew Peter Lyons through reading the *Trib* but he'd never heard of a Belfast connection. He asked a few no-brainers and nodded at my answers. And then, quite abruptly, we had nothing to say. We were like two nervous teens on a date. I twisted my pint on the tabletop. Rose footered with his eyebrow ring. The pub-talk rumbled on beyond the booth. He'd been nettled by my question, and I couldn't hide my chagrin at his age, his clothes, the sleeper in his eyelid. It was a relief when he got up to take a piss.

I looked at my watch. I tilted my glass to get the dregs of my pint. Above my head the ceiling was extravagant – all carved, dark wood, lacquered fleur-de-lis and looping leaves. On the stained-glass windows there were fronds and ferns. Above the walls of the booth rose wooden columns carved like palm trees.

'It's a jungle in here,' I said, as Rose eased back into the booth. He reached to turn the snib: there was a panel of frosted glass in the door, with struts of wood forming the spars of a Union flag: 'How come it survived? Why did no one blow it up?'

'Who knows,' said Rose. 'Pure fluke. They blew up nicer places than this.'

'It's more like a church.'

'It *is* a church, basically.' Rose looked around. 'Italians built it. Craftsmen from Modena. They were over here building chapels and they did this place on the side. Moonlighting.'

'Our Lady of Perpetual Succour.'

A barman's head poked over the partition. Then his arm drooped over and Rose passed him the empties.

'So what are you looking for, exactly?' Rose had taken a notebook from his back pocket. He fished a short blue pen from his Levi jacket and set it on the table, where it rolled towards me and skittered onto the tiled floor.

I bent to pick it up. I'll tell you what I'm looking for, I thought. I'm looking for a proper stringer. A guy with a slouch hat and nicotine fingers. A guy who knows what he's doing.

I held out the bookies' pen.

'Tools of the trade?'

'Fuck off!' He snatched it back and wagged it at me. 'It fits my pocket is all.' He looked up slyly. 'Way things are going, though? You'd make a better living at that game than this. You were saying.'

'OK.' I took a pull of Guinness. You're making a decent living this week, I thought. We were paying him a ton a day, plus expenses. For two or three hours' work. 'First thing. I need details of the three murders. I want the cuttings – the first reports, any follow-ups, reports of the trials. Maybe talk to some of the hacks if they're still around.'

'Fine. I'll take you round the *Tele*, the *News-Letter*. You can check the files. Anything else?'

'I want to talk to the players, guys he'd have known at the time. Get a sense of what he was up to.'

Rose frowned. 'Who, though? Do we know who his contacts were; assuming he had any?'

I opened my holdall and took out the photo. I wiped a beer spill with my sleeve and set the photo on the table.

'Dear dear.' Rose shook his head, leaned over the picture. 'The gang's all here. Look at the nick of that. Where'd you get this?'

I shook my head. 'Doesn't matter. Before your time anyway, eh?'

'How's that?'

'I'm saying you'll not know anyone.'

'Yeah?' He jabbed his bookies' pen at one of the heads. 'There's Kiwi, for a start.'

'Who?'

I craned round to see. A broad-nosed, noble face, the

chin canted high. His blond hair was long, but thinning. A fat brown moustache glorified his upper lip. He wore a black roll-neck sweater under a cracked leather jacket. He was a good head shorter than the others in the photo but you couldn't miss it. Something in the eyes, the way he carried himself: this was the gaffer.

Rose supped his pint. 'Isaac "Kiwi" Hepburn. He ran the Upper Shankill back in the seventies. Old-school Blackneck.' He looked up. 'You know what a Blackneck is?'

I nodded.

'Real stickler for discipline. Compound commander in the Kesh.'

The eyes were hooded, the head slightly cocked. The leather suit jacket barely compassed the chest; stress lines creased the leather round the single button.

'Right. So, what, as in the fruit? The bird?'

'What?'

'*Kiwi*.'

'That's from the Kesh. It was the shoes. He'd always have a tin of boot polish open, giving his shoes another shine. He made his guys line up for inspection, every morning. Checked their fingernails and teeth, the shine on their toecaps. Like the bloody Boys' Brigade.'

Rose grinned. His eyes were a little pouchy. Maybe he wasn't as young as all that.

'He still about?'

'Kiwi? Aye. He runs a boxing club.' Rose glanced at his watch. 'Among other things. And this is your man?' He was tapping Lyons.

'That's him. Peter Lyons, Minister for Justice.'

'Big handsome man. The housewives' favourite.'

'Yeah. What about the others?' I was getting nervous. The pub was still busy and heads popped over the partition now and then to check whether the snug was occupied. A barman might come back looking for empties.

Rose grimaced, his lower lip jutting. 'Nah. Hard to tell at this distance; must be, what, twenty years? Folk'll have changed. But, naw, no other celebrities there.'

I lifted the photo and fed it back into the plastic wallet and the wallet back into the envelope.

'This Kiwi guy; Hepburn, is it? Can you set up a meet?'

Rose shrugged, tilted his head and I saw now – the sunlight catching his hair – little pewtery glints at the temple. 'Leave it with me.' He swirled the last of his pint. 'Let's head.'

The *Telegraph* offices were in the city centre, at the top of Royal Avenue. We walked across town, past the City Hall, up through the shoppers on Donegall Place.

'You think he'll see me?'

'Who, Hepburn? Yeah, he'll see you. He may play hard to get for a day or two but he'll see you.'

'You seem pretty sure.'

'Catch yourself on, Gerry. When the Troubles were here? This guy was a legend, a celebrity. His name in the papers, all the hacks and politicos hanging on his words. What's he got now? He's some baldy old man in a wee red-brick house. Of course he'll see you. Here we are.'

We pushed through the green glass doors to reception. The security guard set a form on the counter, spun it towards me with a jerk of his wrist. I reached inside my jacket for a pen. Rose was at my elbow, his breath sour with whiskey and porter.

'Anything else I can do just now?'

Yeah, I thought. Get a job you like.

'Thanks, John. I'm fine. This is me for the afternoon. I'll see you tomorrow: ten o'clock OK?'

The guard palmed my form and tossed a visitor's pass onto the counter. I clipped it to my jacket. Rose headed off – back to his snug at the Crown, I supposed; 'first of the day' my arse – and I clumped down the stairs to the *Telegraph* library. A cheerful, denim-shirted girl laid down her Harry Potter to show me round. It was much the same as our place. A bank of PCs along one wall. A huddle of chipped Formica desks. Strip-lit aisles and yards of box-files. All the recent stuff was computerised. Anything prior to ninety-five it was actual clippings, accessed via the card index. Murders were filed under surname: normally that of the victim; less commonly that of the lead detective; occasionally – if the guy was a real celebrity – that of the killer himself. My three were simple enough. Gillies, Pettigrew, Walsh: the three victims. I noted the shelf marks, retrieved the slim pink files and dropped them on an empty desk.

It didn't take long. Each file began with the first reports, the deadpan declarative sentences. *A man was found murdered in North Belfast. The body of a man was recovered from a vehicle.* The follow-up pieces carried head-shots: the gormless, unwitting grins of the victims, snapped at some long-gone function. There were backgrounders on recent killings, the back-and-forth of neighbourly death. And in one case only – the shooting of Eamonn Walsh – the report of the trial. (The report wasn't long: a UVF hitman got snagged by forensics and went down for life. His tariff was thirty-five years.) And that was it. Three abbreviated lives, three shakings of yellowed paper.

I put them back in the files. Hardly even files. Three folded oblongs. I fingered the cheap, damp-feeling card, its coarse, pulpy grain. Stacked on the desk the files looked empty. Back home, in the *Tribune* library, a murder file had a certain bulk. It might be three times, four times as thick as this. For all the city's hard-man swagger, its razor kings and ice-cream murders, Glasgow wasn't Belfast. A life meant something in Glasgow, a death mattered, in a way it didn't here. I lifted the files. There was something seedy in their lack of heft. The deaths of these three men were almost weightless. The story moved on. New victims appeared. The photographs changed; a different set of crooked grins, a new crop of dated haircuts.

There was a photocopier in the corner. I bought a copycard from the girl at the desk and copied everything in the files. When I got back to the hotel there was a package waiting for me; cuttings from the *News-Letter*, reports on the three murders, with a note from John Rose: *More to follow. See you at ten.* I took them upstairs and tossed them on the table. I fetched a Red Label from the minibar and sat down to read.

Chapter Eight

'"British as Finchley," she called it. You can see her point, round here. The Troubles might never have happened.'

We were on the Malone Road, heading down towards Queen's.

'Shite,' said Rose. He dropped the Forester into third. 'The Troubles reached everywhere, Gerry. There were people killed on these streets too. The Provies topped a judge outside a Catholic church just round the corner there.' He floored it abruptly to beat the lights. 'The Peelers shot a Blackneck in a stolen car down there, on Elmwood Avenue.' We were passing Queen's, the cheerful red-brick castle with its neat yellow lawn. 'There was a law lecturer, the Provies shot him dead in University Square.' He jerked his thumb out the window. 'Just there. The Troubles were here all right. The difference being, in this neck of the woods you could kid on things were normal. There's no murals here. No flags and bunting, coloured kerbstones. It could be anywhere. Fucking arse-piece!' He leaned on the horn and gave the finger out the window to a minicab that cut us up. 'Except it isn't.'

For the next hour we drove round the city. The Shankill and Falls. Oldpark and Andersonstown. There wasn't much to see. The tight blank streets. Boxy houses stained with rain. Nothing I couldn't have seen at home.

The sky was overcast, a muted, no-weather cotton-wool gauze. Only the hills, swelling dark at the end of each street, lent some colour to the scene. And then we turned a corner.

The mural reared above us, a whole gable end, detailed and luminous, like a rent in the fabric of everyday life. Rose parked the Forester and we got out to look.

I was edgy at first, sniffing the air, alert for some movement, for the challenge that must issue from these tight black windows. My suit was too rich, too blue; its nap practically glowed. I edged close to the car and then edged further off. The car seemed aggressively large in these poky streets, high on its chassis like a preening dog. 'Baby on board'; 'National Trust': the signs in the back made my forehead prickle.

But no one seemed to notice. People clicked their wrought-iron gates, tugged their terriers' leads, lifted shopping from their boots, bumped their buggies onto the pavement. They never glanced our way. Only the teens by the lock-ups, circling on their bikes like baseball-hatted sharks, seemed conscious of our presence. At each lazy revolution their cap-peaks flipped towards us. Their tyres crackled on the gritty ground.

The mural showed a street scene. A typical group of locals – an old woman with a shopping bag, a young mum with a buggy, two teenage boys, a girl dressed for Irish dancing – watched complacently as a British Army foot patrol marched towards the vanishing point. 'TIME TO GO'; 'SLÁN ABHAILE'. It was edged in Celtic patterns, braided knotwork running a border round the image. Nothing was left blank: the backdrop of houses was lovingly rendered, and the drumlins' gradations of olive and lime and bottle and jade. It had the smudgy proficiency of pavement art. I looked around. The cars at the kerbside, the satellite dishes jutting from the walls, the baseball-hatted teens: these things seemed anachronistic, unconnected to the world of the mural, even though the scene it depicted was the scene before our eyes – the same hills, the same sad houses. There was something comforting in the bright image, something kin to the vividly miniature and implausible worlds of snow-domes. It looked like a portal to a greener realm, a window on a technicolour Oz.

For the rest of the morning we toured the murals. North and south and east and west. The Nationalist ones were earnest and kitsch – full of slogans and doves, tags from Heaney and Yeats, historical parallels with Gaza and Mississippi. As if in reaction, the Prod ones were ugly and crude. A brash kind of anti-art. Everything wooden and tight, the lettering clenched and slightly askew. Gunmen in jeans and black jackets, their limbs stiff as guns. There were murals of the Somme, murals of the shipyards. Some of them were oddly jokey. A bug-eyed stomping skinhead in outsize Doc Martens lashing a bulbous drum. A Loyalist Tom bearing down on a Leprechaun Jerry. They were slapdash and happily naff. The newer ones were different again, less partisan and bellicose, they featured footballers and folk heroes instead of hoods and gunmen. George Best and Davey Crockett. On one gable end C. S. Lewis beamed down on the Protestant streets from a wintry Narnian backdrop.

'What's with the saltires?'

This was the other thing. Almost every Loyalist mural featured a bright-blue Scottish flag. We were standing on the Newtonards Road. Above us, the whole side wall of a derelict factory honoured the veterans of the Ulster Volunteer Force. Three black-jacketed, balaclava'd figures toted AK-47s in a tableau framed by billowing flags. On one side was the Ulster flag; on the other a Scottish saltire. Rose seemed puzzled at my question. Conversation had petered out a few murals back and for the last half-hour we'd been driving in amicable silence. He cleared his throat.

'The what?'

'The Scottish flags. The St Andrew's cross.'

I'd seen them all morning. Flapping from flagpoles and telegraph poles, painted on gable walls.

'Like that one there. Look.' I pointed at the wall: a red and white Ulster flag on one side, a blue and white saltire on the other. 'Scottish saltires. They're everywhere.'

We stood before the wall, tilting our heads like connoisseurs.

'The flag of Scotland? Yeah, it's all Scottish stuff now. That's the latest wheeze. We're not Brits any more. We're Ulster Scots.'

'We?'

He shrugged. 'I wouldn't know a haggis from a pork pie, but there you are. There's money in it too. There's a guy they have at Stormont, a species of clerk; he translates all the debates into Ulster Scots. That's all he does.' He laughed. 'They put street signs up – some shitpot town on the Ards peninsula, they put all these signs up in Ulster Scots. Then they had to tear them down.' He grinned. 'The natives thought they were Irish.'

The traffic ground past at our backs. A pair of tourists in crocus-coloured anoraks joined us at the mural. We nodded hello and the guy fumbled in his pocket, producing a small silver camera.

'Can I ask? Would it trouble you?'

The accent was north European: Swedish, possibly Dutch. He showed me the button to press.

'Sure. No problem.'

They shuffled together in front of the mural and the guy put his arm round the girl. I crouched down to get them in the frame. Above their heads a tangle of painted guns. I wasn't sure whether to ask them to smile.

'Here we go,' I said.

'Thank you.' The guy gave a little bow as he took back the camera. He grinned. 'Now we have all of them, I think. What you call a "full house". All of the political murals.'

'Very good.'

'Tomorrow we go to London Derry. We see the city walls. The "Free Derry Corner".'

He gave his funny little bow again. He stowed the camera in his anorak and they strolled off, hand in hand.

Rose was sitting on a garden wall, texting. He looked across and I tapped my watch, jerked my thumb towards the car.

'Had enough?' He slid down off the wall.

For two days we drove around the city. Rose had set up meetings with local hacks – news editors, long-serving staffers. They left their screens and pulled out chairs for me and brought me water in squishy plastic cups. They gave me their time. They were eager to accommodate me – the *Tribune* remains, for some reason, a name that carries weight in the trade – but they couldn't help. They drummed their fingers on their lips and clucked their tongues as they sought to recall the week in question. They'd never heard of Peter Lyons. When I mentioned Isaac Hepburn they brightened and offered variations on the same two or three anecdotes. In the end they were baffled by my urgency. I was like one of those Japanese jungle-fighters, emerging into the daylight after twenty years, still primed for battle. No one had told me the war was over. They couldn't share my hunger for the truth about a Scottish politician and that long dead week in the early 1980s. They'd sooner be discussing house prices. They were just glad it was over. It was time to move on.

I could sympathise with this. I could sympathise with the broken-veined *News-Letter* staffer who quoted the Glasgow homicide rate – wasn't it the highest in Europe? – and wondered if I hadn't enough to get on with at home. But I had a story to write. I wanted to know what Peter Lyons had done. I wanted to know if a fact, properly primed and planted, could still make a difference.

We were driving down the Shore Road.

'No word on Hepburn?'

He grimaced. 'Kiwi's a hard man to reach. I'll try again later.'

I dropped Rose in the centre and headed for Botanic.

The Grania was deserted. An electric fan wafted to and fro on the bare front desk. The empty restaurant was set for dinner, napkins propped like dunces hats, a dark-blue shine on the cutlery.

I took the stairs at a jog. My room had been cleaned. Cushions were propped on the straight-edged bed. Traffic noise buzzed at the open window. A fizz of Mr Sheen in the air. There were new supplies in the bathroom, mint-thin tablets of soap, round-topped bottles of bodywash. The first square of toilet roll folded to a point.

The folder was where I'd left it, under the Bible in the bedside drawer. I fetched a Red Label and spread the cuttings out on the desk in three separate piles. Three hands of cards. Three dead men. Duncan Gillies, Gary Pettigrew, Eamonn Walsh. Three victims of the Troubles in the week before Guy Fawkes Night, 1983. I poured the whisky and added water. Two were non-starters. Gary Pettigrew was an off-duty RUC corporal, killed by an IRA car-bomb as he left his mother's house. (He went to see her every Sunday after church, parking in her driveway while the pair of them ate lunch. This little rhythm, this tick of family life, was enough to get him killed.) Eamonn Walsh was a Belfast solicitor, murdered at home by the UVF. A lone gunman put two bullets in his chest from a range of five yards. The UVF described Walsh as an active Republican, a high-ranking Provo, something the family denied. The gunman was caught on the same night. He worked as a croupier in a riverside casino and wore his work clothes under his overalls when he murdered Eamonn Walsh. The RUC pinched him at the blackjack table; traces of blood in his collar. A red miasma down the edge of his cuff, as if the diamonds and the hearts were bleeding. His sentence was thirty-five years.

The one that intrigued me was Duncan Gillies. The file on Gillies was slightly thicker than the rest. It was thicker because the early reports were wrong. Gillies was beaten to death in an alley near his house in a Protestant district of South Belfast. He was Protestant but his street bordered a small Catholic enclave called The Den. The RUC thought his killing was sectarian. A post-mortem timed the beating to the early hours of Sunday morning. Gillies had been drinking. He'd been at a club, maybe, or a city-centre party, and had taken a short cut through the Catholic estate. He'd been challenged by the locals and set upon, his body dumped at the Protestant end of the alley that connected The Den with the Loyalist streets. There were calls for the alley to be closed. Resident groups in both areas wanted barriers put in place. Another peace line was started.

But then the story changed. A 'source close to the UVF' suggested Gillies's death had been ordered. A graffito went up near the victim's home: 'Lundy Gillies, Traitor to Ulster.' A new theory emerged. Gillies was involved with a prisoner's wife. The usual warnings were given – his car had been trashed the week before, its tyres slashed, its windscreen blinded with paint. But Gillies wasn't listening. He carried on, trysting with the woman in local pubs, seeing her home through the narrow streets. He was flaunting the affair, taunting the hard men, daring them to act. He'd left them no choice. Gillies wasn't murdered by Catholics. His own side topped him, in a bit of internal housekeeping that went too far.

I threw back the last splash of whisky. A muffled jangle in the room behind me: the tinny bar-chords of The Clash's 'White Riot'. My jacket was on the bed; I fished the phone from its inside pocket.

'We're on,' he said. 'Good to go. Tomorrow morning. Get new Duracells in that Dictaphone! I'll pick you up at ten.'

'What's this?'

'I spoke to him,' said Rose. 'Isaac Hepburn. Kiwi. He wants to meet.'

Chapter Nine

Out on Botanic the cafes and snack bars were opening up. Waitresses propped chalkboards on the pavement, the day's specials blazoned in yellows, greens and pinks. A window cleaner was busy across the street. I watched him lather a plane of plate glass and swipe it clean with fluent strokes of his rubberised blade. He was working his way up the street and the windows he'd already done were like a row of shaven chins. He stooped to lift his twin buckets and I thought of the burnished new rotunda by the river and the clicking heels of the girls on the Golden Mile and the hopeful sprig of garnish on my breakfast plate. Maybe the *News-Letter* staffer was right. I was here to pick at scabs. I was greedy for all the old badness, the past's bitter quota of hurt.

I wasn't alone. Across the West of Scotland, in the clubs and lodges, the stadiums and bars, people missed the Troubles. They mightn't admit it, but they rued a little the ceasefires' durability, the Armalite's silence. We had followed the Troubles so closely for so long. There is something narcotic in watching a war unfold on your doorstep, knowing all the while it can't harm you. It's like taking in one of those fabled childhood mismatches – bear against wolverine, crocodile and shark – from behind a Plexiglas screen.

Certainly the newsrooms missed the Troubles. I knew

too well that quickening, that bristling at the desks when word came through of another bomb. A pub raked with bullets. A Scots Guard snipered. An ambushed patrol. How greedily we absorbed it, crowding round the teleprinter, expelling our breath in awed whistles as the rousing news came through on the wire. And then the cheerful bustle, the camaraderie as we readied the layout and left space for the photos and the recapping sidebars, and waited by the phones for the stringer's thousand words.

The violence thrilled us. All the northern carnage. Bombs and executions just out of earshot. Army choppers shot down over hills that looked like Ayrshire. We were close to this slaughter. We understood it. More at least than the English did. People were fighting and dying in the name of those acronyms that littered our walls. It was our war too. Only it couldn't touch us. Nobody here was dying. We weren't being smithereened in our shopping malls and pubs. Our high streets and town crosses retained their integrity, unedited and unabridged by fertiliser bombs. London, Birmingham, Manchester, Warrington: the war came home to England but it never came to us. The Provos had a policy: don't touch Scotland. Who'd want to start things here? So Scotland was exempt; insulated from Semtex and shrapnel. The cross was on our lintels and the carnage passed us by.

I remember travelling to London for a story, sometime in the early nineties, not long after Canary Wharf. We changed trains at Carlisle, the snapper and I. We were waiting on the platform when the snapper lit a smoke, crushed the empty packet and looked for a bin. There wasn't one. Railway-station litter bins stopped at the border. You couldn't have a bin in an English station in case the Provos put a bomb in it.

There was a noise outside in the corridor and somebody rapped on my door. 'Hold on!' I grabbed my jacket. The cleaner, a girl in her twenties with Elvis Costello glasses and the honey-blonde colouring of Eastern Europe, raised her eyebrows at me.

'Yep. I'm ready. On you go.'

The corridor looked like the main road out of a war-torn city, a capital newly fallen to the rebels. I picked my way through a refugee column of carts and service trolleys, laundry bins, gape-mouthed canvas sacks. The carts carried replacement bottles of complimentary shampoo, sugars ranked like banknotes in a till, NutraSweet pink and cane-sugar brown and granulated white; foil-wrapped tea bags, Nescafé sachets, thimble-sized cartons of UHT milk. There were tilting towers of bedsheets and bath towels. From the half-open doors came muted thumps and knocks, the complaint of vacuum cleaners, the mollifying tones of spoken Polish.

In the lobby I sat like a schoolboy in an outsize brown armchair and watched the city. I began to wonder if Lyons had been here at all. He seemed to have left no trace, no spoor, no impression on these streets. A minicab pulled up and John Rose stepped out. I waited for the cab to move off but it stayed put. Then I realised he'd emerged from the driver's side.

I patted my breast pocket. The Dictaphone was there, with a new pair of AAs and a fresh cassette. I'd read up on Isaac Hepburn. I'd googled him. I'd stood for an hour at the 'Troubles' section of Belfast Waterstone's, tracking him through the indexes of half a dozen books. Hepburn was a Loyalist hero. He shot an IRA man in Ardoyne in the winter of '82. This was enough to make him a legend. At that time, the only people killing IRA men were other IRA men. The Provos' nutting squad, the unit that dealt with informers, dumped its regular quota of ruined volunteers on the verges of B-roads in Antrim and Down. But nobody else – not the Blacknecks, not the UDA, not the Peelers, not the Brits – had got close to a Provo in months. They were too well briefed and too canny. They were too bloody good. They slept in different places every night. Their own homes had bulletproof windows; front doors in reinforced steel. They were too special and too ordinary. They didn't cut about in top-range motors and high-end sportswear. They kept their heads down and did their jobs. You couldn't get near them.

But Hepburn did. He found a way. He was friendly with a British Army corporal. They drank in a hotel bar near Thiepval Barracks. This lad was manning a checkpoint when a white Opel was stopped, the driver a mid-ranking Provo. The corporal ran the reggie through the computer and got an address in Ardoyne. He passed it to Hepburn in the bar that night. The next evening Hepburn cycled into Ardoyne wearing a Celtic top. When he came to the address the white Opel was parked at the kerb and the mark was on his way down the path tossing the car keys in his palm. Hepburn shouted his name and the mark stopped with his hand on the car door. The first bullet caught the guy's arm and his car keys splashed to the ground. The next two thumped into his chest and dumped him on the pavement. His head lolled over the kerb. There was a drain right underneath and when Hepburn knelt down and lodged the barrel behind the mark's left ear the blood flowed cleanly through the bars. Then Hepburn stood up, lodged the gun in his waistband, pulled his Celtic top over it, mounted his bike and cycled out of Ardoyne. He crossed the Crumlin Road and was back on the Shankill within ten minutes.

John Rose came in, shaking his head. He dunked his keys in the empty ashtray.

'Sorry, big lad,' he said. 'No go. He's pulled the plug.'

The chair creaked as he dropped into it, his arms bouncing on the armrests. He took his smokes from his pocket and dropped them on the table.

I nodded, reached for my coffee and then sat back.

'OK. See, that's interesting because yesterday this was a done deal. Good to go. Your words.'

He looked around for the waitress.

'Yeah, well, things change. That was true yesterday. It's not true now.' The waitress had seen him. He lifted my coffee cup and pointed at it, then held up two fingers. I never said anything. He got a cigarette in his mouth and fumbled for a lighter. His eyes, when they turned in my direction, had narrowed slightly. He took the cigarette from his mouth. 'It's not the doctor, Gerry. You don't phone up and demand an appointment. You don't get seen within two working days.'

'Right.' I sighed. 'Tell me this. I'm wondering. Do you even know Isaac Hepburn? Do you actually know the guy? Because I'm beginning to doubt–'

The keys hissed as he fished them from the table.

'Fuck you.' He stuffed his cigarettes into his jacket pocket. 'Smart cunt. Fuck you. Let's see how far you get.'

The door thudded open in his wake and his boot heels

rattled the steps. The waitress came over to close the door properly.

The coffees arrived. I finished mine and was halfway through his when the door banged again. He was standing over me, breathing heavily. He wrenched the cup from my grasp and smacked it down on a nearby table.

'Come on to fuck if you're coming.'

He was already out the door. I shrugged into my jacket and hurried out.

We drove without talking. Something in the boot kept rattling around as Rose swung fiercely into the corners.

'What?' Rose said.

'This.' I gestured round the car's interior. The no-smoking signs. The licence on the dash.

'Yeah,' said Rose. 'Like I make a living wage as a stringer. Wise up, Gerry.'

He swung into the car park of an old Victorian villa. The house had long thin windows and pointed eaves that gave the place a morose expression. Rose himself had a face like thunder. He killed the engine.

'I'll wait for you here.'

I told him I would call a cab.

'This is a fucking cab. I'll wait for you here.' He took a book of number puzzles from the glove compartment and turned the radio on.

I climbed an ugly disabled ramp and pressed the buzzer. There was no sign, no hoarding, no banner. It was like that in Belfast: either they spelled it out in foot-high capitals ('YOU ARE NOW ENTERING LOYALIST TIGERS BAY') or they told you fuck all. Only once I'd been buzzed inside did I see the name above the corkboard in the hallway: The Northern Star Athletic Club.

There was a curved reception desk like a dentist's, and a girl in a black polo shirt and tracksuit bottoms came out from a back room and smiled.

I told her I was here to see Mr Hepburn.

'And you are?'

'Gerard Conway.' I said it nice and clean. She looked at me neutrally for a count of three.

'OK, Mr Conway. Why don't you have a seat for a minute? Would you like a coffee? A cup of tea?'

'I'm fine, thanks.'

I sat on a leather banquette by the door. Grunting and slapping sounds came from the gym and an odd hollow boom like a Lambeg drum.

'You're the war correspondent?' A blocky torso was squeezing through the hatch. A fat finger tapped a wristwatch. 'You're a bit late, fella. The war's over.' He wheezed and held out his hand. 'Isaac Hepburn.'

His hair had thinned and the face had filled out and the beard was a tight white goatee. But the eyes, with their hard, hooded brightness, were just as they were in the photo.

'Gerry Conway. Nobody told the doctors.'

'What's that?'

His grip was moist, surprisingly light.

'The war's over? Nobody told the doctors at the Royal. The knee surgeons.'

He tutted. 'Och no, son. It's much more civilised now. Now the bad guys phone the ambulance in advance. They wait till they hear the siren before pulling the trigger. It's a whole new level of service. Why are we talking about this? I'll show you the gym.'

A sparring match was in progress. Hepburn raised his hand and moved into a half-crouch, as if to say *Keep going, boys – don't stop on account of me*. The boxers – a skinny, long-haired galoot with strawberry splotches on his torso and a shorter, thickset, swarthy, purposeful crophead – never wavered. A man at ringside glanced over with no expression and then turned back to the fight.

'What would you like?'

There was a bar at one end of the gym, six feet of lacquered pine with half a dozen tables in front. A big guy in a blue sleeveless vest was sitting at one of the tables with a Nintendo DS Lite. He was jabbing the stylus at the little screen. I recognised the beeps and pings of Brain Trainer. He wore half-moon reading glasses which he tossed on the table when he went behind the bar and frowned at us.

I looked at my watch. 'Let's not go daft.'

I ordered a mineral water. Hepburn had a tomato juice.

We took our seats. Hepburn looked at me and then scanned round the club. He looked back at me. 'Yeah.' I cleared my throat. 'Yeah, this is a nice place.'

'I'm glad you think so.' He sat forward. 'And it's not just a gym, either. We've had some government money – a peace dividend, you could call it – but mostly we raised it ourselves. Raffles, charity boxing bouts.' He knocked on the tabletop, dark mottled red like a tenderised steak. 'Actual granite, this is.'

'Nice.'

The booming noise was the noise of the ring, the boxers' boots on the canvas floor. My money was on the short guy. No one had thrown a punch yet, but you can tell a lot from how a fighter moves. The small guy was everywhere, eel-like, all flourish and swank. He bobbed about with beautiful side-stepping slides; he feinted and weaved. There was a contemptuous excess to his movements, a scornful slickness. The tall guy stumped about in his wake, jabbing empty air, stopping now and then to hitch his shorts.

He was hitching his shorts when the small guy stepped in and tagged him, two head-snapping lefts that tipped him onto the ropes.

Hepburn frowned. The big guy bounced off and wrapped the other in a stiff-armed clinch.

'There's no prejudice here.' Hepburn tapped the actual granite. 'You can't afford bigotry in this game. Once you're through these ropes all bets are off. Everyone's equal in there.'

Try telling the big guy, I thought. He took a dull one on the ear as we watched. He listed a little but kept coming on.

'That's an interesting idea. Beating the shit out of each other brings the warring tribes together. Hasn't worked so far, has it?'

Hepburn smiled tightly. 'You're a cynic, Mr Conway. That's your job. If we were all as cynical as you we'd still be at war. Once you've been what we've been through, then you can talk.'

I let that go. We watched the tall guy taking more punishment. If he was suckering the short guy it was time to spring the trap.

Suddenly Hepburn smacked down his drink and got to his feet. 'For Jesus sake, Gilmour! Keep your guard up. Try and *look* as if you mean it. Move your feet. Move your feet.'

The big guy paused to absorb these instructions, his red and white face tilted blankly in our direction, and the little guy stepped in with a body combo – rat-a-tat jabs to the ribs – and a big looping head shot. Gilmour pitched forward. He tipped over like a bucket and stayed there on his elbows and knees, a rope of mucus swinging from his lip.

'Aw, for fuck sake!' Hepburn turned away in disgust. The barman looked up and grinned, hunching his shoulders and rubbing his palms together.

'How much?' I said to Hepburn.

'Fucking score. And you –' the barman made a show of stifling his grin – 'get us a real bloody drink.' They both looked at me.

'I'm fine,' I said, putting my hand over my glass.

When the drinks arrived – a whisky for Hepburn and another water for me – there was a twenty on the table. The barman palmed it. He whistled something jazzy under his breath.

'Fucking flyman.' Hepburn looked sourly round the gym. Then he looked straight at me. 'What did you want to talk about, son?'

'I thought John had told you. It's a mutual acquaintance. Guy called Peter Lyons.'

Hepburn relit his roll-up. He looked at the Dictaphone when I set it on the table.

'I don't think so, friend.'

I lifted the Dictaphone and stowed it in my pocket, but I thumbed 'record' as I did so.

'You don't know him?'

'Did I say that?'

'But you don't want to talk about him.'

He studied his glass.

'What did you see me for then?'

'A favour. Young Rose out there is a family friend. I knew his daddy.'

'No other reason?'

His eyebrows rose coyly. 'You mean do I know your work? Am I a *fan*? Sorry to disappoint, Mr Conway.'

'That's all right. I'm not a big fan of your own work. It must take you back a bit.' I spread my palm towards the table – the notebook and drinks. 'When did you last do this? It must be a while.'

'I'm sorry?'

'Since someone found you worth interviewing.'

He snorted. 'You think I've missed it that badly? Is that what you think?'

'Yeah, that's what I think. You used to run this estate, from what I hear. What did you call yourself: brigadier? Battalion commander? Nowadays? I'm not sure you even run this gym. Of course you miss it. That's what the will he/won't he stuff was about. That's why you're dicking me around right now. You probably don't even know Peter Lyons, you can't even place the name.'

Hepburn was smiling. 'Very good, son. This is where I lose the rag, is it? Give you the starting prices on Peter Lyons. You think we don't know the techniques? We wrote the fucking manual, son.'

I tipped my chair back and stared at the ceiling. The chair legs cracked on the floor when I leaned forward. 'Frankly? Who gives a shit any more? Wrote the manual! I'm not in the market for anecdotes. Tales from the H-blocks. I've got the fucking History Channel if I want that. I came to you for help. Either you'll help me or you won't. Right now it looks like you won't. That's all right. Thanks for the drink.'

The barman was looking up from his console. He was too far away to hear my words but he didn't like the tone. Hepburn looked over and shook his head and the guy eyed me levelly and went back to his game. Hepburn wetted his finger and thumb and doused his smoke with a tiny hiss. He let out a sigh.

'He's done well for himself, hasn't he?'

'Lyons? He's doing OK.'

'What is he now?'

'Justice Minister. Prisons and police.'

Hepburn laughed. 'Prisons and police. Fat lot he'd know about that. And what are you after him for? What's he done?'

'I was hoping you might tell me that.'

Hepburn nosed his whisky and set it down untouched.

'You think he's done something but you don't know what.'

'We got a tip-off.'

He stopped his glass halfway to his lips. 'Should've let you buy this after all. Must be a queer load of money in the Scottish papers. You're over here on the strength of a tip-off.'

'It's not just a tip-off.'

'I know it's not, son.'

'What?'

'You've got a photo of some guys in fancy dress. It's not *much* more than a tip-off, is it?'

I looked at the door.

'Don't blame him. He lives here. You fuck off home tomorrow or next week; he's got to eat.'

I took a drink of water. I didn't say anything.

'I'm in it too, I hear. Captured for posterity. Do you think I could see it?'

I took it out and slid it across the table.

'Jesus Christ.' Hepburn grinned. 'That fucking tache. I thought it gave me a military bearing, like a wing commander or something. I look fucking gay.'

He shook his head and passed the photo back.

'How well did you know him?' I said.

Hepburn was still shaking his head. I thought he hadn't heard, so I asked him again.

'Do you know what a tout is, son?' He fished the roll-up – it was barely an inch long now – from his shirt pocket.

'I'm not asking for his life story. I just want to know what he was like, what brought him to Belfast every other week. What he did with you guys.'

'Uh-huh.' He was lighting it now, tilting his head to keep the flame from singeing his moustache. 'That's all you want is it? Let me tell you something.' The voice was quieter now, but the guy in the vest was paying attention. 'Let me tell you something, friend. I did sixteen years. I did sixteen years in a British jail. If I'd talked when they pinched me, I needn't have done a day. I could have walked right out the door. But sixteen years is what I did. So why would I talk now? Why would I do that? If you want to ask about the prison thing, in general terms, with no names mentioned, I'm happy to oblige. If you want my own story, I'll talk about that. But I can't talk about anyone else. I don't know what John Rose told you, but that's not what we do.'

The boxers had finished showering. The big guy

looked tougher with his street clothes on. He paused at our table. Hepburn jerked his chin at him.

'How you doin', kid?'

'I'm sorry you lost your bet, Mr Hepburn.'

'Don't worry, Gil. Next time, eh? Watch the right.' He feinted a little, poked the air with two short jabs.

The big guy nodded. He hung around for a few seconds, as if Hepburn might do the intros. Then he hitched his shoulder bag.

'I'll see you again, Mr Hepburn.'

The door banged behind him.

'Good kid,' said Hepburn. My face must have betrayed me since he added in a regretful undertone: 'If a fucking donkey.'

'I'll get going as well.'

Hepburn got to his feet, held out his hand in that regal backhand grip favoured by pontiffs and mobsters.

'I didn't mean to bite your head off, son. I'm sorry I can't help. Anyway, it's twenty years ago. I couldn't tell you what I had for my tea last night, let alone twenty years ago.' He took a card from his wallet and tapped it into my breast pocket. 'You might need some help over the next few days. If that happens, you let me know.'

The barman looked up from his Brain Training, watching me over his reading glasses.

'Thanks. I'll do that.'

In the car park I turned my phone on and it rang straight away.

'Gerry. Thank Christ. I thought you'd vanished.' It was Martin Moir. 'Lyons has been in. He's trying to get a hold of you.'

'Yeah?'

'He came by the office. He knows you're on to something.'

The rain came down just then – big spare bulbous drops that spotted the dry ground. I held out my arm and watched the splotches bloom on my sleeve.

'Shit.' I ran through the possibilities. 'Maguire? Neve McDonald?'

'That told him? Who knows? Stick a pin. The thing is, he's on to us.'

'Yeah, but what does he know?'

'I'm not sure. What do *we* know? He knows you're in Belfast, Gerry; that's enough. He knows you're not over for the Walk.'

The rain was pleasant on my scalp, the big droplets bursting in cool hard slaps that pasted my hair to my crown.

'It's not so bad. Rix never liked him anyway.'

'There's that.'

Moir paused. He seemed to be holding his breath.

'What? What else?'

He breathed out. He said evenly, 'Tennant was in.'

Barbara Tennant – houndstooth-suited, spike-heeled and burnished, the harpy with the weathergirl gloss – was a new appointment to the *Tribune*'s board, where she'd taken her late husband's seat. The board met once a month in Edinburgh. You only ever saw a board member in the building when something was wrong. Tennant was trouble. She was also a partner in Lyons's law firm.

'She see Rix?'

'What do you think? Half an hour. Forty minutes maybe.' Moir sighed. 'He's going to need to see something, Gerry. Soon. He needs a result.'

The rain was easing off now, just a few dark plashes spotting the ground.

'Yeah? Would tonight do, do you think?'

'Really? You'll have something by tonight?'

'I'll have something by tonight.'

'Great. I'll tell Norman. I'll tell Rix. I'll bell you later.'

I climbed in beside John Rose. He lodged the sudoku book in the glove compartment and turned the ignition.

Chapter Ten

'You forget there were so many,' Malachy said. 'Nearly thirty. And they have this makeshift morgue with the bodies covered in blankets, old curtains, anything. And the blood. You see this guy, he's literally mopping it up, it looks like footage of a flood, a guy with a bucket and mop.'

'Jesus.' Simmonds shook his head. We all took a sip of our pints. There was a daytime talk show on the telly and I wished someone would turn it down or off. We all kept glancing at the screen and feeling bad about it. At least I did.

'It was bad,' Malachy said. 'The footage. But know what was worse? They played audio tapes. Jesus. The screams and the wailing. These pitiful shouts for help. Like fucking lost souls, the moans of the damned.'

We were in the Duke of York. This was the last of the journo pubs that Rose had promised to show me. Malachy Kane was Ireland correspondent for one of the London dailies. He was just back from Belfast High Court. For the past two weeks he'd been covering a trial. One of the big bomb blasts back in the nineties. The criminal case had collapsed a few years back. Now the victims' families had brought a civil suit against the suspected bombers.

'You've never heard a noise like it. It's worse than the

visuals: you're trying to imagine what could cause people to produce a noise like that.'

'I don't remember that,' the tall guy said. Tall and bald, a face like a boxer's. He'd been introduced as Down-in-the-mouth Macpherson. 'I was there. On the day. We got there within the hour. All I really remember is the shoes. Shoes all over the main street. The blast had knocked out a shoe-shop's windows. But it wasn't just new shoes. And both kinds – the new shoes and the old ones – were all mixed up together, on the pavement and the street.'

'You do remember,' Simmonds said. 'You think you don't remember but you do. It's all in there,' he tapped his temple. 'And it'll all come back. Believe me. You'll wish you didn't remember.'

'Cheers, Willie.' Macpherson raised his glass. 'That's a cheery fucking thought.'

Simmonds shrugged. 'I'm just saying.'

Macpherson and Simmonds ran the Northern bureau of the *Sunday Citizen*. The *Citizen* was a Dublin-based red-top that specialised in exposés of organised crime. The Northern edition had a narrower brief: go after the paramilitaries. Macpherson was editor and Simmonds his chief reporter. Most of the journalists I'd talked to over the past few days had no interest in the Troubles, they didn't even like to waste time talking about it. Macpherson and Simmonds talked about bombs and assassinations the way an exile talks about home. They looked like they could stand here talking all day and sometimes, according to John Rose, that's what they did. Dublin gave them a pretty long leash. Certainly, the pre-vailing interpretation of lunch-hour seemed spiritedly vague. Another round of beers appeared on the bartop.

'Excuse me a minute.' My phone was ringing. 'I need to take this.'

I walked on up to the pub's far end.

'Gerry, what's the word?' Fiona Maguire was sounding upbeat. 'That couldn't be a *pub* I hear in the background?'

'Listen, I can't talk, Fiona. I'm with someone.'

There were pictures on the bare brick wall, a line of caricatures, middle-aged men with drinker's faces. The little sign above them said *The Twelve Apostles*.

'You're not just sitting in the Crown drinking Guinness?'

'The very thought. I'm in the Duke of York.'

'Just tell me you've got something, Gerry. There's a big hole in Sunday's paper with your name on it.'

I told her I'd file something by Thursday or Friday. 'I'm on the case.'

When I rejoined the group they were talking about Hepburn.

'Kiwi was different,' Simmonds was saying. 'Kiwi's got class, a bit of style. There's a bit more up here –' he tapped his head again '– than your average bear.'

Macpherson was looking at the ground, grinding something with the toe of his brogue. He looked up.

'Why don't you ask Gerard Dolan about Hepburn's class.'

Simmonds shook his head.

'Who?' I said.

Macpherson kept staring at Simmonds.

'Gerard Dolan,' Malachy Kane said, in an undertone to me. 'Kiwi shot him in eighty-one. Before he did your man in Ardoyne.'

'Shot him in the stomach,' Macpherson said. 'Eighty-two, not eighty-one. In front of his wife and wee lad on the Springfield Road. Took him ten hours to die. This guy's a nightwatchman, not too bright.' He turned to me. 'He's practically special needs. And Hepburn calls him a top Provo. Shoots him in the belly.'

'I'm not saying he hasn't done bad things.'

'You think they're different? Because what. Because they sent guns to Spain in the thirties? You think they're good socialists because a couple of guys on the Shankill have read *The Motorcycle Diaries*? They're a People's Army? Are they fuck. O'Neill had it right: a sordid conspiracy of criminals.' He tugged on his broken nose with his finger and thumb and tapped the bartop. 'A sordid conspiracy of criminals.'

'Isn't he retired, now?' I said. 'Isaac Hepburn. I met him yesterday. He looks like Father Christmas.'

'You've met Kiwi? Send him my regards.'

'You know him?'

'I'm joking, big lad. He hates my guts. He likes John, though.'

We all looked at Rose.

'That's right,' I said. 'He told me he knew your father.'

Rose looked at me and looked away.

'It's more than I did.'

'What?'

'No, it's just: my dad died when I was a baby.' He swirled the dregs of his pint. 'I never knew him at all.'

I didn't know what to say to that and neither did anyone else.

'Jesus.' Simmonds waved a twenty at the barman. 'Let's get another round in before we depress ourselves to death.'

'No wonder,' Macpherson said. 'No wonder, Willie. The whole thing's fucked. And it's the prisoners. If we could have taken the prisoners, shipped them all to Greenland, we might have had a shot. We might have turned this place into somewhere halfway normal. But after Good Friday here they all come. These raging fuck-ing egos. They've got no trade, no skills. They've never worked a day in their life, most of them. And they think they're owed, for the time they've spent in jail. Me, I think jail time's what you pay for the stuff you've already done, but they see it different. So who pays them?' He tapped himself on the chest. 'We pay them. You and me. All these grants and subventions. Funding schemes for community projects. Let's call it what it is. It's a bribe: we'll give you money if you keep on not killing people.'

'Is Hepburn involved in this?'

'Have you seen his motor?'

I waited for Macpherson to smile but he didn't.

'What do you drive? He drives a new Saab—'

'It's not new,' someone said.

'He drives a new Saab on the profits of a crummy box-ing gym? Fuck off. The government pays for the gym and how does he pay for the rest? The suits and cars and what all else.'

'Let him enjoy it while he can,' Malachy said. 'It's not going to last much longer.'

'How's that?'

'The money's running out.' Malachy turned to me. 'The government money? The money for these projects? It comes from Europe, mostly. And we're not a priority any more. There's other places with better claims. Plus, here's the other thing. Bribing the hard men not to kill people? People will just about stomach that. But the hard men have to toe the line. Where's the mileage in bribing someone to be a good boy and he's out cracking heads and breaking people's legs with a bat full of six-inch nails?'

'That's why he hates us,' Macpherson said. 'Because we tell the truth about what he gets up to. And then the politicians start cutting the funds.'

'Is Hepburn going to lose it?' I asked. 'The funding for his club?'

'If I've got any say in it?' Macpherson swirled his last inch of Deuchars and downed it. 'Fucking right he is. Come on . . .' He punched my shoulder. 'I'll show you the office.'

'Nice shop,' I said, as we left the pub. 'It's not the Crown, though.'

'Yeah.' Macpherson was checking his mobile for messages. 'It's been blown up twice. Probably you figure you can skimp on the decor.'

After the roar of the pub the Cathedral Quarter was eerie. It was darker than I remembered, mazier, with its arcades and entries, its dog-legs and closes. For all his bulk, Macpherson moved nimbly and I struggled to match his pace as he barrelled down side streets and under archways, skipping up and down from the kerb to dodge pedestrians. I was short of breath when he jouked down an alley and fished for his keys.

'This is us.'

I stepped back to get a proper look at the building but the alley was narrow and dark. A blank facade of blind red brick. The beer heaved in my gullet and I belched stertorously. There was no neon sign, no lettering over the entrance, no glossy plaque by the door. Beside the intercom button, on a tiny ellipsis of clouded plastic, was a printed sticker. It was about the size of the joint on my little finger, white lettering on a red background: *Sunday Citizen*. (Our own place in Glasgow has a Zeppelin-sized sign, blinding the commuters on the Kingston Bridge.)

Macpherson's electronic key fob released the lock and he shouldered the heavy door. I climbed behind him in a smell of damp sacking to the outer office, where the fob set a green light blinking on the lock. While we waited out the ten-second delay, Macpherson rapped the glass with his knuckle. 'Bulletproof.' I nodded.

Inside there were six or seven terminals in a sad narrow room. The light was bad – the alleyway clogged the daylight and the strip lights blinked in their baking-tray fittings. It looked like an office corridor out of working hours. 'Come here.' Macpherson was stood by the door. He was swaying a little. 'Come here and look at this.' There was a plaque on the wall, between ruched red velvet curtains. The plaque bore the name Brendan O'Dowd and a date in 2001. You could comb your hair in its polished glare.

'Aren't you meant to be at peace here? Wasn't there a ceasefire or something?'

Macpherson peered at the plaque. He rubbed out a thumbprint with the cuff of his jacket. 'Yeah but *we're* not on ceasefire. We keep writing the news.' He tapped the black lettering. 'That was our Special Reporter. Guy with three kiddies. They shot him in the head. That's what they do here.' He turned now and looked at me accusingly: 'They shoot people dead for telling the truth.

It was Loyalists killed him but both sides *are* as bad. Both sides are as bad. They're scumbags, Gerry, a shower of murdering bastards. But the good people won, thank God. The good people won in the end.'

They hadn't won much, I thought. Our third-floor storeroom at the *Trib* was bigger than this office. But Macpherson walked me between the terminals and flourished his wrist and swept his arm in demonstrative arcs. There was nothing to see. At one point I paused by the water cooler in murmurous wonder till Macpherson urged me on with a spell-breaking grip of my shoulder. Macpherson was bright-eyed, euphoric. He was proud of what they did here. People were willing to kill him for the stories produced in this room.

'We're not white knights.' We were back at the ruched velvet curtains, the tour having drawn to its close. 'We don't wear our underpants outside our trousers. But I've never shot anyone. I've never hit someone with a baseball bat. I've never blown up a building. The lines are pretty clear here. The good guys and the bad. It's not hard to tell where you stand. These *are* the good guys.' He swept a hand towards the terminals, where three silent staffers pecked at their keyboards. The nearest of these – a dark-haired girl with a weak chin – caught my eye and raised her eyebrows.

'I've got no delusions,' Macpherson said. He frowned at the staffer. 'I'm a hack, Gerry. I'm not a journalist. We know our limits here. We do touts and paedophiles. That's what we do. Sex and Semtex. Come here.' There was a pile of papers fanned out on a table by the door. 'Here's this week's paper. Take it with you.' He thrust it at my belly. I scanned the headline: 'SWINGER

QUEEN'S DAD WAS UVF BOSS'. 'And this is last week's. It spun like a movie headline as he tossed it towards me. 'BORDER BUTCHER: TOUT GUNNED DOWN BY REBEL HOOD'. Is that enough? You want some more? Let you see what we do. OK. We've got a file on your man, too. Mr Hepburn. Jen?' The girl raised her head from her screen. 'Could you get the Kiwi Hepburn file, please? Run a copy off for Mr Conway.'

I flicked through the papers. Jen came up and handed me a cardboard folder. 'Thanks very much.' I folded the two papers and stuck them inside.

I had a couple of twenties in my hip pocket.

'Can I make a contribution to the Christmas fund?'

'Get yourself to fuck, big lad. If I'm ever in Glasgow you can do the same for me.'

He buzzed me out of the time-lock door and I clumped on down to the alley. I was about to take a piss against the wall when a car drew up at the alley's far end.

Chapter Eleven

I did up my fly. The black Saab was blocking the alley. When it didn't move off I went to walk round it.

'Conway!'

The passenger door swung towards me.

'Conway.' It was Isaac Hepburn. 'Get in the car.'

There was a rip in the cream leather seat; someone had patched it with black masking tape. The car stunk of stale baccy.

'Where we going?'

'You'll see. Somewhere quiet. Don't worry.'

Seat belts confuse me after three or four pints. When I finally got it to click we were speeding through the streets and I grabbed for the hand-grip. A lot of booze was sunk in my gut, and a slew of tight corners had slopped it around. I belched softly. I clutched the folder in both hands.

'Jesus, you smell like a pot still. I thought you stuck to the fizzy water.'

'Yeah, well, I had kind of a lapse.'

'Well, these boys can put it away.'

He glanced in the rear-view and changed lanes.

'What boys?'

'Your newshound buddies. Mutt and Jeff. Jeez, I wish I could draw a wage like theirs for sitting in the pub. Hey, did they tell you who used to work there?'

'They mentioned it.'

We stopped at a red. A young mum stepped out, pushing a buggy. Her hair was up in a scrunchie; she wore a white bra-top and sweat pants. The pants rode low and the scarlet 'T' of her G-string blazed wickedly over her waistband.

'Can it even be comfy? That cheesewire riding your crack all day. Never mind the hygiene angle.'

On the far pavement she stopped and bent over the buggy. Her buttocks glimmered brown through the tautened weave.

'That's just what I was thinking. The hygiene angle.'

He looked at me.

The mum straightened up and the lights changed. The car lurched forward.

'Did you miss it?'

He moved up through the gears.

'You mean inside? Not really. There's ways and means. Conjugal visits and all that. They let me out for forty-eight hours when my daughter was getting married. Plus it's like anything else. You get used to doing without. There's not many things you truly need, when it comes right down to it. That's one thing you learn. Some things are indispensable, but that's not really one of them. What you got there?'

'This?' I looked at the folder. 'Nothing. Old newspapers. *Sunday Citizens*. Macpherson seemed keen for me to read them.' I lifted the folder's flap to let him see the masthead.

We were on the motorway now, heading for the river.

'Look. I wanted to help you, Gerry. But that wasn't the place.'

The flyover hoisted us over the water. The city was like a city seen from the air: tight streets, toy houses, low hills. Everything intricate and small-scale.

'You can't talk in your own club?'

'The club? The club's the last place I can talk. This whole city, Gerry. You can't be too careful.'

He peered in the rear-view then as if someone might be tailing us.

'Tell you a story, son. A while back, not long after I got out, I was having a meal in the city. Nice restaurant. Next table but one, who's sitting there but the Peeler who put me away? He sends over a glass of wine. Then he stops to say hello on his way out. "No hard feelings," says he. "You had a job to do and I had mine. I'm glad the war's over." And, fuck, he's right. I'm glad it's over too and I shake the Peeler's hand. But that's what happens here. Take a shit on the Shankill and the Falls holds its nose.'

We were driving past the shipyards, the looming yellow cranes. George Best International Airport. It felt like an outing. There was something in Hepburn's solicitude – he asked at one point if I wasn't too hot, did I want the cold air on – that reminded me of weekend trips with my dad. My father left home when I was ten. Every weekend he took us on trips: Calderpark Zoo, the Magnum Centre, Culzean Castle. He was always checking that you were comfortable, that the car wasn't too stuffy. He kept little bags of Edinburgh rock in the glove compartment. I half expected Hepburn to produce one now but he turned off the bypass and parked in a residential street. I lodged the folder under my arm.

'Leave it in the car,' Hepburn said.

'No, it's OK.'

'Suit yourself. There's a park just down here, we can find a bench.'

There were playing fields at the park's far end. A game was underway and we walked in dappled sunlight down to shouts and cheering, the smattering handclaps.

'You do remember him, though?' I said. 'Peter Lyons.'

'Course I remember him. He was a good guy. He helped us out. We don't have a lot of friends, son. Maybe you've noticed that. Peter Lyons was a friend.'

'And then it all went wrong. How did that happen?'

'I don't know. I wouldn't say it all went wrong. People got tired of him pretty quick. He was an ideas man. What did we need ideas for? We knew what we wanted. We wanted things to stay the same. It's the Taigs want to change everything, let them have ideas.' He laughed and shook his head. 'That's how we saw it at the time. Fucking stupid, but there you go.'

'But what did he do? What was his function?'

'Function?' Hepburn snorted. 'He just hung about. He kind of annoyed folk, tell you the truth. This attitude. Bit of a know-all. The Jocks are like that sometimes, no offence. They think they know the score but they've no idea. Here's this guy from Glasgow telling us what's what and the most action he's seen is a fight at the football. It jerked people's chain. So some of the guys, they took him on a job one night. Low-level stuff. A disciplinary. A fella was out of line, or late with his payments: who knows, at this distance? But they took your buddy along. They thought they'd get a laugh when, fuck knows, he would break down or something. Watch through his fingers and beg them to stop. But the laugh was on them.' Hepburn nodded, leaned towards me. 'He lapped it up, from what I hear. Took a real pride in his work. They had to rein him in at the finish up.'

We reached the touchline. A team in red and white were playing a team in green and gold.

'But what happened?'

'I'm telling you what happened.'

'No. I mean why did Lyons leave? Did you fall out or what?'

A skinny winger came toe-tapping up the line and fisted it into the centre where his team-mate caught it and hooked it over the bar. A thin cheer rose on the far touchline.

'I don't know, son. He drifted away. It's different for you guys. Over the water. You can take it or leave it. You can walk away. We don't have that option. We have to see it through.'

'You mean jail?'

'Yeah, but the thing folk don't realise is the Kesh was the start. The Kesh was the *start* for us. Folk think it was the end. You took a decision, you made a choice – to get active, get involved – and somewhere down the line it brought you to the jail. Thirty guys in a Nissen hut. But that's shite. We never chose anything. We did what everyone else was doing, guys from our backgrounds. You went with the flow. When you got *inside*, that's when the thinking started. When the big hydraulic gates crushed shut? That's the first time I thought: the fuck's this all about? Twenty years? Run that by me again?'

The greens were surging forward. A big upfield punt was caught at full stretch by a red defender, but the forward was quick enough to block his clearance. The blocker's momentum took him skidding into touch.

Hepburn helped him to his feet.

'But did you not fall out?' I said. 'You and Peter Lyons? I heard something happened, there was some sort of row. He came back from Belfast in a hurry. He was pretty shook up.'

'This was when?'

'Nineteen eighty-three ... November: round Guy Fawkes.'

'Eighty-three? I was inside by then. I was already out of the picture.'

'Yeah but, what happened? I've looked into this. There was a beating around that time, another punishment thing, and it went too far. The guy died. Duncan Gillies, his name was.'

'Yeah, like I say, I was inside by then.'

'But you must remember; you must have known what was happening.'

'How must I have known? In broad terms, maybe. But not the day-to-day minutiae.'

'Minutiae? A guy got killed.'

'A lot of guys got killed, son. That's why they called it a war.'

A player trotted over to the touchline and lifted a squeezy water bottle, his throat pulsing as the stream hissed into his mouth. I wished I'd had time for a piss.

'You're saying you don't remember it? Duncan Gillies?'

He didn't answer. The reds were coming into the game a bit now and for several minutes we watched in silence.

'I know the thing you're talking about,' Hepburn said finally. 'You're asking if your man was involved?'

'Yeah.'

He was looking off downfield, watching the reds take a free. 'I couldn't say.' He turned to face me. 'I mean that, Gerry. I honestly don't know.'

I folded my arms and spat on the grass.

'It's true.' He touched my elbow. 'It's true, OK? I was still in charge at the time. Or supposed to be. Truthfully, though? I wasn't that interested. It changes you, the jail. We were born again. I'm not talking about religion. Some guys got religion, right enough. They read the Bible from skin to skin. But even the rest of us, every man in those huts. You werenae the same man when they opened the gates. I didn't really care what was happening outside, who was running what, who was shooting who. That shite doesn't mean much inside.'

The ball bounced into touch just beside us and Hepburn went after it. He moved with unlooked-for grace, his shoulders working in the blue checked jacket, and he trapped the ball before it stopped, trapped it neatly and punted it onto the pitch. He walked back, unbuttoning his jacket. Would he be taken for a grandfather, I wondered, or maybe the father of one of these lads?

'You find things out,' Hepburn was saying. 'You find out what matters. I'll tell you what matters to me.' He was nodding, as if I'd contradicted him. 'Trees.' He grinned madly. 'Trees! The way they move, the leaves and branches. Don't laugh, son. It came to me inside the Kesh. What did I really miss? I missed lots of things. My family. I missed my rum and pep at the Rex. But the thing I remembered, the thing I missed most, was the tree out the back garden. How it moved in the wind. Coming down for a glass of water in the middle of the night, there it would be, through the frosted glass. It wasn't even the tree, it was the tree's silhouette, just its shadow on the glass. The waggle of the branches, the little flitter of the leaves. Before I put the light on I'd stand for a minute and watch the tree. And inside, when things got bad, when I'd lie awake in that tin hut with the smells of thirty men, that's what came back to me. The tree out the back.'

He looked at me.

'This was my great breakthrough, son. Brilliant, eh? I'm doing twenty years for defending Ulster and what do you know? It's not Ulster I care about; it's a fucking tree. What do I with that?'

'What did you do with that?'

'Nothing. I did my time. I did my duties. Muster parade. I cleaned the hut. I played footie. Later on I did the OU. And Good Friday came and they let us out. But that was it. That was me finished. I was out the organisation. I'm bye with it now.'

'Just like that.'

'Just like that. It's not like the movies, son. You're free to leave. They don't shoot deserters.'

I nodded.

'What they gonnae say? You havenae done enough? I did sixteen years.' He snorted. 'You think I need to impress somebody, flash my medals? Fuck that.'

He picked some grass from his trousers and wiped his fingers with a hankie.

'Sixteen years.'

The whistle blew; a long trilling blast. The teams straggled off and the managers started their team-talk. The one on our touchline pointed and waved, sometimes gripping a player by the bicep. The players said nothing. They sucked their orange quarters and watched him, their eyes suspicious above the busy mouths. When he finished they nodded and lined up to drop their orange skins into a bucket. Then they trotted out to the goalmouth to warm up.

A man in a club tracksuit approached us waving a book of raffle tickets. His comb-over flapped in the breeze like Bobby Charlton's.

'Pound a go, gents,' he said. 'Never know your luck. Pound a go.'

Hepburn took five.

'Just write your details on the stubs,' the man said. 'Or even just the name of your boy.'

He turned to me.

'Oh no,' I said. 'I'm just over on holiday. But here . . .' I fumbled in my pocket for a fiver. 'Here's a donation.'

'Dead on.' He moved on down the touchline.

The whistle blew for the second half.

'What did you put?'

'On the tickets?' He spat demurely on the grass. '"Aidan".'

'"Aidan"?'

'It's a safe bet.'

We left before the end. The guy in the tracksuit nodded as we passed.

We were walking down the hill to Hepburn's car. As we got closer to the car, Hepburn slowed, as if he'd forgotten where he'd parked.

'Anyway,' Hepburn was saying. 'Anyway anyway.' He raised his eyebrows. He clapped his hands together and rubbed them briskly.

'What?'

'What do you think, Gerry? The fuckin' money.'

'Whoa, whoa. Hang fire here. Who said anything about money?'

'I did. I said something about fucking money.'

'OK, and why is that?'

He blew out some air and shook his head. 'That's a good one, Gerry. That's fucking priceless.' He took his hand from his pocket and pointed his finger. 'Don't fuck me about, son. You get the gen, you pay for it. That's how it works.'

I could still hear the game, the players' shouts, their comical urgency. I looked in the direction of the park and then back at Hepburn's expectant face. His finger was still pointing.

'Aye, if that's what you've agreed, that's how it works.' I wished he would put his finger down. The thumb was cocked, pistol-style, and the finger was aimed at my head. 'But we agreed fuck all. You wait till now to bring money into it?'

Hepburn shook his head. The finger dropped to his side. He thrust his hands into the pockets of his jacket and yanked them out again.

'Naw, you need to try harder than that, Gerry. What do you think I was doing it for? Public spirit? The repose of my soul? Nobody's trying to stiff you here, Gerry. I just want the rate for the job.'

I stopped walking.

'Oh there's a rate, is there? You know the rates? What are you, a tout?'

I didn't see him move. I felt a sort of wind at my back and then my shoulder flared in white tearing pain and something sharp and hard punched my cheekbone. My glasses skewed and the folder smacked onto the ground.

The hardness slapped my cheek once more and it sounded like a dog was gnashing my ear.

I seemed to be lying on the ground and standing up at the same time. Something cold and hard on my face. I tried to crane round but the hardness slapped my cheekbone again. I was nudged from behind and my thighs banged into something; metal, a ridge, a car's bodywork. He had twisted my arm up my back and cracked my face on the bonnet of a car. I was still there, bent over the car, Hepburn's fist gripping my short hair, and the dog sounds were back again, the snarling in my ear.

'Now you listen to me, you fucking Fenian piece of shit.' Twice more he cracked my face on the hood. His spittle was drizzling my face. 'That word you used? You know what that word means? It means this.' He stabbed his fingers at the bone behind my ear. 'It means one to the fucking back of the head.' He was shaking me again, my face slamming the hood in time with his words. 'So you ever' – bang – 'ever' – bang – 'put that word and my name in the same fucking sentence.' He drew in a long noisy breath and let it back out. 'I'll do you,' he said softly.

He stepped back and I crumpled off the bonnet onto the ground. I just lay there, spent.

'A grand,' Hepburn said.

'What?'

I raised my head and something struck me in the eye. Hepburn was walking away.

'That's your bus fare, son.' He threw the words over his shoulder.

I sat up on the hard ground. I fixed my glasses. Beside me was a greeny ball of paper. I reached out my hand and clutched it tight in my fist and held it to my chest. I looked round for the folder. It was lying in the gutter. I leaned over and pulled it towards me. When I sat up it all came up in a rush, all the whisky and Guinness in a hissing spate, hosing the ground between my knees. As I got to my feet, as I loped off, light-headed, to the station, dragging the back of my hand across my mouth, I kept seeing Hepburn's pointing finger. When I got to the station I opened my fist. Moulded by sweat to a soggy nub was a crumpled Ulsterbank tenner.

Chapter Twelve

The restaurant was large but I spotted John Rose straight away, his bleached poll glowing like a struck match. A pained look crossed his face and I smiled to show it was all right but he turned away. A waiter blocked my path and in the time it took him to hoist two bowls of chowder past my nose I nearly turned for the door. But Rose had seen me so I carried on, picking my way through the tables with my smile tightening.

It must be a do, an occasion, a party of sorts. Twelve or thirteen men, their jackets slung on chair backs. I was conscious of the mess on my face, the green-and-red graze on my cheek, still tacky to the touch. Was this a birthday lunch? Somebody's retirement? A glinting cityscape of bottles extended down the tablecloth.

The faces were turned to the head of the table where Down-in-the-mouth Macpherson was telling a story. Bent low, his chin almost flush with the table, his big hands waggling like antennae. Buttery sunlight caught the facets of his bald head. The story was reaching its climax. I hung back but Macpherson waved me forward, procured an extra chair, and summoned a fresh glass of red, all with his fluent hands and without disarranging his syntax. In a minute I was seated, like one of the boys, with a great globe of wine in my hand, nosing its rich vanilla. 'No problem, my darling,' Macpherson said.

'Just give me a minute to pack!' He reared back. The glasses clanked under the wave of mirth that crashed over the table. The diners came to life all at once, laughing in great winded heaves. I smiled foolishly round, nodded gormlessly at the faces as they raged in savage glee, gagging for breath, the red mouths chewing the air.

When groans and sighs brought the table back to earth, everyone looked at me. I felt my sobriety like a skin colour, like a separate nationality. I gulped at the great glass of wine and some of it slopped on my shirt. I wiped it down with a napkin.

Macpherson did the intros. Simmonds was there, and Malachy Kane. The others dipped their heads or smiled tightly or tipped two fingers to their temples in mock salute while Macpherson said their names.

'Gerry's from the Glasgow *Tribune*,' Macpherson said. 'He's working on a story. Is that right, John boy?'

Rose stiffened.

'You holding out on us, Rosie?' someone said. 'That's not very Protestant, boyo.'

'You find out who you're friends are,' said someone else. 'A time like this.'

'Give him a break, fellas,' said Macpherson, tipping more wine into my glass. 'I'm sure there's nothing in it. I'm sure this big lad from Glasgow would tell his friends if there's something they ought to know. Though it looks like he's already seen some action.'

They all looked at me. I tried a laugh. 'I'm saying nothing.' I fingered my raw graze; gummy, like a sucked sweet.

'Give us a clue then, John boy?'

Rose was flushed. 'Uh-huh. Here's a clue.' His mouth

worked silently for a bit. 'Four across. Eight letters: mind your own business.' He slurped some wine. 'Get to fuck.'

There was a pause while everyone counted.

'Actually, John, it's–'

'Yeah I know it is. Now fuck off.'

Their laughter rose to a mocking cheer as Rose told it off on his fingers.

'Let's just say,' said Macpherson, 'there's a certain Antipodean dimension to Mr Conway's researches. Let's leave it at that.'

The meal was over anyway. A waiter brought a pay-pad and Macpherson punched his number while the others passed the bill around, wincing camply at the damage.

'Aye, laugh, ya bandits,' said Macpherson. 'It's your turn next month,' he said, pointing at a grinning moustache at the far end of the table.

The men rose in ones and twos, patting their pockets, fiddling with their phones, wielding their car keys like tiny stilettos. They fished in pockets for their share of the tip, and a messy cairn of notes and coins piled up on the tablecloth.

Soon they were gone, all except John Rose and me and an angry fat man who slumped in his chair as if he'd been shot and sneered at his very full glass.

Rose was collecting his things, getting ready to leave. I tried to gather my thoughts. The table was littered with glasses and bottles and it was hard to remember that I'd drunk just two glasses of wine. Suddenly, as though the diners had been quietly tipped off and had stolen away, the restaurant was empty. The clash of cutlery filled the air, the bare brick walls throwing the waiters' voices around, giving their footsteps a tinny ring. The place looked like a warehouse again, as if all the wine and drapery, the ponderous napkin rings, were melting away and soon we'd regress to the bare brutal walls.

'What's the occasion?' I asked him.

'Nothing much. It's a wee group we have. The Stringers Club. We do it once a month. None of them's stringers any more, except me. Most of them aren't even hacks now.' He looked at the debris on the table. 'They just act like it.'

I watched him notice my face and decide not to ask.

'Oh you're still one, are you?' I said.

'What?'

'A stringer. I thought you might have jacked it in.'

He drew me a look, then shrugged and shipped another gulp of wine.

He hadn't shown up that morning. We'd planned to visit Duncan Gillies's mother, to see if she could tell us anything about her son's death, if maybe she had heard about a Scotsman being involved. But after forty minutes I gave up waiting and went to the library. I was livid. Rose was drawing a daily wage as a fixer and he couldn't drag his carcass out of bed. I needed to talk to him, too; I needed to ask about Hepburn, find out how to play it. But after an hour in the library I took a coffee break and thought about it. He'd probably been up till all hours, driving his cab. He was knocking his pan in to barely break even. And here's me, the fancy dan from Glasgow, snapping my fingers and watching him jump. Of course he'd get scunnered. Anyone would. So I called his cab company and after phoning the *Tribune* to check my credentials they told me where I'd find him. I came to the restaurant to make it OK, let him know that I wasn't pissed off.

'It's no biggie,' I told Rose. 'We were due a break. We'll do it tomorrow. It's not a problem.'

Rose looked at the floor.

'What, tomorrow's out too?'

He fiddled with his eye-ring; his gaze tracked lazily round the room.

'Well, Jesus, John. You've got to do *some*thing for the money. It's not a retainer.'

'See, that's the thing. The money? It's not worth it any more, Gerry. It's not worth the grief.'

The fat man surfaced briefly from his chins as the waiter reached for his glass. He shook his head with surprising vigour and jabbed a minatory finger in the air. Then he slumped back down and got on with his scowling.

'Grief? John, c'mon. I gave out a bit yesterday. I'm sorry about that. But I had to see Hepburn. You can see that, can't you? I needed to see him. Look.' I dropped my voice. 'I saw him again yesterday.'

'Yeah?' Rose checked his watch.

'John, it's not good. He wants money.'

Rose's frown deepened a little.

'He told me some stuff. About Lyons. He was dropping hints. About the Gillies thing. But now he thinks we've made a deal and he's asking for money. A grand.' I gripped his wrist. '*A grand!*'

'OK, Gerry, calm down.' Rose glanced at the fat man and then back at me. He centred his glass on its coaster. 'So where do I come in?'

'What you talking about, where do I come in? What the fuck do I do? What do I do?'

'Gerry, you do whatever you want.' He shook his head. 'Why you even telling me this? You asked for the meeting. I set it up. You were pretty fucking insistent as I remember. I got you the meeting. I had to pull some strings but I got you the meeting. Now you're not happy with how it went. Fine. That's not my problem: that's your problem. Tell me this: did I mislead you? Did I give a wrong impression about Kiwi Hepburn, that the guy was a Lollipop Man or something, a fucking Sunday School teacher? Did I? The guy's a gangster, Gerry. He's a class-A thug, a sociopath. You want to meet these people, I'll set it up. That was the deal. You want me to babysit too? That's a whole different thing.'

He drained the last mouthful of wine.

'Well that's very handy to know, John. Thanks for looking out for me. What is it, did he speak to you? Are you feart? Is that it? Are you scared of Hepburn?'

'It's not that.' He looked at the ceiling. He practically rolled his eyes. It was as if there was a third party present, to whom my obtuseness was apparent. I looked across at the fat man but his eyes were closed. Rose was embarrassed; not for himself but for me.

'What is it then, John?'

He fingered his empty glass, flicked it with his finger so the crystal sang.

'There's other things involved, Gerry. If you could go after Hepburn and leave it at that, no one would care. But you can't. You can't get Hepburn without pulling other people into the picture. And they won't let you do that. There's too much at stake. Don't ask me any more because you don't want to know.'

He shook his head and shucked himself into his jacket. He made a fist and knocked it against my bicep.

'You be good now, fella. Take care. It was nice working with you.'

His chair scraped as he stood to go.

'So that's it?'

'What else do you want?'

'You're sure about this?'

He laughed: 'Oh yeah.'

'OK. Fine.' I thanked him for all he'd done. I told him the paper would pay him anyway. He paused at the door.

'And, Gerry?'

'What?'

'Your story. It's going nowhere, right?'

'Well, it's going to be harder now, if that's what you mean. I could have used your local knowledge and all that. But fuck it, you know?'

He let the door swing to and walked back. His hands were light as they rested on my shoulders.

'Trust me, Gerry.' His eyes looked into each of mine in turn. 'It's going nowhere.'

He double-clapped my shoulders and turned on his heel. The fat man opened one eye and reached for his glass of wine.

Chapter Thirteen

I found the mural and parked beneath it. A British Tommy in tin hat and puttees, tramping into the foreground with a rifle clamped to his chest. His frame had the ominous angularity, the spidery slouch, of a cartoon skeleton; something from a heavy-metal album cover. But the face was rubicund, cheery – the smutty, rum-flushed phiz of a squaddy in a Great War postcard. Behind him were vague muddy battlefield scenes and a hopeful sunset, with a lot more yellow than pink. In the bottom corner, in white lettering on the dark battlefield: 'THE SOMME'. And in a ribbon arching above the lot, the old Laurence Binyon line about when we would remember them.

The street was quiet. The Forester's door cannoned shut and my heels knocked the tarmac as I crossed the street. The number was stencilled in orange on a white tile by the drainpipe. Twenty-six was the right-hand side of a squat ex-council semi. All sharp angles and tight red brick. A sentry-box porch with its canted roof. I crossed the garden – a blanket-sized pit of white chips – and thumbed the bell. It jangled woozily in the dimness behind the door and above my head a clacking noise, an odd hollow knocking, started up.

I stepped backwards onto the path.

Above the porch, on the slated upturned V, was an

ornamental windmill. A tiny figure in a flat cap, wielding an axe. When the blades turned in the wind he bent to his work, chop-chop-chopping a block of wood.

'I don't want it.'

I lowered my gaze to meet a pair of flat green eyes in a long joyless face. She wore black slacks and a yellow short-sleeved sweater, patterned with small perforations. The skin across the nose had a waxy tightness. She'd been a looker, no question. A breaker of hearts in the distant seventies. An unlit ciggy jiggled in her fingers.

'What?'

'Landscape gardening. Jehovah. Patio doors. Whatever it is you're selling.'

'Yeah? That's too bad. I've come about Duncan.' I told her who I was and who I worked for. When I dug a card out of my wallet and held it out she took it and dropped her hand to her side and kept her eyes fixed on mine. 'There's something I'd like to talk about,' I told her. She flapped the card a bit as if she was drying it and held my gaze.

'It's about Duncan,' I said again. 'Could I maybe come in?'

The living room was off the tiny hall. There was an armchair in the far corner, under an alcove, and a sofa along one wall. In the middle of the back wall a door led through to the kitchen.

I sat down on the sofa. Mrs Gillies stood.

'Go on and sit down,' she said sourly.

'Sit down yourself,' I said. 'You're making me nervous.'

I meant it as a joke but my mouth was sticky, my breath coming through in a turbulent rush.

She perched on the armchair, knees tight together and at right angles to her body. She lifted a lighter from the alcove shelf and lit her cigarette. She kept the lighter gripped in her fist.

'I'm sorry,' I said. 'I'm sorry to bring this all back. I know it's not easy.'

She blew smoke at the ceiling.

'Excuse me.' She rose quickly and stepped through to the kitchen. I thought at first I'd touched a nerve, but I could see her through the open door as she took the oven gloves down from a hook and opened the oven. A big orange casserole pot appeared on the hob. She lifted the lid and stirred the contents and put it back and slammed the oven door.

'Sorry,' she said, without conviction, as she took her place on the armchair and lifted the cigarette from the ashtray. A thin grey reek – as of half-cooked meat – threaded itself into the room. It smelled like my mother's stovies, those lukewarm slabs of tattie and carrot and square pale sausage I forced down every Sunday in the early eighties. I told her I might have some news, some fresh information on Duncan's death.

She uncrossed her legs and leaned forward to tap some ash. She recrossed her legs and stared out the window. She managed to contain her excitement. I pointed this out.

She smiled pleasantly. 'That's because I don't believe you.'

'Right.'

The room was hot. A bulb of sweat slipped coldly down my ribs. I asked for a glass of water.

'There's whisky, if you want it.'

'I've got the car.'

'I saw that.'

I shrugged. I lifted my hand and brought finger and thumb together until they almost touched. She nodded and turned to the sideboard. When we were holding our drinks she crossed her legs and leaned forward.

'What age are you?'

I told her.

'And your name is what again: Collins?'

She reached for the card and we both said my name at the same time.

'And you come from Glasgow, Mr Conway?'

I told her I did.

She cocked her head and pouted.

'So tell me, Mr Conway from Glasgow. Why would you know anything about it? Why in hell' – it was barely a whisper, the merest exhalation of breath – 'why in hell would you think that?'

'I'm a journalist, Mrs Gillies. I get paid to find things out.'

She frowned. 'And you've found out, what, exactly?'

I put my glass on the floor.

'I know one of the men who did it. At least, I'm pretty certain. Did you ever hear that a Scotsman was involved? Did you ever hear something like that?'

'Mr Conway, are you here to tell me what happened to Duncan, or to ask?'

There was something bad in the smell from the kitchen, a ribbon of foulness it was hard to ignore. I started again. 'Mrs Gillies.' The green eyes swung lazily round. 'Mrs Gillies, a group of men beat your son to death. They hit him so hard for so long that he died. I want to find out what happened.'

Maybe it was just timing; the meat was on the turn between raw and cooked. In ten minutes it would be all cooked through, the badness gone.

'They weren't *trying* to kill him. It was an accident, it was a fluke.'

'A fluke? They hit him with bats. He had seventeen separate fractures. A punctured lung. They ruptured his spleen.'

Her eyes narrowed. 'I did the identification, mister. I know what he looked like. I know what they did to him. One of the animals still lives round the corner.'

'I'm sorry. But then you know what I'm talking about. It was no accident. If they didn't set out to kill him they didn't go out of their way to make sure they didn't.'

The meat didn't smell any better.

'Would you mind if I opened a window?'

She flapped her hand impatiently and turned her head to take another drag.

I wrestled with the latch. It wouldn't come.

'Aren't you a little, *delicate* for your line of work, Mr Conway?' She rose and set her cigarette down and tugged up the sash with her thin bare arms. She sat back down and plucked her cigarette from the ashtray and held it beside her head, gripping her elbow in her hand. The smoke plumed up in a straight grey line.

'If it was me,' I said. 'If it was my son who'd been bludgeoned to death, I think I might feel bitter. I might even want them caught, the guys who did it.'

'The Christian thing is to forgive.'

She looked at me with those flat green eyes.

'*Do* you forgive them?'

'What are you, a priest? What do you care?'

A clock boomed portentously. I craned round. Against the back wall was a grandfather clock, ludicrously huge in the tiny room. I waited for the air to settle.

'The men who did it. Do you know their names?'

'Of course I know their names.'

'You said one of them lived around the corner. Were the others local?'

'Uh-huh.'

'And no one else was involved, that you heard of?'

'No one else was involved. That I heard of or not.'

I jumped in my chair. My heart buzzed and fluttered. It was my phone, wheezing and trilling in my shirt pocket. I dug it out and turned it off, but not before I'd clocked the number on the screen: *Norman Rix*.

'I'm sorry.'

The spire of smoke wavered as the shoulders rose and dropped.

'You've got the wrong end of something, mister. There was no Scotsman. You're away the wrong road.'

I slipped the phone back in my pocket. It hung there, fraught with the unappeased wrath of Norman Rix. I would have to talk to him later. I would have to have something to tell him. I tried again.

'See, I think maybe you weren't told the proper story.' Her head drew sharply back, twisting around as if a hornet were circling her nose. She reached for her glass. I pressed on. 'I mean, I don't think you know the full story.'

The glass stayed where it was.

'There was no Scotsman.'

'That's what I mean. Things were hazy, lots of confusion around. Thing like this? Rumours are started, people muddy the waters. It's what happens with events like this. People speculate, they paint little scenarios.'

'Mr Conway. You're not listening. There was no Scotsman.'

'But what I'm saying, there could have been. They could have been lying. Maybe they were covering up. Which people saw it? Maybe they got it wrong. Who were they?'

'I don't know.' Her beads clicked as she shook the question away. 'People. They didn't see any strangers.'

'But how do you know they're telling the truth?'

She tapped her ash impatiently. Her head gave an odd little jolt and something fizzed in the flat green eyes. She stared right at me. 'Because it was me. All right? Because I saw it all. From that window there' – she gestured to the hallway. 'I saw it.'

'What?'

'It happened right there in the alley. I saw it. There were three of them did it and I knew them all. And there wasn't any phantom Scotsman. OK?'

She stood up and turned to the table. 'I need another even if you don't.'

I left my chair.

'Saw it or watched it?'

The glasses rattled. She turned, defiant and scared, and I gripped the skinny wrist.

'You knew!'

'He had it coming.'

'You set it up!'

'Running around with a prisoner's wife. It's not like he wasn't warned.'

'You set it up! Your own son!'

181

I had backed her against the table. The bottles rattled and trilled. The front legs of the table were an inch off the ground. We stopped then, frozen in some dramatic dance-step. I wanted to laugh. The woodcutter chipped at his block for a frantic few seconds and then he stopped too. She shook her hand free and the table settled back with an outraged crash. She poured a shaky drink and gulped it. She poured another and then one for me. She sat down heavily, glared at me over the jiggling rim.

'They were only going to scare him. That's what they told me. Knock him about a bit. That woman was poison. She was pure poison for him. I wanted it stopped. I didn't want—' She stopped; her teeth knocked the glass as she threw back the rest.

'You didn't want him hurt?'

'It's not how it seems. Everyone knows that the wives – well, you can't expect a woman of that age to live like a nun. But they're discreet. They do it out of town. They go to the mainland. This was right in people's faces. They couldn't just ignore it. If I hadn't told them where he'd be they'd have got him anyway. Someone would have put a stop to it.' The two fingers that gripped her cigarette came to rest against her temple. 'I thought I'd get it stopped before it got that far.'

I finished my drink. The whisky was rough, flaring in my gut.

'Even as a boy,' she said. 'He never cared for politics. He never ran with the Tartans. He liked clothes and girls and football. Normal stuff.' She shrugged. 'Normal anywhere else.'

She stood up.

'I'm sorry to disappoint you, Mr Conway. The guy

you're talking about?' She took my empty glass, cradled it to her chest. 'He wasn't involved.'

The air had freshened. The clouds had that swelling, bulbous look, like frozen explosions. The fat-cheeked squaddy wore a sneering, knowing expression as I gunned the engine and took the corner. I pulled up short. Right across the middle of the street, ten or twelve feet high, was a blind brick wall. The Peace Line. Something shocking and raw in its blank red expanse, like the stump of an amputated limb. I three-point-turned and retraced my route.

I wasn't driving anywhere in particular but I wound up at the river. I locked the car and went for a walk. In front of the Custom House the skateboarders were taking turns to grind the handrail down to the plaza. When I turned my phone on it rang straightaway. I didn't recognise the number. At least it wasn't Rix.

'They seek him here.'

'Hello, Peter.'

'They seek him there. You're not taking my calls?'

I watched the skateboarders bump down the rail.

'What do you want, Peter?'

'Is this not supposed to happen when you're on the way *down*? People stop taking your calls. I'd say you've got this a bit back to front.'

'What do you want, Peter?'

He spat a tiny laugh.

'The fuck's going on, Gerry? You're in *Belfast*? What the fuck?'

A fat adolescent boy waddled past. He had both hands clamped to a burger and was tearing a chunk with his teeth. He looked like he was playing the harmonica. His T-shirt said: *I Hear U, I'm Just Not Listening*.

'I'm working on a story.'

'Yeah, I know. You didn't think to ask me about it? You don't think I deserve at least that?'

'You'll get a chance to comment when the time comes.'

'Oh I think I'll do more than comment.'

I let that pass.

'I don't know what you think you're going to find.'

'Yeah? See, I think maybe you do.'

'You're a real prick, Gerry.' He was lighting a cigar: I could hear the struck match and the rapid puffs as he sucked it alight. He might have been blowing kisses. 'What's brought this on, anyway? This sudden urge to do your job. Why start now? Let me find your stories. Is that not how it works?'

'Are we done?'

'Is that not what happens? I find the stories and you write them? It's a bit late in the day for editorial independence, I would have thought.'

'Turn it up, Peter. I'm doing my job.'

'Right, the job.' Lyons's voice tightened. 'Let me ask you something. You do this piece. Assuming you get a story. Assuming it's the biggest scoop since Woodward and Bernstein. You think you're gonna walk into Rix's job? You think I'll let that happen? You do this story and I promise you, Gerry, you're fucked.'

'I'm fucked anyway.'

'What?'

'The whole thing's fucked. Papers is fucked. Nobody wants the fucking job.'

'Yeah? You might want one sooner than you think.'

'You might want one too, Minister.'

We both chewed the air for a bit. I could hear him puffing on the big cigar. He smoked Romeo y Julietas, the long ones, Churchills. He looked like Fidel Castro when he smoked them. I looked like Groucho Marx.

'You know what, Gerry? I'm more sad than angry and that's the truth of it. How long have we known each other? What have I done? Have I said something that pissed you off? What's eating you? Tell me what it is and I'll fix it.'

'It's too late, Peter.'

'It's never too late. Where are you anyway?'

'You mean right now? I'm, I don't know. Down at the harbour. Near the big clock.'

'Albert Square?'

I looked for a street sign.

'Yeah, I think so. I'm not sure.'

'I once saw a lassie near there, chained to the railings. Shaven head, the full bit. Like something out of World War Two. It's a serious town, Gerry. You want to watch yourself.'

'Well, I'll bear that in mind, Minister. Thanks for your concern. Can I go now?'

'Listen to yourself, Gerry. Listen to the pair of us. What are we even arguing for? We've got so much to do together. Let's sort this out. When the time comes – and we're talking six weeks, two months tops – I'm going to need someone. Team leader. I've got my guys in place, more or less, but I'll need a top man. Think about it. Pays a lot better than papers. You said it yourself, Gerry, papers is fucked.'

I was glad I couldn't see his face, the plausible tilt of his head, the coaxing half-smile.

'Good. First you're getting me fired, now you're giving me a job. Make your mind up, Minister.'

His sigh was like a boot heel scraping on flint.

'Naw. Gerry Conway. My mind's crystal fucking clear. I'm the next First Minister of Scotland. I need a Director of Communications. What you need to decide is, do you want the job, or are you gonnae piss it all away on a nothing story? You let me know.'

The line went dead.

Back at the Grania, the bald desk clerk coughed as I passed reception. There was a message: a Mr Hepburn had called. I opted not to notice the question in his eyes.

'He left this,' the clerk said.

'Good man.'

It was a folded page of hotel stationery. 'Conway' it said on the outside. And inside, 'Don't be a stranger', and below that a mobile number. I stuck it in my pocket and headed for the lift.

Chapter Fourteen

When the Skinners bought the *Tribune* I was tempted to resign. The night editor and the health correspondent earned a round of applause and two rounds of drinks when they loudly jumped ship at a meeting in the Cope. But the bows they took to milk the applause showed naked, white-fringed, liver-spotted scalps and the new regime would have culled them anyway. For a week or so the fourth floor crackled with sedition. Meetings were called at short notice; councils of war in the Cope's upstairs lounge. There was lots of heckling and cinematically loosened ties. The Father of the Chapel, a sub called Bill, got up on a chair to smack his fist into his palm amid beery acclamations. We actually staged a walkout and for two days running the daily was eight pages short and packed with literals that had us spraying each other with shandy as we read them out in the Cope.

Eric and Helen Skinner – they were brother and sister, not husband and wife – came from an ex-mining village in Ayrshire. They made their money in discount carpets before moving into papers. Their stable was mainly local: town and village weeklies in the Scottish Lowlands and the North of England. Their titles thrived. They worked to a formula. Hire a couple of hungry up-and-comers to gather local news. A jaded newsdesk staffer to put the thing together and bash out strident leaders. And then fill up the paper with agency rubbish – gossip, showbiz, sport. It worked with their other titles and now it would work with the *Trib*. Before the deal was even done, the newsdesk were dusting off their résumés. Questions were raised at Holyrood. Shadow ministers bandied portentous truisms about the importance of a vigorous press to a functioning democracy.

In our meetings at the Cope we used the same words – diffidently at first, but with growing conviction as the bevvy flowed. Democracy. Truth. Scrutiny. A Free Press. We cared about these things; the Skinners just cared about money. Then we headed back upstairs to file our expenses.

Within a week it was over. Like everyone else who had threatened to leave, I stayed. I had just enough to lose by going. And it turned out the Skinners weren't as bad as we'd feared. They knew their reputation and they worked hard to change it, emailing *Tribune* staff – from editor to copy boy – with a list of high-minded pledges. They dined the politicians, soothing scruples at Rogano's over Loch Fyne oysters and peachy Riesling. And they set up an editorial board for the *Tribune* and the *Tribune on Sunday*. Once a month in the function room of an Edinburgh hotel (not, God help us, in Glasgow, far less the *Tribune* building), they took their places: senior editors, marketers from the Skinner Press, and – this was the bit highlighted in excited press releases and intoned by Eric Skinner to the Media Commission at Holyrood – four representatives from 'civic Scotland', respected figures from the nation's public life. This hand-picked quartet would guard the *Tribune*'s mantle and defend the paper's mission. No one was surprised at the appointments: Fergus McCrone, former *Scotsman* editor and Arts Council stalwart; Madeleine Grant, broadcaster, diarist and author of *Scotland's Secret Gardens*; Edwin Reilly, the Booker-shortlisted novelist and veteran Home Rule agitator; and Jarvis Tennant, former Principal of Glasgow University. Then stomach cancer killed Tennant and after the funeral his equally eminent wife – Barbara Tennant, QC, human rights lawyer and occasional *Tribune* columnist – accepted his seat.

The fact that Barbara Tennant was the former colleague of Peter Lyons in the law firm of Leggat, Lyons and Ross prompted nobody's eyes to narrow. Scotland's a small country. A degree of overlap and incestuous messiness is unavoidable. But Barbara Tennant was now on our shoulder, the scrutineer of the *Tribune*'s morals. And Tennant was out to get us.

I made the call next evening; I couldn't put it off any longer.

'Who's this? Do I know a Gerry? You fucking dipshit, Conway. I thought you'd retired. What is this, your fucking holidays?'

'Hello, Norman.'

'Four fucking hours I've been trying to get you!'

'There's no signal.'

'Yeah? Here's the signal. Get your arse back to Glasgow. It's finished. All right? Get back here and do your job. First ferry.'

I was in the hotel room. The telly was showing golf, with the sound turned off. Sun bouncing off the fairway, the grass a poisonous green.

'Don't lie down to her, Norman.'

'What?'

'Just, show a bit of balls, that's all. What can she do? She's not even management.'

'Whoa, Gerry. What the fuck. Who are we talking about here? Barbara Tennant?'

'It's OK, Norman. Martin told me. She's been in to see you. You're going off the deep end here, Norman. There's no—'

'Gerry. Gerry!' He was laughing. 'Believe me. Barbara Tennant is the least of my fucking worries. Barbara Tennant? Fuck Barbara Tennant.'

'What then?'

'Wolfe was in.'

Kenny Wolfe – 'White Fang' to his admirers, 'Cry Wolfe' to the rest of us – was the Party's chief spin doctor. He was never off the phone, to Rix or Fiona Maguire, to the PCC, grousing about nationalist bias or misattributed quotes, demanding retractions and clarifications. I once wrote an editorial that stopped short of consigning the Nats to eternal perdition. Wolfe was on the phone that morning, demanding the name of the writer. Rix stonewalled him. 'Right,' said Wolfe; 'I'll remember this. Tell whoever wrote it he's got a thistle jammed up his arse.' This time he'd arrived at the *Trib* at 9 a.m., and spent forty minutes jabbing his fat finger in Rix's face. I dwelt on that image for a second or two while Rix ranted on.

'He's calling it harassment,' said Rix. 'First Martin's gangland splash and then the leader attacking Lyons. And now you in Belfast. It's vindictive, he says. We're defaming the poor guy. We're out to bring him down. He's already got the luvvies on the case' – the luvvies were Tennant and the rest of them – 'but now he's going higher. He's written to the Skinners. He's threatening the PCC.'

A heavyset blond guy in fawn slacks and a patterned sweater was stumping up the fairway, fiddling with his glove. This was part of golf's appeal: physically, there wasn't that much to choose between the Sunday morning hackers and their million-dollar idols.

'You'd have to wonder, Norman. Why the petted lip, right at this moment? He's shitting it. He knows we're on to something.'

'Does he? He knows more than I do, then. Or you, unless things have changed.'

'Norman: that's the whole fucking point. They know something we don't: that's what I'm here to find out.'

Rix didn't say anything for a bit. The golfer was reading the green, squatting down with the putter in his fist, like a grotesque parody of a pole-dancer.

'I know, Gerry. I know. Wolfe's a fucking madman, I know. But this time he means it. He's out his fucking tree.'

The blond guy was addressing the ball. His knees quivered as he readied the shot.

'So tell him to fuck himself. You're a big grown-up man, Norman.'

'Yeah? Here's a better idea. Why don't *you* tell him to fuck himself? And while you're at it you can explain to the board where the money's gone. You remember that money? The government money that kept rolling in, all those public info spots that are going to the cunting *Scotsman*, now that you've gone and *fucked it up*. You want to tell them about that?'

'He didn't say that. Come on, Norman.'

'Oh, he didn't?'

The blond guy was still quivering.

'So call him out. Fucking splash it. That's a story in itself.'

'Be your age, Gerry. You think I wear a wire to speak to Kenny Fucking Wolfe? He'd brass it out. He never said it anyway. In so many words.'

I started to speak but he cut me short.

'Save it, Gerry. It's finished. You're coming home.'

The putt sank. Blondie stooped to retrieve it, the spikes on his sole catching the sun. He doffed his visor and tipped it to the crowd.

I put the telly off and reached for the minibar. A plastic miniature Red Label and a fridge-cool Toblerone.

I knew I was wrong. I knew I'd fucked up. But I was having a hard time liking it. Maybe I could go over some things again. I phoned Isaac Hepburn but it went to voicemail. I left a message. I bit down on the Toblerone and hurt the roof of my mouth and tried him again. Finally I drove to the gym and the guy in the blue vest – the same guy who served us drinks while Hepburn promised to help me – seemed fresh out of sympathy.

'I don't know. Do I look like his social secretary?'

'Look, he told me to get in touch. Just give me an address. I need to see him.'

'You're not listening, fella. I don't know where he is.'

'Yeah, fuck you too. Brain Trainer? I'd take it back, it's not fucking working.'

I didn't wait around for his reply. I stomped out to the car and sulked. There was a knot of teens in the car park, hanging about on the disabled ramp, sharing a bottle of cider. I felt like asking for some. I was going home. I had run out of options.

Back on Botanic the hotel car park was full. They were

nose to tail down both sides of Cromwell Street. I drove around and finally found a space on Eglantine Avenue. Walking back to the Grania, I spotted a cab and flagged it: 'City centre, mate.' In the Cathedral Quarter I found a pub I'd never used. Another well-dressed, disapproving barman – this one looked like a border guard or a driving instructor – raised his eyebrows. I scanned the whiskies and spotted the bulbous neck and angular shoulders of a Lagavulin bottle. I made it a double, with a Guinness to chase.

There were plenty of whiskies. I thought of Mrs Gillies and her tray of coloured bottles. The green eyes and the firm-set mouth. The preposterous clock. Her skinny fore-arm, when she pulled it loose, had felt about ready to snap. My palm still burned where I'd gripped her. I couldn't shake the feeling that I'd touched her inappropriately, intimately somehow, as if it was a breast or a buttock I'd grabbed and not her wrist. I slugged the whisky and quenched its sour burn with a sluice of Guinness. After all, what had I done? I'd forced her to tell the truth. But the truth, I now realised, is not common property. Some truths are private. Mrs Gillies had paid for the truth I'd exposed. That truth was hers and I'd taken it from her.

I took a bite of whisky, held it in my mouth till the Guinness joined it. I'd established a rhythm with these alternating mouthfuls: the malt cut through the waves of stout like the prow of a sharp little boat. I was getting drunk but I wasn't feeling any better. I had fucked up – nobody's fault but mine, as Blind Willie Johnson says – but still I felt cheated. I could see it, in my mind's eye, the thing that hadn't happened: Peter Lyons leering with glee as he planted more leather in Gillies's kidneys. It had seemed so in keeping. In keeping, at least, with the Lyons of my weekly column – the debonair street-fighter, the lush-toned showman who still liked nothing better than a spot of toe-to-toe. I always had fun writing him up. I resisted the leonine conceits of the red-tops, who routinely had the Justice supremo tossing his mane or batting away opponents with a swipe of his massive paw, but my copy ran to extravagant lengths. *When Peter Lyons smiles at you, it's time to run for cover. Yesterday in the chamber, Malcolm Jesmond, the hapless Member for Pentlands West, found this out. The hard way.* The Lyons I constructed was a hard man, a smiling enforcer, dishing out punishment to the weak and the wayward. When this image was given flesh by Isaac Hepburn's memories, I felt almost proud. It was like watching a character come to life.

Even as I was driving to meet Mrs Gillies, I'd been shaping my opening par. The sentences were arranging themselves, slotting into place, as if those words in that order had always been there. Now I had nothing. No leads. No pegs. No story.

The jukebox had started: something tinny and Irish. The maudlin swoop of tin whistles, a bodhrán's flatulent blatter. I was sick of the whole place, this tinpot Dodge with its crummy back-to-backs, its pot-bellied hard-men. I drained my Guinness, the final inch of yellow dregs. The wershness made me grue.

Out on the street it was almost dark. Warm, with a fresh salt lick in the wind. For a moment I wasn't sure where to go: was it right or left to the Grania? I paused on the pavement and the door rattled at my back, three guys pushing past, one of them stopping to light a smoke.

He called something to the others as he jogged to catch them up but a bus heaved past and it covered his words. The destination board said 'City Centre' in neon tangerine and I started off in the other direction.

I couldn't shake the image of Mrs Gillies taking my whisky glass, sneering at me through blue cigarette smoke. Had Lyons got to her? Had he told her what to say? It seemed unlikely that he would go to such lengths, but who could tell? And Rix: why couldn't he see it? If Lyons was this desperate it meant there was a story. Why wouldn't Rix let me follow it? I thought of my phone call with Lyons, the dangerous rasp in his voice. I could hardly blame him. He thought I would toe the line. Why wouldn't he? We'd made a deal. The terms were never stated but we both knew what they were. He fed me stories and I made him look good. For a jump on the other papers, I wrote him up in my column. It suited us both. We would rise together, Lyons to the ministerial Lexus, me to the editor's chair. Only it hadn't worked out like that. Lyons was already fixed. In six weeks' time he'd be Scotland's First Minister. It seemed a poor enough prize, but that was his call, not mine. And where was I? No nearer the top than I had been last year. I was clinging by my fingers to a job I'd grown to hate.

'Got a light?'

That Belfast flatness; a querulous whine. I looked round. He detached himself from a doorway with a roll of the shoulders and stepped up to me. Short, the ginger stubble on his skull barely cresting my chest, the scalp flecked and grainy in the streetlamp. A lot of chest and shoulders under the T-shirt.

'A light.'

An edge of irritation now, but still I didn't speak. I sensed, at some level, what was happening, but I was a beat behind the action, distracted by some bothersome detail, some shortfall in verisimilitude, a glitch in continuity. And then it came to me. *He's got a light.* It was the guy from the pub; I'd seen him light a fag just up the street.

He looked away, almost sadly it seemed, and as the bald head dipped I saw the others, his two compadres, shuffling into view, stopping at the corner in a sheepish jostle. There was an alley there, they'd been hiding in the alley, and when I turned back to Ginger that's when it came, once, hard, flush to the jaw, a blow that jellied my legs, and though I stepped back, once, twice, I didn't go down. I swayed on the kerb, my toes scrabbling for purchase, the knobbly stone with its chewed-caramel surface rocking under my shoes' thin soles. Then I stepped back once more, right into the street, let's get it out in the open, and put my dukes up with a flourish like some cigarette-card pugilist.

The three exchanged glances and stepped off the kerb, Ginger coming straight towards me and the other two cutting behind. I edged down the block a few yards, further from the alley mouth and when Ginger lunged I stepped inside and socked him, hard and then again, deep winding digs in the gut. He folded up and back-pedalled across the road, his feet moving with comical deftness, and for a brief, euphoric moment I thought, *I can do this, I can take these fuckers*. Then his two mates caught him under the arms and propelled him back over the road. He was grappling, he had my arms clamped to my side before I could swing a punch and then we fell, together, toppling in the roadway.

In the moment of falling – a long, almost tender interim, during which I fell as you fall in dreams, endlessly, with a distracted anxiety – everything changed. The fight went out of me. Something inside, some internal committee of the will, just opted not to bother. We bumped to the ground and Ginger was already scrambling to his feet. I could have struggled up after him but I didn't. I just lay there, with my eyes closed and my legs drawn up, fingers laced on the base of my skull, my body tingling as it waited for the blows.

For a second, all I could hear was his breathing, Ginger snorting and blowing like a winded horse, and then the ground slid away from beneath me and then it slid away again. He was booting my guts, shifting me a little with each kick, and I hunched tighter, balling my body, shielding my front. He stepped around me now, picking his shots. Kidney. Spine. Head. Head again. One of my knuckles burst as his toecap smacked it. Then there was nothing. The horse sounds again. Then a guttural rush, like a throat clearing phlegm and the ground was moving again, my heels jiggling over cracked tarmac as they hauled me into the alley, my skull smacking brick as they tossed me down.

His face was in mine, a sour porter stench. I opened my eyes to the moving mouth, the working lips and teeth, the darting tongue. Our eyes locked. He had finished speaking. He put his finger out slowly and touched the tip of my nose. Then they were gone, six legs clipping off round the corner, and I lay there letting the sounds he'd made, the tight, level tones, resolve themselves sedately into words.

Chapter Fifteen

The rain had come on, a light smirr ticking into my hair, wetting the backs of my hands. It misted my brow and cheeks, fell coldly on the cut above my eye. I closed my eyes and the water rinsed my lids, sifting into the lashes. It felt good, therapeutic, to lie in the rain, in the dark of the alleyway, cars hissing past on the street. There was a smell down here in the dark, stale piss and petrol, not unpleasant. I moved my tongue. My mouth tasted rusty, like matchbox cars.

In a minute, I told myself. A minute, Gerry; give me a minute. A voice in my head was telling me to move. I didn't want to move. Once I moved I would know how bad it was and there would be no way to change it and go back to not knowing. I would move soon. Three more cars. I counted them off. When the third hissed past I flexed my right ankle, stretched it out like this was 7 a.m. and I was waking to the traffic report. It felt OK. Now the other. I shuffled my hips to bring the leg out from under me. Fine. Then I eased up on one elbow and braced my palm against the ground and a white pulse of pain wrung my shoulder. I braced my arm again, as if I might trick the pain, catch it off guard.

The shoulder, then. OK. What else? The head. I raised it six inches. A dull cold ache at the base of the skull, a bluish pain, metallic. Shoulder; head. And the finger, of course. The middle finger on the right hand, already standing up from its fellows, fake-looking, a plastic banana.

'Take a telling,' he'd said. Those were the words. His mouth half an inch from my own, a lover's closeness.

Take a telling.

The beating had discomposed me. I was no longer a unit but a rackety assemblage, a jerry-built contraption of a man. I stood up in stages. Then I leaned for a while on the wall and pushed myself off and stumbled towards the street, man of iron, a spatchcocked thing, my bones clanking like stair rods.

The car was parked on Eglantine. It wasn't too near the hotel, but that was good. I wasn't going back to the Grania, not till I knew it was safe.

At first I kept a look out for buses. But it hurt too much to keep craning round, so I just walked, one foot in front of the other, watching my toecaps through half-shut eyes. There were cabs around – they shushed past with their roof-signs glowing – but I knew well enough to leave them alone. The cabs were affiliated; probably there was some way to tell which ones were which, some arcane pattern of mudguards or spoilers, but I didn't know the codes. And maybe word had gone out. Short dark hair. Six-two. Glasgow accent. No, a cab was too risky.

I kept on up the road, moving like a busted bike. My toecaps alternated. It looked like a competition, some tightly contested race in which the lead kept switching. The streets spooled off on either side: Georgian terraces, pale and tall, South Belfast's acres of rotten brick. Cracked pavements and rhododendrons. Wheelie bins numbered in white emulsion. Lime trees veiling the street lights. This was the nice part of town, the part that looked normal, right through the Troubles.

I kept thinking the car was nearer than it was. Next junction, I'd tell myself, and then it wasn't and then finally it was. Eglantine Avenue. I paused on the corner. There were cars down both sides of the street. The ones beneath the street lights shone like beetles. I could see the Forester, halfway down on the right-hand side. The street was deadly still. It looked posed and unconvincing, the cars somehow suspicious in their silent rows.

A door opened halfway down the street and a man came down a path and got into his car. I hunched my shoulder as he slowed for the junction, buried my face in my neck. I was standing right next to a church. There were trees in the churchyard, great spreading evergreens, and I hobbled over the wall. The nearest tree was huge, with long drooping boughs; a great green dark gloomy bell. I ducked under a low branch and stood up in the heart of the tree. It was pitch-dark and safe in the soft blackness. I reached behind me and felt the rough ribbed bark. I couldn't see my feet but I could see right out to the road, where the Forester squatted under the light. Tiny lime hyphens marked the numerals on my watch. I'd give it twenty minutes.

Half an hour later I still hadn't moved. The rain had raised the scents of the trees and a rich spicy musk rose around me. It might have been the Forest of Arden, a pastoral dell, if it wasn't for the distant hiss of cars and the gentle tick of blood onto the grass. From the cut above my eye the blood kept coming, beading my lashes. Out beyond the leaves was the foreign city with its repertoire of hurt. Even now, someone might be watching, hard eyes trained on the Forester. There was no way to tell. No curtains twitched, no silhouettes shifted in the parked cars. I ran my tongue over swollen lips. I could have used a drink. A ball of Bush, a pint of stout. Things would look better then. The pains in my head and my shoulder and hand. The cold paste of fear in my gut.

I left the tree and climbed back onto the pavement. The street was still empty. When I pointed my key the car gave its electronic yelp and the parking lights blinked and the locks *shunked* open with that slumping effect, like the car had been holding its breath.

I eased myself into the seat and dug out my phone. I flipped it open, traced the buttons with my thumb while I pondered my options. John Rose had stopped taking my calls. I didn't trust Hepburn. I could call the cops but what would I tell them? Or I could call no one at all, just drive to the ferry and shitcan the whole job. The way the pain sang in my skull and my shoulder, the way my ribs ached when I took in a breath, that seemed like the smart thing to do. But then I'd have no story. And what the pain told me, what the blood dripping onto my thigh made clear, was that somebody wanted me gone. I still didn't know what the story was, but now I knew that there was one.

I scrolled down my contacts and hit the button. Moir picked up on the second ring.

'Shit,' he said, when I'd finished telling him. 'Shit, Gerry, you're supposed to be home by now. What the fuck?'

'Feel free to sympathise, Martin.'

He asked where I was.

'Eglantine Avenue.'

'Right. Don't go back to the hotel. Stay there, I'll call right back.'

He rang back in five minutes. I could stay with his parents. They lived in Antrim, up in the glens. They would give me a bed, get me cleaned up. I could take it from there. He gave me directions, his parents' phone number.

'Christ,' he said. 'We're supposed to be finished with this.'

'But was it even them? Maybe it wasn't. It could have been somebody else, couldn't it? Something random.'

'Of course it was them. Jesus, Gerry. "Take a telling"?'

'But out of nothing? Not even a warning?'

'Gerry,' he said. 'That was the warning.'

I told him I'd phone when I got there. My eye was still bleeding. There was a box of tissues on the back seat. I lifted a handful and mopped the blood from my eye. There was a bottle of Volvic in the drinks holder and I got out the car, leaned over the gutter and sluiced the water over my hair and face. I got more tissues and wiped myself dry.

My hand was on the key when I thought of something and snatched it back. Maybe they *had* found the car. Maybe they'd found it an hour ago. In a minute I was lying in the road once again, playing the flash on the undercarriage.

Nothing looked blatantly wrong. But then I wasn't sure what to look for. It was twenty years since I'd seen underneath a car. As kids we played street football after school. Around five o'clock, the dads would start coming home, and the street would fill up with parked cars. Austin Princesses, Ford Granadas. We played on, but the ball would get trapped under bodywork, wedged in the chassis. You had to lie on your side and kick at the ball till it worked itself loose.

I moved the flashlight back and forth a final time. I remembered the sound it made, the trapped ball, a dragging rasp as you kicked it free.

Fuck it. I eased out and smacked the grit off my jeans. I got back in the car, closed my eyes and turned the ignition.

The roads were quiet. I took the Lisburn Road, heading for the city centre. I was having to clench my eye every couple of seconds to clear the blood from the cut, and the city lights flared white and loud on the throbbing nub of my headache. I couldn't indicate – my busted hand was too sore – and I must have been twice the legal limit. If a cop car clocked me I was finished.

I turned onto the Antrim Road, past the lines of sleeping houses. It was quieter here. I put the foot down, risking forty as the road spooled northwards out of the city.

Blood was spilling now from the cut above my eye. It was running down the lid and pooling in the canthus. I kept wiping it clear with the heel of my hand but it filled straightaway. Salty and stinging. I waited for a lay-by and pulled in. The cut looked deep; black and gaping in the rear-view. I pressed a tissue to my eye and scrabbled around in the glove compartment. There'd been a box of plasters in there at one stage but it wasn't there now. I pulled the handle to let the seat tilt back and let it recline as far as it could. Then I just lay there with my head tipped back. After a bit I put my fingers up to the cut, tapped it lightly; rubbery, it felt, like the yolk of a soft-boiled egg.

When the blood congealed I set off once more, into the

country now, through sleeping villages and darkened fields. I looked out for the turn-off. I hadn't shaved since Thursday and my five-day beard was all gummed up with blood.

I drove on. No villages now, just the narrow road and the flickering trees. Twigs licked the Forester's sides and the shadows of branches crashed down on the hood. Before each corner I leaned on the horn. The headlights' beam threw a curve into the verges and I seemed to be tunnelling, barrelling down through the soft dark earth.

Then the sign flashed up and I tugged on the wheel and the car bumped onto a rutted track and here was a man stepping into the path with a hand to his eyes against the headlights' glare and the other arm lifted in warning or greeting.

Chapter Sixteen

The water was close to the brim, hot as I could bear it. The heat caressed my arm, my ribs, the graze on my hip I hadn't noticed till the water hit it. I closed my eyes, half-opened them again. My knees rose like atolls, stippled isles in a pine-fresh lagoon. The tub was deep. The heat kept me still. The slightest movement, the smallest flexing of my splayed knees, made me gasp. I slid lower down and the hotness flared, snapped at my skin like a testy dog. My mind soaked like a rag in a pail. I let it drift, lavishly blank. Only my legs remembered something, an ancient ache, some boyhood game of football and the long soak afterwards, caked mud lifting in flakes from my roughened knees, bruised shins and the soiled water cooling, the clatter of pots as my mother cooked lunch.

A loud knock roused me, the door juddering on its hinges. I slipped, trying to right myself, and reared sharply up in a great sucking splash. Water shipped over the porcelain lip in glassy curves, hissing onto the granite tiles.

'You OK in there?'

I palmed the water out of my eyes. Half the bath was on the floor tiles.

'Fine. I'm fine. No bother.'

He paused. I could hear him shifting his weight, the floorboard's groan.

'The food's about ready. I've laid out some stuff on the bed. Underthings. Socks. There's some shirts of mine in the wardrobe. Trousers as well. They might be on the short side, right enough, but see what you think. We'll be in the kitchen when you're right.'

'That's brilliant, Mr Moir. I'll be right down.'

He sniffed. 'Dead on.'

He creaked off downstairs. I wallowed a little, sluicing the suds off my legs and chest, then I pulled the plug and stood up, steam clouding off my parboiled flesh. A rough towel hung on a hook on the door. I patted myself dry. My belly and thighs were a deep dull pink. I wrapped the wet towel round my waist. When I opened the bathroom door steam billowed out and the air of the landing felt cool and wet on my shins and the backs of my arms.

In the spare bedroom there was underwear laid out on the floral duvet. A white vest and a pair of pale-blue Y-fronts and black ribbed socks side by side. I put on the Y-fronts and padded to the wardrobe. There were racks of shirts and trousers on wire hangers and above them was a hat. Sitting on the top shelf, an officer's cap, dark bottle green with a red-and-gold badge. It was lighter than it looked, its greeny-black fabric soft to the touch. I hefted it by the lacquered visor and tried it on. It was too large; the visor hung low and only my mouth escaped from its sinister shade. The badge was a harp with a crown on top. In the full-length mirror, naked but for underpants and hat, I looked like an underground clubber, some militaria fetishist.

I put the hat back on its shelf and flipped through the hangers. Woollen checked shirts and thick-ribbed cords in the colours of winter vegetables. I chose a shirt in a pale parsnip yellow with carroty checks. I hauled a pair of beetroot cords from their hanger. There was plenty of room at the waist but I threaded my own belt through the loops and pulled it tight. I stepped in front of the mirror. With my scrubby beard I looked like a farmer, some sly rural wiseacre, slow-moving, reticent. As I limped downstairs it was hard to shake the impression that this was my home, my wife turning from the oven with a plate gripped in a dishtowel, my well-scoured table at which I sat, my chair that scraped on the cold stone flag.

One place was laid. Mrs Moir crossed and set the plate before me. A bottle top skittered to the floor as Mr Moir prised it off. He set the bottle on the table in front of me and fetched an empty glass and set that down too.

I leant down and snuffed it up, the rich bland smell of the food. My glasses steamed up and I took them off and set them down on the scoured pine. I lifted the cutlery and suddenly my eyes were stinging and my throat dry.

'Fantastic. Just . . . It's fantastic. Wonderful.' I gestured blindly round the kitchen with the knife and fork. 'All of it. Really . . .' I shrugged.

'Eat. Don't talk. We can talk after.'

I bent to the food. Damp steam warmed my upper lip. Cabbage and mashed tatties. Rashers of bacon. That cabbagey smell. Thick, waxy wedges that squeaked in your mouth. The tatties fluffed and floury. The bacon thin and crispy, dark red rashers that splintered when the knife pressed down. I poured some of the beer into the glass and swirled it round and washed the bolus of food down my throat. I took another forkful, another swig of beer. I ate in silence while the man and the woman leant against the draining board and watched.

When I finished Mr Moir lifted my plate and crossed to the sink. A pile of dirty dishes was stacked on the work-top. He filled the sink and squirted some washing-up liquid.

'You want dessert, Gerry, some cake?' He spoke over his shoulder, his voice raised above the splashing water, the clatter of plates. 'There's sponge cake, Madeira.'

'I'm fine, thanks.'

'Coffee?'

'Let him be, Brian. Let his food settle.'

'I'm just saying.'

'No it's fine. I'll take another of these if you have it.' I waggled the empty bottle by its neck. I was pleasantly drunk now, the beer mingling with the whisky and stout from before.

He put a plate on the draining board and wiped his hands on a towel and stooped to lift a bottle from a crate beside the door. He opened it and set it on the table.

'Thanks.'

He went back to the basin, lifted a tea towel.

'Three of them, Martin said. Is that right. Three?'

'Brian! What did I tell you?'

'Let the boy talk if he wants to. Do you want to talk?'

'I don't mind.'

'Of course he minds.' She slammed the oven door. 'You're not involved any more, Brian. It's none of your business. You've no concern here.'

His shoulders moved as he dried a plate.

'I'm only asking, Deirdre. I'm asking the boy a question. He can answer for himself. He's a big strong boy.'

The food lay packed in my guts. I'd eaten too fast. I could feel the beer sluicing down, irrigating the packed mass.

'I don't know about that,' I said, jerking my thumb at my sore eye.

Mr Moir smiled. He was stooping to stow the plate in the space beneath the worktop but he craned his neck and smiled. *There's a gun in the house.* That's what flashed through my brain. Just as clear as if he'd spoken. There's a gun in this house. Something in the gesture or the smile. I knew it as sure as I knew my own name. There's a gun here somewhere.

I poured some more beer and swirled it around and watched Mr Moir's broad back. He was balding a little. The hat, I thought. The hat implied the gun. The hat vouched for the presence of the gun. It needn't even be the gun from his uniform. It might be a different gun altogether. But the hat needed a gun to balance it. There was a gun in the house.

'Where'd it happen?' he said.

'I don't know. Behind the cathedral somewhere. I was in a pub, the John Hewitt, I think. Then I left.'

I looked round the kitchen. The bread bin was too obvious. In a jar, then? One of the tins marked 'Flour' or 'Salt' or 'Tea'? The drawer of the big wooden dresser?

'It's a hard town,' he said. 'Your town's hard but Belfast's different. You want to watch yourself.'

'So they keep telling me.' I took a long pull of the beer. It was cold and sweet and brown-tasting. I set the bottle down.

'I saw your hat.'

'I know you did.'

He looked at me steadily, leaning on the sink with his arms crossed tight. I took another drink.

'Ask it,' he said.

'What?'

'Ask me what you're thinking.'

'I'm not thinking anything.'

'Ask me if I've killed a man.'

I held his gaze. I didn't speak.

'The answer's no. Does that surprise you? I never killed anyone. I've seen people killed. I've seen that happen. But I never fired a gun in anger.'

I shrugged. What did he want, a medal? I'd never fired a gun in anger either.

'But I still carry one.' I thought for a second he was about to produce it, fetch it from a saucepan under the sink. 'I still carry one. D'you know why? Because the war's not over. They've stopped bombing and shooting. For the most part they have. But do you think I feel safe? Down *there*?' He gestured at the window, where the road to the village passed by. 'Not a chance.' He patted his heart with the side of his fist. 'My war'll stop when this does.'

Next morning he was still wired, still keen to talk about it. All through breakfast he moaned about the new regime, Provos in suits, killers with cabinet posts.

'I'm not bitter, son. I'm not complaining. People died. Fine. I signed on in seventy-one: my eyes were open. I watched people die. Mates, guys I worked with every day. Watched them die for the uniform. For the badge.'

He waited for me to speak. I sipped my tea and nodded.

'Must be hard,' I said.

'Hard? Oh aye. And then they say, right, change of plan, guys. Thanks for all you've done but we need to switch things about a bit. We need to change the name.

We need to change the badge. Because, you know, some people are upset. Some people have *taken offence*.'

He frowned, his brow pursed with concentration.

'And who's upset again? Right, it's the people who were trying to kill us. The people who shot and bombed us for twenty-five years. These crybabies. They're big enough to put a pipe bomb under your car, but they faint away at the sight of a cap badge. Take offence? I should hope so. We sure as fuck meant to give it.'

'Yeah but it's not just them, is it? It's not just the bad guys who don't like you.'

'Oh no.' Moir waved his hands. 'That's what we're good at, son. That's our specialised subject. Everyone takes offence at everything. But once you've changed the name and scrapped the badge, once you've given in, given them everything they want and they're still not happy and they go back to killing people, what do you do then? Sorry, guys, could you come back and start dying for us again? Good luck with that.'

The phone rang and Moir nodded, once, as if the call had underscored his last remark. It was Martin. He was coming over. He'd be with us later that night.

The Moirs were suddenly busy. Mr Moir whipped off his apron and washed his hands at the sink. Mrs Moir vanished upstairs to change the sheets on Martin's bed. Mr Moir seized a fistful of cutlery and started laying the table. His movements were precise and ladylike. He seemed to feel he'd overstepped the mark in some way, that his ragged bluster was out of place in this sun-shot room, and now he centred the place mats and straightened cutlery to show how really reasonable he was. I drifted outside to smoke.

For the rest of the day I kept to myself. I walked round

the farm. I read some Wodehouse in my room. It was close to ten when Martin arrived. He'd helped put the paper to bed and caught the late ferry. A copy of the early edition was in his holdall and I leafed through it while Martin ate some supper and fielded a string of questions about Clare's pregnancy. When his parents climbed to bed I told him the story, filling in details I'd scrimped on the phone. I told him about John Rose and Isaac Hepburn and Duncan Gillies's mother. I told him again about the beating and the drive north. We were in the yard now, sucking on Bolivars. The night was mild – I was wearing a short-sleeved shirt of Mr Moir's – and not quite dark. An icy stripe of blue sharpened a stand of trees on a nearby hill and the yard felt secret and safe in the soft blue gloom.

'What about the guy who gave you the photo?'

'Hamish Neil? I don't know. His number's gone dead. I'll try to find him when we get back.'

'And Hepburn?'

'Who knows? One day he's plaguing me for a thousand quid, the next he's not taking my calls.'

We talked it all out. We would stay for a few days, use the farmhouse as base. Martin would look up his contacts, do some digging in the city. He was pacing the yard, talking it through, working out his movements. His cigar end weaved like a fiery bee in the failing light. It was his gig now; he was taking over. I couldn't care less. For the time being, I would stay here in Antrim, drinking tea and walking in the glens. That suited me fine. I was in no hurry to get my name on a plaque on the newsroom wall.

Next morning it was sunny when I woke. Moir was in the doorway in a dark-blue suit.

'What's the occasion?'

'Church,' he said. 'You fancy coming?'

The kirk was on a shelf of land near the brow of the hill. We climbed the road, single file, stepping onto the grassy verge when a car swung down on its way to town. When the engine sounds died and the crickets started up we set off once more, slow as marriage, so that Martin and his father wouldn't sweat in their Sunday suits. The little gate clinked behind them and the Moirs joined the others at the church door, old men and women with their faces tipped skywards, catching a final few rays. I climbed on up the twisting road.

From the crest of the hill the valley fell off and then rose again to the headland. The service would last an hour; time enough to reach the headland and get back. I hoped the Moirs weren't offended. I could have faced any number of things on that bright morning, but an hour of earnest Presbyterian decency wasn't one of them.

Out on the point a little chapel shone, its spire brilliant white in the sun. I set off down the slope.

When I came to the base of the hill I saw that it wasn't a chapel at all but a disused lighthouse. A stony path led to the top. The stones hurt my feet so I climbed on the grass, which was thick and deep, wind-bent into spongy clumps that buoyed you up and sapped you at the same time. Little black spiders skittered through the whitened stalks, just below the surface. The sun baked my scalp and the breeze smelled pleasantly of whin-blossom and wild garlic.

At the top I startled a black-faced ram; he scuttled off with a kilt-swing of his heavy fleece. This was the only coast, I reflected, the only plot of land from which

Scotland could be seen. There it was: Lowlands, Highlands and Islands, ranged in gradations on the other side, muted and cool and innocently blue. I could see Ayrshire and jagged Arran. Cumbrae and Mull and the Paps of Jura. It seemed both near and impossibly far.

They had rowed it, I remembered. The Covenanters – the *original* Covenanters. Those principled, grim Presbyterians, hated and harried by prelate and king. This stretch of water – the Sea of Moyle, the North Channel, the Sheuch – was the hinge of their kingdom. During the Killing Time the Scots sought refuge here; Peden the Prophet had sojourned in Ulster when the red-coats flushed him from his Ayrshire glens. At other times, the Irish sought succour in Scotland. Forbidden to worship in their own meeting houses, the Antrim Presbyterians rowed across to Ayrshire on Sunday mornings, and rowed back to Ulster after divine service.

A sheep was bleating on a distant farm. Its thin hard protest rose on the air, shrilling the green peace.

I walked back down to the church. Across from the gate was a green wooden bench, its fat planks tacky in the heat. The final hymn was in progress, its muffled vehemence making no impression on the peaceful scene. A butterfly rose from the long grass and tumbled up between my knees. Then the door opened and the minister stood on the greeny cobbles, his white hair astir, Geneva bands curling in the breeze. His parishioners filed out, each shaking his hand and trading a few words. They gathered on the cobbles, fishing for hankies and squinting into the sun. I was sorry I hadn't joined them. The minister's smile was open and warm and I regretted that I, too, couldn't grasp his hand and swap meaningless words about the weather. Then the Moirs appeared and I crossed to meet them.

We ate lunch at the farmhouse, big hunks of bread and an old-style broth with lentils and ham and square, white, black-eyed slippery beads of barley. Martin came downstairs with two rod cases and propped them by the door. Then he disappeared and came back with a big triangular net.

'You're sure about this?' I asked him.

'What?'

'Fishing on a Sunday?'

'Fuck off.'

He went into the kitchen and came back with a bulky cool-bag and dumped it with the other stuff. At some point I'd have to tell him I couldn't fish. He'd loaned me some gear: green waders and a waterproof waistcoat with too many pockets.

In the car I asked Moir if his father had taken him when he was young. No, he said, his dad never fished. Never had time. He'd taught himself in the summer holidays. Bought his first rod from the tackle shop in town and got the man to show him how it worked. Keep your wrist between ten o'clock and two. Then he'd just practised. All summer long on the banks of the river, forwards and backwards, ten to two, working the rhythm.

We turned down a dirt road through straggly pine trees and stopped in a clearing. I could hear the river as we fetched the gear from the boot. When we set off down the bank the noise got louder, the soft low roar of the falls. Then we stepped out of the trees and there it was: a yellowy Niagara, drumming into a deep brown pool.

Chapter Seventeen

Upstream from the waterfall an island cut the river in two. Martin stopped on the banking and rooted in the cool-bag. We sat on the grass with our sandwiches – chicken and dill pickle – and drank off a beer. The beers were cool but not cold and Martin gathered the cans in his arms and clumped off down the bank. He lodged the cans in the shallows, twisting them into the gravel bed. He stamped back up and lifted his rod.

'You take this stretch,' he said. 'I'll try the other side.'

He waded on out to the island and disappeared into the trees.

I was glad he wouldn't be there to watch me fish. I'd fly-fished as a boy, but I was never any good. My rhythm would slip and the line would get tangled and bellyflop down in a knotted clump.

I lifted the rod and side-stepped down to the edge. The surface was glassy and still, but green weeds were streaming in uniform lines. I almost faltered, stepping down off the bank, when the water pushed at my boots. The current was heavy and fast. I could feel the weight and the cold, the stream's heavy thrum through the waders' lined rubber. I froze for a moment, finding my feet.

The boots Moir had loaned me – they flared above the knee, in musketeer fashion – were slightly too small. They squished my toes and forced me to walk on my heels. The stones underfoot were soft with moss. I could feel their shift and give as I edged out into the stream. When the water reached my thighs I stopped wading and made a pass or two with the rod, but the long loops of line overtook one another and tangled down in the usual mess.

Back on the bank I eased down and opened a beer. Sunlight was glazing the water. I took off my shirt and laid it on the grass. A ladybird clung to the shoulder. I pointed my finger in its path and it clambered onto the nail. It was tiny and moved with surprising speed. Above the knuckle its orange legs waggled as it crested each hair. It pressed on up my arm, labouring over the hairs like a minuscule ship in a boisterous sea. When it reached the elbow it turned and started back down. I pressed my other index finger in its path and it raced up this, moving faster now as if eager to get to the end. It couldn't see far enough to make its escape. I brought my arm up to my mouth and puffed, a breath that wouldn't have doused a match, and it sailed off into the grass.

Moir came across from the other side. I could tell by his face that he'd caught one.

'Let's see it,' I said.

He grinned and opened his knapsack and held it wide. A green mottled thing, its brutal mouth gaping.

'We'll eat that tonight,' he said and then looked at my knapsack. I shook my head and he grinned again and took another look at his fish. Then he laid the bag in the shade of a tree.

'Have a beer,' I told him.

'In a minute.'

Moir went back in. He waded out to the middle and

started working the rod – forwards and back, forwards and back – like a charioteer lashing his horses. Each time it landed his fly kissed the water and kicked up a spritzing corona of spray. Pretty soon he had a bite. He stepped smartly backwards to the bank, yanking on the rod and reeling it in, yanking and reeling, till he hoisted it clear, flexing and flapping, water spouting from its flukes, a beautiful grey-green fish. He swung it round to land it on the grass and his eye caught mine: a leer of manic triumph raked me.

It was bigger than the first one.

He took a knife from his pocket and shucked the fish open and shook its guts into the water. He packed it in the bag and then fetched two beers.

'Don't worry,' he said. 'You need to know where to look. If you don't know where to look it can take you a while.' He said he'd been fishing this stretch of water since he was ten years old. It took him six months to get his first bite.

The late sun was still warm, beating on my scalp. I climbed down to the water, dropped to the bank and thrust my arms into the stream. The cold made my vision swim, chilled my forearms to tubes of glass. The pulse in my wrist ached with cold. I splashed my face and the back of my neck. Then my phone was ringing and I dried my hands on my T-shirt.

'Gerry!'

'Hello, Elaine.'

'Gerry. What happened? Martin told me. Are you OK? What happened?'

'I've got a black eye and a sore shoulder. I think I'll live.'

'You're OK? Really?'

The cold still sang in my hands and arms and I pressed a fleshy forearm to my brow.

'I'm fine. Honestly.' I laughed. 'Don't worry.'

A rasping sigh tore through the earpiece.

'Are you not too old for these games?'

'What games is that?'

Moir was climbing the bank with more beer.

'Fighting in pubs. Falling down drunk. You're a grown man, Gerry.'

'I wasnae drunk!' Moir tossed a can and I caught it in my free hand. 'I wasn't drunk. I got jumped in the street. Three guys gave me a doing.'

'Did you know them? Was it to do with what you're working on?'

'What did Martin say?'

Moir looked over.

'He said he didn't think so. But then he's a shite liar. Right you! Get back up those stairs!'

'Oh put him on. Elaine! Hey, Elaine! Put him on. Are they still up?'

'It's past his bedtime, Gerry. He's got to learn.'

'He's up now. Put him on.'

'Two minutes!' I could hear her stamping through to the kitchen. I set the beer down and got to my feet and started climbing the hill.

'Hullo, Dad.'

'Hullo, kid! How we doing?'

'Fine, Dad. Dad, are you on an island?'

'I'm in Ireland, kid.'

'*Ire*land?'

'Yeah.'

'Is Ireland in Scotland?'

'No, champ. It's a different country.'

'Is it nice?'

'It is. Do you know what I'm looking at right now?'

'No.'

I was halfway up the slope. You could see a dancing strip of sea and a block of mauve that was either Ayrshire or a stand of cumulo-stratus.

'Scotland.'

'You can see Scotland from there? Cool. What does it look like?'

'I don't know. Sort of purply-blue. Far away.'

'Can you see our house?'

'Well, I don't – actually, yeah. Yeah, I think maybe I can.'

'Hold on. I'll be back in one minute.'

Like a drumroll, the footsteps faded out and back in.

'Did you see me?' He was out of breath. 'Did you see me waving?'

'Of course I did.'

'Are you waving back?'

Yeah. I'm waving.'

'I didn't see you.'

'Of course you didn't. That's 'cause it's foggy over here.'

We ate Moir's trout with new potatoes and carrots from the garden. After supper we sat outside with the last of the beer and played knockout whist till the daylight failed.

Next morning Moir drove into Belfast after breakfast. I couldn't sit in the house all day so I walked into the village. I felt like someone passed unfit for service, kept from the action by flat feet or weak eyes. Young mums with buggies; kids by the war memorial; old men in khaki and brown: I skulked among the non-combatants. In a shoe-shop window I caught my reflection. The beard. The battered face. The shaggy hair. A man on the lam, a fugitive from justice.

There was a barber's on the Diamond. I slumped on a splay-legged bucket seat while a jug-eared teen and an ancient, crease-necked farmer took their turns in the chair. I watched them bow their heads to the clippers. In a barber's chair everyone looks like a baby.

'Give me a number two all over.'

The barber raised his eyebrows in the mirror.

'You sure?'

'What the hell.'

He shrugged and lifted the clippers from the bracket on the wall. He rooted in a box for the proper attachment. The clippers buzzed fatly into life.

'Holiday?' he said. He pressed my head down and started on my neck.

'Yeah.'

'Golf?'

'No,' I said. My voice was hollow and deeper than normal, talking into my chest. 'Fishing.'

He nodded. 'Any luck?'

'Yeah, I got a good-sized trout last night.'

'Did it put up a fight?' I glanced up; he was looking at my face, the swollen eye, the purple crust on my cheek-bone.

'Well, it got a couple of jabs in but I floored it in the end.'

He grinned. A radio played quietly in a corner: the archaic RP of Radio 3 purling softly on between big-band classics.

He ran the clippers in fluent swipes along my skull and the hair hit the cape in whispering clumps.

He did one side and then stopped; tugged to free the clippers' cord and drag it round the other side. I looked up. The mirror was a split screen: one half shaved to a quarter-inch crop; the other half rumpled and lush. I turned sideways. Before and after. The man with two heads.

When the other half was shaved he put the clippers away. A Tibetan monk peered into the room with a startled expression. The barber undid the burgundy cape and lifted it clear with a matador's flourish. The monk came out into the late-morning sun, blinking and rubbing the back of his neck.

On the way back to the farmhouse I stopped at a chemist's for a packet of razors. I shaved in the bedroom's tiny sink. The air on my naked cheeks felt wet and cool. There was nothing else to do after that so I lay on the bed. The sun warmed my face. It glinted on the chromium buckles of my holdall, stranded there on the desk by the window. A yellow corner of card poked out: the *Telegraph* folder. They were still in three bundles: Gillies, Pettigrew, Walsh. I took the Gillies pile back to bed and lay down again to read the cuts. I practically knew them by heart, but there might be something I'd missed.

The cuts told the same jerky, join-the-dots story. The body in the alley. The suppositious Catholic mob. And then the correction, the revelation: Gillies was shagging a prisoner's wife and a UVF nutting squad beat him to death. And that's where the story ended. The only question that mattered, the question of attribution, had finally been answered. With the killing rightly ascribed, chalked up to the proper mob, there was no more to report. This was a war: no one gave a damn about the perpetrators' names, no one wanted to read about the rank and serial numbers.

I put the cuts down. There was little enough to go on, but the image wouldn't leave me. Lyons sweating and grunting, elbowing through the scrimmage to land another kick on the writhing form. Lyons as part of the kicking, stamping mob that murdered Duncan Gillies. I gathered the sheets together and put them back in the folder.

Then I started on one of the other files: the murder of Eamonn Walsh, the report of his murderer's trial. It was a long report. I'd read it several times but this time a three-line par towards the bottom pulled me up short. I sat up in bed. I read it again. It was a par about the daughter, Walsh's daughter, the seven-year-old girl who'd been found in the street in her bloodied nightdress. She'd been interviewed by police. She said there were two men in the house that night. She hadn't witnessed the killing, but she'd seen two men in the hall as she came downstairs. No one else saw the other man. The killer maintained he was working alone. The wife, who saw the killer's arm drop to his side and then heard the report and then watched her husband die, confirmed that there was no one else involved. The girl's testimony was dismissed as the confused recollection of a traumatised child.

I read the story again. A little door opened in the long blank wall that encircled Peter Lyons's time in Belfast. The door might lead nowhere at all but I had to go through it. And maybe he'd be there – the man in the hall, that flickering presence, that pentimento.

It was four o'clock. A breeze was jiggling the conifers that lined the driveway. Moir would be back before long. There was a stack of paperbacks on a shelf above the bed but I couldn't settle to read. I lay on the bed with my iPod and thumbed through a dozen tracks – Charley Patton, Robert Johnson, T-Bone Walker, Sleepy John Estes – searching for an opening chord that didn't bore me to death. At one point the door whooshed open. There was nobody there. I eased up on one elbow and something landed on the bed. It was a cat, a skinny tortoiseshell with a flattened band of fur around its neck where a collar had come off. It picked its way up the duvet and stepped onto my chest. Its claws caught in my T-shirt and it started to sharpen them, alternately tickling and scratching my chest. Then its nose came right down to mine and it sniffed my mouth. Its breath smelt of fish. It stared into my eyes with a look of such anxious concentration that I laughed out loud. Its paws hit the carpet with a thump and it skedaddled out the door.

My eyes were stinging from the fur and I washed my face in the little mirror over the sink. The haircut had left a tan-line, a half-inch of yellow right around my brown face. It gave me a naive, startled look, like a child's drawing edged in chalk.

'Jesus, what happened to you?'

Moir was in the doorway. He must have come back while the water was running.

'Martin, come here. We need to talk.'

'Were you tarred and feathered? Did they chain you to the railings?'

I passed him the cut without comment. I waited in the middle of the floor while he took a seat on the bed. He glanced at the headline. He looked up neutrally and then started to read.

'What am I looking for, Gerry? I think I'm missing something.'

'Can you not see it?' I snatched the sheet from his hand, stabbed my finger at the paragraph.

'He's the man, Martin. It's Peter Lyons. The second man. The man in the hall.'

He read it again.

'But there was no man. That's what it says. The girl was confused.'

'Think about it, Martin. Use your head. What's the MO? How many of these hits are one-man jobs? It's fucking him, I know it.'

'Like you knew it was him who helped kill Gillies? OK. OK.' He held his hands up. 'Peter Lyons is the mystery man. Let's look into it.'

His grin was getting wider. It was only now it struck me he'd been grinning since he came in.

'What?'

He kicked off his shoes and lay back on my bed. *His* bed.

'You're gonna love this.' He crossed his legs at the ankles and linked his fingers on his chest. 'I went to a pub on Donegall Pass. It's a UVF shop. I knew some of the faces from way back. So I'm sat at the bar and three guys come in. They take a corner table and one of them's getting the drinks in. He's standing right beside me and he catches my eye in the mirror. He nods at me and I nod back. I'm thinking "I know this guy" but I can't place him. Then he orders the drinks: big Glasgow accent. And it hits me: it's one of Maitland's boys. I've spent the last five weeks tailing these guys round the East End. And one of them's right here.'

'One of Maitland's crew?'

'It's him all right.'

'One of Maitland's guys is in Belfast?'

We waited for this to make some kind of sense. When it didn't I sat down on the bed.

'And who were the other guys? Who was he with?'

'They're Blacknecks,' Moir said. 'I don't know them specifically, but I know the look, I know the form. He's drinking with the UVF.'

'The Maitland Crew and the UVF? I'll tell you one thing,' I said to Moir. 'I'm coming with you tomorrow.'

'You're the boss,' he said. 'I'll take you to Donegall Pass, see if they show up again. And I wouldn't worry about your friends from the other night.' He frowned at my cropped head, the newly beardless chin. 'They'd never make you anyway, looking like that.'

Chapter Eighteen

Behind us came a rumble like a tube train. Then the fat hollow smack as the ball met the pins. We picked out our shoes from the rack.

'You've done this before, by the way?'

I couldn't find elevens. Lots of tens and a single pair of twelves, but no elevens. I lifted the twelves.

'Bowling? I'm a fucking master, I'll kick your skinny arse.'

We didn't take the lane right beside them but the one beside that. Across the empty lane I could see them, in the corner of our eyes, as I bent to tie my shoes.

We'd followed them from Donegall Pass. That morning we drove into Belfast and ate brunch at Nick's Warehouse in the Cathedral Quarter. Around lunchtime we drove down Donegall Pass and parked across the street from the drinking club. We didn't have long to wait. At ten to one Moir poked me in the ribs. Across the street three men in jeans and T-shirts were climbing into a scarlet Porsche Cayenne. We followed them here to the Lagan Arena, a huge new leisure complex on the waterfront.

I haven't bowled in anger more than twice in my life. In the eighties I resisted the hype, and then later, when the alleys had bars and restaurants attached, it somehow was never my thing. Tenpin bowling, for me, was still Tom and Jerry: Tom's tail knotted through the fingerholes, Jerry's arched back as the ball runs him down. Moir, of course, is a natural. His first roll sends the ball on a smart tight curve to the heart of the pins. The skittles burst like an asterisk. He gives a camp little bob and pumps his fist. My own roll fades lamely, clipping two pins on its way to the gutter.

'You fucker.' I plugged the holes in a bilious lime-green ball. 'You're a bloody pro.'

Moir laughed. 'Enthusiastic amateur. Though I do play for a team back home.' 'Home' meaning Glasgow. 'We've made the City play-offs two years running.'

'That's great, Martin. First rate.'

As Moir leaned into his next shot, I glanced over at the three men. The tall guy waiting to bowl had short grey hair, a waxy, pockmarked skin and kindly pale-blue eyes. He cradled the ball to his chest, hefting it tenderly. His biceps bulged whitely. Behind him, sucking on a bottle of lager, was a big ugly baby of a man – short, fat, bald, his tight pot belly like a bowling ball, and hairless pudgy forearms in a bright-red outsize T-shirt. The third man, shaking his head at the shot he'd just completed and stooping for his drink, sported a ponytail. He wore a black dress shirt and jeans.

'That's him.' Martin nodded at the ponytail. 'The Glasgow guy. Tarrins or Torrance. A name like that. I've seen him in the scheme. He's close to Maitland.'

As if the name 'Maitland' had caught his ear, the guy looked over. I turned away too sharply and hurried to play my shot: the ball caught my thigh and smacked fatly down before trundling with comical languor down the lane. Time appeared to have stopped altogether before the ball flopped hopelessly into the gutter. I rubbed my palms on my jeans; my forehead, too, was prickled with sweat.

Moir, however, was all bounce and swagger. He seemed a new man in this context, less diffident and goofy. He was home, of course, on his own patch, and the game we were playing was his. But I sensed, too, that his other life, his 'Hey You' experience, was playing a part. As he stepped to the line with the ball, he was in character. The Moir who pistoned his hips when the pins scattered, who shook the heat from his fingers with a feline yowl: this was a new Moir altogether.

When he'd taken his shot I leaned forward to whisper something and Moir pulled back, laughing loudly.

'Talk normal, Gerry. Whisperers get noticed. Who's going to hear you?'

He threw his arms wide. He was right. The stolid thunder of the balls, the pins' hollow knocking, the judder and clang from the games arcade, the sound system's rousing soft-rock: the place was bedlam.

And yet, if anyone was audible it was Moir. He greeted every strike with a ludicrous whoop, groaned abjectly when even one pin was left standing. At one point, in a lull between songs, he knocked his glass to the floor and it shattered with a prodigious pop.

The ponytailed man, about to roll, pulled out of his shot and glared across. Moir had his hands up. 'Sorry, big man.' He half-salaamed. When the girl arrived he made a big show of helping to clean things up. As he mopped at the spillage and dropped in the basket the bright shards of glass, Moir turned to me with a grin. 'They know who I am now.' He jerked his head at the stain on the floor. 'I'm the dick who spilled his drink.'

I was still getting caned ten minutes later, when Moir went for a piss. 'My phone's on,' he told me. 'Call me if they go anywhere.' I sat down on the red banquette. I took my phone out and checked for messages. I texted Roddy. At the edge of my vision, above the phone's bright screen, the figures shifted. Black shadows, bending and straightening. With a flick of my thumb I put the phone to its camera setting, tilted the screen and there they were. I almost laughed. I pressed the button and that moist crisp click, like a celery stick being snapped in two, seemed recklessly loud. But the figures kept moving, reaching for drinks, stooping to bowl. I took some more shots. I kept both thumbs on the keypad; to anyone watching I was busy texting.

I shuffled in my seat. I was getting plenty of shots but none of them was right. What I needed was the Scottish guy in the frame with at least one of the Blacknecks. I wanted the evidence: the Glasgow godfather's right-hand man getting chummy with the South Belfast UVF. But when one was bowling the others were lifting beers or stooping over the ball-return. Finally I got it – the Scotsman and the fat baby. But when I viewed the photo the fat man was in profile. The zoom brought him closer but no clearer: his cheek dissolved in a pixellated blur. I had to get closer.

I stood up and rolled my shoulders. I moved to the edge of our lane. Baby Boy stepped up to roll and the other two reached for their beers. The Scotsman said something and the grey-haired man's smile showed a big friendly gap in his teeth. Then the Scotsman beckoned the other man closer. The grey-haired man cocked his head and the Scotsman stooped to whisper in his ear. They were facing me now. Though tilted slightly forward and shadowed a little deeply, their heads were almost touching. This was it. This was the shot. I edged a little closer. I had them in the viewfinder but now somebody was coming, a blur of white in my peripheral vision – the waitress, she was coming for the empties – and before she could block me I took another step. I was on the vacant lane now. I raised my hand to frame the shot. By now I no longer had both hands on the phone. There was no pretence now: I was taking a picture. I pointed the phone and clicked and had barely snapped it shut when they erupted from the lane, grabbing fistfuls of air as they broke towards me, the Scotsman, the grey-haired man and Baby Boy not far behind.

The crash when I turned was the waitress's tray. I hopped over the smashed glasses and set off up the lane, fists pumping, my too-big bowling shoes snapping on the varnished wood. The sudden loud burst of static was the sound of six bowling shoes crunching through glass.

Through the jangling gloom of the games arcade and into the light of day. The central plaza. Light. Air. Milling families, balconies in shiny tiers, the escalators' italic slant, the big glass bell of the atrium roof. I seemed to see it all from above, in brilliant vista-vision. Brighter, sharper, louder than it was. Pounding through the plaza I was gauging speeds and distances, calculating angles. Like the arcade games players I was thinking two steps ahead: the parents with the double buggy and dawdling three-year-old; the volatile knot of teens horsing around by the water-feature. Someone stepped out from behind a telephone kiosk dragging a wheeled valise and I vaulted the thing without breaking stride.

I was making for the escalators. It occurred to me to

stop and simply shout, holler for help. Maybe one of the guards would come running, the security men in their rust-coloured shirts; their vizored caps and regulation goatees. But here were the moving stairs and I took them at a running jump, landing too high and almost toppling back as the mechanism lurched upwards. But I clutched for the guardrail and steadied myself and pounded on up the ribbed steel steps. Towards the top a woman held a girl by the hand. I was gaining on them, they were blocking the way, but as I came up behind them the escalator debouched us and I slalomed past and off across the floor.

I didn't look back. Ahead of me was the cinema, a multiplex that took up most of this storey. At the entrance I slowed and forced myself to walk, crossing with care the carpeted foyer. The place was airy and open plan. I passed the ticket counter with its vacant snake of red-roped stanchions. The kiosk for sweets and popcorn, the Häagen-Dazs concession. All the programmes had started; there was no one about. Down a dark, carpeted corridor to the screens, I broke into a trot. On either side were lighted numerals like the ones outside airport departure gates. No ushers stood by the doors: the screenings were underway. I glanced back down the empty corridor and pulled on one of the double doors.

It was pitch-black in the theatre. Green *Exit* signs floated in the gloom. Then the scene shifted – a bright exterior, a city street – and the whole auditorium was washed in grey light, showing banks of seats, the attentive heads. Two rows down there was a vacant seat in the middle of the row. I squeezed past the knees, the bodies half-rising with little irritable grunts and sighs. I slumped down low and turned up my collar, leaned my cheek against my knuckles.

The film was a romantic comedy. The American actor and his European girl – her accent sounded German – were sitting in their car in a city-centre street. The car – it could only be hers, although the man sat behind the wheel – was comically small and British. They bickered in low voices while the man consulted a map spread out on his lap. A gendarme was striding towards them, his silhouette already primed with comedy – the pillbox hat, the girlish short cape. But now the Yank was stamping on the pedals and the Mini screeched out from the kerb and wobbled towards the roadblock, picking up speed as the gendarmes scattered.

It wasn't a rom-com; it was an action thriller. For the next ten minutes the cops pursued the couple through the Paris streets. The mini slalomed through pedestrians, stuttered down flights of steps, outfaced oncoming traffic and went crashing along the banks of the Seine. I was counting in my head, as slowly as I dared, each block of sixty drawing me closer to safety. I stayed till the finish. Twice the door opened and somebody left or came in but I stared straight ahead.

When the credits came up we all filed out. I kept my head down, clamped my phone to my ear. Through the foyer, panicking a little as the crowd thinned, and then down the escalator and out to the car park. I made it to the car and there was Martin in dark glasses, perched on a stanchion. He started to laugh. I laughed too. We were snorting and sniggering like schoolboys as we hauled on the doors. Holy fuck. Moir produced a hip flask and we each took a burning pull. We didn't stop laughing till we hit the Antrim Road.

Chapter Nineteen

Death knocks. That jump in your guts when you spotted the house. The cellophane glint on the pavement, footie scarves tied to the railings. That's what I dreaded most, in my early days at the *Trib*. Send a boy to do a man's job. That's how it works – at the *Tribune* and everywhere else. Boy struck by bus. Boy stabbed in brawl. You're almost a boy yourself but the Desk sends you out to the house. You get to put the lovely questions. How does it feel? What was he like? Did he play sports? Was he good at school? It was nothing but grief. Even if you did get a quote, you never got credit; the chief reporter would write it up. There are plenty of things I'm not proud of, but I've never felt as toxically cheap as when I swallowed my phlegm and thumbed those doorbells.

Get a collect. That's what the Desk told you. If you do nothing else, just get a collect, get a photo. Sometimes they shouted and raved; women lashed out with their chipped fingernails. A man tossed a hot mug of tea in my face. But mostly they were helpful, cowed, pitifully pleased by the attention, asking you in and offering coffee. Wounded as they were, they tracked your gaze from dresser to mantelpiece, hoping to learn from your eyes what their possessions said about them. They wanted a sign, some clue to why it had happened, why trouble had come to their door. You felt like the cops. We perched on their sofas in our outdoor clothes and made them feel guilty.

At the first lull you'd cross to the dresser. 'Is that him? May I? What a happy looking boy. Could we borrow this? We'll bring it straight back.' Sometimes they wouldn't want to give it. In that case the snapper might sneak a photo of the photo but this was tricky and the quality was never good. Much simpler just to swipe it. On the way out you're shaking the mother's hand and the snapper hangs back and two days later she works out what's missing: the school photo's gone from the top of the telly.

That's why I jacked it. That's why I moved to politics, took the job with the swivel chair. I couldn't hack it any more. I couldn't push the doorbells, face the bruised looks, the questioning eyes. I wanted out. And now I was back. The same damp chill in my stomach. The same cold sweat on my brow. No matter that this death was twenty years old. No matter that the woman was expecting me: the jump in my gut was exactly the same.

I got there early. I found the house, a big lemon-yellow place on the shore road. Ballyholme Esplanade. The nice end of town. Two doors down an old guy perched on a kitchen chair, painting his front gate. He dipped his brush in the Hammerite pot and watched me pass.

I had forty minutes to kill. I turned the car around, found a parking spot in the town centre. The shops on the seafront had candy-striped awnings and I walked down the shaded parade. Coils of sand twisting over the pavement. Gulls screamed and hooted, dwindling in yellow air. From up ahead came a muted metallic clatter and a harsh sizzling fizz. I ducked into the gloom.

'You frying?'

A teenage girl at the counter, her bleached hair up in a scrunchie. Further along, a balding guy in a white tunic, busy with the fish. The bald guy looked at the lassie and then at me. I saw him notice my eye.

'Ten minutes,' he said. 'Ten minutes we ready. What you want? A fish supper?'

'Aye.'

'Ten minutes. No problem.'

When I came back the place was full. A squad of site workers in boots and dayglo waistcoats were horsing around but the owner waved a package at me – 'fish supper' – and beckoned me to the front of the queue.

Along the seafront the houses were painted in ice-cream colours. Strawberry, lemon, pistachio, mint. Gulls stamped about on municipal bins, flapping at apertures, tugging scraps of paper like hankies from a sleeve. The benches on the esplanade had little plaques attached. I looked for the dates, the ones that might have been Troubles deaths, the ones that certainly weren't. I chose the most recent:

SALLY McALISKEY, 1973–2004. FOREVER
IN OUR HEARTS.

The batter was crisp and the haddock was fresh, its flesh moist and milky-blue. I ate the fish first and then started on the chips. One of the chips had a blackened end. I left it till last and then tossed it into the road. A gull appeared and flapped awkwardly up as a car approached. Then it stalked back into the road. Another car passed and the gull rose again in a bad-tempered tangle to come stilting back with tight embarrassed steps. Finally a van ground past and smeared the chip to the road and the gull launched up and lifted out to sea, trailing disdainful orange feet.

The old boy was still painting his gate when I parked in front of the house. He craned round, hands on thighs, to get a proper look. He was wearing shorts: I caught a glimpse of pale bluish shin and a rumpled dark sock.

Three steps to the doorbell. I stepped back down to the path, felt the old guy's gaze on the back of my head.

I took up my death-knock stance. Head slightly bowed. Hands clasped in front of the crotch. The upward glance as the door swings open.

'Mrs Derwent?'

'Mr Conway.' She nodded, as if she'd known what I would look like. She held the door wide. 'I want to thank you for coming.'

The hall was dark after the bright daylight. When she closed the door behind me my eyes took a second to adjust and for a spell I wasn't sure where she'd gone. I put my hand out vaguely.

'This way.'

She was halfway down the hall. I followed her into a bright white kitchen with French windows. She strode to the windows and drew them a little closer and then she turned and presented her hand. She was small, a neat little false blonde with coppery skin and glossy green eyes. She was heavily pregnant.

'Have you eaten?'

The circular table was set for two. A big ceramic salad bowl frothed greenly in the centre.

'Actually I had a fish supper at the front,' I said. She frowned. 'Though I could certainly manage a little, what is that – Niçoise?'

'Good,' she said. 'It is. Please.' She gestured to the free chair as she took her own.

We ate in silence for a while, passing the pepper and salt and the bowl of Parmesan. Then she asked about my job, what the paper was like, did I like working there? I better like it, I told her; I was good for nothing else. When the salad was finished she rose and crossed to the sink. There were blueberries in a colander on the draining board. I watched her move. You always did this with the victims, scrutinised their movements, trying to trace some residue of trauma. As if she'd roll her hips another way, her gait would be different if her dad hadn't died on their living-room carpet. And in any case she was moving now with that universal late-pregnancy waddle, leading with the pelvis.

'When are you due?' I asked her. She set a bowl of blue-berries in front of me.

'August 18th. If I last that long.'

'You do look – I want to say ripe but that's not right.' I lifted a handful of blueberries. 'Blooming.'

She smiled.

'When you called,' she said. 'After you called, I put the phone down and cried. I'm not sure why. I think it was maybe relief.' She picked through the berries in her bowl. 'I've always known this day would come. I knew it wasn't finished, that even the legal, the public part wasn't done with. I even thought . . .' She paused and looked up, almost shy now. 'I even thought you might be him.'

'The other man?'

She nodded. The door opened then and a boy came in, a toddler, his face pouchy and smeared.

'I was scared, Mummy.'

'Why were you scared? I was right here. Did you have a good nap?'

He nodded. 'Yes. Mummy I want juice.'

'OK, Kyle. Did you say hello? This is Mr Conway.'

'Gerry,' I said.

The boy looked gravely at me and started to whine for his juice.

'Right, Kyle. OK.' She rose with difficulty and waddled to the worktop. 'You want coffee?'

'Thanks.'

We took it in the garden. We sat at a wooden table under a multi-coloured parasol and the boy played beside us on a tartan rug. She spoke about her childhood, the Belfast house with its gloomy green-black shrubbery, the doorbell like a blinded eye. Her parents had a good life, she said. Her father's law practice was thriving and they entertained a lot, there were parties most weekends. The doorbell – that white porcelain hemisphere that scared her when she passed its vacant gaze – would keep on sounding. She remembered the voices, how she would creep downstairs and listen from the landing. On other nights there were clients – 'clients' was a word she learned early: spare, self-effacing men, who would stand in the hall till her father was ready.

Of her father himself she remembered very little.

'I remember when he came to say goodnight. How the cover tightened when he sat on the bed. The scratch of his chin and the smell of cigarettes. His silhouette in the doorway when he switched off my light. But I don't really remember him. Kyle, sweetheart.' The boy looked up from his toys. 'Kyle: run in and get the picture of Grandad. Bring it to Mummy.'

It was black and white: a youngish dad with a plump baby girl in the crook of his arm. His free arm hangs down, a smoking stub wedged in his fingers. He wears a stripy shirt, flat-fronted trousers without a belt. His side-buckled shoes are shining like shellac. There's a back gate behind him and a white explosion like a too-bright cloud edging into the shot at the height of his head. I lean closer, spot the washing line bisecting his head: it's a shirt or a bedsheet, twisting in the breeze.

'They said he was an IRA man,' she said.

'Was he?'

I passed the photo back.

'I don't know. I don't think so. My mother died last year and she always said it was a lie. He was never a Provo, she said. But he was a Catholic. And he was good at his job. Of course Republicans would want him to defend them. Why wouldn't they? He got a lot of them off. He even got compensation for some of them.'

She told me about that night. How she crept down-stairs and saw a man in the hallway. The open door and the night air cold on her bare legs. The man's smile. His funny accent when he spoke. And the noise in the living room, another man bustling out and the two men vanish-ing into the night. And the mess in the living room. The chaos. The blood. The burnt smoky smell.

'At first,' she said, 'I thought it was a joke. A kind of game.'

She smiled and I thought of the photo, her smiling dad. I liked the look of him. Pursed, ironic lips. The dark curls thinning at the front. His head cocked forward so he's looking up at us, peering over invisible spectacles, and the stoic mockery in his eyes comprehends it all – himself, the photographer, the very genre of the family snapshot. When the shutter clicks he will do something daft, snap the fag-end to the ground and hoist the girl onto his shoulders, jounce her round the garden, her fat limbs jiggling to the rhythm.

'And the man in the hall,' I said. 'Would you know him? What did he look like?'

She shook her head. 'I was seven years old. He was nice. He was a nice man. He smiled and he wore glasses. He spoke funny. A thick accent. I think he had a green coat but I couldn't be sure.'

The boy came over and stood beside her. 'Mummy, can I go inside and play with my aminals?'

'OK, honey.' He toddled off. 'It's like telling a dream. You know when you have a dream and then you tell it to someone, you put it into words? And the words change it? You need words to tell it, but the words take over and you can't get back to the actual dream. That's what it's like. I don't really know what happened any more because I've told the story so often.'

'But there *was* a second man? You didn't dream *him*?'

'He wasn't a ghost, Mr Conway. He was standing as near to me as you are now.'

The boy came over and climbed on her lap for a kiss. Then he went inside to play.

'But didn't they investigate?'

'What's to investigate? They had the killer. They had a result. Why keep digging? It was easier to decide the wee girl was seeing things. She was confused. Anyway, when no one believes you, you stop telling. Sometimes I thought they might be right, I thought I'd made him up. Then I thought he was an angel. They told me an angel had come down to take my daddy up to heaven. I said, "I know! I saw him." "That wasn't the angel," they said. "That was the bad man. The bad man shot your daddy and the angel took him to heaven." "I know," I said. "I saw them both. I saw the bad man and I saw the angel too."'

She placed her hands on her belly then and winced, a sweet grimace, as the child inside her kicked.

'You know the worst thing? The neighbours. Neighbours are supposed to rally round. But people changed, once it happened. The people in the street. Even though he was innocent, that didn't matter. It was like we'd brought it to their doors, just by being ourselves. Being Catholic. The other kids stopped having me round.'

She shifted in the chair, pressed her palm to the small of her back.

'Are you OK?'

'I'm fine,' she said. 'To be fair, the neighbours weren't alone. My aunties came to visit a lot. After it happened. They were just as bad. We should move south, they said. Or go to England.'

She said 'England' as she might have said 'Japan' or 'Kazakhstan'.

The boy was back in the garden.

'I've made a display, Mummy. Come and see. Come *on*!'

She grimaced at me.

'Of course,' I said. 'No problem.'

We laboured up the lawn like a refugee column of two. The boy kept racing ahead and then rushing back, urging us to hurry.

In the living room he stood beaming over a plastic

menagerie of animals. The animals were arranged in family groups: dogs and monkeys and horses and bears. Leopards and pigs with their litter of young. He lifted a lion and an elephant and held them out.

'Which one do you want to be?'

I pointed to the lion. He thought about it and then handed me the elephant.

'Are you a goodie or a baddie?'

'Eh, I think the jury's still out, son.' The blank look. I smiled. 'I'm a goodie. What do you reckon?'

'Well.' He considered it. 'Yes, you're a goodie. We're both goodies.'

We played for a bit on the carpet, moving the creatures around. At one point he stopped and put out his hand to touch my face.

'Kyle! Stop that!'

'It's OK.'

He brought his hand up to my cheekbone, his prim mouth rigid, eyes full of commonplace wonder.

He patted it lightly, the contusion, the purplish crust, and he peered into my eyes to check my reaction.

'Is it sore?'

'It's a bit sore.'

'Will you die?'

'No, I'll be OK.'

He nodded. He turned to his mother.

'He won't die. It's a bit sore, but he'll be OK.'

'Is that right?'

'Yes.' Then he jumped up in anguish. 'Need to go! Need to go!'

'On you go then!' The feet pummelled up the stairs. 'And wash your hands!'

I got to my feet.

'I should go too.'

We stood on the path in the hot sun.

'You've got a photo, I take it.'

I slipped it out of my shoulder bag.

'Which one is he?' Her fingertip circled the heads. I took her finger in mine and brought it down onto Lyons's face. She took the photo in both hands and brought it up close to her nose.

'Who is he?'

I shrugged, but the photo was blocking her face.

I cleared my throat. 'It doesn't matter,' I said, and put my hand out and tugged the photograph down, gently, tugged it out of her hand and slipped it back in the envelope. 'It doesn't matter.'

She crossed her arms over her chest.

'Do you know him, though?' She looked out to sea, shielding her eyes with her hand. There was a ship out there, a tanker right on the skyline, low and long and red. The kind of ship that never seems to move. When she looked back to me she kept her hand where it was.

'I do, yeah.'

She nodded. The boy skidded round the corner and hid behind his mother, shy again now that the stranger was leaving.

'Will he go to jail?' she said. 'When you write your story?'

'There is no story.' I fastened my bag. 'There's not enough evidence. Or any evidence, really. I'm sorry I've wasted your time. I've brought it all back and I can't help you.'

'But if it's him,' she said. 'If you know it's him. Can't

you do something anyway? Name him as a suspect?'

'He's not a suspect. We can't prove anything. Look, even if I wrote the story they'd never put it out. My editor would stop it.'

She looked back out to sea.

'I'll keep on trying,' I told her. 'If there's anything else you remember, give me a call. But I can't write the story just now. There's just not enough there. I'm sorry, Mrs Derwent.'

'It doesn't matter,' she said. 'It's all right.' She put her arms behind her, feeling for the boy. 'It's nice to know anyway. That I wasn't mad. That I didn't make it up. Come on, Kyle and say bye-bye.'

The blond head poked out for a second. Out on the street a car door closed.

'Come out and say bye-bye.'

Her skirt twitched as the boy pressed tighter in and then the head flashed out, eyes shining wide. I hunkered down and when the head poked out again I roared and pawed the air in a tigerish swipe.

The boy squealed. When he peeked out next I did it again. And then again but this time the head stayed put. The smile fell and the eyes – big now, unblinking – seemed to flatten and pale. A gate clicked behind me and the boy was rushing past.

'This is my husband – Ian.'

The man came up the path with the boy in his arms, the little legs clamped round his waist.

'This is the man from Scotland.'

I got to my feet.

'Gerry Conway.'

He hoisted the boy and tried to free his hand. We

shook hands awkwardly. He looked at his wife.

'I'm fine,' she said.

'Great.' He lowered the boy to the ground. 'And did you get what you needed?'

'Yeah. You know.' I raised my shoulders, weighed two invisible somethings on my palms. 'Yeah. Listen, thanks for everything. I'll let you know if anything . . .'

'Fine.'

They waved in unison from the doorstep as I pulled away. The old guy over the way had gone inside. His paint pot still stood on the pavement; his empty kitchen chair.

Chapter Twenty

The disused railway line. Out by Fardalehill, on the western edge of town. As kids we used to go there after school. It ran from the lemonade factory to the woods at Knockentiber. You left the council blocks and crossed a field of sleepy Friesians. A barbed-wire fence creaked and moaned as you held down the strands. Then a running jump to clear a muddy burn and up a shallow banking to the track.

The place had an air of recent abandonment. Brown rust bordered the shiny rails. Broken glass and faded Coke cans. The sleepers chipped and rotting in their bed of stones. On hot days we'd head for the woods, down the straight long track in the stink of creosote. It could give you a headache, the flare of sun in the polished steel, the flat rails turning a molten gold.

Walking was hard. The sleepers were too far apart. The stones kept poking your soles, rocking your ankles with their rumbling shift and give. Sometimes we'd scoop up a fistful – they were narrow and sharp, like Neolithic tools – and heave them in the air, making them zing off the blinding rails.

There were weeds between the sleepers, great green wagging thistles. No trains had run there in years, but you felt a shiver when you walked that track, a tingling in the space between your shoulder blades. Every eight or nine yards your head was drawn back, angling to catch it – a tremor in the rails, an angry diesel bearing down with an outraged blast of horn.

There were shafts along the track at intervals of fifty yards, neat oblong wells sunk into the banking. No one knew what they were for. One cold spring day we were crunching up the track, Davey Merchant and I, when we found a dead cow. A big black Friesian, trapped in a shaft.

All you could see were the shoulders and back, a dull blue sheen on the matted hair. The hide was like a square of choppy sea, rising in little peaks at the spine and the shoulders, the haunches and neck. You couldn't see the head, just the column of the neck; the impact had forced the head between the knees.

We looked at each other and then down at the fence and the sagging wires. The animal had strayed. It had pushed through a break in the fence, wandered the tracks, its hooves sinking into the stones, and at some point the stones weren't there and the cow stumbled into the void. It looked like a set-up, a practical joke. In all three dimensions, the cow precisely fitted its oblong shaft. It occupied its slot the way a Bible fits a slipcase.

There was no stench, no massing of flies. The beast was newly dead. We looked out over the fields, all distant and stilled and smoking in the early sun, but the fields gave nothing away. It was hard not to posit some element of design, some malignant bias in whatever force had weakened the fence at just this point, had drawn the heavy beast up the banking, its sharp shoulders working, and brought it to this cow-sized grave.

We stood there for a minute or two. We bounced a couple of stones off the broad back and prodded it with the toes of our Sambas. Then we tramped off up the track.

All this came back to me on my last night in Belfast when I saw Isaac Hepburn for the final time. I'd been driving back from Bangor.

FOR GOD SO LOVED THE WORLD, THAT HE GAVE HIS ONLY BEGOTTEN SON, THAT WHOSOEVER BELIEVETH IN HIM SHOULD NOT PERISH, BUT HAVE EVERLASTING LIFE. JOHN 3:16.

That was daubed in foot-high letters on the side of a barn. I thought it over while I drove to the city. I hadn't seen Hepburn since he'd cracked my face on the bonnet of a car, but for some reason the crude white letters brought him to mind. It worried me that he hadn't been back in touch about his thousand pounds. It made me wonder if something had happened. It occurred to me, too, that if he wanted to earn a grand, instead of just extort it, there were things he could do. Like tell me who else was present when Eamonn Walsh got shot. I decided to pay him a visit, give him the thousand right there and then if he would tell me what he knew about the Walsh assassination.

I parked in the Donegall Quay multi-storey and checked my wallet. Nearly four hundred. There was a Northern Bank on Donegall Square and I took out the rest of the cash and went for a coffee at the Linen Hall Library. The sheet of paper Hepburn had left at the hotel was still in my wallet. My throat dried up as I punched the number but it went to voicemail. I left a message asking Hepburn to call me. There was no point driving back to Antrim if I was hoping to see Hepburn that night, so I killed some time in the library and then took in a rerun of *Badlands* at the Queen's Film Theatre. By ten o'clock I was in the Cloth Ear Bar of the Merchant Hotel. My phone sat mutely on the table beside a glass of sparkling water. Hepburn still hadn't called. I could try the gym but he wouldn't want to do business there, at least not when other people were around.

I toyed with my fizzy water for another hour and then fetched the car from Donegall Quay and drove to Hepburn's gym. It was after closing time now but maybe I'd catch him before he went home. I parked round the corner. The street was empty. Tarmac glistened in the sodium glare. Puddles threw up tangerine smears. The teens on the disabled ramp – that parliament of crows – had flapped off to another perch. A big-bellied bottle of cider stood daintily on the top step.

The storm door was closed, the fanlight dark. I pressed the intercom, held it down for a count of five. Beyond the door the sound ground dully on but the grille failed to crackle into life. I glanced back at the street; the lighted pinks and greens of curtained windows. A late bus changed gears on a distant street.

Down the side of the building was a narrow roadway. I followed it to the car park at the rear. A cough-drop-shaped security light burned in its strutted cage. The ground had a slimy cast in the orange light. There was a single car in the lot, a Saab 9-5, black, four years old. Nothing moved. The building's back wall had a sullen, shuttered look. But a window on the lower left was a lighter grey than the rest. If I stood on my tiptoes I might just see in.

There was nothing to see. Security bars. A dim pearly haze through net curtains. A wheelie bin stood by the door. I dragged it over and scrambled up on top, but there was no gap between the curtain and the top of the window.

I jumped back down. I squeezed my good hand between the bars and knocked the window, clacking my ring on the glass. Nothing. No shadows swayed. The curtains just hung.

I stepped back and studied the building again. There were three steps up to the narrow back door. I jumped them and rattled the handle. Next to the door was a big boxed-in unit for the air-conditioning system. On the far side of this, above a low step, was the fire door. Craning out over the air-con, I could just make out a hopeful strip of shadow. The door wasn't flush with its jamb. I stepped round the air-con unit and clenched my fingertips on the half-inch strip of fire door and strained, one-handed, like a climber on a ledge. The door gave and I worked my fingers into the gap.

There was no alarm, no shrilling of bells. I stepped inside, let the door bump gently shut, the latch half-engaging with a cushioned click, the push-bar nudging the small of my back.

For a moment everything was black. A squall of panic rose and fell. Take it easy, Conway. Breathe deep. Then I turned to my right and collided with someone.

I threw my arms up in the dark, ready to grapple, to parry the blows. Nobody moved. My breathing rasped like a pack of dogs. I sensed a displacement of air, as if a large body had passed nearby. I put my hand out again and a cold, tacky surface kissed my palm. I put out my other hand, put my arms right around the thing and hugged it. A punchbag. I was in Hepburn's gym.

There was a flashlight in the Forester's glove compartment and I thought about nipping back. But I stayed where I was and the room slowly bloomed into view, the planes and the contours asserting themselves. The big square scaffold of the ring. The heavy bags, one gently swinging.

My breathing eased. I wiped my palms down the crease of my trousers.

I opened the door to the rest of the club. It was lighter here, the street lights piercing the slatted blinds. There were doors across the hallway. I stepped up to one, its push-panel glinting dully and shoved it firmly, once, without crossing the threshold. Before it swung back, the door disclosed a steel double sink, a row of implements on hooks and a slab-topped table in the centre of the room. The next door had two panels side by side: a forked little man and a woman's triangular skirt.

I didn't go in. I moved down to a door marked PRIVATE. STAFF ONLY. A TV was on; tinny histrionics and incidental music. I held my breath and used one knuckle to knock. I used it again a bit harder. The voices on the telly didn't object, so I turned the handle.

It was somebody's office. A gunmetal desk and a blue swivel chair. A standard lamp explained the haze I'd seen from the car park. The telly – it sat atop a four-door grey filing cabinet in the corner – was tuned to a hospital drama: gesticulating doctors breezing through crash-doors. I crossed to turn it off and tried in turn the four locked drawers of the filing cabinet. There wasn't much else in the room. A PC workstation against one wall. A gas fire. A wastepaper basket of scuffed red metal. A desk-tidy on the floor, its holdings of pens, rulers and paperclips strewn on the carpet. On the back wall a Mondrian calendar, open at May. Above the fireplace a large naked oblong of unfaded paint where something had been moved or knocked from the wall. I moved around the desk and found it on the floor, a framed photo, face down, its glass cracked in a sun-ray pattern.

Some of the glass dislodged as I lifted the frame, ragged shards tilting onto the floor. I shook the rest into the basket and laid the frame on the desk. The photo showed a boxing ring after a fight. A handsome man in a dinner suit and black bow tie stood between two sweaty fighters, his arms around their shoulders, his one-button tux still buttoned. He had wavy hair and a professional smile and he looked like a minor celebrity, a regional newscaster or football pundit. The boxers wore coloured vests. Their gloves were off. Their chests and faces shone in the overhead spots. The one in the red vest had a glazed, sleepy look. His right eye was hooded and his other eye looked at the floor. His bandaged hands hung stiff at his sides. He wanted to be anywhere else but having his photograph taken. On the newsreader's other side, the blue-vested victor was all smiles. He stood loosely, in a slouch that was almost sexual, and his gaze – bright-eyed and knowing – met the camera full on. Behind the three figures was a jostle of bodies, among them Isaac Hepburn, a towel tucked into his tracksuit top, his smile pointing just where it should.

I laid the photo on the desk, next to the shattered frame. The desk had three drawers, each of them empty. The room smelled of rolling tobacco, the brownish whiff of Old Holborn. A tin ashtray held the skinny white dowts of three roll-ups. Two of the dowts were folded and crushed; the third was straight and a little longer than the others. Next to the ashtray a bottle of Bush and an empty shot glass. When I turned the glass over a drop slithered down to the rim. I raised the glass and shook it, took the hot, pill-sized fizz on my tongue. I unscrewed the bottle and filled the cap, a medicinal jolt, and tossed it back. It sizzled right down to my gut. It felt right at home. I gave it a friend and then re-screwed the cap.

The whiskey put a brighter slant on things and I breezed out of Hepburn's office and glanced through the rest of the rooms. I wasn't even sure what I was looking for. At first I was trying to find Hepburn. Then I thought I might find something I could use against him, a clue, some giveaway spoor of his criminal doings. The lounge bar was dark: a tiny marina of upturned chairs. The reception desk was tidy and bare. Nothing moved in the cool of the toilets; the urinals shone bluely and I walked down the row of stalls and pushed open every door.

Back in the gym I was heading for the fire door when I remembered the seats. The padded benches down one wall doubled as storage bins; their cushioned seats came off and boxing kit was stowed in the space underneath. When I lifted the first seat, the leatherette slurped as it came unstuck, and the reek billowed up – salty, urinous, the heady fermentations of sweat. A crumpled punchbag. A mound of gloves with laces agape. In the second was a stack of rubber mats and a white snarl of skipping ropes. Then I bent to the third.

It looked at first like a piece of kit, a punchbag or a rolled-up mat, but there was something in the roundness, some telltale slope or curve that made me reach into my pocket. By the Zippo's wavy flame I could see the rise of Hepburn's shoulders under the light-blue weave of Hepburn's jacket. I reached down for the grey hair and tugged on it. The head was the head of a deep-drowned man. The eyes rolled whitely, the lids half-closed like the eye of the beaten boxer in the photograph. There was a ligature of sorts, a cord or wire cutting into his neck. I dropped the Zippo and the seat clattered shut.

The sound cannoned through the empty gym. Was it just the seat banging shut or was it something else, a door closing in another part of the club? I hunched there on my knees, bracing myself against the silence. The wooden floor was biting into my knees but I held myself rigid, breathing in minuscule sips, until the panic died. I was halfway across the gym when I remembered my Zippo. I felt around on the floor in front of the benches. Nothing. It must have fallen in as the seat banged shut.

The seat eased up with another squelching kiss. The Zippo wasn't there. I slipped my hand between Hepburn's shoulder and the rim of the seat-box and started to paddle blindly with my fingers. They brushed something warm and metallic and I dragged it up against the wooden side until it clattered onto the floor. It gleamed in the darkness: the Zippo. I stowed it in my pocket and stood up. Then something occurred to me and I dropped to my knees again. I opened the lid once more and worked quickly through Hepburn's pockets.

There was a bunch of keys, a slippy pouch of rolling tobacco, a roll of dental floss, a box of matches, and a silvery clamshell phone. There was a wallet with the usual plastic and a sheaf of Ulsterbank twenties. At least they hadn't robbed him. I put the wallet and the money back with the rest of his things.

Back in the lounge I found a bar towel and worked my way through the rooms, rubbing the doorknobs and surfaces, the whiskey glass and bottle. I took the bar-towel with me when I left and wiped down the wheelie-bin's handles and lid, the windowsill, the back-doorknob.

It was colder now and darker in the alley. I stopped in the last patch of shadow, my guts sore with fear. Whoever had got to Hepburn might be coming back. Or they might still be here. But I still couldn't move. Every time I made to leave, the slam of a door or the hissing of tyres would flare out of the night. Then I'd wait so long that the silence itself took on a charged, suspicious air. If I didn't move soon I'd be stood there all night. Finally I blundered out, stumping like a fire-walker, and turned right. I'd gone five yards when a figure turned the corner up ahead. I tried to slow, to swing my gait a little, make it look like I'd been trudging for miles.

The walker came on. We were almost abreast. I caught a jagged, Cubist image of a face – pale-blue eye, a droopy grey moustache – before I dropped my head to check my watch. We passed without comment or sign but I sensed that he had stopped, that he was minded to hail me. My knees twitched, as if they might break loose of their own accord and send me sprinting free. At the corner I glanced back. The man stood on the pavement looking after me. I turned the corner briskly, crossed to the car, tugging the keys from my pocket, tugging so hard that the lining tore, and when the engine caught and I lurched from the kerb it was still in my nostrils, the reek of Hepburn's gym, the sour citric staleness of sweat.

Book Three

Chapter Twenty-One

The air in the newsroom was stale. The air-con was down and the open windows – great square affairs that tilted a mere six inches, like a man looking out for a bus – might just as well have been closed. I sat stock still at my desk. I used to find it easy to look busy when I wasn't. Now it was too much work. Now it was as wearisome to look busy as to be busy so I didn't try. I didn't try anything much but it was hard to ignore them. The smiles. The sympathetic nods. The solicitous looks. I could feel it like something physical, my dwindling status. Like the turn of a season it was vague but striking. A warmth, a vernal friendliness, from people who hated your guts. Nobody now was cursing my luck over lager tops at the Cope. Nobody now had me filling Rix's shoes. My fingers slumped on the keys. A bulb of sweat swayed down my spine. Neve McDonald clicked down the floor and the fullness of her buttocks, chewing past in a tight wool skirt, was like a calculated insult.

Fuck it. I had no stories, I had no leads, but I sat at my desk in the fetid heat and tallied them up, my dubious blessings. I was still alive. I was still in one piece, bar the ghost of a limp and a fading black eye. I thought about Isaac Hepburn. Hepburn in a kit-bin. Hepburn in a steel drawer. Hepburn in a wooden box. He never did get his thousand pounds. It hadn't quite worked to everyone's mutual advantage, this arrangement of ours. To his mutual advantage anyway. He tried to sell me Peter Lyons. Then somebody killed him. But were those facts connected? If he tried to sell Lyons then he must have sold other stuff too. And if he sold to me then he sold to somebody else. The guy was a tout and in my experience touts got rumbled. And when that happened, touts got hurt. From what Macpherson told me, half the Shankill was leery of Hepburn.

I remembered the way he spoke about the higher-ups, the Blackneck brass. Bacardi generals. Chocolate soldiers. He was cocky, Kiwi Hepburn: reckless and righteous. He bristled with entitlement. In his own eyes, he wasn't a tout. He felt they owed him and he was taking some of it back. And you couldn't blame him. A lot of guys did well for themselves while Hepburn was buffing his boots in a draughty Nissen hut. But you couldn't expect other people to see it like that.

I planted my elbows on the desk and slumped towards the machine, rigid fingers vizoring my face, the balls of my thumbs rotating my temples.

The cops had questioned me, of course. A PSNI detective flew over within days of Hepburn's death. I took him to the *Trib*'s cafeteria and he set his little Dictaphone on the sticky table. I had visited Isaac Hepburn in the week before his death. Was that right? It was. What was the purpose of my visit? He peered at me with professional intensity; a big flake of sugar from his yum-yum was stuck to his moustache. I told him I'd been working on a story. When I declined to say what it was he didn't insist. It didn't seem to matter. He turned the Dictaphone off and finished his yum-yum. It was a nothing case, he told me. They'd been waiting for this to happen. Hepburn was a tout. He'd also got smart-mouthed in two or three of the wrong pubs and said some careless things about former comrades. His finale was a surprise to no one.

'It might have been a surprise to Hepburn,' I said.

The cop picked the sugar from his moustache: 'It shouldn't have been.'

He thanked me for the coffee and left for his plane.

The heat was getting tiresome now. Sweat was spotting my silent keyboard. I sifted through the crap on my desk for a packet of tissues. The day's papers were scattered everywhere. That morning's *Scotsman* carried a piece by Kirsty Dewar. A crackdown on knife crime: stop-and-search powers to be upped throughout Strathclyde. The story had Lyons all over it. It should have been mine. It would have been mine – its pre-packaged sentences and banal quotations would have been up there on the screen, ready for Sunday's paper – if I'd never gone to Belfast. I tried to feel resentful about this but I knew it was all I deserved.

I didn't deserve to write a story. Last week I'd walked in on the biggest scoop of my career and I was too scared to touch it. I ought to have written the piece of my life. I ought to have sat down that night in the Grania and tapped out Sunday's splash. I ought at least to have called the police and given my statement. But I crept away from Hepburn's gym and drove up the Antrim Road like a sneak, like a timid adulterer. The houses were dark. It felt as though I were fleeing the city, as though a great catastrophe were coming and instead of raising the alarm I was slipping out through a wicket gate. Whenever I eased off the clutch my knee juddered wildly. There and then I decided: I'm telling no one. Nobody knew where I'd been. It was an impulse that had taken me to Hepburn's gym and not even Martin had known.

When I got back to Antrim on the night of Hepburn's death the farmhouse was dark but the porch was aglow with yellow light, like a glassy Tardis. I filled a tumbler with whiskey – it was Bush, the same brand as Hepburn's – and threw it back. I filled it again, right up to the brim, and carried it up to my room.

Next morning when I came down for breakfast Martin was hunched over the *News-Letter*, jabbing a fork at his plate like a painter stippling a canvas. I sat down at my place. Mrs Moir had made scrambled egg and the lumpy cooling mush on my plate – a morbid electric yellow – sent me scrambling to the sink. Afterwards I ran the cold tap and sluiced it all away, paddling my fingers in the mess to break it up. Then I turned my head beneath the icy flow.

In my sprint to the sink I had upset a chair. Sheepishly, I righted it and sat down. I must have a bug, I told Martin. I was sick, I was coming down with something. Martin buried his nose in his coffee and raised his eyebrows. He nodded to the worktop where the whiskey bottle stood beside its upturned cap. I gestured helplessly – the universal who-me shrug of the bang-to-rights busted. Moir went back to his paper.

After breakfast we took some air. In the stand of trees above the farm we caught our breath and lit stubby Bolivars. From up here the farmhouse looked forlorn and unconvincing, like the picture on a place mat.

'Would you ever come back?'

'You mean when the folks kick it?' He frowned and

rattled the matches in their box. 'I don't know. I doubt it.'

He dusted a patch of earth and eased himself down and lay back, propped on his elbows. 'At one time I thought I would never come back. Or just for Christmas and holidays.' He shielded his eyes from the sun. 'Now? I don't know. Things have changed, but still. Would you bring up kids here?'

'No. I wouldn't.'

'Clare would never wear it anyway. It's nice, though.' He waved his cigar at the landscape. 'All this. We moved out here when I was fourteen. My mum worried about security, the isolation. But of course it was much safer than town.'

They lived in Coleraine, he told me. When Moir's father drove him to school in the mornings, he varied their route. A different permutation every day. As Moir threw his satchel in the back, his dad was on his knees on the pavement, checking the underside of the car. They didn't go to restaurants in Coleraine. If they wanted to visit the swimming baths or the pictures they drove to another town. Sometimes they drove west, crossing the border. That was the tremendous irony that shadowed his childhood, the truth that the family could never acknowledge: the only time they felt safe, the only time they felt normal, was in the other country, the hated Free State.

'The doorbell.' Moir sat up, remembering. 'From I was yay-high, from I was a tiny wee lad, I knew that the doorbell was trouble. The doorbell would ring and everything stopped. Ma turning off the telly. Da standing at the window, peering through the net curtains. It was the postman. Or the gasman. Or a guy with a red-white-and-blue

263

rosette. And my da would stamp off down the hall to open the door, breathing through his nose.'

He sighed and stood up, squinting out to sea.

'What's the word, then?' I said eventually. 'What happened yesterday?'

Moir had seen him again, he told me: the ponytailed Scot, Maitland's lieutenant. He dogged him from a drinking club in Donegall Pass to a coffee shop near the university and on to a crime bookstore on Botanic Avenue. The guy browsed the Elmore Leonards and bought a James M. Cain. Moir followed him to a spruce B & B on the Lisburn Road, waited in the car for half an hour and then came home. He couldn't keep tailing the guy on the off chance that something might happen.

He stubbed his cigarillo on a tree. We walked back down to the farmhouse in silence. Finally, grudgingly, he asked for my own news. I told him about Emer Derwent. Yes, there was a second man and the man could well have been Lyons. But so what? How could she identify him at this distance? It was hopeless. Perhaps if the gunman was still around – he succumbed to lung cancer in 1999, a bare year after his release – there might have been a chance, but I'd been working on this story for over a week and all I had now was what I began with: a photograph and an old-fashioned hunch. I also had an old-fashioned body, a dead former Loyalist Godfather, but that wasn't part of my story. We had come to the end of the line. 'SLÁN ABHAILE': I remembered of the words on the Ardoyne mural: 'TIME TO GO'.

There's something intimate about cowardice, something deeply and shamefully yours. A virtuous act is impersonal; it belongs to us all. 'I just did what anyone would have done' is the stock response of your have-a-go hero. But cowardly acts aren't like that. They carry your tang, your DNA; they are knit tight into your flesh. When we boarded the ferry that afternoon my cowardice hung about me like the smell of shit. I was surprised that other people couldn't smell it, didn't shy away in righteous disgust.

I'd like to pretend there was some other motive. Some misgiving, a sense of propriety, some diligent qualm that stopped me writing about Hepburn. What I found in the kit-box, I might have decided, wasn't a scoop or a page one lead. It was a dead human being. A human being who had stood me drinks and revealed his unexpected love of trees and – OK – cracked my face on the hood of a car and tried to extort a thousand pounds.

But I'm a journalist.

Isaac Hepburn was all of these things. Isaac Hepburn was also a story. His death in a sweat-stained boxing gym: that was my bread and butter. What stopped me was fear. If I wrote the story my status would change. I would cease to be a bystander, an impartial spectator; I would step into the story – if I wasn't there already – and who knew what might happen? The kit-box wasn't just Hepburn's coffin: it was a portal, another innocent-looking stick of furniture – looking glass, wardrobe – that led you into a secret realm. In the stories, the hero tends to take a breather on this threshold, weighing the lures of alternate worlds, before pushing through to a fabulous fate. I paused too. But because I'm a coward and not a hero I gently lowered the kit-box lid and skulked away from the gym.

I had closed the door. I'd come home to Scotland, glad

as hell to roll off the ferry onto Galloway soil. Still, though, there was a question of accounting, of tallying the cost. Financially, things were clear enough. I had squandered a couple of grand, depleting by another few mites the *Tribune*'s dwindling war chest, and I couldn't come up with a story. I could live with that. The moral account, though, was less cut and dry. I had tramped through Belfast for a week, sowing confusion, salting old sores. Had I done any good? Had I left the city better than I found it?

The word 'truth' comes in handy at junctures like this. I'd been seeking the truth. But even the worst redtop goon, the crummiest door-stepping keyholing scum-sucker, was better than me. He didn't pretend to be George Washington. He didn't care about the truth. He hurt people. He messed up their lives. He boosted his paper's sales. I hurt people too, but I hurt them in the name of truth, so that was OK. But the truth didn't help Mrs Gillies. The truth didn't help Emer Derwent. And nothing I did had made anything better.

I fetched a can of Coke from the vending machine and pressed it to my neck, rolling it backwards and forwards till the chill wore off and the can was slippy with sweat and condensation. Forget the whole thing is what I wanted to do. Go back to the turgid round of committee reports and Garden Lobby briefings and the childish contentions at FMQs. But when I turned to my empty screen I kept seeing Emer's wee boy, poking out from behind his mother's skirt, and I kept seeing a curly-haired man with a chubby little girl in his arms and wondering what he would do when the shutter clicked.

The story I wanted wasn't the story of Hepburn's

death. The story I wanted was whatever had happened in 1983, whatever Peter Lyons had seen or done on the damp winter streets of Belfast. And that story was closed off, sealed up, a tin missing its label. I'd been close to the story – at times it had seemed like the fading shape of a dream or a word on the tip of my tongue – but I couldn't reach it. I thought of the blank brick wall of the *Citizen* building, the blind frontage of the Northern Star Athletic Club. Belfast was that kind of place. You had to know what you were looking for before you could find it.

The cursor pulsed on the snowy screen. I didn't even cover the death, Hepburn's killing. We were on our way home when the story broke. Moir took a call on the ferry. He stalked off down the observation deck, slowing and speeding up and then slowing again as he took in the details. 'We have to go back,' he told me. 'Turn right around and go straight back across.' I spat over the railing. Ireland had vanished, the eye no longer able to partition land from sky. What good would it do? I asked him. Would it turn back time? Would we get there before the story broke? Face it, I told him: we've missed the story. We didn't get the story we came for and we've missed the story we could have got. Let's give it up as a bad job. In the end we had a bite to eat in Stranraer and drove on up to Glasgow.

John Rose did the story, filed eight hundred words the following day. You had to admire his cheek.

Moir didn't have time to brood. He was busy again with his gangland stuff. His team were preparing another splash. They were in the office more often now, the Hey You, talking strategy with Rix, working out the angles. They stayed in character, lounging on desks in their jeans and stressed leathers, popping gum and rubbing their four-day beards. They swaggered to the lift in loose formation. People kept out of their way, flattened themselves against corridor walls.

The heat was vicious. I was mopping my breastbone with a hankie when Moir stepped out of the lift. He was pointing right at me, grinning and wagging his finger. He bounced over, laughing, and gripped my bicep. He was pumped, his pupils as fat as a cat's.

'We've got him! Gerry, we've only got him!'

I buttoned my shirt.

'Who? Maitland? When?'

'No, Gerry. Lyons! We've got Peter Lyons!'

He laughed again.

'Come here!' He hauled me out of my seat and pulled me over to his desk.

'Watch this.' He commandeered a chair and pushed me into it. He drew his own chair in and tapped his space bar.

'You ready? Watch this.'

He scrolled through some emails and found the one he wanted. He clicked on a thumbnail photo and it scaled up onto the screen. He turned the screen towards me.

A big bay window framed the shot. Two men in conversation over a low coffee table. The one on the left wore glasses that caught the light, but the hair and nose and the bandsman's jawline left no doubt: it was Peter Lyons. The other had a ponytail. His glossy black shirt looked oddly familiar.

'It's not, is it?'

'Our friend from the bowling alley? You got it in one. William James Torrins; racketeer, enforcer, bad-bastard-in-chief to our beloved Walter Maitland.'

'And boon companion of the Minister for Justice.'

I looked at Martin. His grin just kept getting wider.

'When was this?'

'Yesterday evening at six o'clock.'

'Fucking dancer! Congratulations, Martin.'

Moir looked suddenly solemn.

'This is yours, Gerry. This is your story. You're going to write it. You have to write it.'

I stood up. The castors squeaked as I wheeled the chair back to its proper desk.

'Did Rix put you up to this?'

'C'mon, Gerry.'

'This is Rix's idea.' I turned to face him. 'You never hear of a dry patch, Martin? I thought you were bigger than this. Here's a thought: whyn't you let me write my own stories, all right? And you write your own. How does that sound?'

'This is your story.' He gripped my shoulder. His smile was expansive, evangelical. 'This is *your* story. You set it up, Gerry, you put us onto Lyons. All I did was keep my eyes open.'

'You kept your eyes open.'

'I did. I tailed him. Ever since Belfast I've been on the guy's case. He was at Maitland's place this morning. When he left I tailed him. I had a hunch' – he laughed at the cop-show idiom. 'I had a hunch and when he got to Bearsden I knew it was good. I thought he might be headed for the Drum but he drove right into Bearsden. I tailed him to a big villa on Roman Road and belled Gavin Doig. He took that with a long lens without leaving the car. Gerry, it's your story.'

Four hours later the story was done. It was my story

now. It had my meanness and spite salted through it. It fairly shone with crooked irony. It was full of words like 'complicity' and 'clandestine' and 'conflict of interest'. I made no allegations but I managed to make it plain that the Justice Minister was in the gangster's pay. I mentioned the famous suits, the hand-tooled brogues, the collection of contemporary Scottish art. I mentioned the Havana cigars. I mentioned the seventy-pound haircuts. (Last Easter Lyons's wife had sent him for a haircut and he spent the first ten minutes of a lunch date at Ferrante's bitching about the price.) Aspersions, hints, asides, insinuations: the piece was a shiny cage of gossamer threads, each of them tied to the photograph, the image that would 'rock to its tottering base the ruling coalition and quiver the collective backbone of the Scottish legal establishment'. Torrins became Maitland's *consigliere* and I catalogued (with help from Moir) the juiciest items on Maitland's CV. I called in my contacts and lined up the quotes. I had an unnamed QC declaring that Lyons should resign. I had an unnamed cabinet colleague intimating the same. I had the Nationalists demanding that Parliament be recalled so that Lyons might make a statement to the house. 'There may be a perfectly innocent explanation for all this,' the QC observed in my closing par. 'But we sure as hell need to hear it.'

The story was done. It was Friday afternoon: the desk would get it legalled tomorrow. The last thing to do was to contact Lyons and give him right of reply. I didn't want to do it. For two years, on any given Sunday, Peter Lyons had known without opening the paper at least one of the stories that would go out in my name. I wanted to damage Peter Lyons, I wanted to hurt him. But more than that I wanted to surprise him. I wanted his phone to ring on Saturday midnight. I wanted his people to get him out of bed: 'Have you seen the paper?' I wanted to have him jump in his car and drive to an all-night garage, to stand there in the forecourt with the paper in his hands, lost to the shouting drunks and passing cars, the distant whine of sirens. But that could only happen if he didn't know what was coming. I didn't want to phone him but I knew I had to.

I had his mobile number, of course, and his home numbers in Glasgow and Edinburgh. But I was going to do this by the book. I checked my watch: four o'clock. What I ought to do now was phone the Government Press Office at Victoria Quay and ask for the Justice Desk. Then the Justice Desk's director, or one of his junior POs, would take my details and contact Lyons. In an hour or so, Lyons would call back. I'd tell him what we were going to run and he'd give his comment.

That's what I should have done. What I did instead was answer some emails, shut down my Mac and go for a walk. The sun was still warm and a nice breeze came up off the river. I slung my jacket over my shoulder and walked right into town, into the cool high canyons of the city centre, the big blocks of glass and steel and shadowed sandstone. I walked right up Hope Street in bright sunshine and onto Sauchiehall Street. A busker with an electric guitar and a baby amp was playing 'Three Times a Fool' by Otis Rush and I stopped to listen. I'd been planning to walk to the Mitchell and say hello to Doug Haddow but I cut up Rose Street to the GFT.

I sat in the GFT bar with a bottle of Beck's. An Italian film was starting in forty minutes. I had another Beck's and bought some chocolate raisins at the kiosk and took my seat. The film was good. It was a Mafia movie with almost no action. A stylish, well-groomed middle-aged man is living in a Swiss hotel. He doesn't do much. He walks the corridors, takes his meals, plays cards with an elderly bankrupt couple who used to own the hotel. Sometimes he phones home, but his kids never want to talk and he has nothing to say to his wife. Mainly what he does is smoke cigarettes with ferocious, disdainful elegance and stare gloomily out of the window. And once a week he takes a suitcase full of money to a bank and has the tellers count the contents by hand.

Piece by piece, we learn his story. Eight years ago, the man was working as a broker. He made a catastrophic loss on the stock exchange. The money he lost belonged to the Mob. To pay them back he is living this half-life, cut off from his family, holed up in the barren luxury of a Swiss hotel, toting his valises to the bank. The Mob knows he didn't mean to lose the money, so they haven't killed him; but they haven't let him live properly either. He's in limbo, and he shows no real interest in redeeming his life until a waitress at the hotel begins to talk to him. Normally he's rude and uncommunicative with the hotel staff but this girl gets under his guard. He falls in love. And this man, who for eight years has shown no emotion, no spark of volition, decides to act. He knows it's hopeless, he knows he can't beat the syndicate, but he acts anyway. When a pair of renegade gangsters steals one of the suitcases, he shoots them dead. But he doesn't give the money to the Mob. He keeps it. He buys the waitress a new BMW. Finally he's summoned to Sicily to explain himself. Modestly but resolutely he explains his position: he is keeping the money. The Mob have taken enough of his life; he is taking the money as compensation. The gangsters are perplexed, bewildered. In the end, irritably, almost reluctantly, they kill him.

After the movie I walked up Garnethill, past the Art School to Charing Cross. I stopped for a drink in the Arlington Bar. Further up Woodlands Road I stopped again at the Halt. In the lounge I met a guy from my old five-a-side team. I bought him a drink and he bought one back. After a while we started on the whisky and pretty soon it was shutting time. I walked home, stopping at the Philly for a fish supper.

Next morning I was fragile. It was after ten before I made it to the office. At lunchtime Martin Moir stopped by the desk.

'What did he say then?'

'Who, Lyons? I don't know, I'm still waiting to hear from him.'

At ten to three Fiona Maguire came over and asked the same question.

'I'm on it,' I told her. 'I'll let you know.'

At quarter past three I went out for a smoke.

At half-past three I dialled the number.

'Victoria Quay, Security.'

The civil servants don't work weekends. On Saturdays the building's normally empty apart from security personnel. I asked the guard to page the duty press officer. He took my name and details.

'What's it in respect of, Mr Conway?'

'It's a query for Justice,' I told him.

'Let me try the desk,' he said, and then twenty seconds later: 'There's no answer from Justice.'

'Maybe it's deaf as well as blind,' I said. Calls are logged anyway, but there was no harm making sure the guy would remember me. He said he would page the duty officer. Now I just had to sit and wait.

When you leave it this late there's always a chance. There's a chance that the PO doesn't get the message. There's a chance he can't get a hold of the subject. That was the best case scenario. Even if Lyons did get the message, it would come too late. He'd have no time to dream up a story. I hung around for half an hour then I went to the canteen.

I lingered as long as I could over a chewy bagel and hazel-nut latte. Back at my desk there was no blinking light on the phone. There were no new emails, nothing on the mobile. I called up the story and shined it a little.

'Any joy?'

Maguire was back.

'I think he's hiding, Fiona. He's in the bunker. I put in the call to Victoria Quay and there's still no word.'

She lifted a snowman from my desk – a botched ceramic thing that Roddy had made in school – and turned it over in her hands.

'We can't run the story, Gerry. If we don't get a comment we're pulling it, OK?'

'But he's hiding, Fiona. He knows I'm looking for him.'

'You called him when?'

'Earlier on. This afternoon. Look, I don't see–'

'What time, Gerry?'

'I don't know. Three o'clock.'

She glanced at the base of the snowman then replaced it on my desk. She wiped her fingers lightly, and delicately sighed.

'Stop pissing about, Gerry. Phone his mobile. Do your job.'

He answered on the sixth or seventh ring.

'Peter, it's me: Gerry Conway.'

'Hold on.' I could hear him closing a door, setting a glass on a table.

'I've been trying to get a hold of you,' I said. 'I phoned you earlier.'

'That's right. You phoned Victoria Quay. At half-past three on a Saturday afternoon. I'm assuming that it couldn't possibly relate to a story in this week's paper or you would have phoned me long before now.'

'Yeah, well, you assumed wrong, Peter. It's about a story.'

'I see. Have you stopped giving right of reply? Does Barbara Tennant know about this?'

'I'm talking to you now, amn't I?'

'You certainly are. I take it you think you've found something in Belfast?'

'A little nearer home, Peter. We've got a photo–'

'Another photo! Jesus, Gerry, you've missed your vocation. You ought to be working in Boots. With a wee white labcoat. What is this one? A wedding party? A First Communion?'

'It's a more of a portrait, actually. The Minister relaxes. You're entertaining at home. Your guest's name escapes me at the moment. He's about thirty-five, wears a ponytail. Oh yeah: he's called William Torrins.'

Lyons said nothing. I could hear laughter in the background, a door swinging shut.

'You can't place the name? Maybe you've heard of his boss. Fella called Maitland? He's nearly as famous as you.' Lyons had forgotten to breathe. 'You still with us, Minister?'

'What are you doing with this, Gerry?'

'We're doing a story. We want you to comment.'

The breathing was back.

'Look,' he said finally. 'I'm not going to comment on this just now. Hold off and I'll talk to you next week. I'll give you the story next week. That's a promise.'

'Give me it now.'

'I can't do that, Gerry. There's things I need to sort out. I need to talk to people. There's an explanation for all this. That's all I can say. Just trust me, Gerry. Hold off for now.'

'We're running the story.'

'If you're running the story you're running the story. But if I were you, Gerry, I would hold off.'

'Thank you, Minister.'

I talked it through with Maguire and Rix. Maguire didn't like it.

'Why didn't he phone back when you called Victoria Quay? Why's he not demanding to see the copy? Why is Kenny fucking Wolfe not bending our ear? He's playing us, Norman. The prick's up to something.'

'Of course he's up to something.' I turned to Rix. 'He wants to kill the story for a week till he works out his excuses. What the fuck, Norman: take a flyer.'

Rix looked at me. 'A week?' he said. 'He wants a fucking week?' A sneer bunched his cheeks. His vowels were getting longer, more London. 'Come off it, Fi, he's fucking about.' He folded his arms. He was wearing a white shirt, a shirt so white it threw a strip-light glare, seemed louder, somehow, than the others he sported, the lemons, the scarlets, the pinks. 'Cunt's at it. He wants a week to make up a story and wriggle out of it. Fuck this. Gerry: file the story.'

I added a single sentence to the final par: 'The *Tribune on Sunday* approached Mr Lyons for his views, but the Justice Minister declined to comment.'

Then I filed it to the newsdesk.

Chapter Twenty-Two

We put the paper to bed at seven-thirty. I was eating out that night – I'd been invited to a dinner party near Charing Cross – so I went home to shower and change. The dinner was a boisterous affair. I brought some stupidly expensive wine – two bottles of Central Otago pinot – and half-a-dozen push-the-boat-out Romeo y Julieta Churchills, which were snatched up by the men and two of the women as soon as the poached pear galettes had been despatched. It's hard to remain sedate and even-handed with a foot of smouldering Havana in your fist and before long we were going at it, waving our arms, shouting each other down and flapping at the smoke the better to jab imperative fingers, quoting stray lines of Scorsese, hogging the biscuits and cheese, lobbing grapes in each other's wine and shrieking at Logan's impression of Norman Rix.

Someone nipped out at eleven, returning with an armful of *Tribune on Sunday*s. These were passed out round the table with the night air still cold on their folds and we all fell silent for a moment as if a new party game had been coined. 'Minister and the Mobster' was the headline. I got the byline, with 'additional reporting' from Martin Moir. There were grunts and appreciative snorts and then, as if on some sort of cue, nine or ten newspapers folded at once amid general drunken acclamation.

More pinot was splashed into glasses and a ragged round of toasts was proposed. There was 'The Lyons Tamer', 'The Editor in Waiting' and others equally silly. Tam Logan got up on a chair and pledged 'The Brave Men and Women of the Ulster Volunteer Force'. I looked over at Moir but he was laughing hard and he scraped to his feet with his arm braced on a chair back and roared out 'For God and Ulster!' The others liked the sound of this and for the next hour conversation was intermittently pierced by this hollered slogan and we'd all hoist our glasses in the air.

At one point a fireworks display banged and whistled into life and we watched from the big bay window the bursting colours over Cowcaddens, glittering detonations in the tones of Christmas tinsel.

It was three o'clock, the party still in loud disputatious flow when I escaped, a half-full bottle of pinot sloshing against my thigh. 'For God and Luster!' came the slurred shout from an open window and I flapped my free hand and tramped away towards St George's Cross.

The wine purled sweetly in my gut alongside the Bolognese and the pear galettes, and the story, too, seemed lodged there in my belly, a round warm source of nourishment and succour. The Churchill on my tongue, its aftertaste of warm vanilla mixing with the cool night air, was like the savour of accomplishment.

Cabs shushed past like a parade of bowler hats but the night was fine and I kept on walking. At Holyrood Crescent an ebullient Goth swapped a handful of chips for a slug of wine and then a trio of lurching herberts in Ben Sherman checks arm-locked me into a block-long rendition of 'Danny Boy'. A spirit of carnival bonhomie had taken possession of Great Western Road. The bouncers were smiling. A flat race had broken out beside Kelvinbridge Underground: two whooping lassies on their boyfriends' shoulders jiggled and jounced up the white line, spurring their staggering mounts with heel-digs and slaps. Even the bearded jakey huddled near the Underground on a filthy tartan rug was happy. Someone had given him a kebab, and a grey-whiskered, tail-thumping Lab was sharing the spoils. I leaned down and placed my third-full bottle of pinot on his rug and the jakey looked up and smiled, the most beatific, gorgeous smile. Beneath the grime and greasy hair he was shockingly handsome – strong teeth and pale clear eyes: the Jesus of Kelvinbridge.

Across the bridge my path was blocked by a hen party, a clacking, shimmering, hooting confusion of shoulder straps and Shalimar, lipstick and gravelled laughter. The bride-to-be was jostled in their midst, her quilted jacket thickly sewn with tissue-paper roses, the blues and greens and whites and pinks, her Bo-Peep bonnet winningly askew. She carried a chanty hung with L-plates, and her gaggle of strappy-sandalled handmaidens shoved her towards me. It was £2 for a kiss and I found a fiver and dropped it in the chanty. 'Give him his money's worth!' somebody shouted and when Bo-Peep's sheepish osculation was over one of the henchwomen thrust her aside and shouted that she would make up the difference, probing my throat with her strenuous tongue while the whooping and cheering crescendo'd around us.

Outside one of the clubs a sleepy-looking doorman distributed flyers: 'Sunday Night is Funk Night'. One of the hen party swooped past and snatched the whole wad from his grasp and, with the gesture of freeing a bird, launched them into the air. For two or three seconds they tickertaped round us, rippling and swooping like dayglo dollar bills and the punters who had up till now ignored them were suddenly in full pursuit, snatching them in fistfuls and tossing them back in the air, kicking through the dayglo leaves.

Every two or three blocks the gold lighted windows of Pakistani grocers gleamed like caves in the tenement cliffs. I stopped at the last one for milk and rolls and two chicken samosas and a *Tribune on Sunday* and every other Sunday paper.

'You are planning a long lie,' said the shopkeeper with a mock-forensic air as I lodged the bale of newsprint in my armpit and walked out into the night.

Inside the flat I buttered two rolls and put the samosas inside. Somewhere between the party and my flat I'd been garlanded with a pink Hawaiian lei. I hung it on my utensils rack. I poured a glass of milk and sat at the kitchen table.

The samosas were good – peppery and moist, with big potato cubes and hard little peas – and I slurped two glasses of milk while I ate them.

None of the papers – not one of them – carried the story. I looked again in case I'd missed it. A little knot started forming in my stomach, tightening as the pages turned. Why had they left it alone? As soon as a first edition hits the street, the other Sundays have it taxied to their office. If there's anything big in another paper, you just lift it. You switch things about a bit and call your own contacts for a quote and then you put it out as your own story. The tabloids do the same thing but slap

'Exclusive' on it too. The other Sundays would have seen the story, which meant they'd preferred not to touch it.

I stood at the kitchen window and thought about this and smoked a Café-Crème and decided: big deal. It was nice to knock Moir off the front page, if only for a week. I swilled the last inch of milk, wadded the papers into a slippy newsprint log and dropped it into the pedal bin. I set the alarm for nine and went to bed.

I woke at 8:59 and waited for the numbers to change and the Radio Scotland news to come on. It was pretty far down the running order – maybe the fourth or fifth item – but at least it was there. *Justice Minister Peter Lyons is under fire after an alleged secret meeting with a Glasgow criminal.* The phrasing of the item was pedantically circumspect – 'According to the *Tribune on Sunday*', 'The newspaper alleges'. What they were reporting was not the incident but the allegation. But at least they hadn't ignored it.

I turned off the radio and got to work. I emptied the ashtrays and opened the windows and put all the paperbacks back on their shelves. I emptied and stacked the dishwasher. I took the rubbish down to the back green. I rinsed the bath and squirted thick green liquid under the rim of the toilet. The boys arrived as I was hoovering the living room.

'Dad!' James was wrestling out of his jacket. 'Dad, I got a set-, a setter-. What is it again, Mum?'

'A certificate.'

'Dad, I got a certificate! It says I'm a dolphin.'

'That's great, son.'

'Everyone's a dolphin,' Roddy said. 'You don't even have to dive.'

Elaine checked herself in the hall mirror, rubbing lipstick off her teeth. She was wearing a sleeveless print dress patterned with languid, sexual poppies. Her heels, belt, bag, nails and lipstick were a blatant glossy red.

'You look nice.'

'Thanks.'

They were driving to a wedding in Dundee, which is why they were able to drop off the boys. They would pick them up tomorrow on their way back to Conwick.

'Adam in the car?'

'Yeah, we're double-parked. He says hello. So what's the plan for today?'

'I don't know. Hello back, by the way. What do you think, boys?'

The boys looked at each other.

'Swimming!' shouted James. They thundered through to the living room and the telly's strident contention started up.

'Heavy night?'

'How's that?'

She leaned towards me and sniffed. Her own smell – or anyway that of her perfume, an overripe musk that might have seeped from those lurid poppies – reached me.

'I had a glass or two,' I said. 'In celebration.'

'Yeah, I saw the piece,' she said. 'Roddy, don't put your jacket on the floor!'

'And?'

'Yeah.' She bent to retrieve Rod's jacket. 'It was very well done.' She smoothed out the jacket and draped it on a chair.

'But?'

'But. I don't know, Gerry. The guy's your *friend*.'

'He's not my friend! For Christ's sake, Elaine. He's a contact. He came to the house a couple of times. Jesus. And so what? What if he was my friend? I turn a blind eye? I don't write the story?'

'I don't know.'

'The guy in the photo? He works for Walter Maitland, Elaine. Walter Maitland the gangster? The guy's a criminal, a flat-out bad guy. And our Minister for Justice is meeting him for drinkies? I mean, for Christ's sake.'

'Oh that's nice, Gerry.' She nodded at the living-room door. 'You want them saying that in the playground? All I know is Peter Lyons was very nice to us. He's been good to you, too.'

'OK. Thanks, Elaine. Why don't you leave the editorial comments to me. All right?'

Roddy came through with the Hawaiian lei round his neck. He was doing a hula dance. Elaine looked at me. She hitched her shoulder bag.

'You be good now, boys. I'll see you tomorrow. Give your mum a kiss.' She went to the window and waved down to Adam. 'Can you have them back for twelve? Adam's folks are coming for lunch.'

'Message received.'

I took them swimming. Before we left I tried to catch five minutes of the lunchtime politics show but the boys were eager to get to the pool.

After the swimming we went for burgers.

'I want it. I want the green one!'

James reached over the tabletop, clutching for the plastic toy. Rod held it out of his reach.

'Want the green one! Want the *green* one!'

Every time we come here there's a fight over the toys, the hunks of plastic junk that come with the food.

'Just give him it, kid. Would you?'

Roddy couldn't believe it.

'What does it matter, Roddy? He's just a wee boy. Keep him happy.'

'Fine!' The toy skittered onto the table and James snatched it up. Roddy folded his arms in a comic-book huff. 'Why does *he* always get what he wants? I never get anything.' He leaned across to his brother. '*Idiot.*'

'Hi! Less of that.' I should have given him a proper row but I only had a day and a bit with them now and there wasn't time to waste on falling out.

He threw me a look.

'Hey. C'mon. We're having fun, right?'

I passed out the food. I put a straw in James's Sprite carton, unwrapped his cheeseburger and made a tear in his bag of fries. In its warm wrapper, my burger felt soft and moist – it seemed to grow heavier as I held it, lique-fying in my palm, its fibres collapsing. I put it down and opened my coffee.

As I knew it would be, the coffee was scalding, and though I tried to take the slightest of sips, merely vacu-uming the topmost layer of liquid with a short intake of breath, it was enough to burn my mouth. The groove of my tongue was throbbing.

The boys brought skinny fries to their mouths. In the kitchens, a fat server in a maroon polo shirt was moving back and forth. No one in the restaurant was talking.

'So. Roddy. James. Carradale: we all set?'

I was taking them in a week's time, their rearranged trip.

'Suppose so,' said Roddy. 'Are you really taking us this time?'

James looked up for the answer: big unblinking serious eyes.

'Of course I am, son. Look, I'm not going to let you down this time. I promise.'

They nodded and bent to their food, and the silence washed back in and swamped us. It has to do with the lighting, I thought, and with the absence of plates and knives and forks. It generates a lassitude, like you're not eating properly so why make the effort to talk? It's like the lethargy of a long car journey once the conversation has petered out.

Finally James spoke up.

'Dad?'

'Yes, kid?'

'Is there bunk beds in Carradale?'

'I don't know, kid. Maybe.'

'I'm having the top one. If there is.'

I looked sharply at Roddy and he bit back whatever he was going to say. I took a swig of coffee. Probably it was cool enough by now, if I hadn't burned my mouth.

The restaurant was more than half empty. *Have It Your Way* read the signs along the wall. *You're the Boss.* At a table near the door, a man and his son sat in companionable silence, chewing, reaching for their drinks. Why was I so scared of silence? Why this need to fill things up with talk? A surge of sympathy, of maudlin solidarity for the chomping boy's father – like me, I decided, a Sunday dad – surged through me.

My phone rang loudly and I fumbled for it. My fingers are too chunky for the little phone pockets they have in

286

jackets and I have to tweezer the thing out between two forefingers or else squeeze it up with my fingers and thumbs like a man losing grip of the soap. It was Moir. He offered his congratulations.

'It was your story, Martin.'

'No, I'm serious. You did a great job.'

'Well.' The door opened and a woman with what looked to be pillows in her shopping bags struggled through. 'It's nice of you to say.'

'I'm a little surprised, though.'

'That no one picked it up? I know. What's that about?'

'You want me to phone my guy at the *Record*, see if they'll run with it? I could give them the photo as well.'

The woman made for the table with the father and son. She kissed them and sat down, settling her bags on an empty seat.

'Could you, Martin? I've got to go.'

The next morning we slept late. I made scrambled egg and listened to Five Live while the boys squabbled over DVDs.

'Choose one you both want to watch.'

When the noise started to swamp Victoria Derbyshire I went through to sort it out. James was trying to place a DVD in the open tray and Roddy was blocking his way.

'If you put that on you're not coming to Brandon's party with me.'

'Yes, I am!'

'No, you're not.'

'Dad said I could go!'

'Hey! I never said anything of the kind.'

They looked at each other. 'The other dad,' said Roddy.

'Oh. Right. Well, that makes sense. Why don't you watch Laurel and Hardy?'

They did. They'd always loved Laurel and Hardy. It was one of my few parenting triumphs. When I was still at the house I'd made it my mission to convert them. Two or three times a week after dinner, I'd put one of the shorts or maybe *A Chump at Oxford* or *Way Out West*. They'd both become hooked. They knew whole routines off by heart. I left them guffawing at *Brats* and went through to butter the toast.

Elaine and Adam arrived at noon. They stayed for coffee. The wedding was fine, Elaine said, but the guests had spent a chilly half-hour on the pavement, with hotel bathrobes over their pyjamas, when the fire alarm sounded at three in the morning.

'There she was,' Elaine said, 'on her wedding night. Out on the street with no slap and her hair in a scrunchie.'

'It's a wedding night they'll never forget,' said Adam. He was obviously hungover. That apart, he didn't look too good. There were swathes of grey in his limp black hair and his profile, when he stood up to stretch, was gratifyingly paunchy.

I caught Elaine's eye and nodded at Adam's belly. She shook her head – *would you ever grow up* – and rattled her car keys.

'Say goodbye to your dad, boys.'

James rushed into my outstretched arms and I straightened up, his arms in the quilted anorak tight round my ears, his knees squeezing my ribs. Roddy's hug was slacker. Already he was growing distant, contained. Even his wave, as the car pulled off, was lazy, a louche flourish, next to James's eager, clockwork to-and-fro.

The day was breezy and fine. On Great Western Road I bought another armful of newsprint and this time the shopowner confined himself to a knowing tilt of the head. Moir's contact had come through: Lyons was on the *Record*'s front page: 'MOB JUSTICE'. I read it as I walked. They had the shot of Lyons and Torrins; on the inside pages the UVF colour party and the ancient photo of Lyons in a sash. They'd given it a good show. None of the other papers carried the story at all – I went through them front to back at the kitchen table – but at least now we weren't alone.

On Monday night I went to bed early. I woke with the phone ringing.

'Shit, Gerry.' It was Moir again. The alarm said 12:53. 'That guy with Lyons: William Torrins? He's not a gangster at all.'

I closed my eyes. My brain sifted the possibilities and came up with the answer as Moir said it.

'He's a cop.'

Chapter Twenty-Three

I slid right down and pulled the duvet over my head.

'Fuck.'

'I know. My guy in Justice phoned me. Lyons is holding a press conference tomorrow. I thought you'd like to know. I'm sorry, Gerry.'

'Thanks, Martin.'

Fuck. I got back out of bed. I opened a beer and sat at the table.

The bastard had known. He let us run the story. He let us run it, knowing that once the truth came out it would hurt me more.

I barely slept that night. I sat up with the quilt around me, drinking Rolling Rock and watching *The Sopranos*. I woke on the sofa with a neck that seemed less cricked than broken. I felt like I'd been hanged.

The press conference was scheduled for eleven, in time for the lunchtime bulletins. I was tempted to go along, sit there in the front row, do my penance on the cutty stool, but I couldn't face it. I made it into the office at five to eleven. The telly was on, the whole newsroom waiting for the broadcast. Neve McDonald pointed the remote and turned up the volume.

When they cut from the studio, the press conference had started.

'For any politician these would be serious allegations.'

Lyons is at a lectern, gripping its sides. 'For a Minister for *Justice*' – a little blitz of hissing – 'they are doubly grave.'

Here he pauses; a big deep breath.

'I therefore have no option but to reveal that William Torrins' – he relishes the name, rolls it around his mouth – 'is a serving police officer. *And* a witness in a criminal case being drawn up by the Crown Office. This case has been in preparation for many months, and has involved much painstaking work by police and prosecutors. As Justice Minister, I have taken a direct and personal interest in the case. I asked DS Torrins to brief me on the state of the inquiry, and that is why he was visiting my home.'

Another pause; Lyons scans the bent heads of the press pack. Now he looks like a dominie, an old-school heidie at morning assembly.

'DS Torrins is currently in hiding. William Torrins is a very brave man, a man who volunteered to infiltrate a dangerous criminal network operating in the East End of Glasgow. He is now in fear of his life and has been moved, with his wife and children, to a safe address.

'Through his irresponsible and reckless style of journalism, Mr Conway has not only compromised a major criminal investigation; he has jeopardised the safety – indeed he has endangered the life – of a serving police officer.

'Now' – here's the toss of the hair, the trademark angry flick – 'let me make one thing perfectly clear.' A long lull as Lyons scans the heads once more and lets the silence deepen. 'The freedom of the press is a value very dear to my heart. A functioning democracy – and especially a new democracy, like our own – depends for its effectiveness on a free and fearless press. Politicians *should* be subject to robust scrutiny. But there is a world of difference' – here he shakes his head, and holds up his finger – 'a *world* of difference between robust scrutiny and the kind of scurrilous innuendo peddled by Mr Conway.

'Organised crime' – another finger; he's not a dominie any more, he's a courtroom lawyer, Clarence Darrow, Atticus Finch. 'Organised crime is a cancer in our cities. It is a cancer that Mr Conway's paper, to its credit, has done much to highlight. In a recent editorial, the *Tribune on Sunday* went so far as to single me out, demanding that I show a firm hand in dealing with this menace. This is precisely what I – together with Strathclyde Police and the Crown Office – have been endeavouring to do. We now find that the action demanded by the *Tribune* has been sabotaged. Not by the political process, not by the judicial system: sabotaged by one of its own journalists.

'As far as I understand it, Mr Conway's job is to tell the truth and report the news. My own job is to make this country a safer place to live. In an ideal world, these jobs would complement one another, and Mr Conway and I would be allies, not enemies. That hasn't happened. In performing his job so recklessly Mr Conway has made my own job that much harder. And we in Scotland are less safe tonight because of the story his newspaper carried on Sunday. Thank you for your time.'

There were no questions. Lyons swept from the room with his fringe swinging, his lip snagged in a righteous sneer. A youthful aide skipped to the lectern to lower the mike and field the shouted queries of the hacks. Back at the studio the anchor spun round to her studio guests.

'Jesus fuck.' Martin slumped to the desk, his fingers laced on the back of his skull.

Maguire appeared behind us, noiselessly, like a junior demon. She jerked her chin and I rose to my feet. Moir turned back to the screen.

'You too, Wonder Boy.'

Rix was looking out the window, knuckles on the sill. I got the feeling he'd been holding this pose, waiting to wheel round and fix us with his baleful stare. He nodded at the chairs and Moir and I sat down. Rix leaned against the window and crossed his arms, his big frame blocking the light. Maguire stood by the door, like the duty officer in a nick.

For a moment nobody spoke. Then the room lightened as Rix left the window and crossed to the desk. His shirt was a violent fuchsia, a bordello hue. He hunched forward with his elbows on the desk, as if to make a proposition.

'One question, gentlemen. Just so we're clear. What time did you contact the Minister for Justice to give him right of reply?'

I looked at Moir.

'Don't fucking confer! Just answer the question.'

'It was late, Norman. Three o'clock.'

'You didn't think to phone before then?'

'No. Not really.'

He sat back, clasped his hands behind his head. 'Not really? That's interesting.' The black ovals at his armpits widened like eyes. '"Not really." The fuck does that mean?'

I looked at Moir but his eyes were locked on the floor. I shifted my feet.

'Martin warned me to ask him. He told me to ask him in time but I left it too late. It's my fault, Norman. I should have called earlier.'

'You warned him to do it?' He turned towards Moir: Moir nodded, once.

'But you left it too late. What was it, you had better things to do? Your fucking watch stopped? What the fuck, Gerry?'

'I don't know. Because of Belfast. Because he made everything so bloody hard for us in Belfast, because he did everything he could to stop me getting the story.'

'I see. He's supposed to help us bring him down is he? He's supposed to stick his head in the noose?'

'You know what I'm saying, Norman.'

'Yeah. You're saying he pissed you off. You're saying he fucked things up for you in Belfast so you wanted to drop this on him. "Fuck him. Let him find out when he opens the paper. How do like them apples, Mr Lyons? That's what you get when you fuck with Gerry Conway."'

He had me cold. I didn't even need to nod.

'You wanted to nail Lyons. You wanted it so bad you stopped doing your job.'

I shrugged but he wasn't finished yet.

'And if Fiona hadn't forced you to do it, you wouldn't have phoned him at all. As it is, you put a gun to our head by leaving it so fucking stupidly late. A gun to our head.'

He leaned back and his armpits glared at me again. He shook his head. I could feel him fixing me with a stare but I looked off to one side, to the blue patch of sky in the window. He was just a big vague redness in my peripheral vision, a big fat shapeless human heart. After a while the heart aimed at Martin.

'What's your line, Wonder Boy? What you got to say about this?'

Moir cleared his throat and said nothing.

'All the work you've done. Your Maitland stuff. Two months' work? Three? All the surveillance, the fucking leg-work. And it's all for nothing. He's blown it out the water. Your friend here. You might as well not have bothered. You should have just sat on your arse.'

'I don't know about that.'

'Your buddy's gone and fucked it up.'

Moir was pouting at the floor, his shoulders working like a boxer's. I felt he might be gathering his forces for a stri-dent rebuttal, a righteous vindication of my professional honour. I cleared my throat.

'So what happens now?'

'What do you mean, "what happens now"? We take a fucking caning. Anyone that wants to can line us up and dish it out. And we have to sit here and take it. We'll be eat-ing shit for breakfast, lunch and dinner.'

'I meant with me.'

'What happens to *you*?' He snorted. 'I don't know, Gerry. I genuinely don't. For now, what you do is go home. Take a couple of days off till we see where we are with this. OK?'

At least I didn't have to sit at my desk not writing. I could do that quite proficiently at home. Moir chummed me down in the lift and walked me to the car park.

'Gerry, I want to tell you I don't agree with Norman. I hope you know that. I don't think for a minute that you've ruined my investigation. In fact, if anyone's to blame, it's me.'

'I wrote the piece, Martin. I got the byline. It's my fuck-up.'

'OK, but it's my fault you wrote it. I brought you the photo. I feel terrible, Gerry. If I ever thought–'

'Martin. Just leave it. All right? Don't beat yourself up. Rix is right. I saw what I wanted to see. I should have checked it out. I should have done my job. It's not your fault I didn't.'

'Anyway I'm sorry.' He stood stiffly there in the car park. In his jeans and trainers, his hard-man leather jacket, he looked like a schoolboy dressed for a play, the head-boy male-lead in a Year Six production of *Grease* or *West Side Story*.

I clapped him on the shoulder. 'Me too, Martin. I'm sorry too.'

When I got to the flat it was all I could do to avoid going to bed. I stood in my bedroom doorway looking reproachfully at the rumpled sheets for a long minute. Then I went to the kitchen. There was no bed in the kitchen. I made a cup of coffee and sat down at my computer. As an afterthought I took the coffee back to the kitchen and tipped a capful of Red Label into it. I sat down again, booted up, and clicked my way through each of them in turn: the websites of the Scottish daily papers.

Everyone led with the story. For the tabloids it was the threat to Torrins ('Marked Man', 'Fears For Undercover Cop'), graphically embellished with bullets and crosshairs. The qualities led with Lyons's fightback ('Minister Comes Off Ropes') and the tottering case against Maitland ('Journalist Jeopardises Gangland Prosecutions'). A columnist who threw up in my kitchen sink last Hogmanay was calling me 'the unsavoury face of Scottish journalism'. A *Scotsman* leader regretted that falling sales could prompt a once-proud paper to junk its professional standards. Then there were the posts, endless poisonous kite-tails of stinging barbs, dwindling into cyberspace. I trawled a few of these. The posters greeted my downfall with their usual judicious mix of bile and condescension. There were plenty of asterisks and transposed letters. People who misspelled my name and questioned my parentage reproached the laziness and moral bankruptcy of the MSM.

After an hour or so of this I took two Solpadeine and went to bed.

But even the Catholics in Glasgow are Calvinist. At seven that evening I threw back the sheets. You have to show face. The stool of repentance might as well be a bar-stool.

The Cope was crowded. Tuesday was Quiz Night and the teams were clustered round the tiny tables, answer sheets and pencils at the ready. I kept my head down and made for the bar. Before I could order, one of the sports guys was gripping my elbow. What was I having? He put an arm round me and actually clapped me on the shoulder. He brought me over to his booth. Logan was there with the answer sheet in front of him. A couple of subs and some of the magazine girls raised their glasses and shoved up to make room on the banquette. From the warmth of their welcome I might have been the pub-quiz king of Greater Glasgow, the Napoleon of general knowledge. And in fact, when the MC tapped his microphone and started reciting his questions, our table came off pretty well. At the half-time interval Neve McDonald came over with two White Russians and squeezed in beside me – she practically perched on my lap – and handed me one. It was mud-coloured and tasted like malted milk. For the rest of the quiz she stayed there, her thigh pressed close to my own, her breast nosing my ribs as she breathed Kahlúa fumes in my ear.

Public obloquy was proving underrated. In fact, as I conceded to myself that night, watching the green numerals on Neve's digital alarm while she snored daintily beside me, the situation was not without an upside. You live for so long with the dread of exposure – the fear of being busted, surprised in a lie – that the feeling, when it happens, is mostly relief. Disgrace was like a landscape I'd visited in dreams. It was a Dead Sea in which I could float at my ease with no effort at all. My attitude to those *Tribune* colleagues I observed from this perspective, as they tramped importantly around on the shore, maintaining their reputations, was not envy but pity. I lay back in the buoyant dark and closed my eyes.

On Thursday I took a call from Jenna, Rix's PA.

'He wants to see you tomorrow. Is eleven OK?'

My shirt was still damp. I'd hung it up the night before and it still hadn't dried. I stood in clouds of hissing steam, running the iron back and forth, but when I buttoned it up the fabric clung coldly to my shoulders and ribs.

I put on a suit. I knotted a tie and yanked it off again: I already had the bloody job. My razor needed charging: the light blinked red and it sluggishly growled like a rousing dog. The charger was in a dresser drawer, entwined with all the others – the phone charger, the digital camera charger, the charger for the camcorder. At least it should have been, but I wrestled with the braided mess of cords for five minutes before I gave up. Fuck it. I ran the razor over my chin but the blades tugged the hairs instead of cutting them. I splashed some water onto my face. I tipped my head back and dropped some Murine into my eyes to try to dissipate the redness. A taxi beeped in the street.

I stopped at the full-length mirror in the hall. I looked like I'd slept in my clothes. I grabbed my keys and clattered downstairs.

There they all were: Rix, Maguire, and the skinny, fastidious bloke from HR whose red blepharitic eyes were the echo of my own. I tried to remember, as the door settled silently behind me, whether I'd been in the boardroom before. The carpet was so thick and soundproof that it made you doubt your own corporeality. No one had turned on the chandelier, and the great oval table blazed in the bright daylight. An ugly cast-iron tangle of wings protruded from the wall at the room's far end: the earthly incarnation of the eagle on our masthead.

A glass of water had been stationed at a chair opposite the other three. It looked like a prop from a stage play, suggesting an interrogation suite, perhaps, or a Congressional hearing. I took a drink and set the glass back down and the three of them watched intently as if I was here to test the water and was pondering my verdict. I flexed my shoulders and my damp shirt slimed across my back.

'Gerry, This is John Mulholland from HR. He's just here to see that everything goes by the book. Do you want your Union rep present?'

'Tam Logan? Do I need him?'

'It's up to you.'

'Actually, yeah. I do want him.'

Maguire left to get him. We waited in silence till they

appeared. Logan smiled apologetically and looked around the table. He didn't seem to know at which side he should sit. Finally he opted for my side but sat where the table started to curve.

Maguire pulled her chair in and smiled.

'You got everything you need, Gerry. Would you like a coffee before we start?'

'Let's just do this.'

'OK.' She smiled again and opened the folder. 'As you know,' she said, 'we published a story in last week's paper that turned out not to be true. We implied a criminal collusion between the Justice Minister and elements of organised crime in the Glasgow area. In the preparation of this story, our own procedures were neglected or at least imperfectly observed. There was a delay in contacting the Justice Minister. He requested more time to respond to our story but it was decided –' and here she looked drily at Rix '– it was decided to run the story. And now we have this . . . situation.'

'It's a fucking mess is what it is, Gerry. A shitstorm of your making.'

Maguire turned to look at him and Rix raised his palms.

She turned back to me.

'We have a situation. And the question now is, how do we resolve it?'

They all looked at me. Even Tam Logan craned round in his seat.

'How do we resolve it? It's an error. We retract it.'

'Have you seen the papers?'

I shook my head.

'Do yourself a favour,' Rix said. 'If you pass a

newsagents on the way home? Keep walking.'

'So what's your answer, Gerry?' Maguire was arranging her papers, aligning their edges. She looked up at me. 'What do we do?'

'I'm not sure.' I sighed. 'Short memories, I guess. It's old news in a week's time. It's a nothing story. It hasn't got legs.'

'But you're the story, Gerry. You've become the story.'

I sighed again. 'I know. I know. Look, all right, I'll do the apology. OK? Sack cloth and ashes.'

Maguire and Rix exchanged a look.

'Gerry,' said Rix. He grimaced and tapped the table with his knuckles. 'It's a bit late for apologies.'

I looked across at Maguire. She was staring at the floor.

'You're firing me?'

'You fired yourself, Gerry. What choice do I have?'

'But you read the story.' My voice was up in the rafters; I cleared my throat and started again. 'You read the story. You let it go. We got it legalled . . .'

'You got it legalled, Gerry. A slight problem: the story was bullshit. It was a bullshit story. You looked at something and you saw what you wanted to see. It didn't even occur to you that there was any other angle.'

A security guard had appeared in the doorway. He waited with his hands clasped over his groin, like a footballer in a defensive wall.

'I'm sorry, Gerry.'

'But you OK'd it. This is *your* fucking business. You let it go. Tam! Tell him!'

Logan grimaced and spread his palms.

I looked round the faces and scraped to my feet. 'For this? For one mistake?' I shook my head. 'Why?'

Rix's face darkened. His big hands rose from the table and grasped at the empty air.

'Because this is the *Tribune on Sunday*.' He gestured at the eagle as if he was introducing us. 'Because we're a newspaper of record, Gerry. Because we're not the fucking Drudge Report. We don't just shit everything out whether it's true or not and let the reader decide. If something appears under that bird it means we think it's true. We think it's *true*. You knew there was a good chance that it wasn't fucking true. Or you should have done. That means you're a chancer, Gerry. Or else you're a wanker. What you're not is an employee of Tribune Newspapers.'

The security guard gave a little swivelling nod, as if to say 'There you are then', and stood aside to let me leave. Tam Logan half-rose in a pained leering cringe as I passed him. The guard followed me to the newsroom and waved his hand at the stuff on my desk. I swept it into a plastic bag and wedged the photos down the side. I unplugged my laptop and stuck it under my arm. A sort of burning numbness held me while I did this. My ears were ringing. I could smell something too, a sour, meaty musk like the odour in Hepburn's gym. I thought the shock had conjured this smell till I realised it was him, the security guard, standing too close with his rancid pits, his unwashed easy-iron nylon. I grabbed a fistful of pens and we left, the guard treading my heels all the way to the lifts. I passed Neve McDonald with a nod. One or two others reached out for languid, consolatory high-fives. I looked out for Moir but his desk was empty.

The guard rode down with me and followed me to the revolving door. I escaped into fresh air, the bright noonday sun, the glinting river. I sat on the steps and called the cab firm the *Tribune* used. 'Cash or account?' the controller asked me. 'Account,' I said.

I lit a Café-Crème and watched the sun on the water. The cab pulled up and I gathered my things.

The driver looked at my plastic bag, the laptop clamped in my oxter.

'Conway?' he said doubtfully.

'That's me,' I said. I told him the address.

Chapter Twenty-Four

A tenement has its own life, its own rhythm. After nine o'clock and the *shunk* of car doors and the briskly revved engines ours was mostly quiet till eleven, when the postie skliffed upstairs and the letter box brought up the morning's offerings on the hall carpet. Around the same time the upstairs baby roused from its mid-morning nap and bleated resolutely till footsteps crossed the ceiling. At noon the music began – this was the students on the second floor, three skinny boys with Highland cow fringes, who were keeping their flat through the summer vacation – and rumbled on and off until the wee small hours. It was companionable, like the wood pigeon on the roof whose three low notes whistled in my fireplace.

Summer had brought new life to the close. Often there were voices in the stairwell, a hackney throbbing in the street, laughter on the front steps, the stertorous *mmmms* of other people's buzzers, and it came to me one day, as another cab three-pointed under my window, that the students were dealing drugs. On fine nights they sat on the steps, like small-time hoods in a gangster film. They'd been cold to me at first – a hack is barely better than a cop – but since my sacking they'd begun to nod when we passed on the stairs and then one humid night, with the radios blaring and the sky a savage pink over Byres Road, I scuffed down in my slippers and scored some weed. I

smoked it right there, sharing with ~~the~~ guys, and we wilt-
ed like flowers to let the Mormon~~s~~ ~~co~~unt the steps in
their white shirts and shiny shoes.

In the mornings I slept late. I ran befo~~re breakfast, long~~
hot safaris up Great Western R~~oad~~ ~~past~~
Knightswood and Yoker. After showering ~~I wa~~lked
to Byres Road for filled rolls from the deli. I ~~d passed that~~
deli a thousand times but only now did I ~~see~~ ~~own~~
splendour of its sanded floors, its hanging bratw~~urst~~
curve-glass cabinet with its logs of salami, its tray~~s~~
parate olives. There were nectarines, too, and pea~~ches on~~
the stalls outside the shop. Each morning from a m~~ound-~~
ed cardboard tray the colour of uncooked liver I chos~~e a~~
red and yellow peach and carried it to the park. At m~~y~~
favourite spot on the grassy bank below Park Terrace ~~I~~
savoured the moment, brushing the down with my lips,
and then as slowly as I could – my teeth stretching the
integument – bit till it burst in a sharp yellow flush and
my teeth sheared a sopping chunk and the juice ran down
my neck.

I got to know the city again. I rode the subway, alight-
ing at stops I'd never used: Shields Road, West Street,
Kinning Park. I hung around Buchanan Street and
Princes Square and noticed again how Glaswegians
dressed for work the way Edinburghers dressed for the
theatre. I smartened up. I bought a Paul Smith suit and a
pair of brown Loake brogues.

I was happy. For eight or ten days I was happy. I even
met a girl, a trainee architect from Auckland, over on a
placement. We fucked clumsily on the settee and then a
little more adroitly on the bed. Every couple of days we'd
meet up for DVDs and beer and uncomplicated sex.

Then one August...

I'd stopped off at...

scalp and the la...

sleepy as I w...

shut. When...was

kerb and...

thumb...

to u...

...y I was walking back from town.
...bins on Byres Road. The sun on my
...p the hill. I climbed with my eyes
...them a cab shone like a scarab at the
...was poised at the top of the steps. He
...er as I climbed the path. I squeezed past
...nd he grabbed my arm and tugged me
...e, I thought, for his fix. I shook my arm

...rry Conway, it's me.'

...a moment. The bleached hair. The wedge of
...smile. He looked older and the eye-ring had

...ose.' I looked at the cab. 'What you doing

...ait there. Wait just a minute.' He raised a yellow finger. 'There's someone you should meet.'

He paid the driver. The cab door opened and something tumbled onto the pavement: a great skinny raggedy
crow of a man. He was sixty years old, six foot tall and
junky thin, and he stalked up the path beside Rose in
black skinny jeans, wrapping his black combat jacket
around him as a bird might settle its wings.

'Gerry Conway, this is Vincent Rose. My favourite
uncle.'

'I'm your only uncle, John boy.'

We shook hands. Uncle Vincent looked like he was
moulting: his hair and beard all black and patchy, and
something was wrong with his smile. The cab roared off
and left the street in silence.

'Right. Well, you better come in.'

The beers were still cold. I stuck three in the fridge and we took the others through to the living room. Clearly John Rose had brought news: they hadn't come from Belfast to split a six-pack. Still, they were guests. We would drink some beers and they would tell me the news when they were ready. I was trying to muster a likely scrap of small talk when Rose leaned forward and tapped the old guy on the forearm.

'Vince here's got something to tell you.'

I nodded. Vincent had taken the chair by the window. With the sun behind him he looked like a witness on a TV documentary, his features shadowed to hide his identity.

'I was out of the country,' he said. 'When you were over in Belfast. Canada. I go there every year. Two weeks in July. Tell you the truth, I don't like the Twelfth. I've a daughter in Toronto and I go there every summer when the jungle drums start beating. It gets me out the road. Anyway. It's last week before I catch up with this one –' he nods at John '– and he tells me the news. I think I can help you, son.'

He leaned forward and planted his elbows on his knees. His skinny wrists stuck out of his cuffs.

'I was the driver,' he said. He cleared his throat. 'I was the driver. The night Eamonn Walsh was hit. It was me drove the car.'

I looked at Rose. He nodded. Vincent set his beer down on the table.

'The guy you're on about? Peter Lyons? He was there. He watched the door while Walsh was shot. I knew the guy, like: Peter Lyons. Actually –' he lifted the beer bottle between finger and thumb '– I'm not much of a drinker. Could you do me a glass of water?'

I fetched it; my hands were shaking a little as I carried it across and when he leant to take the glass something flashed in his lapel: a little silver stylised fish.

'Thanks.' His smile showed a ridge of gum, leprously white, and I saw what was wrong. What the patchy moustache didn't quite cover: the scarring from a harelip.

'He asked to go on the job. He wanted to go. He wanted more responsibility. It was his idea.'

'Holy Christ.'

Vincent turned sharply away, made a little moue of displeasure.

'He was there.' I stood up. 'I was right. He was there at the shooting. Jesus Christ.'

Again Vincent bristled. He sat back stiffly. 'Go easy, eh?'

'What?'

'The blaspheming. All right? Just go easy.'

'Vincent's a pastor,' Rose said.

I laughed before I realised Rose was serious.

'Oh. Right.' I sat back down. 'I didn't realise. I'm sorry if I–'

'Hey. Forget it.' He smiled his damaged smile. I could see how it might help him, the spoiled lip, in his chosen field. It marked him out. He was blemished, branded, elected to grief. A man with special insights into suffering and shame.

'What was it, a prison conversion?'

'What?'

'Did you find religion in jail?'

'I've never been in jail.'

I looked at him.

'It's not obligatory,' he said. 'They have to catch you first.'

He took another sip of water.

'You've left it kind of late,' I said. 'To make your atone-ment.'

'I don't follow.'

'Isn't that what you're doing? Making your peace. With God, your conscience?'

His gum shone white in the gloom.

'Wrong testament, my friend.' He turned to John Rose. 'Does he know what they did to your father? Do you know what they did to his father?'

'No.'

'They killed him. Johnny's father. My wee brother. Those Lundy bastards killed him. They pulled him out of his pub and shot him like a dog. When Johnny here was a babe in arms.'

'I was nine years old, Vincent.'

'Right. He was just a kiddie.'

'"They"? Who's "they"?'

'His comrades. *Our* comrades, so-called. Kiwi's mob.'

'Kiwi Hepburn killed your father?' I turned to Rose. Rose shook his head.

'Not Kiwi,' Vincent said. 'Kiwi was inside by then. But Kiwi's people. Over nothing. They're jackals up there. Hyenas. Someone ought to put them down.'

'They killed your father? What for?'

'I told you!' The white mouth flashed again. 'Nothing!' He drained his glass of water and wrapped his coat around him. 'It was a fight in a pub. Johnny wasn't even there – Johnny senior. There was a pub we drank in, at the top of the Shankill. One night this Volunteer from Donegall Pass comes in. They had lost some hardware at the time, down Donegall Pass – the Peelers had found their cache. And this blowhard at the bar starts riding the guy, cracking funnies. About does he want to buy some popguns and water-pistols. Is he in the market for pea-shooters. At the finish up, the guy hands him a beating.' Vincent paused. 'Of course the guy who gets hit is a brigadier. Next night, two cars head down the Pass, guys from the Shankill. They stop at a pub and take the first guy they find and haul him out onto the street. It's Johnny Rose.' He pointed at John: 'Johnny's dad, my brother. He's never been in their fucking pub. He's never met the brigadier, doesn't know him from Adam. He just wants to get back to his pint. But they do it anyway. They take out a gun and force him to his knees and shoot him in the back of the head.'

'And was Lyons involved?'

'I'm not sure who was involved. I was working in the bakery that night. I know some for definite who were there. Peter Lyons? I don't know. He might have been there. He was one of that shower.'

His face was still mostly in gloom and I went across and tugged on one of the curtains. Vincent's features bloomed into view, still snarling.

'They're fucking animals. All of them.'

'I'm sorry.' I sat back down. 'Hey. What happened to Mary Whitehouse over here?'

'What?'

'Fuck this, fuck that. You're worse than me.'

He looked at me incredulously. 'They're only cuss words, mister. They don't mean anything.' He shook his head. 'But that's what it was like. Back then. That's what could happen. You're stood there with your pint and smoke and then, bingo, your brains are on the pavement. And it's not even a brawl. You haven't bumped somebody's pint or looked the wrong way at their wife. There's no reason. Or, there is a reason, but what's it got to do with you? It's like Death roaming the street, Death himself in a fucking cape and scythe, picking people out. Him, and not him. This guy, not that guy there.' He looked at Rose and jerked his thumb at me: 'And he thinks it takes a jail term to bring a man to God.'

I walked them down to the street. They were heading for the cab rank at Queen Margaret Drive. We all shook hands.

'How come you were never in jail?'

'I kept a low profile. I was the driver. That's all I did. I had a proper job too – I worked in a baker's. There were Volunteers in my own street who thought I was a civilian.'

I thought of Gordon Orchardton: you never knew who for sure was in it and who wasn't. But if that was so, then how could Vincent Rose finger Lyons? How would he prove he'd been active?

'Gerry.' The pair of them were frowning. 'What is it, Gerry? What's wrong?'

'No, it's just. If you weren't convicted, how do we know you were even involved? Who would believe you? You could be anybody.'

We stood around for a bit and thought about this. Vincent took out his cigarettes and offered them round.

'Look,' I told them. 'Thanks for coming over. It means a lot. But I haven't got a story. I can't stand it up.'

Vincent looked off down the street. The sun was in his eyes and he lifted his hand to his brow and when the shadow crossed his face it stopped just short of the mouth. I looked at him.

'Hold on,' I told them. 'Wait there.'

I found it in the bureau. The Colour Party photo. There it was. One of the balaclavas: the brutal mouth-hole showed a twisted, puckered lip, raggedly partitioned by a scar, and the gapped front teeth beneath it. I clattered back downstairs and passed them the photo.

'There he is,' said Vincent. 'The Frankenstein Kid. I didn't need the balaclava, did I? I would frighten the weans without it.'

'There you are then,' John Rose said. 'There's your story.'

I took the photo from Vincent.

'What about you, though – you'll go to jail too.'

'Who's going to jail?' Vincent said. 'Nobody's going to jail.'

John Rose said. 'You don't go to jail for anything prior to Good Friday.'

'Of course.' I remembered this. If the crime took place before 1998 and it's a terrorist offence, you're safe. You'll stand trial and they'll convict you, but you're out on immediate licence.

'Sometimes you do a few days,' Vincent said. 'A token gesture, but that's it. The conviction stands – you've got that on your record – but you don't do the time.'

'And you'd take the conviction?' I asked him.

'To get at those bastards?' He shrugged.

Ulster has its Disappeared. People who went astray, mislaid like a scarf or a pair of glasses. Lost, like a half-drunk glass of wine, set down on a shelf and forgotten. A troubling skelf in the back of the mind. But the Disappeared weren't many. Mostly the dead turned up. The rhetorical power of a bloodied corpse – stricken, bested, conspicuously wrong – depended on the body being found. Dumped at a roadside, slumped in an alley, left where it fell on a cinderblock path. And this is how it mostly worked: for every killing a body, for every body a claim. If you were an ambitious police detective during the Troubles, this was your whole problem. From the standpoint of detection there was never much to do. Before you'd got the body to the morgue, the killers were ringing the press to claim the credit. A steady stream of self-solving murders. No suspense. No manhunt. No salacious details leaking out. Murders, not cases.

The cops just aimed to tidy up, to prove what they already knew. Within hours of a killing, the police knew the story. Paramilitary organisation, relevant brigade, probable ASU, likely triggerman. It then was a question of forensics, of looking for the tell-tale spoor or snag, the fingerprint or fibre. Sometimes they got lucky. They got their match, the forensic click. They got it after Eamonn Walsh was shot. The triggerman was Davey Craig, a Woodvale volunteer who worked nights as a croupier at a riverfront casino. On the night of the murder he's due to work the late shift. He meets with the others at a safe house in the Upper Shankill where a man they've never met is waiting to brief them. They learn who the 'get' is and where he lives, the layout of the house, the quickest escape routes. The weapons are handed over. They drive to the job for a dummy run. Then they do it for real. Afterwards they drive to another safe house where they strip and shower and their clothes are taken away and burnt. The car is dumped on waste ground, the guns returned to storage.

This was the procedure, but on the night of Walsh's murder Davey Craig didn't follow procedure. He wore his work clothes – a burgundy shirt and tie, black formal trousers – under his painter's overalls and he went straight to work from the job. When the RUC pinched him at the blackjack table they found carpet fibres from Walsh's house in Craig's turn-ups, a mist of Walsh's blood on the cuffs of his blood-coloured shirt.

Davey Craig got thirty years. He claimed he was working alone. He wasn't interested in doing a deal and the cops didn't care. They had their result. But now the driver had turned up out of nowhere and the old pentimento, the man in the hallway, was showing up too.

I checked on the boys. They were lying side by side, hands on their hearts like cadets in a passing-out parade.

I sat down at my Vaio. I lit a Café Crème and booted up. I scrolled down my bookmarks to Scottishwire.com. It's a site for hacks. It carries job ads and media goss and sometimes it breaks a story. The website listed an editorial telephone number with an Edinburgh code. It answered on the second ring.

'Scottishwire.com.'

'Who is this?'

'Kevin McCarthy.'

'Kevin, it's Gerry Conway.'

'You still with us? I thought you'd dropped off the edge of the world.'

'I thought so too.'

'Are you looking for a job?'

'Are you looking for a story?'

Chapter Twenty-Five

There were three arraignments within the year. Lyons was tried in Belfast alongside Vincent Rose. And in the High Court of Glasgow Walter Maitland bore an air of benign abstraction through six laborious weeks of depositions. In blue pinstripes and silver tie, with a half-inch of snowy cuff that he pulled back to glance at his watch, he might have been a guest at a wedding, not a soon-to-be guest of the nation.

The Maitland trial was a circus. I went along on the opening day, braving the scrum of white Lacoste tracksuits and black leather jackets. It was ten years since I'd reported court but nothing had changed. The first thing I saw, on pushing into the Press Room, was Lachlan MacCrimmon's Harris tweed jacket: rough, grey, unyielding, its sleeves like rolls of carpet. Probably he didn't hang it up at night, just propped it in a corner. Or maybe, since no one could remember seeing him free from its speckled custody, he slept in the thing, rolling himself in its smoky folds as his Hebridean forebears rolled themselves in plaids. Inside the jacket, when it turned from the coffee machine in the corner, was Lachlan himself and he gave a friendly little shout and plunged across the room.

'Gerard Conway, all grown up. The big fixtures always bring them out.'

Lachlan had been covering the city's courts for twenty-five years, crossing the river from the High Court to the Sheriff Court and back again. His little office on Ballater Street housed the Clyde Court Agency and supplied copy to every paper in Scotland. He covered everything – murders, misdemeanours, claims for damages, rapes, traffic violations, breaches of the peace, fatal accident enquiries – in the same unflustered prose. There was an odd dichotomy between the disciplined crispness of Lachlan's prose and the rumpled disorder of his person. His shaggy curls and beard were long, brown, and speckled in patches with grey, as if his hair were turning tweed. His tie – the job required a tie and so he wore one – it was a brown, soft, woolly, square-ended affair, folded not knotted, that seemed, when he fingered it, like an extension of his beard. The effect was less of a man in a suit of clothes than a creature in its mottled, moulting pelt. The grunts and snorts that accompanied Lachlan's ferocious note-taking – he had the fastest, cleanest shorthand of anyone I knew – only buttressed this impression of an upright, friendly bear.

'Lachlan MacCrimmon. Where you been hiding?' It must have been close to ten years since I'd seen him.

'Here and there, Gerry. Here and there.'

In Lachie's case, 'here and there' was a very precise specification. His whole life took place in the square mile bounded by Ballater Street and Clyde Street and the Victoria and Albert Bridges. This was his domain – a little rim of tarmac round a stretch of dirty river, with a courthouse at either end. If 'here' was the High Court on the Saltmarket, then 'there' was the Sheriff Court on Carlton Place.

'Better motor, Gerry boy. We'll never get a seat. Drink up—' he had passed the coffee to me and fetched himself another. We both drained and crumpled our styrofoam cups. In the corridor Barbara Tennant came scurrying out of the advocate's Common Room with one arm in her gown. The smiled she flashed at Lachlan as she wrestled with her sleeve darkened and fell as she spotted me. She clacked on up the corridor.

The courtroom was raucous and full, the public gallery packed like Parkhead, like the old terraced Jungle. Ushers craned like meerkats, scouting for empty seats. Lachlan breenged forward to the press benches and pushed right in, the clamped knees collapsing like a line of dominoes as he passed. I hurried in his wake, excuse-me-ing and thank-you-ing, and dropped onto the six-inch of bench that his shuffling hams had cleared. Then the judge came in and we all stood up and squashed back down again. I couldn't move my arms from my sides, but Lachlan had his elbows cocked, his notebook open and pencil poised.

The big trials are the dullest. I'd forgotten this but it's true. There is so much to get through, such a tiresome parade of truculent witnesses, sullen, dogged, sedulously reticent, rolling dully onwards like an overloaded cart. Within a day all the excitement and spice has been flattened under the creaking legal wheels.

Maitland's QC was Russell Spence. I knew Russell from the paper: he legalled the *Toss* on Saturday mornings, sitting at Maguire's desk with a tall Starbucks suspected by the subs to be laced with single malt. I waited for the silent treatment – it was me and Moir, after all, who'd put his client in the dock – but he gave me a nod and mouthed the word 'Gerry' when he spotted me at Lachie's side.

Spence was good. All the QCs were good but Spence had that special, impermeable arrogance. Nothing a courtroom could throw at him, no blurted revelation or startling retraction, could ever discompose him. Whatever happened, something in his profile – the tilt of the jaw, the line of the mouth, the angle of an eyebrow – declared that this, precisely, was what he had looked for. I once watched him browsing a holiday brochure on the last day of a murder trial. I was sitting right behind him on the press benches. A blue, blocky legal tome was propped in his lap, but inside it were glossy shots of the Côte d'Azure. When the prosecution rested, Spence clapped shut the volume, rose to his feet, tugged on the points of his waistcoat and subjected to elegant ridicule each plank in the prosecution's argument. The acquittal took barely an hour.

This time there were no holiday brochures. This time even Spence was on the back foot, though he covered his tail with the usual aplomb. For nearly two weeks I sat beside Lachlan MacCrimmon and watched Russell Spence and tried to stay engaged. I didn't succeed. When the verdict came in I was watching it on the evening news from a barstool in the Cope, the channel's crime reporter wearing his hangdog face, his grey suit spotted with rain.

QCs are indiscreet. They're so much smarter than everyone else that they don't see the need for circumspection. The night the verdict came in, Spence was in Babbity Bowster's. He was drinking thirty-year-old Springbank at £12 a nip. I pretty much failed to mask my stupefaction when the barman rang it up, but I carried the drinks to his table and sat down.

I sat there for most of the night. As the Springbank bottle dipped in twelve-quid increments, Spence gassed on about Maitland. In due course I was able to piece it all together, construct a serviceable version of events. Some of it I got from Spence, that drunken night in Babbity's, some from Lachlan MacCrimmon, some from Moir and the Hey You, some from the trial itself, and some from the cuts of the Belfast trials. There are gaps, of course, and a necessary dependence on lies and suppositions, half- and quarter-truths. But this, as near as I can make it, flawed, skewed and half-cocked, is what I believe it comes down to.

Walter Maitland was a gun-runner. He shipped weapons to the UVF from the early seventies right through the worst of the Troubles. Every three months a cattle truck rattled out of a Brigton yard, headed south for the ferry. Under the wooden boards, running with shit and piss, were yellow crates stamped 'CORNED BEEF'. Inside them, under an innocent layer of tins, was a novelty race of firearms: World War Two Webleys; sporting shotguns with doctored stocks; converted starting pistols; 'spitters' knocked together by night-shift workers at light engineering firms. And maybe, too, there'd be some weeping sticks of gelly from the Ayrshire pits. These crates were unloaded in Antrim and the contents found their way to the back-rooms and cellars of drinking clubs in Donegall Pass and the Upper Shankill. Maitland wasn't the only supplier: Toronto was the Loyalist's Boston, and the Blacknecks had a supply line from Canada. TA depots were also popular for hit-and-run night-time raids. But the guns from Glasgow were regular and, for the most part, reliable. For twenty years they put the ginger into robberies, kneecappings and assassinations right across the Province.

Maitland was now a key associate, someone to culti-vate. There was a courier, a high-ranking Blackneck who made regular visits to Cranhill on the pretext of watching Rangers games. He slipped back and forth between Ireland and Scotland like the phantom 'e' in whisky, dropping off payments and making arrangements for the next consignment. There were drugs as well as guns, and sometimes drugs instead of guns, in the boxes under the slippery hooves.

Naturally, Maitland was careful. There were no photo-calls with balaclava'd colour parties, no souvenir snap-shots. But every few months he'd take the late-night crossing from Stranraer. He stayed on the Upper Shankill and drank in the kind of establishments where inquisi-tiveness is discouraged. It was in one of these shebeens that Maitland heard a voice from home. Peter Lyons was drinking with Isaac Hepburn. The two Glaswegians shared a drink and hit it off. They swapped numbers and kept in touch. When Lyons started the New Covenanters, Maitland weighed in with heavies and hardware. When Maitland strayed within reach of the law he had Lyons, fresh out of law school, to hold his hand. He even had Lyons represent him, in a libel suit in the early eighties. (A journalist had described Maitland as 'Glasgow's Godfather', and Maitland promptly, primly and unsuc-cessfully sued him.)

The Irish visits were quick and discreet, and nobody knew of Maitland's Blackneck dealings but two of his closest lieutenants. Russell Spence himself, Maitland's counsel for twenty years, had known nothing of this till the trial began. But the UVF was a leaky boat. There were touts at every level. When Special Branch learned who all was arming the Blacknecks they beelined for Cranhill. It took them two days but they finished the job. They turned Walter Maitland. The deal was simple. Maitland would keep up his UVF contacts and feed what he knew to his Special Branch handler. In return, the Branch would keep the Provos in the dark about Maitland's career as a UVF armourer, and Maitland would be free to ply his dubious trades – smack, crack, rackets and girls – without fear of interruption by the Procurator Fiscal.

For a while it all worked out. Everybody's happy. The Brits get their intelligence and Maitland stays alive and out of the Bar-L. There are minor arrests, just to make it look good, the odd overnighter in the cells, but nothing that might stick. Then the ceasefires come. And then the ceasefires hold. And when the peace beds down, the questions begin. Who needs a tout with nothing to sell? When does Walter Maitland's Get Out of Jail card expire? Next thing the planes strike the towers. Now Maitland's terrorists are not merely idle; they're the wrong terrorists. No one's interested in these guys any more. And here comes Martin Moir and the Hey You boys and suddenly Walter Maitland is the star of a weekly serial, an overwrought confection of knives and guns and girls and rackets that runs in instalments on the *Toss*'s front page. Now people are clamouring for action. And the man they expect to clean up the mess is Maitland's old Shankill mucker, Peter William Lyons.

But there's nothing wrong with Maitland's memory. He takes to phoning Peter Lyons to reminisce about old times, the Belfast days, the New Covenanters. The name Eamonn Walsh figures strongly in these telephone trips down memory lane. Naturally, Lyons gets the picture. He agrees to help Maitland however he can. He can't stop the prosecution: Maitland accepts that. But maybe Lyons can take a direct interest in the case, find out what's happening, and feed it back to his friends in Cranhill. The go-between here is DS William Torrins, the undercover cop who briefs Lyons on the case. There is some dubiety as to whether or not Torrins is alive to the true situation. In any case, the situation itself cannot survive the Scottishwire post on the decades-old murder of Eamonn Walsh.

I had my answer. I had known it all along but I was happy to have it confirmed. Properly framed and presented, a fact could indeed change – if not the world at large, then at least our little West of Scotland corner. Walter Maitland got twenty years. He'll be seventy-two when he's up for parole. His goons pegged similar scores: seventeen, sixteen, eighteen years. There were no victory speeches on the High Court steps, no raucous bands of cheering supporters, no private parties in East End pubs.

Peter Lyons got life, convicted in Belfast alongside Vincent Rose, as accessory to the murder of Eamonn Walsh. Lyons and Rose were released on immediate licence. Lyons was disbarred from practising law and expelled by the Party. He'd already resigned his ministerial office and his parliamentary seat.

The Hey You got a special commendation at the Scottish Press Awards. They all filed up in their Mafia suits and Martin made his little Oscars speech. We were sitting at his table, myself and Mariella, the girl from Auckland. I raised my champagne flute when he thanked 'the incomparable Gerry Conway, who I'm proud to call my friend and mentor'. Two weeks later Martin filled my old berth as Scottish Political Editor. I took them to Ferrante's, Martin and Clare, to celebrate his appointment, and we drank Sancerre and laughed and I tried not to count the number of calls they made to the sitter to check on baby Esmé.

What did I get? I got plaudits and pints at the Cope. I got to look my shaving mirror squarely in the face. But before all that I got a holiday. In the last days of August I took the boys up the West Coast. Five nights in Argyll, at the Carradale Hotel.

The boys were still young enough to enjoy Carradale for what it was, which, admittedly – two hotels, a village shop, a nine-hole golf course, a working harbour and a white mile of beach with foreshortened views of Arran – wasn't much. But for me, principally, it was deep-green reveries of fernie hillsides, following my dad's rhythmic back along pellet-strewn paths, wading through waist-high bracken, and a ram's skull white in the grass, the great knitted seam down its brow and the fossilised whorls of the horns.

Three summers running I'd come here as a boy, and now I did with James and Roddy what my father had done with me. We walked the hills and the beach and squatted to poke through smelly rock pools and climbed the Point to the old ruined fort. And every lunchtime at the harbour we watched the lobster boats come in. Some of the local boys came too and we all stood in a line on the concrete quay, like the front row of the stalls, while the crew rinsed and sorted their catch. Sometimes, a stray, unusable haddock was trapped among the langoustines and when this happened a crewman would take it to the stern and dangle the fish by its tail. Presently a seal – it was always the same one, a marled, bone-coloured fellow with stubby whiskers and wet black eyes – would lift his chin above the black water and then dive to come curving up as the fish dropped.

The days bled into each other, blissfully empty of news. The only excitement came on the morning of the second day. We were down at the bay, scouting for jellyfish, when Rod found a bomb on the beach. It was a canister bomb from the Second World War and no one seemed terribly fussed. It sputtered and hissed in the outgoing tide. The police arrived and loaded it into a strongbox and drove off, their Land Rover gouging deep tracks in the sand. Back at the hotel our landlady explained. There's a huge MOD munitions dump in the North Channel between Scotland and Ulster. From time to time a phosphorous bomb turns up on an Ayrshire beach or gets trapped in the nets of a trawler but nothing gets done. The stuff is too volatile. It's more dangerous to move it than to leave it where it is.

It spoiled things a little, tilting a gin on a clear summer's night, watching Arran become its silhouette, to know that beneath the twinkling firth, rolling and bumping in the salty dark, was a mess of rotting ordnance.

On our last day I packed the bags and loaded the car and we took a last walk to the harbour. The day was fresh, with a salt lick of wet in the wind. One of the boats had come in, the *Clyde Valley*, its scarlet hull the brightest thing in Carradale. The boys ran ahead down the quay and I followed after, shouting them to stay back from the edge.

A man and a teenage boy were on deck. The boy had fetched a hosepipe from the quay and was rinsing the catch. A great red muddy plastic basket, big as a dustbin, brimful of langoustines. They flexed weakly, waggling their feelers, as the water sluiced over them, back and forth. The hotels would serve them that night, to tourists from the south and golfers from the city. The skipper stood at the gantry with another basket, sorting lobsters by size.

The seal wasn't there. We scanned around but the harbour basin, choppy despite the breakwater, was empty. The boys stared out to sea, James laughing at the strong blasts of wind that rocked him on his heels.

The reedy peep of my mobile pierced the air.

'Mr Conway. It's Hamish Neil.'

I walked a few yards down the quay.

'Hamish Neil. I was beginning to think you'd left the country. Or maybe you were a ghost.'

He laughed.

'Oh I'm real all right. And I'm not going anywhere. Congratulations, anyway, is what I'm phoning for. On the piece. It was something of a triumph.'

'I'm not sure if losing your job is much of a triumph. But thanks.'

'Oh come on, Mr Conway.' His voice seemed fuller than I remembered, tonier and more sure of itself. 'No false modesty now. You'll hardly be idle for long. A man of your proven abilities.'

The boys were playing tig, jouking back and forwards on the quay.

'I hope you're right,' I said. 'Listen, I meant to ask you. Now that you're on. What was your angle in all this? What was your beef against Lyons?'

'Peter Lyons? I've no opinion of Peter Lyons, black or

white. No, my interest lay with the other principal.'

James was straying too close to the edge. I motioned him back.

'I'm not sure I understand.'

'Let me put it like this. Have you ever worked for someone who didn't know when to go? Someone who just keeps on, when the time has come to hand over the reins, keeps on and keeps on, taking all the credit for the work you do?'

'We're talking about Maitland? You work for Walter Maitland?'

'He left me no choice. I couldn't *move* against him. Imagine the mess. And as long as Peter Lyons was in his pocket, I knew the police wouldn't move either. No, I needed someone to bring it all out, bring it into the open.'

'Wait a minute. You think I did this for you?'

'Don't feel bad,' he said. 'You did a good thing. It's better this way. Better for business. Better all round. I'm sorry about our friend in Justice. I'm sorry about your job. But believe me—'

'You think I did this for you? You think it was a favour. I did it for—'

'What *did* you do it for, Gerry?'

'I did it for the truth. I did it for the girl. I did it for, I don't need a reason. I did my job. That's why I did it.'

'And you did a good job. That's what I'm saying. I just wanted to thank you for your help, Gerry. I won't forget it.'

He rung off and darkness rinsed the air as a cloud crossed the sun. A cold wind rose off the water and rippled my shirt. I zipped the boys' fleeces.

'Come on,' I said. 'We're going.'

I had James by the hand when Roddy spotted him, out near the middle, the doglike head erect above the water, the world's unconcern in the round black eyes.

The boy on the boat had seen him too. He laid the hosepipe on the gunwale and stooped to lift something from the deck. We looked round for the seal but he was gone. James tugged at my jacket and pointed at the empty water.

'Hold on,' I told him. 'Look.'

The boy stood at the stern, holding a long silver fish by the tail. He dropped it. The fish hung in the water, spiralling brightly, and the dark shape curved up from below, the great pale belly just breaking the surface, and carried it down to the depths.

Acknowledgements

I am grateful to Lindsay McGarvie and Stephen Khan for sharing their knowledge of the journalist's trade. Lee Brackstone and Derek Johns provided crucial editorial guidance. For help and advice of various kinds I would like to thank: Patrick Crotty, Helen Francis, Doris and Ronnie Fyfe, Eamonn Hughes, Hugh Jordan, Henry McDonald, Jim McDowell, Valerie McIlvanney, William McIlvanney, Catherine and Ian Nicol, Fiona Rennie, Ray Ryan, Ian Sansom, Linda Shaughnessy and Graham Walker.

ff

Faber and Faber – a home for writers

Faber and Faber is one of the great independent publishing houses in London. We were established in 1929 by Geoffrey Faber and our first editor was T. S. Eliot. We are proud to publish prize-winning fiction and non-fiction, as well as an unrivalled list of modern poets and playwrights. Among our list of writers we have five Booker Prize winners and eleven Nobel Laureates, and we continue to seek out the most exciting and innovative writers at work today.

www.faber.co.uk – a home for readers

The Faber website is a place where you will find all the latest news on our writers and events. You can listen to podcasts, preview new books, read specially commissioned articles and access reading guides, as well as entering competitions and enjoying a whole range of offers and exclusives. You can also browse the list of Faber Finds, an exciting new project where reader recommendations are helping to bring a wealth of lost classics back into print using the latest on-demand technology.